melissa hill

A Gift to Remember

**SIMON &
SCHUSTER**

London · New York · Sydney · Toronto · New Delhi

A CBS COMPANY

First published in Great Britain by Simon & Schuster UK Ltd, 2013
A CBS COMPANY

1 3 5 7 9 10 8 6 4 2

Simon & Schuster UK Ltd
1st Floor
222 Gray's Inn Road
London WC1X 8HB

www.simonandschuster.co.uk

Simon & Schuster Australia, Sydney
Simon & Schuster India, New Delhi

A CIP catalogue record for this book
is available from the British Library

HB ISBN: 978-1-47112-761-8
TPB ISBN: 978-1-47112-762-5
EBOOK ISBN: 978-1-47112-764-9

Typeset in Sabon by M Rules
Printed and bound by CPI Group (UK) Ltd, Croydon, CR0 4YY

To Dad, with lots of love

Chapter 1

She is too fond of books, and it has turned her brain.
Louisa May Alcott

Anyone who says that money can't buy happiness has clearly never been inside a bookstore. And certainly not one like Chaucer's, Darcy Archer thought proudly, glancing around the gorgeous place she was lucky enough to work in.

The space was snug and inviting, with a vaguely Dickensian feel to it by way of its floor-to-ceiling hardwood shelves and filigreed gold signwriting above each section. The Victorian panelled bay window and festive-themed window display evoked old-fashioned storefronts of times gone by, as did the scroll-effect store sign hanging just outside the entrance.

Catering to its well-heeled Upper West Side neighbourhood, the little shop carried an eclectic mix of literature in a variety of genres, early edition classics as well as popular bestsellers for adults and children. Booklovers and gift-seekers alike adored Chaucer's; its cheerful, experienced staff and homey atmosphere made it the perfect place to spend an afternoon wandering amongst the shelves or hunting down an elusive title.

At this time of year, with just over a week to go before Christmas, the store was decked out in its holiday finest: fairy lights strung along the shelves, homemade glitter snowflakes hanging from the exposed rafters above, and the evocative aroma of cinnamon wafting from the tiny café on the first-floor.

'Excuse me, I'm looking for a book . . .'

Darcy glanced up from the shelving cart to see an older woman hovering uncertainly nearby. She looked to be in her late fifties, well-maintained and manicured, dressed in an expensive coat and scarf and clutching one of the last decade's most luxurious handbags, which Darcy knew, thanks to her fashion maven Aunt Katherine, was easily worth at least three of her monthly pay checks.

Looking for a book in a bookstore? If she only had a dollar for every time she'd heard *that* one, Darcy thought to herself.

But she gave the woman a warm smile. 'Let's see if I can help. What's the title?'

The woman bit her lip. 'That's it – I can't remember, but I know it's by a female author with three names . . . and there are four daughters in it, although one has a boy's name, I think. And it's Christmas-time, and as far as I know they want to buy themselves presents, but then think better of it and buy one for their mother …' The woman's voice trailed off, and she stared at the shelves helplessly.

Darcy slipped a stray lock of raven-black hair behind one ear. No matter what she did with it – which admittedly was little – it would never stay put. 'Is this a new release?' she asked.

'Oh no, my dear, it's a classic.' The woman's eyes refocused and her voice grew almost haughty. 'I'm surprised you don't know it. Have you been working here long?'

Darcy had to smile. Actually she was manager of Chaucer's and had been working in the store for almost six years. Yet she was supposed, with minimum description, to magically identify the book in question amongst the millions published.

Still, she did love a challenge …

'Now, you say there are four sisters, and an author with three names?' she said, gently guiding the woman towards the classic literature aisle. The customer nodded. Overhead, a smooth jazz rendition of 'It Must Have Been the Mistletoe' played softly through the speakers. 'Well, I'm going to go out on a limb and say you may well be looking for *Little Women* by Louisa May Alcott.'

The woman grimaced. 'I'm not sure.'

'There are four sisters in the book, and one of them – Jo – has a vaguely masculine name.' Darcy pulled a thin red book from the shelf, the pages edged with gold, and presented it to the woman.

'Oh,' she said, taking it. 'That is *beautiful*.' She examined the book from bottom to top and inside and out, marvelling at its rich leather binding, and the original illustrations scattered throughout.

'Is it intended as a gift?' Darcy asked.

The woman smiled. 'Yes. A Christmas present for my twelve-year-old granddaughter.'

Darcy guessed that the girl's grandmother was acting on a recommendation and had never had the pleasure of reading *Little Women* herself.

Which was a shame.

It was one of Darcy's favourites, and Alcott's famous quote about books turning the brain described her pretty well. Darcy was indeed too fond of books – a condition known as 'bibliolatry'. She always had at least one book on the go close by, and felt almost naked without a novel on her person. Darcy had been enveloped in a story every single day of her life for as long as she could remember, and tended to use every opportunity – waiting in line, eating, occasionally even while brushing her teeth – to indulge in her greatest pleasure.

It was one of the reasons she loved working in Chaucer's.

Darcy had first made the move as a teenager to Manhattan from Brooklyn where she lived with her Aunt Katherine, to attend Columbia University and get a Master of Fine Arts in Writing – the closest form of study relating to her passion that was available. Only to quickly discover that trying to create stories herself was a world apart from the joy of reading them. Easy reading definitely didn't equate to easy writing, and the weight of her own expectations, combined with insecurity regarding the extent of her talent (or lack thereof), soon resulted in writer's block, after which Darcy had to admit defeat. Following graduation, she spent some time working on *Celebrate*, a glossy New York women's magazine. Her Aunt Katherine – via her hugely successful corporate events business – was good friends with the Editor-in-chief, and had pulled in the favour for Darcy.

After two miserable years of cutting down bland, 3,000-word descriptions of shoes and handbags into even blander 300-word descriptions, as well as struggling to fit in amongst her über-cool and effortlessly chic workmates, Darcy had just about given up on turning her passion into a way of life – until one day, when she had stumbled into Chaucer's with the aim of finding a guidebook that could help with her hopeless lack of fashion nous. Being unable to pass by a bookstore without venturing inside had always been one of her major weaknesses, but this time it had turned into a blessed stroke of luck.

There had been a 'Help Wanted' sign on the door and, on impulse, Darcy had applied there and then. She was interviewed on the spot, upstairs in the café, over a cup of caramel mocha. The following morning when she got the call from the owner telling her the job was hers, she felt as though all her Christmases had come at once. Imagine spending her days surrounded by books, being able to pick one off the shelf whenever she wanted, caress the spine, smell the paper ... heaven!

Darcy quickly discovered that working in a bookstore was in reality more about unpacking boxes and rearranging shelves than sitting curled up in a corner sampling the merchandise. Even so, she felt that she'd finally found her calling. She quickly forgot the long hours, the lousy pay, the paper cuts and the doom-laden prophecies that books were finished.

This sudden development came as a blow to her Aunt Katherine, who considered it a huge step down in both pay and career prospects. And while there was certainly some truth in the former, Darcy wasn't the least bit interested in climbing the media ladder. Unlike the formidable, high-achieving Katherine Armstrong, Darcy just wasn't made that way, and when growing up had always been happiest with her nose in a book. One of her earliest and fondest memories was of her mother reading to her before bedtime, all tucked up and cosy together on Darcy's bed. A love of reading was something her bookworm parents had instilled in her right from the start, and the family had spent many happy times curled up together escaping into wonderful fictional worlds.

Like her mother Lauren used to say, books were solid proof that ordinary people were capable of creating magic.

Sadly, Darcy's beloved parents had both died in a car accident when she was twelve years old, after which she and her aunt had been thrown together by circumstance and familial duty. As per her parents' wishes, Lauren's sister Katherine had taken her niece in and overseen her upbringing until Darcy finished school and then at seventeen moved to Manhattan to attend Columbia. During their years together the two of them had somehow muddled along – as well as a traumatised teenager and a single, thirty-something career girl could.

A formidable figure in New York society, for over fifteen years Katherine had been at the helm of Ignite – one of Manhattan's most prominent event-management companies with offices close to Union Square. Hence her interest in her niece's career, and while Darcy had known from the outset that nobody got into bookselling for the money, for the sake of passion she was prepared to forego a healthy pay cheque for one that just about kept a roof over her head. Her response to her aunt about quitting the magazine six years before had been a quote from Albert Camus: *When work is soulless, life stifles and dies.*

'Oh, for heaven's sake, Darcy! Albert Camus won't pay the bills, whereas a nice two-page advertorial on the latest Dior collection *will*,' Katherine had said. 'If you must, then at least aim to work in one of the conglomerate bookstores or publishers even. Yes, I'm sure being surrounded by books sounds great in theory, but really, what kind of prospects can you expect from working in a tiny independent?'

'The prospect of spending my days doing something I love and being happy,' Darcy had retorted sunnily. 'That's really all anyone can ask for, isn't it?'

But Darcy knew her commercially-minded aunt didn't lend herself to impractical notions such as finding joy in work simply for the sake of it, and certainly not without some kind of tangible accompanying reward. She was aware that Katherine had worked (and continued to work) ferociously hard over the years to build Ignite into the successful corporate event management company that it was today, but she often wondered if any of it actually brought her aunt contentment or satisfaction, because she eternally seemed to have her eye on the next hurdle or challenge.

Darcy knew in her heart and soul that finding joy and satisfaction in her work was undoubtedly what *she* wanted. And she had yet to regret her decision. Besides, she had in the meantime worked her way up to manager, a dubious promotion that in reality meant more responsibility and not a whole lot more money. However, what it also meant was that she had greater creative freedom over window displays, shelf arrangements and, most importantly, free rein to choose and order any titles she felt would suit Chaucer's customers.

Now, Darcy watched the woman walk away with a copy of *Little Women* housed in one of the store's trademark purple and gold striped carrier bags and sighed contentedly. Another satisfied customer.

Just then, the front door swung open and Darcy turned to find Joshua, her workmate and relief for late opening hours, standing there with a green elf hat on. An attractive guy in his late twenties, his hair was close cropped against his mocha skin and his grey sweater tight against his thin frame, while his maroon-coloured cords threatened to slide down his narrow hips at a moment's notice. He looked like a walking Gap advert.

'Merry week before Christmas!' he intoned in a voice full of rich humour and warmth. No matter what mood Darcy might be in, Joshua always cheered her up. He'd been wishing everyone a Merry 'something' before Christmas since pretty much Thanksgiving weekend: 'Merry month before Christmas' or 'Merry three weeks before Christmas.'

It had been exasperating at first, but now it was something she looked forward to every week; her own personal Advent calendar.

And he was the best kind of workmate – a fixer. If he suspected or sensed that Darcy or Ashley, Chaucer's other store assistant, were feeling hassled, down in the dumps or full-on exhausted, then look out: the place would be full to bursting with his own personalised 'Joshua bucks' – handwritten coupons he'd slide into pockets or beside the cash register. They were always for cheery little things, like *This entitles the bearer to one free back massage* or *Cover for one half-shift*. In short, Joshua was a sweetheart, a pleasure to manage and great fun to work with. Plus his literary knowledge was extensive and he had a particular talent for obscure cult books which, combined with Darcy's more classic bent, made them a fantastic team.

Dropping his sheepskin jacket behind the counter, he put on the purple and gold striped Chaucer's apron, and Darcy in turn went to untie hers. Up close, he smelled like the hollyberry hand wash he'd been using ever since it went on sale at the nearest Bath & Body Works. Joshua was truly the most effeminate straight man she had ever met, and Darcy had been truly astonished when she'd first met his girlfriend a couple of years back – a stunning long-legged blonde who would have looked right at home on the fashion pages in Darcy's old magazine job.

'So what are you up to this evening, boss?' Joshua asked. 'Besides Today's Special from Luigi's?'

Darcy's apartment was situated over a popular little Italian restaurant just off West Houston Street, a good twenty minutes from the store but worth what she paid in rent to be within cycling distance to work. She'd lived in three different apartments in Manhattan since making the move from Brooklyn, and although by far the smallest, her third-floor walk-up over Luigi's was easily the best location, close as it was to Hudson River Park, a riverside oasis amidst the hustle of bustle of the city.

She loved going down there on her days off, taking long walks along the water with views out to Lady Liberty and Staten Island. And of course in the summer months, the grassy areas amongst the pretty flowerbeds were ideal for reading, and the welcoming river breeze perfect for surviving the worst of the city's heat and humidity.

'Actually not tonight,' Darcy told Joshua. For once she had somewhere to be. 'I'm headed to a book launch.'

'Ooh, anyone we know?' Due to the shop's minuscule dimensions, Chaucer's didn't hold launch parties or literary events, but even if they did, Darcy guessed that this particular author wouldn't draw too many of their regulars.

'Oliver Martin, science-fiction author?' she said to Joshua's blank look. 'He's just hit the *Times* bestseller list and according to Aunt Katherine he's a "big deal".' She mimed quotemarks with her fingers. 'I'm only going because I haven't seen her for a while and we're long overdue a catch-up.' Oliver Martin must certainly be a very big deal indeed if Katherine Armstrong was deigning to attend his book launch.

While her aunt was forever extending invites to various glamour-filled events and gatherings which her company hosted all over the city, Darcy tended only to favour the ones with a literary bent. She loved meeting authors, although it had to be said that the more successful ones were often insufferably pompous, but still it was nice to occasionally be able to dip her toe into the glossier side of her industry.

'And you're going like *that*?' Joshua glanced meaningfully at her.

Darcy looked down at her grey trousers, forest-green woollen sweater and chunky leather boots. 'What's wrong with it?' She pulled out the elastic from her ponytail and fluffed out her black curly hair, letting it fall loose around her shoulders. A pointless action as it would very quickly be flattened by her bike helmet on the journey downtown.

Joshua smiled fondly. 'Like I keep telling you, if you tried making an effort now and again – maybe some eyeliner and a touch of lipstick – you could almost pass for Megan Fox's older, chunkier sister. Oh, and lose the spinster glasses, for tonight at least?'

Darcy was well used to his teasing. 'Not all of us are lucky enough to possess your rather ... unique eye for style,' she said wickedly, eyeing his drainpipe trousers. 'The literati will just have to take me as I am.'

It was true that she had no fashion sense whatsoever. Also, there was barely enough room to move in her tiny apartment, and for Darcy the choice was simple. She'd happily sacrifice anything, even food, if it meant she could fit in more books.

While her wardrobe consisted mostly of functional work clothes (in a bookstore, paper dust clung to *everything*), she did possess a few items for special occasions – a seventies-style wrap dress she'd found in a cute little vintage store down in Greenwich, and incongruously a pair of unworn Jimmy Choo heels that her aunt had bought her a couple of Christmases ago.

Still, now that Joshua had openly pointed out her sartorial shortcomings, she guessed she was due for a similar earful from Katherine on arrival at the party, which was being held in fashionable Chelsea.

While Darcy loved her aunt and was massively grateful for everything she had done for her, Katherine's outspoken and no-holds-barred personality had also caused a certain level of heartache, because not only was she focused on an eternal attempt for Darcy to improve her career but also to improve herself in general. Not to mention a seemingly endless quest to matchmake her niece with reputable New York men.

The truth was that Darcy was perfectly content on her own and had no interest in partaking of the often terrifying Manhattan dating scene. It was a million miles from the romantic rituals outlined in her favourite novels, and while it might be wishful thinking, she wasn't willing to settle for any-thing less than being swept off her feet.

While she'd had relationships with guys over the years – mostly quiet, bookish types like herself – none of them had been especially serious, rarely lasting longer than a couple of months.

'No flesh and blood man could ever live up to those fictional heroes you're so crazy about,' Joshua often teased her, and Darcy supposed there was some truth in that.

There was certainly no denying that she'd always been taken with the idea of true love and proper passionate romance like that between Romeo and Juliet, Lancelot and Queen Guinevere, Scarlett and Rhett, and her favourites, Elizabeth and Darcy, her namesake.

Later, saying goodbye to Joshua, she wrapped up warm in her purple North Face ski jacket and woollen scarf, and prepared for what was for her, unlike most New Yorkers, one of the most pleasurable parts of her working day: the commute.

Navigating Manhattan's Upper West Side was something tourists paid good money to do on a regular basis, and Darcy did it twice a day, five days a week for free.

Going into the tiny yard behind the store, she unlocked her bike and put on her safety helmet, fastening it tightly beneath her chin. She was proud of her knowledge of New York's streets – like the nifty shortcut via the Meatpacking District she relied upon to avoid the traffic on Sixth, or how a simple hidden passageway near Chelsea whisked her away from the worst of the Forty-Second Street hordes.

She particularly loved riding around town this time of year, with all the festive shop displays, cosy cafés and trattorias lit up for the season, white and coloured fairy lights blinking, candles aglow, early-evening diners holding hands in window seats, or braving the al fresco tables that sat mere inches from the kerb, bundled up in thick woollen coats and gloves as they smoked a crafty cigarette.

Darcy cruised along steadily on the bike, marvelling at the colour of the sky, that bleak city blue she loved so much in the last few hours before complete darkness fell upon the city. Manhattan's music filled the air, a mix of honking horns and hissing pipes, vendors shouting and people chattering.

It was all a blur as she sped by, obeying traffic signals as she hugged the kerb. She was zinging now, the lights green, the air cold and crisp, her eyes open and alert, her long legs loose and limber. She felt truly alive.

She knew that cyclists in Manhattan, with their natural proclivity for speed and deft weaving through traffic, were generally considered by most New Yorkers – and taxi drivers in particular – as being only barely above sewer rats and cock-roaches in the food chain, but Darcy wouldn't swap her beloved three-speeder – and the addictive sensation of almost flying through the streets – for any amount of abuse. In truth, much of the bad reputation was derived from daredevil city couriers who defied traffic laws and sometimes gravity, as they zipped along as if on a kamikaze mission rather than a job.

It wasn't snowing, not yet, but Darcy could feel it teasing her in the crystal sky. Slowing at the corner of Broadway and Columbus Avenue, she passed by a fancy bistro full of equally fancy patrons sitting at tables with white cloths and big glasses of rich, red wine and plates of delectable pasta in front of them. Her mouth watered. The air felt clear as she cycled on through streets lined with people heading home from the market, their upmarket bags brimming with organic carrots and loaves of Cuban bread or carefully boxed truffles: another night of opulence in America's favourite city.

Darcy felt like an impostor here sometimes, particularly on the Upper West Side, amongst the galleries and restaurants and bistros, cafés and high-rises and appointment-only vintage stores and photography studios. She was an ordinary person in an extraordinary place, one who ate Ramen noodles three nights a week and half-price specials from Luigi's the other four, who didn't own a car and took care of what few clothes she had so she wouldn't need to spend her hard-earned wages on new ones. And her entertainment of choice generally took place in her own apartment between the pages of great books rather than in the nightspots of New York.

But still it was all worth it, to live in the most magical city on earth. She smiled. Maybe one day she'd find someone to share in the fairytale.

Chapter 2

Her heart was a secret garden and the walls were very high. **William Goldman**

A little while later, Darcy pulled her bike up to the hip Chelsea bistro hosting the science fiction author's book-launch party. Parking it next to a lamp post, she took her bike lock out of her messenger bag and clipped it around both. Despite the media's harping on about New York crime statistics, in all the years she'd lived in the city she'd never had one stolen. Satisfied, she turned towards the entrance and inside by the door, immediately locked eyes with the only person she was likely to recognise here tonight: her aunt.

A statuesque blonde in her mid-fifties, dressed in head-to-toe Chanel, Katherine Armstrong was holding a martini glass in one manicured hand, and critically assessing every inch of Darcy's windblown appearance.

Feeling under examination, Darcy shook out her flattened hair, straightened her coat and adjusted her bag on her shoulder, just as light snowflakes began to descend from the sky, melting on contact with her increasingly flushed cheeks. She turned her face upwards, briefly revelling in the sensation. Then, steeling herself for the inevitable assassination, she walked towards the front door, all too late noticing the salt stains on the back of her trousers.

Well, there was nothing she could do about that now, she thought as she opened the door to the restaurant and hastily brushed down the legs of her pants, hoping that her aunt wouldn't notice.

Before Darcy made it two steps inside the entrance, had a chance to scope out the room or even take off her coat, Katherine accosted her.

'Darling, why on earth are you still riding that dreadful thing in December, in the middle of winter, when it is starting to snow.' Darcy took careful note that this was a statement, not a question. 'Do you have some kind of death wish?' *This* was a question, though.

She smiled tiredly. 'No, Katherine, I don't have a death wish, and you already know why I ride my bike.' Over the years they'd had countless 'discussions' about Darcy's preference for the bike over any form of public transport, something which according to Katherine thumbed its nose at reason and indeed personal safety. But riding on public transport was actually detrimental for Darcy. Such journeys afforded her the opportunity to immerse herself in reading, and she'd lost count of the number of times she'd gone miles past her stop and ended up late for work.

Her aunt sighed. 'You know, your parents are probably spinning in their graves, may they rest in peace. They entrusted you to me all those years ago, and what do you do to honour their wishes for your personal welfare? You pedal a bike around the streets of Manhattan, just asking to be mown down. Why can't you be like any other self-respecting New Yorker and just take the subway or a damn cab?' Darcy opened her mouth to protest, but Katherine held up one heavily bejewelled hand to silence her. 'I mean, thirty-three is a little old to be clinging on to the hippie thing, isn't it? Which leads me to my next point: what successful man these days would be interested in some sort of tree-hugger when they would have to walk her and a *bicycle* home from a date? It's like something that happens in the schoolyard. Men in this city want women as sophisticated as they are, and how would you even ride a bike to a date anyway? Those Jimmy Choos I gave you would be completely destroyed if you tried to pedal in them. Then of course there's your job . . .'

Darcy shook her head good-naturedly, the litany of her aunt's complaints sailing right over her head. She had heard all of this before, and knew there was no point in trying to argue her case. If she allowed Katherine to get a foothold with the cycling thing, the lack of relationship or gather speed with the job criticism, she knew she wouldn't be able to get past the entry of the restaurant for the rest of the night.

So much for a catch-up. More like an ambush!

'Anyway, sweetheart,' Katherine continued, as she took Darcy's elbow and led her into the restaurant, steering her forward until they were in front of the bar, 'I invited you here because there are some people I want you to meet. Actually, one person I want you to meet in particular. He's the author being celebrated tonight. Oliver Martin,' she said triumphantly, as if she was personally responsible for his success, looking at her niece for a reaction. When Darcy seemed unmoved, she said resignedly. 'You know, given that you work in a bookstore, I would have thought you would know who Oliver Martin is.' She turned to the bartender. 'My niece will have a dirty martini, three olives, blue cheese stuffed, with Belvedere vodka.'

Darcy quickly interrupted with: 'No, actually, I'll just have a glass of Cabernet. Whatever the house is – no big deal.'

Katherine's eyes widened. 'House?' she said, horrified. 'She doesn't want the house. Give her the Clos du Bois. Or the Fourteen Hands.'

'Really, the house is fine,' Darcy insisted to the bartender who was uncertainly juggling bottles, trying to determine who was in charge. He gave a small smile as Darcy mouthed, 'Seriously.' Even so, he must have figured that Katherine was the more redoubtable of the two, because he duly uncorked the Clos du Bois.

Well, at least it isn't a dirty martini, Darcy thought, feeling a small measure of triumph. She didn't like vodka, but no matter how many times she said it, Katherine seemed to believe that eventually it would grow on her. It wouldn't.

'So,' her aunt continued, eyeing the crowd and seeing who

was nearby and worthy enough to talk to, 'seems Oliver Martin is going to be huge.'

'Isn't he a sci-fi writer?' Darcy asked as the bartender passed her a wine glass. 'I haven't read anything of his because I'm not interested in that genre. Not my thing.' It was one of the few genres that she didn't read, as Darcy would gladly read the back of a milk carton if there was nothing else available. However, possibly down to being a self-confessed Luddite, she found it difficult to immerse herself in futuristic technologically-based worlds.

Katherine waved a hand airily. 'It doesn't matter whether or not you are interested in sci-fi. The point is, he has recently become a *New York Times* bestselling author so I want you to meet him. Word is, he is in talks with Spielberg about something too.' She once again grabbed Darcy's arm and directed her through the bodies towards a corner of the room where a large crowd was gathered. Darcy did her best to manoeuvre her glass so as not to slop red wine all over someone's Prada shoes.

'Excuse me, excuse me,' Katherine ordered, elbowing through people as Darcy smiled apologetically and tried in vain to put on the brakes as her aunt dragged her forward.

Finally, they reached the edge of the crowd to where the man of the moment, Oliver Martin, was holding court.

Darcy blinked. The guy standing in front of them might have been a celebrated bestselling sci-fi author, but his wardrobe choices evidently stopped at the door of his teenage closet. Not that she could talk, but at least her choice of clothing bore some

resemblance to twenty-first-century fashion. She turned to
Katherine with a pleading look, trying to convey the message
that this short, greasy-haired man-child, outfitted in a Marvel
Comics T-shirt and chequered blazer belonging firmly in the
1980s was a million miles from her type. While he might have
been presentable enough if he decided on a shave, a haircut, a
change into some adult clothes and a departure from the wide-
frame glasses popular amongst the laboratory set, he was
definitely no oil painting.

Not that Darcy required a man to have movie star good looks,
of course, but what on earth did her aunt think that she would
see in Oliver Martin? Other than they were both book geeks,
they were likely to have absolutely nothing else in common.

'Oliver!' Katherine commanded, putting a proprietary arm
around his shoulders and not in the least bit mindful of interrupting the conversation he'd been having with another guest.
'I want you to meet my niece, Darcy Archer. With you being
new to the city, I thought the two of you should have the
opportunity to get acquainted.'

Darcy opened her mouth to speak, unsure of how she was
going to extract herself from the situation, when Oliver beat
her to it.

'Do you game?' he asked, looking her up and down.

She blinked, unsure of the question, and looked at her aunt
who quickly smiled before she sauntered off.

Darcy smiled politely at him. 'I'm sorry, but I'm not sure
what you mean.'

'Do you game?' Oliver asked again, as if repeating the

question would help her understand it. 'Gaming? On a computer, TV or gaming system?'

'Oh.' She bit her lip, and felt a fresh wave of exasperation come over her. She glanced helplessly over her shoulder towards her aunt, who had by now disappeared into the crowd. What on earth had Katherine been thinking?

'No, I'm afraid I don't. I'm a bit of a Luddite actually.' The Vaio laptop she owned was so old it still ran on Windows 95, and was only used now and again for the creation of flyers for Chaucer's. Darcy was completely bewildered by Facebook, Twitter or any of the social networking systems that seemed to be replacing face-to-face communication. And as an advocate of the written word, computers were almost an anathema to her way of life. To her, time spent online was precious time away from reading real books, and while she knew she was old-fashioned and out of touch, was there really anything so terribly wrong with that?

But upon this admission Oliver's face immediately went blank, as if he had nothing else to say to her. Darcy took a sip of her wine and thought quickly for something to chit chat about. 'So Katherine said you've just moved to New York. Where from?'

'San Diego,' the author replied simply.

'Oh, California, wonderful,' she enthused, nodding. 'Quite a departure from this part of the world. Weatherwise, especially.' She motioned towards the window where snow was now falling heavily outside, the gentle snowflakes illuminated by lamplight and mesmerising in their descent.

Oliver's expression showed no recognition whatsover that the New York climate was any different to where he'd moved from. 'I wouldn't know.'

Darcy swallowed. Did he not go outside then ... ever?

'I'm originally from Wisconsin and only lived out west for one reason: Comic-Con. Ever been?' Again he looked at her expectantly.

'Um, no, never,' she said, her mind conjuring up what little she knew about the event, and she pictured a bunch of grown men dressed up as Spiderman or Thor. Not exactly her scene.

'Oh, you should *totally* go,' he said by way of a command.

She plastered on a smile, and surreptitiously glanced down at her watch. This was beyond awkward. Usually Katherine's choices in matchmaking were a little bit closer to the mark. Was she now so desperate to get her niece paired off that any man would do?

She thought back to the last author her aunt had tried to foist on her a year or so ago – a Valentino-clad egotistical thriller writer who had more in common with the macho series character at the centre of his bestsellers than any real-life person. The guy might have been wealthy, mega-successful and movie star handsome, but he had the personality of a dishrag.

'I'm not sure it would be my scene really,' Darcy told Oliver Martin. 'It's not something I know a lot about. My taste in literature is quite differ—'

Oliver cut her off. 'Oh? So what do you read then?'

'Well, I'm a fan of Jane Austen, the Brontës, and most of the classic Regency romances – as well as Dickens and Shakespeare, of course. I do enjoy contemporary literature too. Really, my interests span across multiple genres and—'

Oliver cut her off again. 'Have you read my books?'

Darcy felt her face flush. Authors almost always asked that question, and nine times out of ten the answer wasn't the one they wanted to hear. She remembered the thriller author's disbelief that Darcy wasn't (like most of the female reading population, it seemed) head over heels in love with Max Bailey, hero of his bestselling series – a kickass crime-fighter styled as a modern-day James Bond. 'It's just ... I don't read all that much science fiction,' she fudged. 'I've heard it's a wonderful book though, and the reviews have been—'

Oliver looked impatient. 'It *is* good. As a matter of fact, it's *great*. I can't believe you prefer sappy Austen to something with real merit. What is it with all you women who'd rather read about Colin Farrell in a dripping shirt than something of substance?'

Darcy's mouth dropped open at the man's blatant rudeness. She was about to retort that Austen was anything other than 'sappy' when at that moment, her mobile phone buzzed in her pocket. 'Excuse me.' She fished it out and looked at the screen. It was a text from Ashley asking if Darcy wouldn't mind moving her shift around tomorrow. The graduate daughter of a successful city real-estate developer, and thus only in the job for the fun rather than the money, Ashley was notoriously undependable, but very sweet and the customers adored her.

It meant that Darcy would be opening up first thing, but

given that the evening had been going rapidly downhill from the outset, there was little point in her staying around here. The request might actually be a blessing in disguise.

She looked back at Oliver and realised that whatever retort she might make would be wasted on this overgrown teenager. He might be the current hot-shot in publishing and be in talks with Spielberg, but he was sorely lacking in manners, and indeed literary knowledge.

'I think you'll find it's Colin Firth you're referring to, not Colin Farrell. And you know what they say: you should never judge a book by its movie.' Smiling tightly, she added, 'You will have to excuse me; I need to make a call. Good luck with your book. Nice meeting you.'

Darcy made her way to the front of the restaurant and typed an affirmative response to Ashley. At that moment, Katherine approached her from behind.

'Where are you going? Why aren't you talking to Oliver?'

Darcy glanced over her shoulder to where Oliver Martin was now chatting animatedly with a man holding an Iron Man helmet, guessing that *that* conversation would be much more to his liking. She wondered briefly if the guy had worn the helmet on the way here.

'Aunt Katherine, please. Before you start, I am not talking to that man because we have absolutely nothing in common. He might be involved in books, and I might be interested in books, but a match that does not make.'

Her aunt sighed deeply. 'Oh, you are just impossible some-times. How are you ever going to find someone? Such a shame. You do know that the movie based on Will Anderson's books opens this week, don't you? I knew at the time that he was an incredible catch, and of course now his career's about to go even more stellar. I think he was interested in you too.'

'The same guy was already madly in love with someone else, Aunt Katherine,' Darcy argued tiredly. 'His own reflection. When are you going to realise that I'm just not interested in men who are all about success and career? I want someone who's fun and intelligent, and who can actually hold a conversation with someone other than themselves.'

'Don't we all?' her aunt replied airily. Then she said more kindly, 'I just want you to be happy, darling. This city's not an easy place to be alone, especially around the holidays, and—'

'But I'm not alone. I have lots of friends, and I have you too, don't I? OK, I know you're heading to St Barts for Christmas this year ...'

Notwithstanding that her aunt would be going out of town, she and Katherine just didn't have that sort of close relationship.

Darcy thought about their first Christmas together, over twenty years ago – not long after her parents' accident. She was still only a child though she felt like she'd grown up almost overnight upon losing her beloved family, and moving in with her mother's younger sister, who in truth she barely knew. Her forbidding and somewhat austere aunt had always frightened Darcy a little, and she seemed to possess little of Lauren's natural warmth and gentle ways.

She recalled how, that first, sad Christmas, Katherine's modern Brooklyn condo had barely been decorated for the season; nothing but a small artificial tree in the corner of the living room and a holly wreath on the door – a sharp contrast to the usual lavish adornments of her family's classic brick townhouse in the older part of the borough.

There was no lovingly prepared Christmas dinner on the day – Katherine ordered Thai take-out. Nor was there a big fuss around the opening of presents like Darcy was used to.

In fact, it was almost as though her aunt had forgotten about the holiday altogether. Darcy wasn't sure if this was down to Katherine's still-raw grief over losing her only sister a few months before, or her bewilderment at the sudden over-whelming responsibility of becoming guardian to a twelve-year-old girl. Most likely a combination of both.

Though given her own heartbreak following the accident, Darcy hadn't felt that there was much to celebrate. Still, Christmas had always been one of her favourite times of the year and the lack of any traditional nod towards the festivities merely served to highlight her loneliness and the gaping difference between her old life and the new.

Over the years, and mostly through her own efforts, Darcy had gradually brought her aunt round to celebrating the season, though Katherine typically preferred to spend the holidays in warmer climes, whereas Darcy couldn't conceive of being anywhere else but Manhattan at this time of year.

And even though in reality she and Katherine had spent only five years living under the same roof, Darcy had always felt that she'd been cramping her vivacious aunt's style, which was why she'd tried to stay as independent as possible and make her own way in life as soon as she could. She wasn't sure why her aunt's sense of responsibility now seemed to extend to finding Darcy a mate. Perhaps if she was coupled or married off, then in Katherine's mind that burden of duty (perceived or otherwise) would finally end? There was no denying that Katherine took a businesslike approach to most things in life. It was part of the reason she'd been so success- ful in navigating Manhattan's cut-throat events scene. Darcy knew that her own lack of ambition was another aspect of her character that her aunt didn't understand, but she was happy with her life and her job and her beloved books. Sure, she could do with a little more excitement in her life, but she fig- ured most people felt like that from time to time.

Katherine put a hand on Darcy's arm in a rare show of ten- derness. 'Of course you have me.' She watched in surprise as Darcy started to take out her gloves and scarf. 'You're not leaving now, are you? But you just got here! I promise I won't introduce you to any other ...'

'No, honestly, thanks, but I think I have had enough for one night. Besides, I have an early start in the morning.'

'Well, if you insist. But you certainly can't ride that bike home now,' her aunt argued, indicating the thickly falling snow outside. 'It's too dangerous and it's getting late. We will order you a cab and they can put your bike in the trunk.'

Moments later, Darcy was tucked into a Yellow Cab with her aunt peering in the window. The cab driver pulled away from the kerb, as her aunt hit one resounding hand on the roof of the car. Darcy waved a weak goodbye.

'You said West Houston?' the driver asked as he turned the corner.

'No,' she said resolutely, 'change of plans. Just take me up a couple of blocks and turn right. I can get my bike out and ride home from there.'

Snowflakes landing on her cheeks was one of her favourite sensations, and she would much rather brave the elements than be cooped up in an airless vehicle.

'In this weather?' grunted the driver.

Darcy nodded. 'In this weather,' she repeated, in a tone that indicated the conversation was over. 'But thanks anyway,' she added, not wanting to be rude.

Moments later, as the driver unloaded her bike and she reached into her messenger bag to get his fare, her hand touched her old dog-eared copy of *Pride and Prejudice*. She felt a sudden longing to get home as quickly as possible, make a cup of chamomile tea, change into her pyjamas and get under the covers with her namesake, Mr Darcy. Her mum had been a big fan of Austen too, she thought, smiling fondly as she recalled when Lauren Archer had first introduced her to her all-time favourite novel. Darcy had been too young to understand much of the subject-matter at the time, but over the years found herself returning again and again to Austen's famous tale, finding comfort in the story and, she supposed, viewing it as a kind of tangible connection to her late mother.

She slung a leg over her bike as the cab driver got back in

his vehicle and disappeared. Alone on the cold street, the snow fell across her shoulders and she tentatively pushed off, knowing she would have to ride with caution.

Darcy stared in front of her and navigated the empty streets as snowflakes danced in front of her, happier now in the knowledge that she was in control of her own destiny and would be home soon.

In the words of Groucho Marx, she thought wryly: *I've had a perfectly wonderful evening. But this wasn't it.*

Chapter 3

Dreams are illustrations ... from the book your soul is writing about you. **Marsha Norman**

The setting sun dropped languidly behind the lake at the rear of the Pemberley Estate. Here it was midsummer, and the heat added to the mood that now enshrouded Darcy as she took a tentative step towards it.

Although she was a lady and shouldn't be inclined to so-called animal urges, it was difficult to curb the anticipation that soared through her chest at that moment. It seemed the faster she breathed, the more her tight whalebone stays drove into her chest, constricting her fluttering heart. But none of her efforts to still herself would take hold. She could barely contain her anticipation.

Would he be here? she wondered

She knew she was breaking all the rules just then – that she was facing damage to her reputation if anyone saw her alone with him. But still, she couldn't seem to care about her reputation. Not in light of the ecstasy she felt when she was in his presence, the heady sense of wonder. This shocked her, considering they hadn't got off to the best of starts. And that was saying the absolute least.

She adjusted her parasol and quickened her pace as the lake came into full view before her. Suddenly, hearing the clattering of hooves behind her, she turned – and the breath caught in her throat.

There he was. His gaze met hers as he pulled his great steed to a stop and swiftly dismounted. His eyes seemed to bore into her soul and she placed a quivering hand against the bosom of her empire-waist gown.

A tentative smile flitted across her face even while his expression remained unreadable in the setting sun. It was he who made the first move. Taking a slow step in her direction, he then seemed to make up his mind about something, and closed the space between them with his long, manly stride.

Before she knew what was happening, he was in front of her, so close she could smell the intoxicating male aroma of the brandy he had been sipping after dinner and the pipe tobacco she knew he kept in his coat pocket.

'You're here,' he said simply.

'I am,' she replied, feeling a blush spreading from her neck to her cheeks. His gaze found her lips and at once she understood what would happen next. As if on cue, his eyes turned a smoky shade of grey and determination crossed his face. He moved his head ever so subtly towards hers and her heart threatened to explode from her chest. He was going to kiss her! Mr Darcy was going to kiss her!

'Miss Archer ...' he said quietly.

'Yes?' she replied breathlessly as she met his eyes.

Buzz ... Buzz ... Buzz ... Buzz.

Confused, and unwilling to miss what he was about to say next, she shook her head, as if trying to shoo away an annoying insect. She looked around out of frustration, trying to figure out just who was interrupting what had to be the most romantic moment of her life

Buzz ... Buzz ... Buzz ... Buzz.

Darcy sat up in bed and pushed her wayward curls out of her face, trying to work out where she was. The ringing phone was lying next to her on her pillow, where she must have left it after texting Katherine the night before to confirm that she was safely home.

She'd spent the rest of the evening reading in bed, and realised that she must have dozed off before setting her alarm. And in her slumber had enjoyed a recurring dream that was just about to reach a most satisfactory conclusion ... only to be interrupted.

Looking blearily at the phone display, Darcy discovered that she had multiple missed calls and – frighteningly – that it was almost 10 a.m.! She was more than an hour late for work, and poor Joshua had been phoning steadily for the last hour and was trying to call her right then.

Feeling panic rise in her chest, she fumbled with the keypad to answer the call. Fully awake now, she hit the accept button.

'Oh my goodness, Joshua, I'm so sorry. I know I was supposed to be in with you first thing, but my alarm didn't go off and my phone was on vibrate and I am a complete putz and I'm *so* sorry. I'm on my way right now.'

'Darcy, thank God.' Joshua sounded concerned. 'Are you OK? I've been phoning for the past hour. I thought Ashley was supposed to be in, but then she told me she'd changed shifts with you and I was just about ready to start calling round the Emergency Rooms. Where are you? What are you doing?' Clearly, Joshua had been too agitated to register any of Darcy's excuses.

She threw back the covers, hoping she could calm down her workmate, who had a penchant for dramatics akin to the stage mothers on the TV show *Toddlers & Tiaras*. Darcy knew that, right now, he was probably wringing his hands and on the verge of tears. Small wonder his earlier career as a trainee paramedic hadn't worked out.

Growing up in a family of surgeons, it seemed inevitable that Joshua would follow in his older siblings' footsteps and take up a career in medicine, but ultimately he proved too much of a delicate soul to handle the inevitable daily chaos of such a profession. Much to his relief, Joshua's parents had grudgingly accepted his decision to cut short his training and pursue instead his passion for literature. Which was how he'd ended up working in Chaucer's, in a job which (most of the time) was considerably less tumultuous than the ER, while taking a Masters in Drama – something that suited him all too well.

Strange though, how her and her colleague's career paths had taken such similar routes, suggesting that you could (and should) never fight your own destiny.

'Joshua, I'm fine, you can call off the search-party. I forgot to set my alarm last night, that's all. And I'm sorry I scared you.' Darcy hurried across the room towards the tiny adjoining bathroom and turned on the shower while trying to pull her pyjama top over her head with one arm. 'I'm just jumping in the shower now. I'll be with you in no time.'

'For all I knew you could have been hit by a car on your way to work and were laid up at Mount Sinai, unconscious, on life support. I mean, don't you understand how much you scare me – especially on that bike?'

Darcy couldn't help but giggle. 'And don't you understand how much you sound like a worry-wart mother?'

Joshua's voice was gentle. 'Someone has to look out for you, you know,' he said, and Darcy was touched by his concern.

'Thank you. I'll be there as fast as I can, OK?'

'And take a damn cab!' Joshua pleaded. 'Don't even think of trying to make your way all the way up here on the bike. It's a mess out there this morning with all that snow. The city put salt down but the roads are still a horror show, and everywhere people are losing their damn minds. Honestly, it's like something out of *The Dead Zone*.'

'Joshua, I'll be fine. My bike has seen worse, believe me. See you soon.'

'Well, don't pedal too hard!' he said in parting.

Having showered and dressed, Darcy clattered downstairs. On the way, she met one of her neighbours, Mrs Henley, a cantankerous type who lived in the apartment across the hallway. Darcy smiled as she passed the older woman, who was on the way up. 'Morning, looks like it's going to be a cold one today!' she called out by way of greeting.

'It's the middle of December – what else would it be?' the woman grumbled, her face typically pinched as she continued upward to her own apartment.

Darcy knew it was her own fault for bothering. In the three years she'd lived in this building, Mrs Henley had barely acknowledged her salutations, or any attempt at neighbourly friendship. She understood that many people including herself embraced solitude and were perfectly happy in their own company, but still the rejection stung. Despite being a city of millions, New York could be a lonely place at times.

Throwing open the front door of her building, she was immediately assaulted by the change in temperature. Joshua had been right about the weather, she thought. Her hair, still damp from the shower, would be in danger of freezing under her helmet in these icy conditions. Well, she didn't have time to go back in and blow-dry it, and if she ended up catching pneumonia, it would have been for the greater good of Chaucer's bookstore. Darcy unlocked her bike from the decorative rail sectioning off the front of Luigi's restaurant to the entrance of her building, and mentally thanked her landlord for having the foresight to have salted the steps the night before.

As she positioned her bike on the path, she began to swing a leg over when, caught unawares by the icy terrain, she slipped and landed squarely on her backside on the hard cold ground.

'Damn!' Darcy cursed as the bike landed clumsily on top of her. Pulling herself to her feet, she steadied the bike while holding on to the rail, deciding that she'd have to be more careful and not go out and prove them all right – those who seemed to believe that she was putting herself in serious danger on this thing.

Taking a deep breath this time, she mounted without issue and with the wheels eventually finding traction, she pedalled off in the direction of uptown. The panicky adrenaline rush she'd been experiencing since she woke began to subside, and Darcy felt her pulse gradually stabilise as she pumped her legs, gliding through the streets with ease. Taking a cleansing breath, she concentrated on the streets, soon realising that traffic was nowhere near as bad as Joshua claimed; at this hour, the worst of the morning rush had dwindled in any case. She smiled fondly; her workmate could really be a worrier sometimes.

Gradually, Darcy slipped into autopilot, something that happened routinely when she was riding. Her body was so familiar with this route – right and straight up on Sixth Avenue towards Central Park – that she could probably do the journey in her sleep.

Her mind started to drift to the list of items to be accomplished at the bookstore that day.

She should probably start with that special order from Mrs Hansen, she thought, remembering an email from one of the store's regulars the day before. And then get those Christmas orders out, or maybe Joshua had done that already? And she needed to ready her yearly festive favours – special Chaucer's colour-themed candy canes to give out with purchases. These always helped spread some cheer amongst customers' stressful last-minute shopping expeditions.

If she could get all of that done before the weekend, Chaucer's would be in great shape for the last-minute Christmas rush next week, she decided, admiring the gigantic Christmas tree baubles atop the fountain between Forty-Ninth and Fiftieth Street, before she sped past the famous *Love* sculpture further along on the corner of Fifty-Fifth.

Then once the holidays were over, she would think again about putting in place her long-held idea to offer customised literary walking tours of the city.

Over the last while she'd spent a lot of time investigating potential routes and assorted literary-related nooks and crannies throughout the city. Such as a former speakeasy in Greenwich frequented by F. Scott Fitzgerald, the destroyed shirtwaist factory near Washington Square Park – the tragedy of which featured in several modern literary works – as well as the various Greek Revival houses made famous by Henry James, which were home to eighteenth-century New York high society and where Edith Wharton had once lived. Not to mention the plethora of cafés, theatres and watering holes oft-frequented by many a Great American Novelist.

She'd come up with the idea ages ago through conversations with customers and tourists who'd shown a keen interest in the city's literary heritage, but had yet to get round to making it a reality. For Darcy, offering to show people around the city's bookish landmarks was something of a natural progression, yet still she struggled to find the courage to *just do it* – and not for the first time, wished she possessed some of Katherine's entrepreneurial spirit.

Darcy's ultimate dream was to open up her own bookstore some day – and try to recreate the kind of bookshop that was once ubiquitous to New York City but over the years had been lost.

Somewhere with panache, but a certain tattiness too: a lived-in, homey quality, with separate areas for new as well as old books, and unusual genres. Quiet little corners to get lost in, making browsers helplessly lose their bearings, the way any great bookshop should. She longed to be able to present the books themselves in ways that made them as irresistible as jewellery or chocolates, as well as provide space for public readings, book groups and launches, plus a café that perhaps at night turned into a wine bar.

It might be idealistic, but weren't all the best dreams?

The traffic signals had mostly been in Darcy's favour so far, but now reaching the top of Sixth Avenue and approaching the busy intersection at West Fifty-Ninth Street, she slowed her pedalling, preparing to stop for an upcoming red at the crosswalk. However, seeing it turn green, she sped up again slightly.

Too late, she became aware of a large dog walking out from behind the tall FedEx van about to move off just in front of her. She pumped hard on the brakes, but realised very quickly that she wouldn't make it, as her bike skidded perilously beneath her.

'Hey, watch out!' came a shout, which Darcy barely recognised as coming from her own lips.

Swerving, she squeezed again on the brakes and jerked back the handlebars, and for a split second felt relief at managing to avoid impact with the dog.

Just before ploughing directly into the pedestrian at the end of its leash.

Chapter 4

Our destiny is frequently met in the very paths we take to avoid it. **Jean de La Fontaine**

Barely avoiding the van, and instead ricocheting off a mailbox to her right, Darcy came off the bike just as her wheels slammed right into the pedestrian.

Several cars coming from behind honked and swerved to avoid her, screeching their brakes and sending her rolling on her side, while the FedEx van driver continued on as if nothing had happened.

Her bike had flown in the opposite direction, and the strap of the messenger bag that she usually draped across her chest now hung awkwardly around her neck and held her to the ground in a vice-grip. She felt cold seeping through her trousers and realised, too late, that she was lying in the dirty wet slush that finds its way kerbside during snowfalls in traffic-filled Manhattan.

Dazed, she sat up tentatively, wondering if she had sprained or broken anything, but she was still in one piece. If she had been a cartoon, this would be the moment that little blue birds would have been drunkenly circling her cranium.

'Hey, is that guy all right?' someone cried out nearby.

Like a tidal wave of memory, Darcy suddenly became aware that the voice, wherever it came from, wasn't talking about her.

She once again felt the memory of a body connecting with her bike. She straightened, the left side of her body howling in protest, and let out a guttural groan of pain.

'Lady – hey, lady! Do you need an ambulance?' called out another voice.

'Goddamn crazy cyclists ...' muttered yet another not so helpful-sounding one.

Darcy's eyes zoomed in on a brown shape situated about five feet from where she was sitting. Shaking her head to clear it, she tried to make some sense of the cacophony of voices around her. She attempted to push herself to her feet, but feeling dizzy, she toppled back down again, splashing noisily in the slush.

She looked back at the toppled mound, noticed the mop of dark tousled hair, taking in that the form also had two legs, at the bottom of which were expensive-looking, black leather shoes that now bore a long scuff across one heel. She saw that the brown lump was indeed a coat, and a nice one at that.

Or at least, it had been nice, before it had been dragged across Sixth Avenue, she thought.

As the scene unfolded and recognition finally set in, to her distress she quickly realised that she wasn't the one who needed help. A woman whom Darcy idly noticed was carrying bags from nearby Pain d'Avignon at the Plaza Food Hall helpfully uprighted her bike and leaned it against a lamp post. A guy dressed in jogging clothes bent down beside her. Probably on his way for a morning run across the road in the Park, she thought dazedly. 'I think somebody called an ambulance,' he said. 'Can you sit here for just a moment?'

She stared open-mouthed at the jogger, in shock and completely unsure about her answer.

Am I hurt? What happened? She focused her eyes once again on the man in the brown coat, and felt relieved when she saw another bystander – an older woman – go over to check on him. Calling out to him, the woman gently nudged his shoulder. But the man didn't move.

Panic surged through Darcy's chest and she made another feeble effort to push herself to her feet. 'Oh my God, is he OK?' she cried out, finally finding her voice.

The woman crouching down beside the injured man looked up at her and said, 'I'm not sure. His eyes are closed, I think he might have blacked out.' She tried to adjust the man, so that he was lying flat on his back.

Someone else cried out in alarm, 'Jeez, don't move him! He might have neck or back injuries or something. Wait for the ambulance, lady!'

At these words, Darcy felt her head start to spin afresh as she considered the implications.

Back injuries. Oh Christ ... had she just broken someone's neck?

Against the jogger's advice, she got up and slowly approached the huddled shape on the ground, a well-dressed man who looked to be in his early to mid-thirties, his face so slack and serene he had to be unconscious. She took in his aquiline nose, dark brows and fine cheekbones. One of his shoes – a sleek black loafer to complement his charcoal-grey trousers and maroon turtleneck – had come off. She got down on her haunches and started to reach for it when the older woman stopped her.

'Don't touch that; it could be evidence,' she warned sternly. 'The cops are on their way.'

Oh God. Could this day get any worse?

Suddenly, Sixth Avenue was like a blur, the kerb hard beneath Darcy as she slumped to the ground once again, one of the man's shoes lying in the gutter, a dog whining restlessly at his feet.

A dog ... she turned to look at the animal more closely. It was a medium-sized grey Husky with almond-shaped ice-blue eyes and white tipped ears, long bushy tail wagging as the animal circled his owner, a red leather leash dragging behind it.

She watched aimlessly, trying to put things together. The guy must have been out walking his dog, and had darted onto the crosswalk from behind the van at the last minute, just as the light turned.

Trying to stand up again, she held her hand out towards the dog, hoping to try and calm him, whispering, 'Here, fella.'

'Hey, don't strain yourself, miss. The ambulance should be here soon, and the paramedics will know what to do,' someone else reassured her.

More voices rose in protest as Darcy got to her feet again, her gaze fixed on the man still lying motionless on the street in front of her.

If she had only been paying attention ... If she had only been focused on riding her bike, and not on everything she had to do that day and daydreaming ... If only she had set her alarm and got out of bed in time, none of this would have happened. Yes, the guy and his dog might have cut it close with the lights, but there was no denying she had been going too fast if she couldn't stop in time. She felt tears in her eyes and a lump swell in her throat and then told herself sharply to stop. She wasn't the victim here; she had no right to cry.

Crouching down again and lightly touching the injured man's arm, she noticed the long gash in the sleeve of his coat.

I'll replace that, she promised silently, despite feeling worried when she realised the coat probably cost more than what she made in a month. *Somehow*, she added, wondering how close her credit card was to its limit. And although his turtleneck was rumpled and smudged from his brush with the pavement, Darcy could tell that this too was expensive. Reaching out, she touched the fine cashmere material, marvelling at the silkiness of its touch.

Soon, she heard sirens in the distance and an ambulance approach. The vehicle came to an abrupt stop, and moments later the doors to the back end were thrown open. The crowd parted.

'Can we get some room here?' the paramedics shouted and Darcy stirred, becoming vaguely aware of a man and woman in blue tending to the fallen pedestrian, and shooing away the dog as they did so. As Darcy stood back, her muscles briefly screamed in agony; there was no question that she was going to be bruised, but otherwise she thought she was OK.

Having checked the injured man's vital signs, the male paramedic began searching through his clothes and brought out the man's wallet, deftly flipping to his ID.

'Aidan! Aidan – can you hear me?' he called out urgently. 'Mr Harris ... can you hear me?'

But Darcy noted with growing unease that there was still no response from the man. Dear God, what had she done? What if he didn't wake up? What if he had kids? What if she had ruined everything for him and his family? And at Christmas ... She swallowed a sob as it built in her throat.

A flash of panic fluttered afresh in her chest as they carefully manoeuvred the unconscious man onto a stretcher, and loaded it into the back of the waiting ambulance.

'You were with Mr Harris?' a woman in uniform asked Darcy, appearing in front of her. A policewoman, she realised gulping. She hadn't noticed the cop car pull up.

'No.' She shook her head. 'I–I'm the cyclist,' she said ashamedly. 'He just stepped out in front of me. I didn't have time to ... will he be OK?'

46

The woman frowned and scribbled something in her note-book, leaving Darcy's question hanging in the air. As she went on to explain how the man and his dog had run the lights and that she'd tried her utmost to avoid him, the cop remained unmoved. Clearly she shared the view of the passer-by about her being just another goddamn cyclist. At this point, Darcy wasn't about to argue with that assessment.

'Honestly, there was no way I could have avoided him. He just came out of nowhere and there are witnesses ...' She looked back in the direction of the bystanders who'd helped earlier, but much to her distress, the jogger and the woman with the bag of groceries were now nowhere to be seen.

'Can you give me your name, address and contact details, please?' the cop asked. 'We'll be in touch if we need more information.'

As the police car finally moved off, time seemed to stand still. Darcy stood there, watching the ambulance doors shut and the vehicle pull away. What would happen now? Was she in big trouble? How bad were the guy's injuries? And when would he wake up, if at all?

Was it normal for someone to remain unconscious for more than a few minutes like that? Did he have permanent brain damage? Would he be in a coma for days, weeks, months – years even? What view would the police take on the scenario? Would they consider the collision her fault and would be she charged with Grievous Bodily Harm or Dangerous Driving or some such?

Her stomach twisted in knots, Darcy turned and looked around dazedly for her bike. The gathering of onlookers had since entirely dispersed, minds firmly returning to work, shopping, the morning run, or wherever their next appointments happened to be now that the drama was over.

Approaching the bike, she ran a cursory glance over it, wondering if she had damaged or bent the frame or the wheels while in the process of running down Aidan Harris.

Then she looked down to see a shopping bag she didn't recognise leaning alongside it and immediately guessed that the woman with the bags who'd so kindly picked up the bike for her must have accidentally left one behind. She was about to reach down to check if her suspicion was correct, when suddenly she heard a faint whine from her right.

Amongst all the mêlée, the Husky dog had been left behind. But of course he had: what ambulance would take a dog along to the hospital?

The poor thing stood beside a garbage can near Darcy's bike, looking lost and frightened.

Though she liked dogs and had had one as a family pet when she was younger, Darcy wasn't familiar with this wolf-like breed. Approaching it cautiously, she remembered the protein bar she always kept in her bag for emergencies. This certainly qualified as one, she thought as she slid the bar from one of the belted pockets on the side. It was peanut-butter crunch, her favourite, and the minute the dog heard the wrapping crinkle he limped forward, front paw still entangled in the leather leash, licking his lips.

'Here you go, fella,' she said cheerfully, peeling back the shiny foil wrapper and breaking off a corner of the bar.

She set it down on the path just in front of him, backing away as much as the passing foot traffic would allow. After a beat, the Husky lurched forward and cleanly snatched it up. Darcy smiled, breaking off similar-sized chunks and holding them out to him one by one.

When the bar was all gone the dog licked its grey and white chops thirstily, guilting Darcy into pulling out her purple water bottle, and emptying some into her hand. The dog, happier now, more trusting, lapped it up, plus the six other handfuls she offered him. The pink sandpaper tongue was stiff and ticklish, and it took all of her willpower not to giggle each time it latched onto her palm.

Eventually, she reached out a tentative hand towards his silken head, curling her fingers inwards in a non-threatening manner. As her hand grew closer he took a moment to sniff her skin. Then he again licked the tips of her fingers, as if enjoying a ghostly taste of the food item that had been there previously. Seemingly satisfied, he relaxed his posture and allowed Darcy to place her hand on top of his head, and caress his ears. Confident that the dog now trusted her, she reached down and picked up his lead.

'There you go, boy, you're a nice dog, aren't you?' The Husky was silent save for his panting, but his tongue lolled to one side of his mouth, and his ice-blue eyes stayed fixed on her own.

She lowered herself to her haunches and put a hand under the dog's bright white chin. A glimmer of light caught her eye

49

and she noted a tag in the shape of a dog bone dangling from his leather collar. She leaned closer to read the name etched on it: *Bailey*.

'So, what now, Bailey?' she asked, and the dog immediately responded to his name with an energetic wag of his tail. Then, much to Darcy's surprise, he jumped up on his hind legs, laying his big paws on her chest. He was so huge they were almost face to face and gulping nervously, she took a quick step backwards. 'Whoa, down boy!' she cried, and to his credit, the Husky did exactly as she asked.

When all four paws were once again safely on the pavement, Darcy fiddled with the Husky's lead. 'What do I do now?' she wondered out loud. 'And more specifically, what do I do with *you*?'

Darcy worked through the current situation in her mind. Yes, she had not only hit his owner Aidan Harris and knocked him unconscious, but she'd done it while the man was evidently out for a morning walk with Bailey. And now said dog was here in front of her, probably wondering what *he* was supposed to do next.

She considered the complexity of her situation. She couldn't very well bring the dog to work with her and – oh hell! Darcy gasped as it suddenly dawned on her where she was supposed to be. She took out her phone to check the screen, and sure enough, there were more missed calls.

All from Joshua.

She dialled his number and waited anxiously for her workmate to pick up, picturing him in a complete panic.

'Where in the living *hell* of all things holy are you?' Joshua shrieked. 'I've called you twenty times now, and no answer! I know it's hard to hear your phone ringing out on the street, but good God, Darcy, what is—'

'Sixteen,' Darcy said numbly.

'What?'

'You called me sixteen times. Just for the record.'

'Whatever. It's well past eleven – where on earth are you?' he repeated.

'Listen, Joshua, just calm down for a second, OK? I'm sorry, I know I'm late but there's been an accident and—'

'Oh my God, I *knew* this would happen eventually, I just knew.'

Darcy wished he would just let her tell the story without interruption.

'No, actually, *I* hit someone, Joshua. On my bike.' Tears sprang to her eyes as the shock and adrenaline gradually wore off and she was now able to properly assess the enormity of the situation. 'I'm fine, but I knocked the guy out cold and I don't know if he's going to be OK.'

Mercifully Joshua listened in stunned silence while she recounted the tale and the fact that right now, aside from being frantic about his condition, she was also trying to figure out how to reunite the injured man with his dog.

'It's my fault he got hit and his dog got left behind,' she said shakily. 'I need to at least find a way of letting him know the dog is safe.' And she very badly needed to know if he – Aidan Harris – was out of danger too.

The best thing for her to do, of course, was to take Bailey to whatever hospital his injured owner had gone to, and take things from there. Otherwise, not knowing whether Aidan Harris was dead or alive would eat her up.

'You're at West Fifty-Ninth Street?' Joshua mused, when she outlined her intentions, 'So I'm guessing they would have taken him to the ER at Roosevelt,' he said, reverting to paramedic mode. 'Either that or St Luke's, but Roosevelt's closer.'

'OK.' He was right; Roosevelt was only a few blocks away.

'Well, if you're going there, get yourself seen to as well,' her workmate advised, his voice soothing now. 'Sounds like Dog Guy wasn't the only one to take a knock. But don't rush off right away, take a breather first. Grab a coffee or something. And try not to panic.'

Darcy nodded. In truth, that sounded like heaven. She definitely needed to sit down somewhere for a little while at least.

'And it goes without saying that you mustn't worry about coming in to work today. I can cover things and Ashley's due in after lunch anyway. Consider it a Joshua buck.'

'Thanks, Joshua.' She sighed gratefully, knowing there was no way she'd be able to face work just then. 'I'll make it up to you, I swear.'

'Don't be silly – just make sure you're OK. But if you even think about bringing some strange dog down here, all bucks will be revoked.'

She smiled. 'I know – you're not a dog person, I get it. I suppose I'll just have to take him round the Emergency Room with me.'

'The good workers in the ER aren't exactly dog people either, sweetie – they've got the humans to think about. Tell you what though, instead of trying to strike it lucky with the hospitals, let me make a call. I know a guy who still works at Roosevelt.'

Darcy brightened a little. 'Do you think your friend would be able to tell me if the man I hit has come round and is OK?'

'I can't promise anything. It's been a while since we've talked, and he could well have moved on since, but I can certainly try.'

'I'd really appreciate anything you can do, Joshua, thanks.'

'Like I said, go and sit down somewhere for the moment – preferably out of this cold. I'll call my friend and see what I can wheedle out of him, if anything.'

Grateful for her workmate's help, Darcy said goodbye to Joshua, while he promised he would call her back as soon as he knew anything.

Feeling a powerful headache coming on, she tugged on Bailey's leash and wandered back towards her bike. As she did so, she again noticed the deli bag and wondered if she should just leave it there beside the lamp post in case the lady came back for it.

But now, lifting it up, Darcy realised it didn't contain deli or bakery products, but something much, much heavier. And looking inside, she saw a package, a gift box that had been beautifully wrapped in thick green paper, and tied with a wide red grosgrain ribbon.

The bag itself, although a little wrinkled, also had an expensive look to it.

But where had it come from? Darcy wondered. Alongside her, Bailey panted and wagged his tail with such enthusiasm it was causing her to wonder if his owner might have been carrying it before he got hit. And thinking about it now, she recalled – a snapshot of the man and his dog right before they connected flashing into her mind – there was indeed something on the end of his arm – the same one in which he held the leash.

Darcy looked from the gift box back to Bailey, quickly understanding that she had more than one thing to return to Aidan Harris.

Chapter 5

What lies behind us and what lies before us are tiny matters compared to what lies within us. **Ralph Waldo Emerson**

Still shaken in the aftermath of the accident, Darcy adjusted her bike and manoeuvred Bailey's lead in such a way that she would be able to walk alongside him and the bike, while at the same time keeping a hold on her belongings and Aidan Harris's gift.

Taking Joshua's advice, and with her bones aching and clothes still a little damp from the fall, she decided to take temporary refuge in a nearby café – one that hopefully allowed dogs inside. Most of the places directly on West Fifty-Ninth were pretty swanky, so she made her way a block over to one of the more casual chains on Seventh, where she guessed she should have no problems finding a table.

Locking her bike outside, she took Bailey's leash in her still-trembling hand and entered hesitantly, breathing a sigh of relief when a smiling cashier called out in greeting.

'Nice dog,' the woman commented, as Darcy ordered a strong cup of English breakfast tea and a cranberry muffin for the sugar hit. The immortal words of C.S. Lewis: '*You can't get a cup of tea big enough or a book long enough to suit me*' automatically popped into her brain. Never a truer saying, as far as Darcy was concerned, remembering how curling up with a book and a mug of tea had always been a comforting ritual for her mother, and a tradition that Darcy had tried to hold onto from their time together. She only wished she had one of her beloved books to help soothe her right now, but in her haste to leave the apartment this morning, she'd forgotten to put the copy of *Pride and Prejudice* back into her bag.

The café was full of Christmas shoppers as Darcy led Bailey towards a vacant table down the back.

He walked patiently alongside her, as if he was used to doing this kind of thing, and she wondered if perhaps he was some kind of assistance dog. She didn't think that was common to this particular breed though, and she also got the impression that the Husky was quite young, not much older than a pup. Well, if his owner did depend on him in this manner, she'd try her utmost to have them back together very soon.

She fretted, going over the accident a dozen, a hundred dozen times in her head.

The light turning green, the sound of her brakes screeching, wheels spinning, the brisk air, the smell of fresh bread from a nearby bakery, the supposedly clear intersection and then, bam, splat, crunch, Darcy's messenger bag digging into her ribs and the man lying there, flat on his back. Out cold.

The image made her flinch but all she could see was him, Aidan Harris: his firm chest and broad shoulders under his maroon crewneck, eyes closed; his dark, silken hair lying on the ground. Adding an extra sachet of sugar to her tea to help counter the shock, Darcy took a sip and eventually sat back, hoping that the weight of the morning's drama would gradually subside, though it was impossible to relax when she was still frantic to find out which hospital Aidan Harris had been taken to, and more importantly, whether he would survive.

Bailey sat on the floor beside her, again as if he was well used to waiting around in places like this, though he was showing an extraordinarily strong interest in her muffin. Feeling guilty, she broke off a piece and fed it to him. 'I'm sure you're used to much classier places than this, though,' Darcy murmured to him, given his owner's expensive clothes and shoes, as well as man and dog's proximity to the surrounding neighbourhood.

Given that the guy was out walking his dog, and wasn't wearing a suit or carrying a briefcase, it seemed unlikely that he was on his way to work. Much more likely that he lived close by this part of town, perhaps the Upper West or East Side? But there was little point pondering such things; Darcy realised she had no clue about anything to do with Aidan

Harris, other than that he liked dogs and had good taste in clothes (and, it seemed, gifts).

She reached for the bag again and carefully removed the heavy gift box. The box had such an expensive, luxurious feel to it; so tactile and firm to the touch with faint wired embossing. The bow was equally exquisite, a rich red, almost maroon in colour. Darcy wondered for whom the gift was intended. Had Aidan Harris been out on an important errand when she'd crashed into him, diverting his plans, and quite possibly his life?

She swallowed hard, tears in her eyes. It just didn't bear thinking about. What if she'd caused serious, maybe even permanent damage? If so, she didn't think she'd be able to live with herself and was trying her utmost to banish the thought when just then she heard her phone ring. She stared at the handset for a moment, almost afraid to find out what news her workmate might have for her.

'Joshua … hi,' she greeted, her voice watery.

'Well, it turns out that I was right, which as you know is a regular occurrence …' Darcy waited impatiently for him to finish his typical long drawn-out introductory spiel, before eventually getting to the point. 'So it seems your victim,' Darcy winced afresh at his choice of words, 'has indeed been taken to Roosevelt ER.'

'Your friend actually confirmed that the man I hit is there?'

'Well, of course not. It would be more than his job's worth to give out confidential information like *that*, but after some cajoling, I did coax it out of him that a pedestrian injured on

Sixth and Fifty-Ninth Street had been brought into the ER this morning. So unless Bergdorf are doing the kind of special that would cause pile-ups round there ...'

'That's wonderful to know, Joshua, thank you,' Darcy said. 'I don't suppose your friend happened to let slip anything about the guy's condition? If he was still unconscious or ...?' She inhaled deeply, not sure if she wanted to know the answer.

'Sadly, my legendary powers of persuasion aren't *that* good,' he intoned. 'Patient confidentiality and all that.'

'I see.' Joshua went on to give her a detailed and sobering run-down on the ins and outs of patient privacy rules before assuring Darcy again that she shouldn't worry about things at the store and that he was very capably holding the fort.

'Thank you, I owe you one,' she said, hanging up, but the phone call had given her little comfort other than confirmation of her 'victim's' current location. Darcy shuddered and tried to look on the bright side. The hospital wasn't too far away, at least – a plus, seeing as she would have to walk there, though in truth she wasn't sure she could face getting back on the bike just yet in any case. The warmth of the café had dried off the worst of the dampness on her trouser legs, and the sugar hit had helped stave off the worst of the shock, so she guessed she should be good to go.

Bailey's lead in hand, and wheeling her bike at her side, Darcy slowly made her way along the snow-filled streets to Roosevelt ER.

She thought again about the privacy issues Joshua had just outlined. Given that she wasn't a family member, it was a long shot that she would find out anything about Aidan Harris's condition, she thought, locking up her bike outside the hospital. But surely if she explained the situation – that she too had been involved in the accident, they would at least let her know if he was or wasn't seriously injured, wouldn't they? Darcy certainly hoped so, but first things first.

She rubbed Bailey behind the ears. 'Time to let your master know where you are, buddy.'

Taking a deep breath, she approached the double doors of the Emergency Room, only to be immediately blocked by a security guard. 'Excuse me, miss. You can't take that dog inside.'

Damn.

'I understand, but he's not my dog – he belongs to a patient here.' Darcy launched into a full account of the accident and how she needed to reunite Bailey with his owner.

'I'm sorry but I can't allow it – no matter the circumstances. Dogs are not allowed in the hospital.'

Darcy exhaled deeply. She guessed she should have expected this, but she had been so focused on bringing Bailey back to Aidan Harris that she hadn't really thought much more beyond that. 'But what am I supposed to do?'

'You can tie him up over there beside the bikes, if you like. Don't worry, I'll keep an eye on him for you.'

Darcy had actually been referring to more longterm issues, but this option would have to suffice for the moment. At the very least, she would be able to get the hospital to pass on the information to Mr Harris that his dog was safe.

She just hoped he was in a fit enough state to receive the message, she thought, biting her lip to stem a fresh flow of tears.

'OK, thank you.' She duly walked Bailey towards the nearby bike-stand and looped his lead through the metal. 'Sorry, boy,' she said, ruffling him behind the ears, but the Husky seemed to understand and simply sat down alongside Darcy's bike, as if he'd been doing the same for years. 'I'm just going to see if I can get you back to your owner, OK?'

The dog just stared back and settled in for a wait. He was so well behaved, she noted, recalling how easy it had been to negotiate the streets with him and her bike. Clearly well-trained, he wasn't in the least bit skittish and Darcy instinctively knew this one was no brainless mutt.

Going through the double sliding doors, she headed straight for ER Reception, all the while noticing little seasonal touches inside, like the small tree blinking in the corner, and a white tree skirt covered with gaily wrapped packages that Darcy guessed were just empty boxes. Coloured lights blinked on and off, and cheesy Christmas carols played from a speaker some-where. Currently someone with a lisp was singing about his 'two front teeth'.

Emergency Rooms were possibly the last places anyone wanted to be in at this time of year, but at least the staff were making an effort.

A sudden image of the airless grey hospital waiting room in which she and Katherine had spent tortuous hours waiting for news of her parents after the crash wormed its way into

Darcy's brain and she tried her best to shrug off the unwelcome memory and concentrate on the task in hand.

Approaching Reception, Darcy swallowed the lump in her throat. Now that she was here, she wasn't sure if she really wanted to know the condition of the man she'd upended earlier. What if his injuries were critical?

She cleared her throat and tried to project a casual air to her voice. 'Excuse me, hi,' she began, smiling at the receptionist who looked at her coolly. 'I'm here about a patient, Aidan Harris. I believe he was brought in this morning, about an hour ago?' She wished to give the impression that she was family or a close friend, in the hope that the woman might inadvertently reveal some information about his condition.

The woman typed a couple of commands into the PC in front of her. 'Harris, you say? And you are?'

But try as she might, when it came down to it, Darcy couldn't pretend. In fact, she was a terrible liar and shared that much with Aunt Katherine in her ability to speak the truth, albeit in a decidedly softer manner.

'I'm the reason he's here,' she blurted out. And then, much to her embarrassment she burst into tears, all her fears and worries since the accident suddenly overwhelming her. 'I collided with him this morning on my bike. The light was green, honestly, and he just came out of nowhere, I swear, and ...' She sniffed tearfully. 'I'm sorry, but he was unconscious when the ambulance took him away, and I've been going out of my mind with worry over what might have happened to him. Is he all right?' she pleaded with the receptionist. 'I know you're not supposed to give out personal information, I get that, but can you at least tell me if he's OK? For all I know, I might have killed him. And I have his dog ... he was out walking him at the time, and I want Mr Harris to know that Bailey is fine, and that I'm taking good care of him.'

The receptionist had kind eyes that looked at her sympathetically. She seemed taken aback by Darcy's distress and heartfelt desperation. 'You're right honey, we're not allowed to give out patient information,' she said, but she picked up the phone. 'Can you wait just a moment? Let me see if there's something I can do.'

Darcy exhaled in relief at this, though the phone call seemed to take forever as she waited to hear some news – any kind of news – about Aidan Harris.

Eventually the receptionist hung up and turned to her. 'Like I said, I'm not allowed to give out patient information.' She took a deep breath. 'So let's put it this way: nobody brought in this morning to this ER with reported head injuries has suffered any serious trauma,' she added meaningfully, her gaze locked on Darcy's, 'and all are now stable,' she finished.

Darcy wanted to cry with relief. The woman was, in her own way, letting Darcy know that he was not in danger.

'Oh, thank God!'

'However, stable doesn't necessarily mean one hundred per cent OK either,' she cautioned. 'Often victims of TBI – traumatic brain injury – become disorientated.' The receptionist eyed her. 'Like I said, I can't give out specific patient medical information – even to a family member – without patient

63

consent. Unfortunately, not all of our patients are in a state of mind to provide that consent.'

This time, Darcy was having trouble following what she was trying to say. So Aidan Harris's condition was stable, but he was disorientated, so not quite out of the woods? Still she guessed that she'd learned just about as much as she could at that point.

'Thank you, and yes, I completely appreciate your position,' she said, playing along. 'Just something else in general. If there are items – pets, for example – left behind at the scene of an accident, how does the hospital usually reunite them with patients?'

'I'd imagine the care of such animals would be given over to family members or next of kin.'

'So there's no chance of my giving the dog back to Mr—'

'No chance whatsoever.' The receptionist's tone was firm but kind. 'Animals are not allowed in hospitals, sweetie.'

'OK.' Darcy thought hard. 'Well then, is it possible to leave a message letting the patient in question or their families know that the dog is in safe hands, and is ready to be returned to them as soon as possible?' She guessed Aidan's family would have been contacted by now and would surely be worried about Bailey and anxious to get him back. 'May I leave you my number and they can call me? And Mr Harris too – I'm sure he'll be anxious to find Bailey as soon as he's back on his feet. I mean ...' She trailed off, kicking herself at her unfortunate choice of words.

'Sure, I'll arrange to have the information passed on,' the

woman replied, but Darcy could tell she was becoming anxious about the line of people beginning to form behind her.

'Thank you, I can't tell you how grateful I am for your kindness,' Darcy said, writing down her mobile phone number on a piece of paper.

'You're welcome,' said the receptionist. 'Have a great day and happy holidays.'

'Same to you.' Darcy smiled, buoyed by the news that her victim seemed to be recovering, and Bailey would be back with his family in no time. It felt as if a huge weight had been lifted off her shoulders, to know that she hadn't caused any lasting damage.

Her day was finally starting to look up. Aidan Harris would be a chance encounter, a quirky story to tell now and then over drinks, a cautionary lesson before life returned to normal once again.

Chapter 6

Outside of a dog, a book is man's best friend. Inside of a dog it's too dark to read. **Groucho Marx**

As Darcy exited the hospital, going through the double sliding doors again, the winter chill cut through her jubilant mood and brought her back to reality. What exactly, she wondered, was she supposed to do with Bailey in the meantime until his family called to take him back?

She was exhausted by now, and all she wanted to do was go home, take a bath, curl up with a book and try to put the morning's dramas behind her. But she could hardly drag both Bailey and the bike all the way downtown, not when her legs were just about ready to collapse from under her.

He was much too big for public transportation and in any case would need to be in a carrier for the bus or the subway. What she was supposed to do?

There was only one thing for it: she'd try to nab a cab driver who'd be willing to take a dog Bailey's size, and hope for the best. She wasn't permitted to keep pets in her building, but she figured it would be easy enough to sneak him in for just a couple of hours.

'Good news, Bailey; it looks like Aidan is OK,' she said, untangling his leash and her bike from where they waited outside. Bailey looked up sharply, and she realised it was the first time she'd mentioned his owner's name in the dog's presence. 'You can go home soon.'

At the mention of the word 'home', Bailey's ears perked up even more, and a small whine emitted from the back of his throat. Darcy frowned as a feeling of sadness crept up on her. Never mind her own concerns, the dog must be really confused about what was happening and why his owner had seemingly abandoned him for some weird stranger.

'I know, buddy, I'm sure you do want to go home.' She put a hand behind Bailey's silky ears and rubbed them. 'But for the moment, my place is going to have to do, OK? So let's go and find a cab,' she continued, resigned to the fact that this might take a while. Her plan was to try and get one on Fifty-Seventh Street going in the right direction. Wheeling the bike alongside them, she and Bailey reached the intersection at Eighth Avenue, two blocks down from where the incident had occurred just hours before. It felt like a lifetime ago. Checking her watch – a treasured gift from Joshua with the Dr Seuss quote, *How did it get so late so soon?* inscribed across the face – Darcy noted that it was now past lunchtime. Small wonder she was feeling tired.

But as she turned right onto Eighth, all the while scouring the street for free cabs, Bailey suddenly stopped.

Darcy gently jiggled the leash and pulled in the direction she wanted to go. 'Come on, boy, it's freezing and we need to keep going if we want to find a cab.' She tugged again but Bailey resisted, and this time sat right down on the pavement.

Puzzled by this show of stubbornness Darcy tugged again, this time a little harder, but Bailey jerked backwards, almost pulling the leash from her hands.

Crikey, what if he ran away and got lost? she thought, panicking. She couldn't lose him now, not after all that had happened. And especially now that Aidan Harris's family would soon find out she was taking care of him. No doubt they were distraught enough as it was about Aidan, let alone finding out that the stupid woman who had knocked him over had also gone and lost their dog in the meantime.

Darcy sighed and engaged the kickstand on her bike, before crouching down to his level. 'Bailey, come on now, come,' she commanded a little more authoritatively.

But when he still refused to move, she took a deep breath and put her hands on her hips. 'Bailey, come. This way. Heel?' She tried several variations of the same command, but still the Husky strained mulishly in the other direction.

Darcy's shoulders sagged. 'Bailey. Come on, buddy, *please*,' she cried in frustration. 'I really need to get you home.'

At the mention of the word 'home' again, the dog's ears perked up once more. He stuck his tongue out and wagged his tail as if to say: 'OK then, let's go.'

She shook her head at his perplexing change of demeanour. 'Yes, but home's *this* way.' Darcy pulled the leash and waved a hand in the direction that she wanted to go. Bailey once again resisted and pulled the opposite way, back up towards Columbus Circle and the Park. He stared hard at Darcy as if telepathically trying to deliver a message.

That famous quote from Groucho Marx about dogs being too dark to read instinctively popped into her brain, and she frowned, trying to figure out what the hell she was missing.

She wondered if maybe he was trying to tell her that home – *his* home – was back in the other direction. Understanding finally dawning, she looked again at the tenacious Husky. 'Are you trying to tell me that your home is that way?' She pointed past Columbus Circle towards the Park. Bailey whined and then gave a sharp bark.

Darcy felt as if she was having a *Lassie* moment. She thought back to her childhood when she would watch the old black and white TV reruns of the show, remembering how the faithful collie always seemed smarter than her owners. No change there then.

She recalled laughing with her mum at how exasperated the dog always looked when her owners would scratch their heads and ask: 'What is it, girl? Did Timmy fall down the well?' Even as a child Darcy remembered thinking, Go on dummies, follow the dog. She's smarter than all of you put together.

She bit her lip. Was it just her imagination or was Bailey now wearing a very definite Lassie-like expression?

Then the thought struck her. Of course! If she could find

out exactly where Bailey lived, then she could return him to his family right away without having to wait for them to contact her. Clever puppy; evidently he was thinking more clearly than she was.

While Darcy didn't relish the prospect of facing Aidan Harris's wife or relatives, given her part in the accident, she would at least be able to return Bailey and the package to them safe and sound.

Then her part in all of the drama would be over, and she could relax for the rest of the day and try to put the incident behind her. Unless, of course, Aidan Harris tried to stick her with a lawsuit for his medical bills, in which case she would put all guilt aside and stand up for herself.

'Oh what the hell,' she muttered, as she adjusted her bike and turned in the direction of the Park. Walking some more wouldn't kill her, and it would surely be a lot easier than trying to persuade a cab to take them both downtown. 'At the worst, it's a crap shoot, at the best, you get to go home soon.' She nudged Bailey on, and let him take the initiative. The dog looked back at her for confirmation, and she smiled. 'Go on then, buddy, you're the boss. Lead the way. Let's go home.'

Bailey tugged on his leash and set off. He barked as he started to trot, looking back briefly at her and breaking into a doggie grin as if to say, '*Finally*, you get it. I thought we were going to be here all day.'

Darcy trailed behind the Husky as he led her with purpose through Columbus Circle past the Time Warner Centre, and the Trump International Tower on Central Park West.

Walking along at a brisk pace, they proceeded about fifteen blocks northwards, past the 'Ghostbuster building' and the beautiful German Renaissance-style Dakota residence, skirting the Park all the while.

As they walked she struggled to not only keep up with the determined Husky, but also manage the bike and come to terms with the idea that a dog seemed completely in control of where she was going. But he was very determined, and his bearing clearly told her that Bailey knew exactly what he was doing.

So even while he seemed sure about where they were headed, she half-wished Bailey was able to give her some sort of clue or indication as to how far away his home actually was, or how long the journey would be. Fatigue was setting in again now, and at this point she just wanted this strange day to be over. Still though, Darcy held firmly to Bailey's leash; she wasn't going to risk losing him after all of this.

As they made their way along the streets, she was aware of the change in real estate. The salubrious historic apartment residences they passed, along with the fact that the sidewalk crowd became increasingly well-heeled, started to weigh on her, and as always she felt conspicuous around these parts, especially in her bedraggled state. She guessed that with her limp ponytail, damp clothes and scruffy coat, she looked as though she had quite literally been dragged through the gutter.

Then something dawned on her and she came to a halt, stopping Bailey in his tracks.

'Do you live in an apartment with a doorman?' she asked him.

Of course, he didn't answer, but gave a slight cock of his head. Darcy wished she could read his thoughts. She looked up ahead, trying to get her bearings. He could just as easily be heading towards Harlem (a distance which Darcy didn't think her feet could take), but then she recalled the clothes that Aidan had been in that morning, and the fancy package he'd been carrying, and suspected that he lived in a upscale part of the city. If it turned out that he and Bailey lived in one of those residence buildings with a carpet and awnings outside, and a doorman or a concierge inside, she wasn't sure how (or if) she would be able to get past them.

She sighed heavily. '*Of course* your owner would have to live in this neighbourhood, Bailey.' The Husky's white-socked paws danced happily, and he was once again off with a much more reluctant Darcy in tow. As he led her closer to what her aching limbs hoped would be their final destination, she couldn't help but admire the impressive Art Deco, Renaissance and Beaux Arts buildings that soared up around her on all sides. She had to admit, Bailey's owner certainly had good taste in his choice of neighbourhood.

A dream location for many, there was arguably nowhere else in Manhattan than the Upper West Side that enjoyed all the conveniences and bustle of a thriving city with the eclectic amenities of the suburbs, combined with sophistication and beautiful outdoor space.

Working at Chaucer's, Darcy was familiar with the high-end

shopping and dining the upscale neighbourhood offered; mouth-watering gourmet places like Zabar's and Fairways, as well as myriad wonderful cafés, gelaterias, salumerias, bakeries and fine restaurants, though much to her regret she couldn't afford to shop or eat in any of them.

Beautiful homes in ornate buildings or historic brown-stones on tree-lined avenues, wonderful farmers' markets, great restaurants and stunning outdoor living in the shape of Riverside Park (not to mention Central Park) all added up to a charmed life for the lucky residents of the Upper West Side.

And just as Darcy started to ponder over what Aidan Harris might do for a living if he could afford to live around here, Bailey came to an abrupt stop. So abrupt that she almost ran over his tail with her bike's front wheel.

The dog threw a cursory glance backwards at her, took a quick sniff of the air and turned to the right. Evidently, he was giving her the heads-up that they needed to turn.

Darcy and her bike followed him down a quiet tree-lined residential side street. Up ahead, she saw a break in the luxury pre-war apartment buildings, and instead saw a neat row of three-storey brownstone townhouses. Bailey quickened his pace and led her directly to the third one on the right, where he stopped and sat at the bottom of the steps.

She glanced down at the dog. 'Here?' she asked, pointing. Bailey's tongue popped out of his mouth and he wagged his tail. 'So that must be a yes,' Darcy said, taking in the exterior of the forbiddingly elegant home.

She bit her lip as she contemplated what to do next. At least she wouldn't have a doorman to contend with. But on the other hand, this was *serious* Manhattan real estate. Darcy wasn't sure exactly how much brownstones went for in this part of town, but she guessed it was major cash.

'Well well, well,' she said to Bailey. 'Do you think that maybe you could have told me before that you guys were loaded?'

Darcy parked her bike next to the stairway that led up to the front door and cautiously looked around. She wondered if anyone was looking out of their window, taking in the fact that she was not a regular in this neighbourhood and already dialling the NYPD.

'That's all I need at this moment, the cops again. I'm just trying to do a good deed,' she muttered as Bailey led the way up the steps. 'Maybe people will just think I'm the hired help.'

The Husky looked at her doubtfully.

Darcy reached for the doorbell and pressed it hard, glancing at the pretty potted maple tree outside. 'OK, let's see if anyone's home.'

Bailey moved skittishly at her feet, as if waiting for her to open the door and let him in. But there was no reply, and after a beat, Darcy rang the bell again. Still nothing.

Her heart plummeted. Damn.

Bailey looked up at her and whined impatiently.

'Believe me, I wish that door would open too. But there's nothing I can do, Bailey; it looks like nobody's home.' Checking her watch, she saw it was still mid-afternoon, so if Aidan's wife or girlfriend (or boyfriend even) was at work, they weren't likely to be home for hours yet. Or of course, she realised, wanting to kick herself for not thinking of this sooner, once they'd learned about Aidan's accident, they were likely to be back at the hospital.

Damn again, she whispered silently. So much for getting all of this sorted out quickly. She reached down and caressed Bailey's silky head. 'Sorry, buddy, looks like you're stuck with me for a little while longer.'

The Husky's tummy rumbled out loud, making Darcy aware of the fact that he likely wouldn't have eaten a proper meal since breakfast that morning. No wonder he was so anxious to go inside.

She'd have to find a way to feed him then, and while she was at it, feed herself too. She'd missed breakfast on account of being late for work and the only thing she'd eaten was the muffin at the café a little while ago.

But Darcy didn't figure on finding anything to eat for either of them around these parts. Not without taking out a mortgage in any case.

'Sorry, Bailey, back to Plan A,' Darcy informed him jadedly. 'You're going to have to forgo your usual creature comforts for a little while. We're going downtown.'

Chapter 7

Books are not made for furniture, but there is nothing else that so beautifully furnishes a house.
Henry Ward Beecher

After finding a taxi willing to carry the Husky with surprising ease – Darcy guessed doggy transport was a common occurrence amongst the pet-loving Central Park West set – soon they were back along her own elm-tree-lined streets, cars wedged bumper to bumper against the kerb. Luigi's was quieter after the lunchtime rush; no line at the counter and only a few late stragglers pressed against the window, sharing a Coke and a slice of pizza. She was relieved, guessing that she wouldn't have to wait too long for the order she'd phoned in on the way.

Two flights full of excitable yipping led her up to her apartment and Darcy fiddled with her keys, eager to get Bailey inside before grouchy Mrs Henley heard the commotion and poked her prominent nose out to see what was going on. In contrast to his staid behaviour earlier, the Husky now seemed positively excited by the change in scenery. Or more likely, by the scent of roasted garlic and meaty bolognese coming from the restaurant.

Darcy had just found her key when she heard feet pounding up the stairs. Heavy, male feet. Terrified that her stowaway would be discovered, she frantically slid the key in, swinging wide the door to sneak him through to her apartment. At that moment Ricardo, one of Luigi's waiters, rounded the corner, a white and red chequered pizza box in hand, the contents so hot, fresh steam seeped out of the side.

Her mouth watered. For the pizza, that was – not Ricardo.

In his mid-twenties, Ricardo was six feet tall and stocky in his wheat-coloured cords and green and red Luigi's shirt beneath his stained apron. The newest addition to the staff at the restaurant, for some reason he had latched onto Darcy.

Maybe he had a thing for (older) bookish types, that whole hair up, reading glasses on and open shirt collar thing that some guys went for, though she felt almost old enough to be his mother, and had told him so on several occasions. Almost instinctively she tightened her tousled ponytail and checked her neckline to ensure there was nothing for him to get in any way excited about. Though it was unlikely. The look Darcy was currently sporting – a combination of flushed cheeks from the freezing cold, frizzy hair and damp dirty clothes covered in greyish dog fluff – was unlikely to be a turn-on for any guy.

'You ordered pizza, Darcy?' he queried, reaching the top of the stairs. 'How come you're not at work today ... and hey, who's the big guy?'

The waiter spotted Bailey inside circling Darcy's Christmas tree and slipped into the apartment uninvited, as if he'd been there a dozen times.

Uh oh.

'Hey Ricardo,' she sighed as he slid the pizza box on her kitchen counter. She was exhausted, her feet ached, her limbs were sore, and right then all she wanted to do was slump onto her cosy sofa and eat. The smell of warm tomato and basil, rising dough and freshly bubbling cheese assaulted her senses and her stomach rumbled.

'Come here boy,' the waiter commanded, dropping to his knees as Bailey barked excitedly, circling him with a harmless growl before leaping into his lap. Ricardo sat back on his haunches, tickling him behind the ears and clearly earning a friend for life.

Darcy winced at the noise, hoping the neighbours wouldn't hear and complain to the landlord. 'You're pretty good with him,' she remarked to Ricardo, turning on a couple of low-level lamps and flicking a switch. Her little Christmas tree (the smallest the street vendor could find) and the homemade ornaments decorating it immediately came to life; fairy lights illuminating her tiny living room and its packed-in furniture, and overloaded shelves all weighed down even more by the plethora of tinsel and festive garlands.

'My brother-in-law has two Huskies, each one crazier than the next. You got lucky; yours seems pretty calm.'

'He – he's not mine,' Darcy improvised quickly. She washed her hands and reached for a slice of thin-crust margherita, hoping she wouldn't have to explain. But Ricardo was patient, waiting for her to finish chewing as he stared at her with questioning dark eyes. 'I'm ... I'm watching him for a friend from work. Just for a couple of hours.' She hoped he wouldn't mention the dog's presence to his boss who was also Darcy's landlord.

'Cool.' He looked at the Christmas tree. 'What are those, key-chains?'

She smiled. 'No, they're books. Well, actually, they're matchboxes covered in coloured paper, but each one represents a different book.' She picked up one at random, turning it over to read the title. 'See, this one's *Moby Dick*. And that one's *Northanger Abbey*. And that one's *The Great Gatsby ...*'

'I get it, I get it; you don't have to read the whole tree to me. It's no secret you have a thing for books.' He looked around and she tried to see the room through his eyes: the bookshelves filled to brimming, tottering piles of read and to-be-read titles positioned in various places around the living area – beside the sofa, beneath the TV-stand, blocking out the weak winter light on the windowsill. She smiled, proud of her collection, and only sorry that she didn't have room for even more.

Having polished off her first slice of pizza Darcy quickly reached for another, and hesitantly offered one to Bailey, not sure if such stodge was healthy for dogs, but by the way he scoffed it down in one go, she figured it didn't really matter. She then offered a slice to Ricardo, trying to be polite, but he made a disgusted face. 'Pizza without meat is like spaghetti without sauce,' he lectured.

'Spoken like a true Italian,' she joked, going to the fridge. There wasn't much in there, but she knew she had some beer left from when she'd had Ashley and Joshua over for a pot luck Thanksgiving.

Darcy paid Ricardo for the pizza and waited until she heard his sneakers pounding down the stairs to turn back to her doorway, only to find Mrs Henley poking her head out into the hallway. 'What's all the racket?' she asked, her face pinched with annoyance.

'Just getting a pizza delivered,' Darcy smiled, forgetting her door was wide open. 'Sorry about the ruckus.'

'Was that a dog I just saw in there?' Too late, Darcy realised her error and slid the door closer to her back. Mrs Henley pointed a bony finger towards the apartment.

'A stuffed one?' Darcy tried to joke.

'Hmm ... stuffed dogs don't breathe, or poke their heads out between your legs.'

Suddenly, Bailey was there at her ankles, sniffing the hallway, looking up at Mrs Henley and giving her one of his by now trademark yowls. Darcy took a deep breath, expecting fireworks, a lecture on building codes and no pet policies, but instead, the older woman was suddenly smiling, waggling her long fingers as if flirting with her schoolyard crush.

'What a gorgeous pooch,' she said, catching Darcy completely offguard. 'I had a dog, many years ago back in Queens before my husband dragged me to the city. We had no yard, and one day he just let the dog run free. I thought it would come back, but . . .'

Darcy stood there, her mouth agape. It was the most her neighbour had ever said to her in the three years she'd lived here, by about a hundred words! Bailey's big paws padded along the hardwood floor of the hallway as he sniffed at Mrs Henley's housecoat.

The older woman knelt slowly, reaching a wrinkled hand out to pat the Husky's silky grey crown. 'What a good boy,' she said, her voice gentle, as if speaking to a child. 'What a good, good boy.' Bailey edged into her hand, sneezing twice before turning around and skittering back across the hall into the apartment.

'Thank you,' Darcy said, accepting the compliment as if Bailey really was her dog.

The two women stood there awkwardly, nothing to say any more without Bailey slinking between them. 'Well, goodnight,' Mrs Henley said then, abruptly shutting her door but, Darcy noted, not slamming it.

Going back inside, she was surprised to find Bailey lying contentedly on the rug beneath the bookshelf, curled into himself like a mink stole and looking for all the world like he belonged there.

'Maybe slumming it isn't so bad after all, eh, buddy?' Darcy whispered, reaching down to caress his silky head before grabbing another slice of pizza.

Bailey woke her early the next morning; impossibly early, it was still dark out.

She nuzzled beneath the covers, simultaneously moaning and marvelling at his energy, bounding and leaping about as if it was the best game in the world.

'Go away,' she murmured, trying to pull the covers over her head, but again, the dog just thought it was another game.

Darcy rose, the Husky circling her legs like a cyclone so that she had to take short steps for fear of tumbling over. It was only as she was using the bathroom, Bailey staring at her resentfully from the doorway, that she realised the poor guy hadn't gone all night.

Dressing quickly, she grabbed her ski jacket and the dog's red leather leash. Then, remembering the reason he was here in the first place, she took out her phone to see if Bailey's owners had called looking for him yet, but there were no missed calls at all.

She guessed that Aidan Harris's family probably had enough to deal with after the accident, but she did think at the very least a courtesy call would be in order, checking to see if Bailey was OK. But perhaps the message with her number hadn't got through to them yet? She made a mental note to keep her cell phone close by at work today.

Work! What on earth was she going to do with Bailey

while she went to work? She couldn't very well leave him alone in the apartment all day. For one thing, he was much too large and it wouldn't be fair to keep him cooped up, and for another, what kind of chaos would she be facing when she came back? In the few hours she'd had him, he'd already shed a massive amount of his grey fur, and she couldn't even begin to imagine the level of damage those sharp claws (or indeed teeth) would do if he was alone and bored in the apartment all day. But she couldn't very well take him to work with her either. Could she?

But at that moment, the only place Bailey was focused on going was outside.

Leash on, he practically dragged Darcy through the door, whining the whole way downstairs, through the front entrance and out into the street. Then at the first fire hydrant he saw, the big guy lifted a leg and let out a steady stream. Darcy was amazed; dogs really *did* that.

'Who's your friend?' asked a familiar voice from the doorway of the restaurant.

Damn. Darcy winced and her heart pounded with nerves as she turned to face Luigi. In his late fifties, her landlord was wiry and thin, with close-cropped grey hair under a battered red and green chequered cap.

Bailey, now finished with his business, rushed to sniff around Luigi's legs.

Already dressed in his apron and cook's whites for the long day ahead, Luigi immediately had the Husky jumping up and down at something in his right hand.

'I'm ... I'm dog-sitting for a friend,' Darcy mumbled, aware that her landlord would likely give her an earful for harbouring a temporarily orphaned dog. 'Is that OK?' she added tentatively.

Much to her relief, he chuckled. 'Would I be offering him a piece of pepperoni if it wasn't?'

So that was what Bailey was practically leaping to the height of the second floor for. Luigi doled out a few fragrant slices of the rich, red meat one at a time, backing toward the front stoop and sitting down until the dog was resting against his leg, happy and full.

'Is that good for him?' Darcy asked, reminding herself to head straight to the Pet Care section at work that morning to get a better sense on what to expect from Bailey's type. She didn't want Aidan Harris's pure-bred canine to have clogged arteries by the time he got him back.

Her landlord shrugged, his salt and pepper moustache twitching. 'It's been my breakfast since I was about knee-high, and look at me now.'

'Thank you,' she said distractedly, remembering she didn't have anything even remotely resembling dog food in her kitchen. Another thing she had to worry about.

Darcy hadn't even had her first cup of tea and already she was exhausted.

They both walked inside, Luigi to the pizzeria and Darcy back up the stairs; Bailey full of pepperoni and straining at the leash, again eager to get wherever he was going as fast as possible.

A shadow filled the second-floor landing, and Darcy was surprised to see Mrs Henley standing at the window in her pink slippers and fluffy housecoat.

'Morning,' she said, looking down at Bailey. 'I see your friend's already done his business.'

Darcy blushed, unsure of the rule on letting a dog pee all over a fire hydrant. 'Boys will be boys,' she chuckled nervously.

Mrs Henley nodded, her grey hair curled tightly against her head. 'Aren't you working today?'

'Yes,' Darcy sighed, looking down at Bailey as he nosed around the door of Mrs Henley's apartment. It was open just a hair's breadth and the sniffing inched it open wider. Darcy noticed that unlike her stuffed-to-the-gills living room, the inside of her neighbour's was as sparse and spare as a hospital room.

Mrs Henley stood back, her mouth a thin slit but her eyes definitely warmer than usual. 'If you're leaving him here, I could keep an eye on him if you like.'

Darcy was floored. 'Thank you, but I couldn't possibly ...' But still she had mixed emotions about Mrs Henley's offer. On the one hand, it would make her day, not to mention her life, a whole lot easier, and her apartment potentially a whole lot safer, but on the other she was responsible for Bailey for now, whether she liked it or not.

'Nonsense, dear,' said the old woman, colour rising in her cheeks. 'It's been years since I cared for anyone, let alone a dog. I rather welcome the challenge. And like I said before, I know a little thing or two about taking care of dogs. He'll be in good hands with me.'

Before she could think about it for too much longer, Darcy handed over the leash. 'Well, if you really don't mind, thank you – it would save my life, I can't exactly take him to work – and I'll pick him up directly after my shift, I promise,' she continued, babbling. She looked again at her neighbour, taken aback by the complete change in temperament Bailey seemed to have brought about. 'I really appreciate it, Mrs Henley.'

'It's not a problem, and please,' insisted the old woman, struggling to keep Bailey from dragging her back into her apartment. 'Call me Grace.'

'Grace ...' Darcy repeated, thinking to herself that it had taken her three years to learn her neighbour's first name.

With a final whine, Bailey stuck his snout back out again, looked up at Darcy and happily wagged his tail before disappearing quickly inside.

So much for loyalty, Darcy thought, faintly chagrined that the dog was happy to go off with anyone. Here was she, thinking they'd struck up some kind of special bond.

She showered and dressed quickly, and having wrapped up warm and fastened her safety helmet, tentatively got back up on the bike, the first time she'd done so since the accident yesterday. She was pleased to find that there was little damage to it, save for a few missing spokes and a faint clicking with each rotation of the wheels. And once her initial nerves had subsided, she soon got back into her stride. It was just like riding a bike, she laughed to herself.

The morning streets were blustery and colourful, and as she passed by Bouchon's Bakery, she could smell the croissants rising, buttery and flaky, and inhaled the scent of fruity infusions from Limoncello's tea rooms. With less than a week to go till Christmas, every store she passed that morning on her way uptown had a blinking sign or festive lighting, making the street glitter in the early-morning light. Customers walked through doors to the sound of Christmas music, sometimes fun and funky, other times jangly and traditional, but always cheery.

'Thank God!' Joshua gushed, as just under half an hour later she came through the door of Chaucer's, having locked her bike out back. 'How are you feeling? Does your head hurt? You could have taken today off too, you know, although I'm glad you're here all the same. It was kinda busy yesterday with the holidays just around the corner, and Ashley not available because of exams, so I'm a little bit behind.' Today he was dressed in fashionably ripped grey jeans and a bright red sweater, which hugged his narrow torso like a second skin. On his head, a matching red Santa cap with a bright white fur dot on the end trembled every time he moved.

'I'm fine,' she said, smiling at the sight of a friendly face. 'Thanks for being so helpful yesterday, though. It was a weird morning.'

'So what happened?' he asked as Darcy pulled her striped Chaucer's apron over her head and got ready to face her day. 'Tell me everything, right from the beginning.'

'Well, as you know, I hit someone on my bike. His name is Aidan Harris.'

Joshua looked at her. 'The guy was nice enough to tell you his name after you hit him?'

Darcy told him the whole sorry tale, starting with how Aidan Harris and his dog had stepped out in front of her at the intersection, followed by her visit to the hospital and then her impromptu trek along the Upper West Side.

'Ooh, a *rich* guy – was he cute?'

Darcy thought about it. She remembered his silky dark hair and pronounced jawline. 'More than cute. He was very handsome, actually.'

'Good, because if you're going to sweep somebody off their feet like that, I think they at least need to be cute.'

Joshua really was irrepressible. 'Are you absolutely sure you're straight?' Darcy teased. 'And I didn't sweep him off his feet, Joshua, I *knocked* him off his feet. Plus now I still have the dog. The hospital wouldn't take him, and I'm not sure what to do until I hear from the family.'

Joshua's high-pitched laughter was almost loud enough to drown out Bing Crosby's 'White Christmas' currently playing on the in-store speakers. 'You? Taking care of a dog? Where is it now – in Lost and Found at Luigi's?'

'Close. Actually my neighbour is watching him for me.'

'Your *crazy* neighbour? That scary old lady who only wears pink?'

'Grace,' she said, almost defensively. 'And she's not crazy actually – just a woman of few words.' Darcy had come to this conclusion on her way to work. Thinking about it, Mrs Henley had never really done anything other than resist Darcy's attempts at neighbourly friendship. Which was reasonable enough in this town where you could just as easily be living beside a grade-school teacher or a serial killer. 'And she seems to really like dogs.'

'And pink,' he reminded her.

'Oh God,' Darcy groaned, her stomach now fluttering afresh at his words. Had she been too hasty in passing off Bailey to a complete stranger like that? Too eager to overcome the work-related dilemma his presence presented? 'Do you think she really is crazy?' she asked him. 'What if I've left Aidan's dog with a lunatic? What if she's selling him on eBay as we speak?'

Joshua put a hand on her shoulder. 'Relax. Ninety-nine per cent of the people in this town are crazy, and they still manage to care for their pets. I'm sure the mutt will be fine.'

Suppressing her worries about Bailey's welfare for the moment, Darcy once again checked her phone.

But much to her frustration there was still nothing from the Harris family, no missed calls, no messages. Well, adorable or not, she couldn't keep looking after their dog for much longer, she thought resolutely. If she hadn't heard anything from them by midday, she'd just have to phone the hospital again and demand to speak to Aidan Harris himself.

The hours passed quickly in Chaucer's and Darcy was kept on her toes by customers seeking out books with obscure-sounding titles – 'Something about tequila and a bird?' which

Joshua eventually deduced was *To Kill a Mockingbird* and 'a teenager who goes nuts on prom night' (Stephen King's *Carrie*) as well as looking for recommendations, the part of the job Darcy enjoyed the most. There was simply no better feeling in the world than a customer returning to the store full of praise for a book she'd suggested for them and trusting her again to choose another.

She'd had a couple of humdingers though. Just before lunch, a stern-faced businessman in his mid-forties brought a special edition copy of *Great Expectations* to the counter.

Darcy smiled as she rang up the purchase. 'Wonderful book. Did you know that Dickens actually changed the ending after a critic told him that Pip spending the rest of his life single was much too sad, and that the masses wouldn't be happy with it?' she offered conversationally. 'So Dickens decided that Pip should meet Estella again after her husband dies, providing a gentle suggestion that they would end up together.'

The man looked at her. 'No point in my buying it then, is there? Now that you've given away the ending.'

Darcy was horrified. It had completely slipped her mind that not everyone had read the classics, and given that the man was buying an illustrated gift edition of the book, she'd just assumed it was an old favourite, or indeed a gift.

She was still trying to get over her embarrassment and indeed the loss of a sale when from inside her apron, she heard her mobile ring.

It was a Manhattan number, one she didn't recognise, and

she looked towards Joshua, who was restocking the bestseller table at the front. He duly gave her a thumbs-up, indicating that she should go ahead and answer it.

'Hello, Darcy Archer speaking,' she said, heading out back towards Chaucer's broom-closet-sized stockroom.

'Ms Archer, my name is Doctor Ingrid Mandeville, I'm calling from Roosevelt General.' Darcy felt a sensation of dread rush through her. Had Aidan Harris's condition deteriorated, or had there been some kind of unforeseen complications maybe? Then she calmed a little, guessing that if this was the case, it was more likely to be the police, than the hospital calling her about it. Not that that should make her feel any better.

She listened as the woman continued to speak. 'Your number was passed to me this morning; I believe you were a witness to a collision involving one of my patients yesterday? A Mr Harris?'

'Well, yes.' Darcy wasn't sure if she should point out that she was actually the one who'd caused the collision, not just a witness to it, but she decided to wait and see what else the doctor had to say.

'This is unusual to say the least, but according to the note, you are currently in possession of Mr Harris's dog?'

'That's right, yes. I'm not sure if the paramedics noticed the dog when they were tending to Mr Harris, but he was left behind so I thought it best to—'

'Well, my patient would very much like to talk to you, Ms Archer. You see, and let it be known from the outset that I am speaking to you with Mr Harris's full consent, it seems he's having some issues remembering events leading up to yesterday morning, and was hoping you might be able to enlighten him.'

Enlighten him? How could Darcy possibly enlighten the guy as to what had happened, unless he really was trying to dispute who was at fault, in order to pin some of the medical bills on her? Yet, he couldn't possibly know that she was the one who'd run into him, could he?

'I'm not really sure how I can help,' she said hesitantly. 'I'm at work at the moment in any case, and if Mr Harris's family could arrange to pick up his dog as soon as possible, I'd be very grateful.'

'Well, that's part of the issue, Ms Archer,' the doctor said simply. 'We haven't been able to contact the patient's family, because he is unable to tell us anything about them. It's a rather serious situation.'

Darcy's eyes widened and her stomach knotted once again. 'A serious situation?' she repeated, terrified. Oh no, despite the receptionist's assurances yesterday, had Aidan Harris since taken a turn for the worse? In which case ... Darcy didn't even want to think about the implications and how much trouble she was likely to be in.

'Yes,' the doctor confirmed, sending her heart plummeting to her stomach. 'To put it succinctly, the only memory Mr Harris seems to possess at the moment is of his dog.'

Chapter 8

Every man's memory is his private literature. **Aldous Huxley**

That evening after work, her mind filled with questions and her insides twisting with fear, Darcy made her way back to Roosevelt Hospital.

Dr Mandeville was expecting her, and she only had to wait a few moments at Reception before the doctor came to find her.

'I realise this is unorthodox, but I really appreciate you coming in and I know Mr Harris will too.' The woman went on to explain how temporary amnesia was often a side-effect of such a collision, but she believed that Aidan Harris's current condition was actually more down to shock following the accident than a fugue state.

'Fugue?' Darcy queried, familiar with the term but not

entirely sure what it meant in terms of what was happening to Aidan Harris. It sounded scarily technical for one thing. Just how serious was the damage she'd caused? She recalled reading once about how Agatha Christie had apparently disappeared one day, only to reappear eleven days later in a hotel in Harrogate, with no memory of the events occurring during that time-span. When she asked if this was something similar the doctor shook her head.

'No. The condition you mention is usually identifiable after the fact, such as when a person comes to after such an episode, and while he or she is in possession of normal day-to-day memories, they have no memory whatsoever of that specific blackout period, be it hours or days. Mr Harris's condition is more along the lines of simple reversible amnesia, typically characterised by loss of personal identity, individual memories, personality, address, loved ones and other identifying characteristics.'

'So did ... did something happen to damage his brain that way – a hit on the head or something?' Darcy was still afraid to admit to the doctor that she'd been the one to run Aidan Harris over, because that would mean she was directly responsible for his injuries, and the implications. She couldn't know whether or not the guy had hit his head following the fall because she hadn't seen it when she'd come off the bike herself.

'No, actually there's minimal physical trauma to the brain itself. This is more of a psychological condition: a dissociative response following a major stress event, not uncommon after shock or psychological trauma, but not as a result of physical trauma to the brain,' the doctor continued and Darcy breathed a sigh of relief.

OK, so at least she knew she hadn't caused any serious damage to his brain then. By the sounds of it, he was just having trouble recalling a couple of things as a result of the accident. Darcy could understand that; she too had been rattled by what had happened yesterday – she still was – and she wasn't the one who'd been knocked out or ended up flat on her back. So it was perfectly reasonable, Darcy reassured herself, particularly following his blackout, that Aidan Harris would be still somewhat in shock following the whole episode.

'Things are foggy for him at the moment but he may well come out of it in a few days, typically once something identifiable – often with an emotional association – triggers his memory,' Dr Mandeville told Darcy as she led her towards an elevator and they both stepped inside. 'But as you can imagine, he's confused and upset that he can't remember who he is, and of course we can't contact his next-of-kin to help illuminate the situation for him either. There were no ICE details in his wallet or amongst his personal effects. In Case of Emergency,' she added when Darcy looked blank.

As the elevator rose to the third floor, Darcy's thoughts went back to the package he'd been carrying, now safely tucked away in a drawer in her apartment.

Was this something that could trigger his memory?

'For now, all he remembers is a dog, and regardless of the

circumstances we simply cannot allow pets in the hospital,'
the doctor continued before Darcy had a chance to enquire.
She led Darcy down a long, quiet corridor before stopping
briefly outside a door. 'When Mr Harris was informed that
you were taking care of his pet, he insisted on speaking with
you.'

Darcy nervously followed the woman into the room, not
sure what to do or say. The automatic door at the end of the
hall hissed open and snatches of 'Jingle Bells' filled the air for
a few moments before the door hissed shut again. The sound,
usually so cheery, this time made her heart yammer even
faster. Was there a worse place to spend the holidays? Did
Aidan have a worried wife and children at home waiting for
him?

The room was bare and unadorned, with not a single floral
arrangement or greeting card. When Joshua had had his gall-
bladder taken out last year and she'd come to visit, she could
hardly move, the room had been so jampacked with bou-
quets, cards and stuffed animals.

Now she wished she'd thought to bring something. But the
request had taken her completely by surprise earlier, and
anyway, she reminded herself, she didn't even know this guy.

Aidan Harris lay silently on the bed in front of her. He was
hooked up to tubes of every shape, size, colour and length,
and Darcy gulped at the sight of them. She thought he looked
cleaner now, shinier somehow, than when she'd last seen him
out cold on the busy street yesterday morning. His luxurious
black hair had been washed and combed back, his face was

cleanshaven, though his skin looked worryingly pale. But it also gave her the chance to learn that his eyes, which she'd never seen open, were a soft hazel.

'Aidan, this is Darcy Archer, the lady who is looking after your dog.'

He turned to look at Darcy and she had to remind herself not to stare. Aidan Harris had arresting, almost piercing eyes, heavy eyebrows and a well-defined jawline; the kind of masculine good looks that might give Rhett Butler or Heathcliff a run for their money.

When he offered Darcy a smile, the skin around his eyes crinkled ever so slightly, and the light tan of his weathered-looking skin suggested time spent in the sun, or outside. He ran a quick hand through the thick mop of hair and Darcy felt overcome by a desire to do the same.

To his hair, not her own.

She willed her hands to stay at their sides. How anyone could look so handsome and regal lying flat in a hospital gown and covered in white sheets was a mystery, and feeling unsettled by his attractiveness, she snapped to in case it was obvious that she was ogling him. Not that she was an ogler. But rarely was she struck in a way that she would feel lost for words.

Darcy, who lived her life through words, suddenly had nothing to say. Aidan Harris looked a bit worried and she guessed he was probably wondering if she wasn't just a little slow or dim-witted. She felt a blush creeping up her neck and looked quickly at the ground; almost as bashful as she had been yesterday morning when Mr Darcy had populated her dreams, reminding herself that this wasn't Regency England and that Elizabeth Bennet would be frustrated by her tied tongue. Shrinking violet types in the twenty-first century were *so* not cool.

Clearing her throat, she said in her best Chaucer's customer service voice, 'Hello, Mr Harris. 'I hope you're feeling better after your accident.'

'Not really,' he replied simply, and there was a world of frustration behind those two words. Darcy once again felt desperately guilty for running him over and figured that if he wasn't aware of this before now, it possibly wasn't the best time to reveal it. His voice was deep and gruff – surprising; she had expected someone a little more … refined. And yet, she yearned to hear him speak again. 'You told Reception you have my dog?'

This time she noticed the slight hint of an accent behind his words – an Irish accent perhaps? His name certainly suggested as much. Yet it was just that: a trace of a lilt beneath a decidedly more recognisable New York twang. Darcy suspected that while Aidan Harris might well have been Irish by birth, he was an immigrant and had likely spent many years here in the city.

'Bailey?' she smiled. 'Yes, he's fine. My neighbour's taking care of him at the moment. He's a great dog. Really well behaved, and so intelligent.'

'Bailey …' Harris nodded absently, as if hearing the name for the first time.

'Does the name mean something to you, Aidan?' Dr Mandeville enquired. 'Can you picture the dog in your mind, what he looks like, how long you've had him, where you were walking him yesterday morning? Is there anything at all you can remember about him?'

As the doctor fired questions at him, the man gripped the edge of the bed, his knuckles white with frustration.

Darcy's heart went out to him, horrified that she had been the cause of all this.

'No, the name doesn't mean anything to me,' he replied, his tone fraught with exasperation. 'Like I said before, all I can remember is something about a dog – a sort of grey dog that looks a bit like a wolf.'

'That's right; he's a Husky,' Darcy confirmed, somewhat relieved that he was remembering *something* at least. No doubt he'd piece together the rest once he and Bailey were reunited, but of course as she already knew, dogs weren't allowed in the hospital. She didn't know how long Bailey's owner would be here, but she supposed she could always take a snapshot of him on her cell phone and show it to him.

Aidan Harris closed his eyes. 'I can picture a dog in my mind, but that's all; why the bloody hell can't I remember anything else?' He slammed an angry fist into the mattress.

'OK, Aidan, let's not force things too much just yet. Why don't you chat to Ms Archer about your dog for a little while, see if anything else rings a bell,' Dr Mandeville suggested smoothly, looking at Darcy who nodded, even though she was still terrified.

It was obvious that Aidan Harris was hugely frustrated about his condition, and given the level of his exasperation over the after-effects of the accident, she wasn't looking forward to admitting that it was she who'd run him over with her bike.

It must be awful, waking up like that and not being able to remember who you were or where you lived. The closest she'd ever come to something like that was drunkenly struggling to figure out which apartment was actually hers after a 'lively' night out with Joshua a while back. She'd escaped a potentially close call by trying her keys in Mrs Henley's door in the early hours of the morning, but luckily for her, her neighbour seemed to sleep very soundly.

Then Darcy thought of something. 'Doctor,' she called out just as the woman was about to leave. 'You probably know this already from Mr Harris's ID, but if it's any help, I think he might live in a brownstone off Central Park West. I can give you the address if you'd like.'

The doctor nodded. 'Thanks. I believe we did get that information from Aidan's ID, however we've been unable to contact any family members there.'

Maybe he lives alone? Darcy wanted to reply, and took a surreptitious glance at Aidan's left hand. No wedding ring.

'How do you know that?' Aidan asked suspiciously, when the doctor took her leave. 'About where my house is?'

Darcy coloured a little as she told him the story of how Bailey had refused to let her take him home until they'd tried his place first. She smiled as she recounted the Husky's exploits from the day before, although she left out the bits where she'd fed him pizza for dinner and pepperoni for breakfast. But then she thought of something.

'So how long do you think you'll be here – at the hospital, I mean?' she asked him, wondering now just how long her house-guest would be staying.

His expression darkened. 'A few days at least because of the damned concussion and the fact that I have no idea who the hell I am. They say they can't let me out in case I go wandering off somewhere – for insurance reasons or some other bloody nonsense like that.'

'Sorry, I didn't mean to upset you.'

'No, it's fine. *I'm* the one who should be apologising, not to mention thanking you for taking care of my dog,' he said, raising a smile which lit up his entire face and made his eyes crinkle at the corners.

Darcy gulped, looking away. 'It's been a pleasure. He's a great dog. I'm sure he misses you though. You should have seen how anxious he was to get into the house yesterday and couldn't seem to understand why I didn't have the keys.'

Aidan Harris frowned once again, and Darcy was worried that she'd said something wrong when he reached over to his bedside locker. Opening it, he took out a transparent Ziploc bag, and from this withdrew a heavy set of keys.

'They gave me these earlier and I immediately started wondering if I worked for Fort Knox or something. Look.' He pointed out a heavy key-ring which to Darcy's untrained eye looked to be made of real gold; a selection of keys were attached to it. Next to this was a miniature baseball key chain bearing what Darcy recognised as a Mets logo.

'So at least you know you're a baseball fan,' she said with a smile, although she would have betted on someone from his part of town favouring the Yankees.

'So it seems.' Harris sighed heavily. 'Inconceivable . . .'

There was a brief silence and unsure what to say next, Darcy asked what sort of food she should be giving Bailey. 'Does he have any particular favourites? Seeing as it looks like we might be roomies for a little while longer.'

She noticed that Aidan seemed to be struggling internally with something. 'I wonder – would you mind keeping an eye on him just until I'm back on my feet?' he asked then. He added apologetically, 'Look, I know it's a lot to ask, especially as you don't even know me, but—'

'It was me,' Darcy blurted out then, and Harris stared at her. 'On the bike. I was the cyclist who hit you. The lights were green and you and Bailey just stepped out in front of me at the intersection . . .'

'Ah, I see.' He was silent for a while, and Darcy cursed herself for saying anything.

'I couldn't avoid you and there were witnesses, if you don't believe me,' she babbled eventually, wishing he'd say something, or show some kind of reaction.

Was he angry, furious even? It was impossible to tell.

Aidan Harris stroked his chin and looked sideways at Darcy. 'So I guess that explains the dog-sitting then; I was just about to ask how you'd come across him.'

She winced and held her breath, desperately hoping he wouldn't chew her out for running him over and being the root cause of all of his current woes.

But miraculously he shrugged. 'Well, seeing as I can't remember a thing about it, I guess I'll just have to take your word for it.'

Darcy looked sheepishly at him.

'But if it's any consolation, I believe you,' he continued, his tone lightening a little, much to her relief. 'When you say that there was nothing you could have done, I mean.'

'I was so worried when I realised you were out cold,' she confessed. 'And was terrified I'd caused untold damage – serious brain damage or something. I mean, I know that not being able to remember things is surely no picnic for you now, but—'

'But how were *you*, Miss Archer?' he asked. 'After the accident, I mean. I hope you came out of it all OK?'

Touched that in spite of everything, he was chivalrous enough to be concerned about her welfare, she smiled and said, 'Please, call me Darcy. And I'm fine. Just a couple of bruises, and a few broken spokes on the bike.'

'Well then, Darcy, I'll take care of that – whenever I get out of this bloody hell-hole,' he snapped, his tone darkening once more.

'There's no need, really,' she protested. 'It's fine.'

'No, it's the least I can do, especially when it seems that not only have you gone out of your way to take care of my dog, but also taken time out of your day to come and see me. I

103

appreciate that, since as you can see, I'm kind of on my own here.'

'It must be very frightening.' She smiled reassuringly, and tried not to betray the anxiety she felt about the logistics of having Bailey longer than she'd thought. It was a small problem compared to the enormity of what his owner was facing just now. 'But even though you can't remember anything at the moment, I'm sure your family will find you very soon. They're probably phoning around the Emergency Rooms as we speak.'

He frowned. 'Unfortunately, even if they are, thanks to some stupid bloody privacy rules, the hospital is not allowed to give out information to anyone unless I specifically tell them who to give it to. But of course I can't give permission for them to speak to specific people because I don't know who the hell is supposed to be looking for me.' He ran a hand through his hair, frustrated yet again, and Darcy couldn't help but sympathise.

'Oh dear.' Talk about a bureaucratic nightmare, she thought, wondering what administrative healthcare genius had come up with *that* one. While it was obviously in place to safeguard patient information and privacy, it created real difficulties for people like Aidan Harris, effectively leaving them in the dark.

'So I really need to figure out who in God's name I am,' he went on, his voice gruff. 'And at the moment the only clue I have is that I own a Husky dog – and live somewhere off Central Park, you said?'

'Yes. A beautiful brownstone on the Upper West Side. With a lovely little potted maple tree outside the door,' she added somewhat pointlessly, but she was trying to think of things that might just trigger his memory for him. Then again, a simple tree was hardly going to yield the strong emotional connotations the doctor mentioned before, was it?

Feeling stupid, Darcy was silent again, not sure what to say. 'I'm really sorry about this, Mr Harris,' she said helplessly. 'Truly, if there's anything at all I can do ...'

Looking thoughtful, Aidan Harris was fidgeting again with his keys. 'Call me Aidan, and if you don't mind, I think there might just be something you can do actually.' He paused and fixed those probing dark eyes on Darcy's own. 'As you know, I'm kind of desperate here, and seeing as you were asking about dog food earlier and you already know where my house is, I wonder if you could do me a small favour ...'

Chapter 9

A man's house is his castle. **James Otis**

Once again, Darcy stood outside Aidan Harris's brownstone off Central Park West, but this time she didn't need to use the doorbell.

In the hope of helping him overcome his amnesia, Aidan had entrusted her with his keys and asked if she could go to his home and find something (or even someone) he'd recognise that would help trigger his memory.

'Perhaps a photograph or a notebook maybe, anything you think that might be important or significant in some way. Please Darcy, I really need to get out of this place. I need to get my life back.'

He sounded so desperate that it was extremely difficult to say no, and while Darcy wasn't convinced that she would be able to walk into a complete stranger's home and identify something that might be significant to them, she knew she owed it to him to at least try. And if nothing else, she mused somewhat selfishly, it would give her the opportunity to nab some decent food for a dog of Bailey's size without having to max out her own credit card.

She was still kicking herself for agreeing so readily to look after the dog and wasn't sure how Luigi would react to finding out that Bailey wasn't just an overnighter. To say nothing of how she was going to keep a dog his size in her tiny apartment, when it was barely big enough for herself and her things as it was. Still, she'd made Aidan Harris a promise and she was going to keep it. Bailey would just have to get used to more cramped living quarters and she would have to get used to giving up her space on the sofa as well as fluffy grey dog hairs on every surface, she thought wryly.

Though judging by the size of Bailey's real home, 'cramped' was an understatement.

Reaching into her messenger bag, Darcy fished out the set of keys Aidan had given her, trying to decide which one of them opened the front door.

Spotting the Mets keyring, she idly wondered if perhaps Aidan had at one point lived in Brooklyn, Long Island or Queens, where the majority of such fans were from. Being a Brooklyn girl, she herself was very much a Mets fan, or at least she had been, she thought sadly, recalling how passionate her father used to be about baseball when she was growing up. She used to watch the games with him on TV and he often promised to take her to the team's then home Shea Stadium. But they'd never got the chance.

Over the years, she'd lost touch with what was going on with the team and baseball in general – Katherine wasn't exactly a sports fan. Thinking about it, the only real thing she could identify her aunt being passionate about was work, which was why Darcy had spent so much of her teens with only her books for company while Katherine was in Manhattan tending to what seemed like a neverending succession of important commitments. Still, she couldn't complain; her aunt had always done her best for her in what must have been very difficult circumstances, and Darcy couldn't help but contrast her own anxiety about having a mere dog as an unexpected house-guest to the utter shock her aunt must have felt back then on learning she was suddenly sole guardian of a twelve-year-old girl.

Moving on to the gold Cartier keyring, Darcy inspected it more closely, noticing that the brand's recognisable double 'C' pivoted within a ring of what looked like very expensive high-carat gold. She let out a low whistle, marvelling at how anyone would spend so much on a simple keyring. But she supposed that if you had money to burn, dropping cash on some kind of status accessory signalling your wealth was par for the course.

Trying the first key attached to the Cartier ring in the lock, she found herself quickly denied, and peered nervously over her shoulder just to make sure no one was watching her. Permitted or not, she didn't fancy explaining herself to any nosy neighbours just then.

Flipping to the next key, she was once again denied access.

Finally, feeling beyond anxious, Darcy selected the third key on the Cartier keyring, put it into the keyhole and turned. To her relief, the lock clicked and gave way.

She went inside and shut the door behind her quickly, again worrying about one of the neighbours calling the cops. Only when the door closed and the house was filled with silence did she stop to think that she might not be alone.

Even though the hospital had been unable to contact anyone at the house, she decided she should have tried the doorbell first, just in case. What if Aidan Harris lived here with a girlfriend? Or a boyfriend, a roommate – or even still with his parents?

If so, she could only guess their reaction to Darcy bursting into their home on a dark winter's evening.

Standing in the hallway, the first thing that caught her eye was the large bouquet of fresh lilies sitting in a vase on a nearby side table, which immediately suggested that a woman lived here. Darcy couldn't imagine any man – even Joshua – going to the trouble of putting fresh flowers in his house. The question was, was that same woman – perhaps Aidan's wife – here at the moment?

'Hello?' she called out, inching forward on the foyer's hardwood floor. A mirror up ahead caught her reflection, her dark hair tied up in her usual messy work ponytail, purple v-neck sweater over black trousers, eyes wide and skin pale. 'Anyone home?'

Her voice, timid yet loud, echoed off the high walls and

crown moulding that bordered every inch of the hallway's white ceiling. Darcy froze, listening. Could hear her breathing.

Otherwise silence.

'Looks like nobody's home,' she whispered to no one in particular, leaning against a nearby doorframe. She wasn't sure whether to be relieved or disappointed; if somebody was here, then she could simply be on her way and Aidan (or Bailey) would no longer need her.

But there was no denying that she was curious to see inside this beautiful house, had always wanted to see what a properly restored and lived-in New York brownstone was really like. This could be her only opportunity to do so. The house she'd lived in with Katherine was a small two-up, two-down Brooklyn townhouse, and of course any apartment she'd ever been in here in Manhattan was little bigger than a shoe box, and possessed about as much charm. Inside, the house was warm, and feeling a slight bead of sweat run down her forehead from her exertion in cycling all the way here from the hospital, Darcy brushed the moisture off with her hand and steadied herself, collecting her thoughts.

So, I'm in. Now what?

She put a tentative hand on the door closest to her and was about to venture further into the house before remembering to wipe the slush off her shoes.

She took in the spotless wooden floors and large patterned Turkish rug laid out before her and assumed that there must be a housekeeper or cleaner. No matter, she didn't want to track in muddy footprints and cause a mess.

After all, she had already messed things up enough for the guy.

Wiping her feet across the doormat, she continued on inside and for the first time began to really take in her surroundings. Right in front of her, hanging in the foyer not four feet away, was a rust and blue coloured abstract painting she immediately identified as a Rothko, having seen the artist's work in MoMA one time. And she was willing to bet it was real. She whistled under her breath. Just who was she dealing with here?

Darcy peered at the oil painting, trying to imagine the value of this piece alone.

'And it's hanging in Aidan Harris's foyer. Oh my,' she sighed.

Looking over her shoulder, as if a thief might appear out of nowhere and swipe the painting from in front of her nose, Darcy subconsciously hugged her messenger bag to her chest.

If these people had a Rothko hanging in the entryway of their house, what on earth would they have in the rest of the place?

And then she got to wondering whether the painting might work, if it had some significance or emotional connotations for Aidan. Some people felt that way about art, although admittedly Darcy wasn't one of them. She enjoyed looking at it but had never felt the urge to have a piece of artwork in her apartment.

No, if she had that kind of money to spend, Darcy would choose a first edition novel over a painting any day. But if

Aidan felt the same way about his painting as she did about books, then surely this would mean something to him, and he would immediately recognise it? A piece like this, from one of America's most revered Impressionist-influenced painters, wouldn't have been easy to come by, and she guessed the procurement of the painting, or the special occasion or landmark that an expensive purchase would surely represent , would be the kind of significant item that Aidan needed.

But what was Darcy supposed to do – take a painting worth a million dollars or more and just pop it on the back of her bike and pedal off back down to the hospital in the snow with it?

Not an option.

Unsure where to go next, never mind what she was supposed to be looking for, she spied a doorway at the end of the short hallway which was dotted with smaller but no doubt also original modernist prints. Trying the handle, the door opened with ease and going inside, Darcy immediately stepped into the kitchen of her dreams.

Not that she was that much of a cook – in truth, she could just about manage to boil an egg – but she adored cookbooks and in particular the beautifully shot photographs of the food and accompanying pictures of typically gorgeous workspaces.

This room looked exactly like one of those, and Darcy decided that she would do nothing else but cook if she ever lived in a house with a kitchen like this.

Floor-to-ceiling culinary elegance beckoned to her, every stainless-steel and granite surface gleaming pristinely. There was no way she would ever be able to keep this kitchen free of fingerprints, even with a platoon of housekeepers at her command, she thought, instinctively holding her hands out for fear of touching something. She noted the imported Rayburn stove, and the glass-doored wine cooler showcasing rows of bottles which she guessed were of a higher vintage than those she usually picked up at the Essex Street Market.

Darcy sighed dreamily as she took in the artfully displayed Cuisinart mixer, funky Alessi fruit bowl and the bevy of other high-end appliances that looked as if they had been plucked from a display at Williams-Sonoma. Yes, this truly was the kitchen of her dreams – of *anyone's* dreams. She shook her head dazedly. Even though her own gastronomic speciality basically required Kraft American cheese, two slices of bread and a frying pan, she knew without a doubt that this kitchen would elevate the simple grilled cheese sandwich to something ambrosial.

She tried to picture Aidan moving around in this space, trying to imagine if he wandered in here at the end of the day once he was finished with whatever he obviously did so successfully at work. The lack of scribbled drawings on the refrigerator and the absence of any toys in the room suggested it was unlikely any children lived here.

She pictured him pulling open the wine cooler and selecting a Pinot Grigio before choosing fresh ingredients from the fridge and going on to prepare some luxuriously gourmet meal.

She looked to the Rayburn stove, which incidentally had a

Williams-Sonoma branded dishtowel (*good eye, Darcy*), seemingly unused, hanging over its handle. She wondered if Aidan grabbed that dishtowel and threw it over his shoulder as he cooked, the way her own dad used to do when he pretended to 'help' her mother at dinnertime.

Did Aidan cook – and if so, what? she mused. The kitchen gave away no hints, at least not concerning what the occupants might have eaten for breakfast yesterday morning. There wasn't a single utensil or piece of crockery in the sink, not even a coffee cup someone might have used that morning. The granite countertops sparkled, and actually the entire space looked as if it had never been used.

Well, maybe they just eat out all the time, she pondered.

But whatever the occupants did or didn't cook in this room, and whether or not they shared it with children, Darcy knew that at the very least there had to be food in those cupboards for Bailey. And seeing as one of the reasons she was here was to get the Husky's chow ...

Darcy needed to locate the food. Which was why she needed to look through some of his master's cupboards, and possibly the refrigerator too, no? Because it wasn't as if there was a bag of dog food just sitting on the countertop, or any signs pointing out where it might be kept.

Wiping her hands on her trousers, she turned to what had to be a walk-in pantry. To her right was the refrigerator, and while commonsense dictated that dog food would be in the walk-in, she thought she'd still better look in the fridge first.

Just in case.

She smiled, acknowledging to herself that she was just snooping, but she had to admit that she was enjoying the experience of being in another person's domain and trying to figure out how they occupied it. It was a similar sensation to being lost in a story, aware that you weren't getting the full picture, and feeling compelled to try and work out where it might be headed.

Having justified her curiosity, Darcy opened the refrigerator door and quickly surveyed the contents: several jars of gourmet pasta sauce were lined up on the top shelf, as well as a cellophane-clad chunk of Parmesan cheese and a small plastic carton containing fresh basil leaves.

Glancing around at the other contents, she spied mostly typical refrigerator fare like milk, mineral water, eggs, butter, sliced meats and some vegetables, as well as a few fancier items like blue cheese and stuffed olives. They also had a taste for champagne, judging by the half-empty bottle of Veuve Clicquot. She wondered if Aidan had been celebrating and if so, *what*?

Still puzzled, she closed the fridge and turned to the walk-in pantry. Flipping on the inside light, Darcy spied shelf upon shelf of expertly organised goods and canned foods: a cornucopia of exotic jars, bottles, baskets and boxes – things like mango chutney, wasabi almonds, sesame flatbreads, hemp oil and maple leaf candy. Clearly these people were among the few New Yorkers who did not eat take-out every night.

Then, out of the corner of her eye, she noticed a basket that indicated the residents took regular grocery delivery from Dean & DeLuca. She let out another low whistle. When you were rich, even the little things like boring old grocery shopping really were so much better, weren't they?

On the shelf below this, she spied a couple of dog bowls that she automatically assumed belonged to Bailey, as well as rows of organic dog food in cans and a bag of dried kibble. Turning her attention to the canned food, she selected one labelled *Confit of Duck and Sweet Potato*.

'Very fancy. I think Bailey might eat better than I do,' she whispered out loud. Taking out a few cans and the bag of kibble, she laid them on the countertop and looked around for something to carry them in.

She pulled out some of the nearby drawers and almost immediately found an integrated garbage bin.

Darcy looked inside, wondering if Aidan recycled. *Please make him one of the good guys.*

Sure enough, there were three separate compartments, one of which was a bin with a collection of recently discarded cardboard boxes, cartons and other recyclable material.

Then, thinking of something else, Darcy opened the cabinet beneath the sink and almost immediately found what she was looking for – a medium-sized garbage sack that would be strong enough to hold the heavy dog food and secure the cans and kibble in one piece on the back of her bicycle. She gave the rest of the contents a cursory glance. All organic cleaning products too. *Good for you.*

So that was the first part of her task completed at least. Now Darcy had to go about finding something (portable) that might help Aidan with his memory issues.

Pictures, she thought, going back outside into the hallway and trying to make a brief reconnaisance of the rest of the house. Not only were photographs the most likely thing to help Aidan, but they would also likely clear up any questions Darcy had about the occupants of the house. Namely whether he shared it with an entire family, or just another person.

Going back down the hallway, she tried another door and happened upon a room that looked to be a formal dining area or reception room. She glanced across the occasional furniture dotted about the place, seeking out photo-frames, and soon hit pay-dirt.

On a nearby sideboard, two framed black and white photographs that looked like as if they might have come from the early twentieth century were positioned on either side of some silver ornaments. The images were of a man and a woman, perhaps Aidan's great-grandparents on their wedding day?

A little further down, she came across a smaller cabinet that held some exotic-looking knickknacks: a carved Oriental-style box, an ivory elephant, an African tribal mask and a sculpture of a man with an embarrassingly large erection. Darcy pinkened, before deducing it must be some kind of fertility statue.

And then – jackpot: a row of photographs of the man she'd crashed into at the intersection, the man now lying in a hospital bed with no clue or memory of his identity.

One seemed to have been taken mid-air while Aidan was in the throes of what looked like a seriously scary skydive. Darcy gulped. Though it looked and sounded like fun, she knew she wouldn't in a million years have the nerve to do something like that.

In another, he was scuba-diving, surrounded by numerous colourful fish in what was obviously some fabulous tropical destination, his thumb and forefinger held up to the camera in an 'OK' sign. Perhaps Australia or the Indian Ocean somewhere? Darcy felt a twinge of envy. She'd always wanted to travel to Australia, ever since reading about it in *The Thorn Birds* – it always sounded so eccentric and exotic – but had never had the opportunity. Not to mention that, given her meagre salary, she'd hardly ever be able to afford it.

Based on what Darcy knew about the place, it was certainly a memorable destination. Picking up the photograph, she placed it carefully in her bag, hoping that the once in a lifetime trip might mean something to Aidan.

Then again, long-distance travel seemed par for the course for people like him, she thought. Maybe if you travelled that much it didn't feel like such a big deal. Darcy knew that if she had the opportunity to visit even a fraction of the countries that Aidan had obviously spent time in, or partake in some of his adventures, she'd treasure those memories for the rest of her life.

Moving on, the next photo actually made Darcy's heart sink.

In this one Aidan was pictured alongside a smiling redhead, the woman's perfect white teeth gleaming as she beamed at the camera, her luscious hair fanned out beneath her ski hat and mask, as the couple stood arm-in-arm atop a ski slope somewhere; snow-covered mountains in the background. Aspen, Vail – Mont Blanc even? Darcy shrugged. As if she would be able to tell. It's not like she'd ever visited any of them and thus could differentiate between mountains situated here in the US, or abroad. She had only ever seen pictures of Mont Blanc, and had certainly never been to France. She lifted this picture up and put it in her bag too.

It meant that her earlier suspicion about the flowers in the hallway were correct; Aidan was indeed attached, she thought to herself, a little surprised at how much this disappointed her. These two were clearly a couple, and such an attractive one at that, Aidan with his tall, earthy good looks and the woman, model-thin with her perfect smile and stunning cheekbones.

Darcy sighed at the sheer perfection of it all: this amazing house with its coveted Upper West Side address, top of the range furnishing and rare paintings, the beautiful companion and evidently, the means to travel to the most exciting destinations in the world.

The guy seemed to have it all – things most people could only dare to dream about. A truly wonderful life.

Darcy stopped in the middle of the room and looked around her wide-eyed, and now even more curious about the man who lived in this venerable Aladdin's cave.

Who in the world *was* Aidan Harris?

Chapter 10

My name is Aidan Harris and I'm an idiot.

Looking once again through my contacts list, I couldn't escape the idea that I was missing something that should have been blatantly obvious.

But then again, no matter how hard I tried to get used to this stupid iPhone and all the incredible things it was supposedly capable of, I just had to admit that I really missed my BlackBerry. I get it that all this new technology is supposed to be the latest and greatest thing, and therefore absolutely integral to modern life, but bloody hell, is a simple keyboard really too much to ask? Some clickable keys that allow me the opportunity to truly feel that I am getting something done? This virtual onscreen keyboard thing is just not cutting it, and besides, my fingers are too big.

'I'm trying to program in my contacts but I can't seem to figure out how to do it,' I said to the girl from the Apple Store who was assisting me.

Jenna was her name: I was informed of this after standing around for forty-five minutes in the basement of that gigantic futuristic glass box that has made its home on Fifth Avenue. Completely incongruous if you ask me, situated as it is right across the road from the beautiful French Renaissance building that houses the Plaza Hotel. Quite literally a whole different world.

And incredibly, with this little box of wonders, it seemed you needed to make an appointment just to ask a simple question. Who ever heard of making an appointment in a cell-phone store? Though looking around at the crowds all worshipping at the feet of the company at its flagship Fifth Avenue store, I was beginning to understand why.

'It's really not that difficult,' Jenna said. Behind the bright smile and perky demeanour, I had the distinct impression she was trying to rein in her frustration with me – a guy who was probably old enough to be her father as he struggled to get to grips with new technology.

But despite what she might think, it wasn't that I couldn't adjust to new technology. I just wanted to perform basic actions with it, without feeling as though I needed a Molecular Physics degree.

I watched for a moment as Jenna did something fancy with

the handset and then suddenly, she was talking to it – was I hearing things or was another voice answering her back?

'OK, Aidan, just talk into it now so it recognises your voice,' she said, as if it was perfectly normal for human beings to talk to inanimate objects.

And was it another indicator of my age that this casual use of my first name rankled? OK, so at thirty-seven years old, I'm not exactly a geriatric, but surely it's not too old-fashioned to expect random strangers to address you in a more respectful manner, rather than behaving like you're best buds?

I shook off my frustration, guessing that the waiting around in the stifling heat of this glass box, compared to the biting cold outside, as well as the enormity of the task I was currently trying to undertake, was making me feel old and narky. Maybe I wasn't being fair; Jenna was only simply trying to help – and being very nice about it too.

'But who am I talking to and what should I say?' I asked her, still suspicious as she held the phone up to my mouth.

The young assistant gave me a friendly smile. 'Doesn't matter. I am just setting up Siri for you.'

'Who?' I asked, decidedly baffled now.

Jenna laughed. 'Siri is your new best friend. Didn't you see the commercials? And oh, there was this great episode of *The Big Bang Theory*, where one of the computer geeks had a quasi-love affair with her. Siri is a feminine computerised intelligent personal assistant and knowledge navigator,' she told me, evidently guessing that most of what she'd talked about had gone completely over my head. She was right. 'She uses voice recognition technology to answer questions, make recommendations, and perform actions on your iPhone,' she continued chirpily. 'Really? You've *never* seen the commercials?'

I shook my head, completely clueless. 'No, I haven't,' I replied. 'But I suppose it's not all that surprising because I don't watch a whole lot of TV.'

Though considering what I do for a living, you would think that I would be much more adaptable to new technology. It definitely would help me keep my days a lot more organised than they have been recently.

I turned my attention back to Jenna, who was now furiously pressing some more buttons. It seemed like she knew what she was doing, so I let her get on with it, while I thought about what else I had to do that day.

Finally she held the phone back out to me. 'Here you go, Aidan. Everything should be working now. All you have to do is hit this button right here,' she indicated the relevant command icon, 'and Siri will get you whatever you need in your phone. Contacts, directions, doesn't matter – she'll pull it all up for you. So if there is a contact you want to add, just tell her what you want to do and she will do it. Does that make sense?'

'I suppose so.' I nodded and took the phone from her. As much sense as a disembodied voice inside of a machine could possibly make. 'What happened to the *old* kind of personal assistant?' I asked her jokingly. 'The human kind?'

She gave me a smile. 'Made redundant, I guess. I mean, unless you are like, super-rich, of course. The rest of us have

Siri. So how would you like to pay today, Aidan?' she asked
then. 'Cash or credit?'

I took a final look at my iPhone, supposedly now in complete working order. 'There's a billing address on file. It's a
corporate account.'

But instead of going off somewhere else to look up the
company details like I expected, Jenna promptly took out a
little portable machine that looked like a credit-card proces-
sor, and poked around at it for a moment.

Finding what she needed, she looked back at me and
smiled. 'Awesome. OK, Aidan, you're all set.'

I paused a little, waiting for her to hand me a receipt but
she didn't.

'I hope you have a great day,' she continued, obviously
eager to move on to the next customer.

Awkwardly running a hand through my hair, and aware
that it was badly in need of a cut, I knew I once again would
come across as deeply uncool. 'Well, do I get a receipt or anything?'

She smiled again. 'I've just emailed to it you. Should arrive
in no time.' As she spoke, the iPhone made a sound signalling
that an email was incoming. 'That's probably it.'

'OK.' I glanced down at the phone screen and saw that she
was indeed correct, then slipped the handset into the pocket
of my coat. 'Thanks for your help, Jenna.'

'No problem, Aidan. And remember, if you have a non-
technical problem in the future, just call on Siri. She can help
you solve any issues you might have, I guarantee it.'

Hmm, *any* issues? I wonder . . .

I made my way up the winding stairway out of the bowels of Apple and up into the glass box, smiling when through the window I saw Bailey outside waiting patiently for me. Sitting next to a tree, with his leash tied around a fire hydrant, he stared at the big structure, probably wondering what the hell this place was and what I was doing in there, but sitting patiently just the same.

He was a really great dog. Sometimes I got the distinct impression that he absolutely knew what was going on. Notwithstanding that his breed was known for its intelligence and high level of observation in any case, Bailey, I felt, was a cut above the rest.

As I stepped outside into the piercing cold air, the dog immediately stood up, greeting me with a wagging tail, his ice-blue eyes boring into mine as if to say, *what took you so long?* Couldn't agree more, fella.

I untied his red leather leash from the hydrant and pulled the iPhone out of my pocket, considering once again Jenna's statement. Around me, the holiday shoppers were busy running from one Fifth Avenue store to the next, on a mission and apparently quite sure of where they needed to go to find what they were looking for. Shirts at Bergdorf, jewellery at Tiffany or Cartier, scarves at Louis Vuitton. I envied them briefly, wishing my own shopping expedition would be as easy.

I looked down at Bailey. 'What do you reckon, buddy? Do you think I can get what I need in time?'

He cocked his head to the side in answer, and I couldn't escape the all too clear expression that appeared in those shrewd, almond-shaped eyes. I pursed my lips and said, 'Gotcha. I get the picture. You doubt me.'

If Bailey could have rolled his eyes right then, he probably would have.

At that moment, my iPhone rang, but this time I didn't panic because now I knew how to answer it. I looked at the screen display but it was a withheld number.

'Aidan Harris speaking,' I said into the handset.

She started up like she always did, right in the middle of a sentence. 'You know, I never understand how I end up getting stuck with these long-distance business trips so close to Christmas. Why can't I have your job? Swanning around New York without a care in the world and all this money to spend.'

'Ha-ha, I wish.' I laughed, not in the least bit offended. 'Where are you off to this time?'

'Hong Kong. For this stupid merger. Of course, the only time that the masters of the universe want to get together is when it is most inconvenient for their staff. So off I go, sayonara and all that.' She sounded exasperated.

'Erm, sayonara is actually Japanese, you know,' I couldn't resist teasing.

'Yeah, yeah, yeah – of course you're the expert in these things, aren't you?'

'I have no idea what you are talking about,' I replied innocently. 'Hope it's not too crazy for you though. And here's an idea, maybe you need to introduce your boss to Siri.' I explained all about my recent brush with the Cult of Apple. 'Having now been schooled on the benefits of a virtual personal assistant, I will never have to inconvenience another human being again.'

She barked a laugh. 'Ha! As if you'd ever rely on anyone else, be it human or computer. We will see just how long *that* lasts.' She paused for a moment and then got round to the true purpose of her call. 'So. The plus side to all of this is that when I get back, I've got more time off so I'll probably fly over earlier than planned, if that's OK?'

'Fantastic. I can't wait to see you.'

'Me too,' she said warmly. 'It feels like ages. It'll be good to see your face, the rest of the crew too. How is everyone?'

'Good. Excited about Christmas and seeing you. Do you know for sure when you'll be arriving?'

'Not yet. I'll give you the heads-up when everything's finalised. So enough about me, what are you up to? Is it snowing there at the moment?'

I looked up at the sky. 'Not yet, but I'd imagine it's on the way. Freezing cold though,' I told her, my teeth chattering in agreement as I walked, and I briefly considered popping into the Plaza for a breather, but then remembered I had Bailey with me, and knew that lovely as they were, the staff at the Palm Court wouldn't take too kindly to such a wolf-like animal frightening away their guests. A Starbucks carryout would have to do for the moment.

'Well, I hope it does when I'm there; nothing like snowfall to make it feel really Christmassy.'

'Let me put it on the list – I'll see what I can do,' I joked, but she must have noticed the undertone of strain in my voice.

'Why, what's going on? What are you up to now?'

I grimaced and explained what I was trying to achieve and more importantly how little time I had to accomplish the task. And while I knew from the outset that it was a big ask, I have to admit – I did enjoy the challenge all the same.

'Whoa, that is a toughie. Are you sure it's a go?'

I shrugged and fiddled with Bailey's leash. 'I certainly hope so.'

'Well, I suppose it's lucky for you that money is no object. I'm sure you'll sort it. Or hey, I know – why don't you ask Siri, seeing as you're such a convert?' she teased. 'I hear she can find *anything*.'

'Ha. Chance would be a fine thing, I'm sure.'

'Look, I'd better go – I just thought I'd give you the latest.'

'Thanks. It's good to hear your voice. Enjoy Hong Kong and be sure to let me know when you're due in. I'll send a car for you.'

'Really? I'd love that.' He could hear a huge smile in her voice and was glad he'd thought to suggest it. 'I'll email my itinerary once I have it, but I'm guessing it'll be Newark. A town car – one of those massive Lincoln numbers?'

I chuckled. 'Better not let you get too used to the perks or you'll be hell to live with.'

'Haha, you know me too well.'

When we'd said our goodbyes and hung up I glanced at the iPhone screen and wondered if she and the Apple girl might actually be on to something. Maybe I should just 'ask Siri' for the fun of it.

I pressed the button that Jenna had indicated, and furtively looked around to see if anyone was watching me. I guess I shouldn't feel weird talking *to* a phone, instead of *on* the phone. After all, probably everyone was doing it.

A cool disembodied female voice greeted me. 'Hello, Aidan, what can I do for you?'

'I need to find something.' When I outlined the specifics of my request, there was a brief pause.

Then finally she answered.

'Based upon your current location, there are five separate locations close by. Would you like directions?'

I raised my eyebrows, surprised. Five? Could it really be that easy?

Then I thought about what I'd asked, and the rather crucial piece of information I'd left out. I spoke again into the phone, adding this important detail.

After another wait, this time there was no response and I smiled.

Siri was at a loss for words.

Chapter 11

She had an immense curiosity about life, and was constantly staring and wondering. **Henry James**

Although Darcy knew she could easily spend all night looking around Aidan Harris's house, she reminded herself that she needed to get a move on if she didn't want it to be midnight by the time she got back home.

She'd promised him that she'd return to the hospital tomorrow to report back on whether she'd found anything helpful, and of course she still had to collect Bailey from Mrs Henley and make him dinner.

She went back to the kitchen to grab the bag of dog food, and was carrying it back through the hallway when she spied a bureau on the left-hand side of the door which she hadn't seen on her way in.

On top of it was a phone with an answering machine.

An answering machine that was flashing a tell-tale blinking light.

Darcy bit her lip, wondering if she should perhaps listen to the messages. Yes, it could be considered an invasion of Aidan's privacy, but wasn't he the very one who'd sent her here, tasking her with finding something that would help him get his memory back?

At the end of the day, the guy was in an accident yesterday and had spent all of last night in the hospital. Surely somebody – be it family, his girlfriend or even a work colleague – must have noticed his absence and was wondering where he was? And if the message happened to be from one of those people, then her job would be a lot easier.

Without further contemplation, Darcy turned to the answering machine and pushed Play. A beep emitted from the machine and then a sultry female voice filled the room.

'Aidan, are you there?' She paused for a moment and Darcy could hear noises in the background that suggested the woman was calling from a cell phone in a busy location. *'I've been trying your cell but it's going straight to voicemail ... I'm not sure what's going on. I know you're busy, but I can't believe you'd forget about this and let me down today of all days.'* A hurt sigh. *'Look, just call me when you get this, OK?'*

Click. The line went dead. And that was it. There were no other messages after that. And no name or contact information offered on the one Darcy had just heard. Who was it? she wondered. Judging by the woman's tone and indeed the contents of her message, it certainly sounded like someone Aidan was close to, not at all like anything you'd expect from a work colleague. Could it be the girl from the ski photograph?

Whoever it was, she had definitely been expecting to see Aidan yesterday, or at least expecting to hear from him. *I can't believe you'd forget, and let me down today of all days ...*

Wondering where the woman might have been calling from, Darcy picked the handset up to see if the Caller ID gave any clues, but much to her disappointment she found that the last call registered had come from a withheld number.

But of course she couldn't be absolutely sure that the message on the machine was the last call, could she?

Outside of that, there was only one other incoming call registered yesterday, a 212 area code. So whoever that was, they were based here in Manhattan.

Should she call the number back and see if whoever it was could shed any light on the riddle wrapped in a mystery wrapped in an enigma that was turning out to be Aidan Harris? No, Darcy decided, she really should talk to Aidan again first, get his take on it and see if what she'd found so far rang any bells for him.

Taking a piece of paper and a pen from the bureau, she took down the 212 number and then played back the original message, transcribing it word for word. Listening to it again, she thought the woman, whoever she was, sounded mightily put out but not especially frantic or anything.

She'd mentioned about trying his cell phone a couple of times, and Darcy made a mental note to ask Aidan about the call log on his cell phone, assuming he still had it. God, she hoped it hadn't been lost in the mêlée and she wouldn't be faced with having to replace that, as well as his shoes and fancy coat. If the guy spent a seven-figure sum on a painting for his hallway and all those luxurious kitchen appliances, what would he be spending on his clothes?

Thoughts of Aidan's wardrobe segued directly to his bedroom and indeed other parts of the house that she hadn't yet investigated. She checked her watch; she didn't have a whole lot of time but should at least take a quick look around, just in case something jumped out.

The one thing that was apparent from her search was that Aidan Harris led an interesting life. At least, that's what his house told her. At the same time it didn't give up any especially revealing clues about the personal life of its owner.

She had found a small study on the second floor sparsely furnished with just a desk and laptop lying open on top of it. Suspecting that her efforts were likely to be in vain, Darcy approached the laptop and switched it on but sure enough, it was password protected.

She quickly tried a few options – his surname, Bailey – but failed. Figures, she thought irritably. Even though she couldn't blame him for not making his computer password as obvious as his dog's name.

There were also rows of expensive-looking rosewood filing cabinets, but each drawer had been locked. Darcy couldn't get her head around the thought that it seemed odd in a house with a Rothko just inside the hallway, to afford such security to drawers likely full of rubber bands and stationery.

But the study made her wonder again what he did for a living. Given his Irish heritage she guessed he couldn't be the offspring of one of Manhattan's wealthier blue bloods, so his wealth might have been earned. But how? Was he some kind of Wall Street hotshot, a hedge fund manager maybe? Those guys were seriously rolling in it and many chose to live in this part of town, much to the chagrin of the aforesaid blue bloods who considered them tacky and nouveau riche. Or he could be one of those millionaire tech types like Bill Gates, someone who had set up a business in his dad's garage and then went on to earn more money than the national debt of some countries?

As with so many other things about Aidan Harris, the answer remained a mystery, at least until the gaps in his memory could be filled.

When Darcy finally made it to the master bedroom, she took a moment to cast her eyes across the expanse of his California King bed, thinking that in her tiny apartment she would barely have been able to fit the mattress through the door. And if by some miracle she was able to get the massive bed into the apartment, there would have been no room for anything else, including herself.

She walked slowly across the room. There had to be a uniquely personal item in this space that would trigger something for Aidan, or perhaps shed some light on who the woman on the phone, or in the photograph, might be.

From her visit to the house, she had gleaned that Aidan Harris was not only loaded but a lover of fine things – food, design and exotic travel. And that he was in a relationship with a beautiful red-haired woman.

But precious little else besides.

She looked at the bed, and tried to determine whether Aidan slept on the right side or the left side. Or in the middle even. Darcy then considered both bedside tables. One was completely devoid of paraphernalia except a lamp. The other, on the right side of the bed, played host to a copy of *The New Yorker* magazine, and the *New York Time*s.

At once Darcy realised that she'd learned another thing. She moved to the side of the bed which showed evidence of someone who clearly read in bed. She sat down, careful not to disturb the elegantly displayed cushions, and picked up the newspaper – yesterday's edition. The copy of *The New Yorker* was last month's, and she took note of the fact there was nothing out of the ordinary about the periodicals, not even an address label.

Then Darcy spied the drawer beneath the side table and she reached forward, fastening her fingers around the polished brass handle. She took a deep breath, hoping first that the drawer wasn't locked, and secondly, that if it did open she wouldn't find anything that would make her blush or invade Aidan's privacy.

But the drawer opened easily.

Darcy felt a surge of adrenaline in her veins as she peered inside, very much feeling like a voyeur now, though hoping she might be on the precipice of discovery.

There was an eight by ten photograph inside. A photo of a

woman – blonde, this time – and completely different to the girl in the skiing shot downstairs. And there was something more about this picture.

Darcy picked up the print, curious. She had to wonder why this one was without a frame and had been apparently shoved in a bedside-table drawer. Could she be an ex, perhaps?

She looked more closely at the blonde woman. She was laughing, her mouth open in a wide smile. She had one foot raised slightly off the ground, as if she was about to skip or break into dance, and her hands were held high above her head as if she was working to cast her blonde mane from her shoulder, or artfully tousle it as a gust of wind blew her way.

The backdrop was slightly blurred but there seemed to be a fountain, or some kind of waterfall, just behind her, and the woman, her hands held high in that curious pose, seemed aware of the camera while also appearing artfully unaware of it.

Darcy felt the teeniest stab of jealousy knowing that she herself could never pull that look off. Then again, there were few women who could. She instantly wondered if this woman was a model of some kind, and secondly what she meant to Aidan – how she was connected to him – and, perhaps most importantly, why he had a picture of her in his bedside drawer.

Now she really did feel like a voyeur. There was something private about this photo. It was one of the first truly personal things she'd discovered in this entire house. Something that wasn't meant to be seen by just anyone.

But why?

She turned the photograph over, wondering if there might be an inscription, or a date mark, anything that might give her some clue as to who this person was and how she might relate to Aidan. Hidden away or not, if the woman was important to him, then she needed to take the photo with her and show it to him at the hospital.

Feeling as if she was in a Nancy Drew novel, Darcy picked up the photograph and placed it safely in her messenger bag, adding it to a growing list of mysteries surrounding Aidan Harris – mysteries that she couldn't yet solve.

Chapter 12

To thine own self be true. **William Shakespeare**

It was well after 8 p.m. by the time she made it back to West Houston Street, and when her next-door neighbour opened the door, Darcy was full of apologies. She'd not had Mrs Henley's telephone number to call and warn her how late she'd be.

'I'm so sorry, I had no idea I'd be so late.' Even though Bailey wasn't actually hers, she felt how she imagined a hassled working mother late picking up her kids from daycare must feel. And looking at him now, she again wondered again how she was going to manage a dog his size in her teeny apartment for yet another night – or perhaps even longer, who knew?

'No need to apologise, it's not as though I was going anywhere in any case.' Mrs Henley beckoned her inside her apartment, which was bright, cheery and ... very pink.

The blinds were pink, the sofa cushions were pink, the lights on the white plastic tree were pink, and from every branch hung pink-coloured decorations.

Bailey danced around her legs, whining and yowling, and Darcy was relieved that she finally had some decent food to feed him with.

'Here you go, boy,' she said, as she slipped him one of the rust-coloured dog biscuits she'd picked up for him at Aidan's house. He jumped up and snatched it from her hand, retreating to Mrs Henley's satiny pink tree skirt to nibble it gently between his big paws.

The older woman emerged from the kitchenette, a tea tray in hand. A conspicuously white tray, Darcy saw, and not a sign of pink in sight but no, there it was … the cocktail napkins.

'I am so sorry,' she apologised for the sixth time since heading straight to the apartment after leaving Aidan's house. 'And thank you, but you really shouldn't have gone to so much trouble.'

The old woman set the tray on her coffee table, and settled onto her pink couch. 'Don't mention it – it's no trouble at all,' she purred, a truly different woman to the one Darcy thought she knew. She turned her eyes to Bailey, curled beneath the blinking pink Christmas tree. 'We had a lovely day, didn't we, boy? I took him over to Hudson Park for a nice long walk by the river, and on the way back we stopped off for a couple of hot dogs,' she told Darcy. 'My treat, but very definitely Bailey's idea. He got very excited when he came across the vendor's cart, didn't you, darling?'

Bailey looked up and lazily wagged his tail before resting his head on his white paws, looking from Mrs Henley to Darcy and back again.

'Like I said, I really can't thank you enough,' Darcy enthused, as the older woman handed her a cup of coffee so black she could see her reflection in the rippling surface. Thoughtfully, she had added several butter cookies to the saucer.

Darcy sipped the coffee, hiding a wince as the first taste of instant hit the back of her throat. Mrs Henley must have spooned in twice the recommended dosage for each cup. Darcy wasn't a huge coffee fan, more of a latte/cappuccino person if she had it at all, but at the same time it was hot and warming. And as Darcy still hadn't had dinner and was starving, she quickly made the four thick butter cookies disappear.

She sat back in the comfy chair across from her neighbour and sighed. It felt like the first time she'd sat down all day. 'Are you all right, dear?' Mrs Henley asked.

Darcy nodded serenely. 'Just tired, I guess.'

The other woman leaned over and poured more coffee into her cup. 'Then you need some more of my special brew.'

Darcy chuckled and leaned over to accept the top-up. 'Nice tree,' she said, trying to get a better look at the pastel decorations.

'Thank you, don't you just love it?' Mrs Henley set the pot down on the tray and sat back, her pink housecoat soft, her pink slippers fluffy. She shivered to herself with pleasure.

'Er yes,' Darcy hedged. 'What's hanging on them? Are

those decorations ... shoes?' she asked, finally recognising the shapes.

Clearly shoes were to Mrs Henley what books were to her. Another revelation about her neighbour, who kept on surprising her.

The old woman wrinkled her nose and waved a hand. 'Ballet slippers, of course. I was a ballerina a long, long time ago. I even danced at the Lincoln Centre once. What a rush it was ...'

'Wow, that's amazing, Mrs Henley. I had no idea.' But how would Darcy know something like that about her neighbour when this was the first time she'd even been inside her home? 'It must have been wonderful.'

'I keep telling you, call me Grace. Yes, it was – incredible actually, but like I said, it was a long time ago.' Her eyes grew misty as she seemed to stare beyond the tree and right into the past.

Her mood had turned contemplative, and still feeling as if she didn't know the woman well enough to press for more details, Darcy stood up, gently patting her leg for Bailey to follow. Time to go.

His head perked up, and having been nearly snoozing a moment earlier, he suddenly shot out from under the tree like a missile and stood by her side.

'Leaving so soon?' Grace asked, but her voice was tired and as she struggled to get up, Darcy shooed her back down.

'Please, no need to see me out. We've taken up enough of your time as it is and I'm sure Bailey has you worn out.'

Grace sat back down and smiled. Bailey, tail wagging happily, shuffled over once more and licked her hand before darting back to Darcy. 'We did have a nice day, didn't we, boy? Same time tomorrow?' she asked, eyes glinting and hopeful as she looked up at Darcy.

'Seriously?' Darcy was taken aback. She was on the late shift at Chaucer's the following day, which meant she didn't need to be in until midday, but she was anxious to head back to the hospital to give Aidan his things as soon as possible; if Grace was willing, she would be able to do so in the morning. Her neighbour's surprising kindness was turning out to be the answer to her prayers.

'That would be great, thank you. I really appreciate it.'

She picked up the red leather leash on the way out and made sure to fasten Bailey to it before letting herself out – otherwise he could go skittering down the stairs and at this point Darcy definitely didn't have the energy for a game of chase. 'You really are a lifesaver. I don't know how to thank you ...' she continued, saying goodbye, but the rest of her sentence trailed off when Grace's snores met her in reply.

Waking early the next morning, Darcy realised that even though she still felt sore from the accident, she also felt properly rested and refreshed. And for the first time in a while, she'd woken up without an alarm clock interrupting her dreams.

Instead, she was greeted with a kiss by the male with whom she was sharing a bed. The first member of the opposite gender who had shared her bed in quite some time, she thought wryly, opening her eyes.

OK, so what if it was a dog.

Katherine was right; her current dating dry spell was lasting a little longer than she'd thought. It wasn't for the lack of trying – on both Darcy's and her aunt's part – and there were a few guys who'd initially set her pulse racing, but she had yet to meet a man with whom she connected – *really* connected – on an intellectual as well as emotional level. So much so that he could occupy her thoughts night and day and she would count the hours until they were together again. Ultimately, if you didn't have that, what was the point? Darcy had long since decided that she wasn't going to settle for second best. She supposed she and her aunt were alike in that way at least. Katherine had never married, and while Darcy recalled her aunt bringing home the occasional suitor to the Brooklyn condo for dinner over the years, she'd got the impression that these guys were always somewhat taken aback by her presence there, and the revelation that Katherine was to all intents and purposes a single mother. Darcy often worried that she was the reason her aunt had never settled down, and this was why she had resolved to get out from beneath her aunt's feet as soon as she possibly could.

She turned over to find Bailey breathing doggie fumes in her face. She let out a giggle as he licked her cheek and she scratched behind his ears. 'Did you know that you are kind of a bed hog?'

Bailey sighed, as if to say, 'Yeah, I've heard that one before. Tell me something I don't know.'

'Well, unfortunately, I don't have a California King like your owner; therefore until we get you back home, you are going to have to learn how to share a little better. OK?'

She sat up in bed and allowed Bailey to lay his heavy head in her lap as she rubbed him under his chin, thinking she could easily get used to having a housemate like this.

'You know, Bailey, I haven't been around a dog like this since I was a kid.'

He looked up at her with his big blue eyes as if suddenly interested in what she was saying and she smiled. 'Having you here makes me realise how much I miss it.'

Darcy allowed herself to reminisce about the black and white Cocker Spaniel that she'd had as a child. Timmy (named after the canine star in the *Famous Five* books) had been a great dog, and Darcy used to devotedly follow the little animal around the family house in Brooklyn.

Having Bailey here brought all of this back – but in a good way.

Darcy quickly ate breakfast, this time giving Bailey a huge helping of his fancy dog food. In truth, it looked and smelled so appetising that Darcy was almost tempted to give it a go herself. But she wasn't quite that desperate.

Having brought him outside to do his business, she dropped Bailey off at Grace's apartment once again, then got back on the bike and headed straight to Roosevelt General.

Entering the hospital room, she once again felt hesitant,

unsure of the specifics of Aidan's condition and wondering for a moment if he might since have forgotten her. But those worries were assuaged when he looked up, immediately brightened by her arrival, and greeted her with a smile that made her stomach do a tiny somersault. 'How are you feeling this morning?' she asked him. She could see that half the tubes and vials and dials and plugs that had been attached to him the night before were gone.

'Right as rain, apart from the obvious.' He knocked pointedly on the top of his head. 'Thanks for coming in, I really appreciate it. How's Bailey? I hope you found the dog food OK?'

She guessed he was forcing himself to make small talk, and was no doubt much more anxious to hear what else she might have found at his house the night before.

Darcy was still thinking about his home and all the treasures within, and had spent hours last night analysing the kind of person he must be. In truth, Aidan Harris's life – or at least the way he lived it – was as intriguing as the first few pages of a good novel, and Darcy knew she wanted to read on in the hope of finding out more. The fact that he also looked like he could have walked out of the pages of such a novel helped too.

But like all heroes in fiction, his perfect other half was also out there somewhere. Darcy just had to try and put the pieces together and help him find her.

Giving him a brief description of the layout and contents of his house, she waited for a reaction, some spark of recognition. But there was nothing.

She then handed him the framed photo of him and the red-head on the ski slope, as well as the picture of the blonde she'd found in his bedside drawer.

'Ring any bells?'

He studied both pictures for a long time, but by his expression she knew that he was still drawing a blank. 'Sorry, no. I don't recognise anyone in these.'

'No need to apologise to me.' Still, she couldn't help but feel bad for him. Clearly, shaking off the memory loss might not be as straightforward as they'd first thought.

Darcy then took out the holiday photographs she'd brought with her; the scuba diving and sky-diving shots. Again he studied them both closely, but after a while shook his head once again. 'Nothing. It's like I'm looking at some-body else's photographs. I really don't remember doing anything like this ever.' His expression was strained, the dis-appointment painfully evident, and Darcy tried to cheer him up by telling him how amazing his house was and what he had to look forward to when he did go home. 'You have a Rothko in your hallway – a *Rothko*,' she repeated reverently. 'Can you maybe remember where or even why you got that? A landmark occasion maybe? Something major in relation to your job, or your work? A big promotion or securing a major account or . . .'

She had no idea what sort of promotion would enable someone to suddenly decide to buy such an expensive paint-ing but this was his world, not hers, so she had to try and put herself in his shoes.

And what a world it must be. The kind of wonderful, privileged New York society lifestyle that so many people dreamed about when first coming to the city. Where the streets really were paved with gold. Darcy had tasted just a fraction of it last night in Aidan's house, and she couldn't even begin to imagine what it must be like from day to day. To think that you could afford to dine in the best restaurants, were likely to be known by name in the fanciest hotels, and invited to incredible parties held in the most prestigious buildings ...

It reminded her of one time when she'd met up with Katherine in the Plaza for impromptu drinks. It was a foggy evening around Christmastime and the two of them had sat in the opulent lounge by the window in ornate brocade chairs looking out at the horse-drawn carriages waiting outside a snow-covered Central Park while a white-gloved waiter had served them the finest champagne beneath crystal chandeliers. From that vantage point, it was as if modern life had retreated, and for Darcy it was almost like going back in time, straight into the pages of an Edith Wharton novel, witnessing what old New York might have looked like, back in the early 1800s.

But once she'd explained about the painting, again Aidan heaved a sigh, telling her, 'I really have no idea.'

The poor guy looked so lost and dejected that Darcy wanted to reach over and give him a hug. But of course it wasn't her place to do so, and this immediately reminded her of the message on the answering machine. She then went on to recount the message word for word from her notes, watching carefully as he listened to the words.

Nothing.

'Someone is definitely missing you in any case, which is good to know,' she assured him, going on to explain about the other missed call and accompanying number. 'I guess it's only a matter of time before your girlfriend, or whoever she is, shows up here. But in the meantime, do you want to call that 212 number, just in case that too might be someone important?'

Aidan looked even more frustrated. 'Well, I would if I had a bloody phone.' He reached towards his bedside locker and took out an iPhone. Even at this distance Darcy could tell that the screen had been smashed to pieces. Ah, so at least that answered her query about why he hadn't been picking up messages on his cell phone.

Darcy grimaced at the damage. 'You can just add it to my tab,' she joked nervously. 'I'm already in for your dry-cleaning bill.'

He waved a bare arm, toned and strong-looking as the rest of him, Darcy noted, gulping a little. 'Don't be silly. You've been so kind in taking care of Bailey for me, and helping me out last night too.'

'It was the least I could do.' But Darcy was guiltily relieved that she wouldn't have to worry about financial – or worse, legal – implications resulting from her part in the accident. Guilt aside, this had been playing on her mind, and she had to admit it was possibly one of the reasons she'd been so willing to help him out in the first place.

That, and the fact that Darcy was unable to resist any kind of mystery.

She took the iPhone from him, curious. Rather like bookshelves, you could tell a lot about a person's life from their phone.

She pushed the big button at the bottom of the screen, but as expected the display remained black. 'It might not be a completely lost cause, though; there may be a way to get some of your data off it,' she assured him, trying to remain positive and upbeat for his sake. The truth was, Darcy had no idea if this was the case, since she had never even used an iPhone before, but Joshua was a real technology whizz and a devoted Apple disciple, and she resolved to ask him about it later at work. 'Just count yourself lucky it wasn't dropped in water; according to my friend that's the kiss of death.'

Aidan looked at her speculatively. 'I'm so sorry, all this time we've been talking about me and I didn't even think to ask anything about you. What do you do, Darcy Archer?'

When she told him she worked for Chaucer's, he brightened immediately.

'So a literature aficionado, eh?' He playfully raised his eyebrows. 'Sounds interesting.'

This line of conversation reminded Darcy of something, and she wondered if it was worth a shot.

'Remember last night when were talking?' she said to Aidan. 'I noticed that you kept repeating a particular word – inconceivable.' She watched his expression carefully as she spoke again. '"You keep using that word. I do not think it means what you think it means",' she added, her voice hesitant, wondering if the words would mean anything to him.

Aidan looked up sharply, and said straight away '*The Princess Bride*.'

Darcy was delighted that he'd recognised the literary reference from William Goldman's famous tale. She sat forward, her face eager. 'Would the book be a favourite of yours or anything?' Granted, she hadn't seen any books at the house yesterday, so wasn't sure if he was much of a reader. 'Or maybe you're a fan of the movie?'

Aidan was shaking his head. 'I have no idea. But if I'm quoting it as you say, it must be significant. I just wish I could remember something more concrete, something that would help get me out of this bloody place.'

Now he looked even more troubled, and Darcy decided it was better to move on and concentrate on things that could help him, rather than have him dwell on what didn't.

'What about your wallet?' she asked. 'Besides your ID, surely you must have something in there that might help?'

'No. It was the first thing I checked when the doctors gave me my things back. Just typical stuff – a couple of credit cards, a gym membership access card, a subway card ...'

'A subway card.' This struck Darcy as curious. 'Why would you need a subway card?' Judging by Aidan's house and prestigious address, he was far from the type that would ever need to brave the subway. She'd automatically assumed he would have either a private driver or use a limousine service.

He shrugged, taking out his wallet and showing it to her as

if to prove he was telling the truth. Then he flicked through another compartment. 'Also a pair of theatre tickets, and get this – a receipt for Gray's Papaya.'

'Gray's Papaya?' she repeated with a surprised laugh, picturing the popular eaterie which was an institution amongst the city's hot-dog fans. Again, not somewhere she imagined a man of Aidan's means frequenting. Then she remembered what Grace had said the day before about Bailey getting all excited at the sight of the hot-dog stand while they were out and about.

'I wouldn't mind, but I don't even like hot dogs,' Aidan continued, 'or at least, I don't think I do,' he added hoarsely, before suddenly he started to cough.

'Are you all right?' she asked, concerned.

'Water would be good, thanks.'

There was a mustard-yellow pitcher on the nightstand, and a stack of white plastic cups sitting next to it. Darcy took one and poured it half-full, bringing it to his side. She spilled a little on his chin before using her free hand to lift up his head. His neck was warm and soft as he drank. The intimate act felt oddly comfortable.

'Not too much,' she told him, having read something like it before.

'OK,' he said, and he stopped. 'Thanks.'

She put the cup back, filling it again in case he got thirsty later, then feeling stupid about it because of course there were nurses for that.

'Well, according to my neighbour, Bailey certainly seems to

like hot dogs, but I could check out the Gray's thing in more detail if you'd like,' she told him once she was sure the coughing had subsided. 'Give me the receipt and I can swing by there on my way home from work later. You never know, somebody there might remember you, or you could be a regular even.'

He put a tired hand up and said, 'No, honestly, you've already done more than enough and I don't want to impose.'

'Seriously, it's no problem. Like I said, it's not far from where I work. And I'm curious to know why someone like you would have been enjoying,' Darcy read from the receipt, smiling a little, 'a Recession Special earlier this week.'

'Beats me. And you keep telling me I'm loaded, but there's only about thirty dollars' worth of cash in here.'

This too seemed odd; she figured that millionaires usually carried more cash on them. But maybe Aidan wasn't the type of person who 'made it rain' everywhere he went.

All of it – the fact that despite his wealth he still did everyday things like take the subway or eat crappy food – merely made her like him all the more. Yes, he might be loaded but he wasn't afraid to slum it with the rest of them either.

She looked down at her watch. 'I'm sorry, I'd really like to stay longer, but I need to get to work.'

'Of course.'

'Don't worry about Bailey. My neighbour's watching him – he's in really good hands. I'll check out the hot-dog place, and come back to you if I find out anything, OK?' She smiled. 'In the meantime, you should give that number a call – see if talking to someone who obviously knows you might be able to jerk something loose.'

Aidan was back to being belligerent. 'Well, I would, but I still don't have a phone, do I? And the doc's still keeping me under observation and won't let me move out of this damn bed, let alone the room.'

Darcy thought about it. 'How much did you say was in your wallet?'

'About thirty dollars?'

She held her hand out. 'I'll sort you out with a prepaid phone as soon as I can. Something to keep you going until you get your iPhone fixed.'

'You'd do that?' He looked so grateful, it almost brought tears to her eyes. 'Honestly, Darcy, I don't know how I'll ever be able to thank you.'

'It's not a problem, and no thanks needed,' she said, though inwardly she was childishly pleased by his gratitude. 'I can only imagine how lost and scared you must be feeling just now, and seeing as it's my fault you ended up being hurt in the first place and got separated from your dog and it's Christmas—'

Suddenly Darcy remembered Aidan's package; she hadn't given it a second thought since putting it her drawer. 'Oh, I almost forgot – I have something else of yours.' She went on to explain about the beautifully wrapped gift she'd found at the scene of the accident. 'I'll bring it to you tomorrow. Maybe whatever it is might trigger something?'

He looked thoughtful. 'Yes, but from what you said you're not sure if it's even mine.'

'I do remember you carrying something though. Do you think you might have been on your way to deliver it or ...?'

Then something struck her – that woman's annoyance and frustration on the phone message the day before. It certainly sounded as though Aidan had been a no-show for something important, a date or a business lunch.

Of course!

'Aidan,' Darcy said breathlessly, feeling stupid for not having made the connection when she played back the phone message yesterday: 'I wonder – would you have been on your way to deliver that package to somebody when I ran into you?'

Chapter 13

I don't approve of surprises. The pleasure is never enhanced and the inconvenience is considerable.
Jane Austen

'So, what's the latest with your victim?'

Later at the bookshop, Darcy had to laugh at Joshua's bluntness. Typical. It was early afternoon, just after lunch – often one of the slowest times of the day in Chaucer's for customers but a good time for stickering and restocking. Upstairs from the café, she could smell gingerbread scones baking and the peppermint scent of the special 'Kringle Cup' roast they'd been offering since the week before. It was making her mouth water.

'He's not my *victim*, Joshua. And he's fine, stable, just ... still not remembering anything.'

He cocked one carefully manicured eyebrow and straightened his reindeer antlers. 'Very Jason Bourne.'

'Stop it, this is serious. It must be scary not remembering anything about your life, or the people you love.'

She smiled as a customer approached the desk with a purchase.

'Would it be possible to arrange a personal dedication from the author, please?' asked a young woman with an officious-sounding voice, frosted blonde hair and an entitled air. 'It's a Christmas gift.'

Darcy had to look twice at the book the girl was buying, trying to determine if she was actually serious. 'From the author of *this* book?'

'Of course,' she replied curtly, through obviously Botoxed lips, as if she didn't appreciate being questioned.

'I'm afraid not, ma'am,' Darcy said, smiling patiently. Several other customers had since appeared in line behind the woman and were waiting with arms full to get to the cash register. Darcy had to marvel at the way this always seemed to happen when she was about to have a tricky customer experience. The girl turned, ostentatious gold jewellery clattering on the counter as she complained loudly, 'Why not? I was told this place was the best independent bookstore in town.'

The other customers standing in line looked on with interest.

Darcy tried her best to keep her voice down as she replied pleasantly, 'Yes, and while we always try our utmost to assist our customers, I'm afraid that's just not possible in this case. You see, Mr Lewis died in 1963.'

'Not good enough,' the woman huffed, walking away and

leaving the seven-volume *Chronicles of Narnia* box set edition behind on the counter. Darcy sighed. Looked like it was going to be another long day.

Later, during her coffee break in the café upstairs, over a gingerbread and cinnamon latte, Darcy took out the piece of paper upon which she had transcribed the missed call number to Aidan's house.

Until she was able to sort him out with his own phone, she'd promised that she would do what she could to find out who might have been trying to get in touch with him. Thinking about it more, she guessed that it must have been the person he'd been on his way to meet. What she couldn't be sure about was whether or not this woman knew about the package – although Darcy did recall how she'd mentioned something about Aidan letting her down 'today of all days'. Could she have been referring to a specific day, maybe a special anniversary or birthday or something?

Based on what she'd already learned about him, she knew she could create 1,001 ideas about Aidan Harris and his life – with her imagination this wouldn't be hard. Was he a hot-shot stockbroker with a love of art and a string of beautiful girl-friends, or a dedicated family man who'd inherited all his good fortune from Irish emigrants done good? But she wondered if his real life story wasn't the most interesting of all?

Darcy knew she wouldn't be able to stop thinking about it until she found out more, and as she dialled the number and waited for a reply, she started to wonder again what the beautiful package might contain.

Seconds later, a female voice answered the phone.

'*Buenos dias*, Kensington Residence, how may I help you?' said a woman with a highly accented voice.

Darcy sat up. *Kensington Residence.*

'Hello, yes. I am hoping you can help me. I am ... I'm Darcy Archer,' she scrambled her thoughts frantically. What was she to Aidan? An acquaintance, a Good Samaritan? 'A ... friend of Aidan Harris's.'

'Yes?' the woman on the other line said, somewhat impatiently, and Darcy could tell right away that the name meant nothing to her. 'What can I help you with?'

Trying to overcome her nervousness, Darcy went on, 'Like I said, I'm a friend of Aidan Harris's. Unfortunately he was hurt yesterday morning, in an accident – nothing terribly serious – and I was at his house and I saw this number come up on his caller ID. So I'm not sure if you know him, or whether perhaps somebody else in the ... er ... Residence might. Certainly someone from this number called Mr Harris yesterday, and I am really just looking for a little help and thought that maybe you might be able to assist me.'

Suddenly, the woman interrupted. 'Mr and Mrs Kensington are not available at the moment.'

'Oh.' Darcy was somewhat taken aback by the woman's curt tone. Then again, she supposed she was babbling. But she wondered now who Mr and Mrs Kensington might be. Not Aidan's parents, given the surname, but might they be his girlfriend's parents? Perhaps wondering why he'd let their daughter down? Then, conscious that her imagination was running away with her, she forced herself back to the conversation.

'Well, perhaps I could leave an urgent message for Mr and Mrs Kensington?' she asked. 'It's just they may have called my friend yesterday, but like I said, he's in the hospital right now, and I really need to get in touch with somebody who knows him.'

'Didn't you just say you were his friend?'

'Yes, but—'

'I am very busy right now,' the woman said sharply, clearly bored by Darcy's sob story. Yet again she was taken aback by the woman's bluntness.

'I guess you might say I'm a "new friend",' she told her. 'Really, I am just trying to help.'

The woman gave a weary sigh. 'Fine, fine, give me your name and number. Miller is in Europe but I will pass it on to Mrs Kensington. She is at her spa day today so she may not call you back right away.'

OK, so it must have been the wife who had called the house then, Darcy deduced quickly, seeing as the husband was away at the moment. Feeling a tiny amount of sunshine break through the fog that was thus far Aidan's story, she rattled off her contact information, hoping against hope that this Mrs Kensington, whoever she was, would call her back quickly.

'OK,' said the woman. 'I will give her your information and she will call you if she wants to.'

Darcy harrumphed at the pompous tone. Why did some people feel that social niceties, like simply returning a call, were beyond them? And why on earth would someone as pleasant as Aidan be associated with someone so rude? No, that wasn't fair, she was stereotyping right now, and it wasn't Aidan's acquaintance she was speaking to. Mrs Kensington could be a perfectly nice person, and the dragon on the line right now – be it her personal assistant or housekeeper or whatever – was just doing her job.

'I certainly appreciate that, Ms ... um, I'm sorry, I didn't catch your name.'

'Maria,' replied the woman grudgingly.

'Maria, I really do appreciate your help. Aidan is pretty disorientated right now and if Mrs Kensington is a friend of his too, then I'm pretty sure she will want to help him.'

Maria clearly had had enough of this conversation. 'Yes, OK, fine,' she said exasperatedly. 'I already said I'd pass your message along. She will be at Elizabeth Arden for the rest of the day though, just so you know.'

At this Darcy's ears perked up and she recalled what Maria had said earlier about a spa day. She was at Elizabeth Arden today? But she stayed quiet and simply bade Maria goodbye. She didn't want to let the woman know that she had inadvertently given out very helpful information indeed.

Darcy was familiar with the Elizabeth Arden salon down on Fifth Avenue; Katherine was a regular although Darcy herself had never been inside its hallowed walls.

If the Kensington woman was spending the day at the salon, then maybe Darcy should call down there after work and ...

And what? She could hardly just saunter in and ask for a

chat. The receptionists at these places were like guard dogs, and while Maria might have been indiscreet, there was no way *they* would be so flippant. Not to mention that Darcy didn't even know Mrs Kensington's first name.

But for the rest of the afternoon, she just couldn't get Aidan's plight out of her head, and knew that waiting around for the woman to return her call would simply drive her crazy.

The mysterious Mrs Kensington was potentially someone who ran in Aidan's social circle, since spending the day at Elizabeth Arden wasn't cheap – far from it. Darcy had read some of the eye-watering prices from a brochure Katherine had left lying around and the cost of a simple facial would almost keep Darcy in groceries for a month.

Almost.

But seeing as there was a *Mr* Kensington, the woman certainly couldn't be Aidan's girlfriend or someone he lived with. Then Darcy shook her head, annoyed with herself for being so naïve. Married people had affairs all the time, didn't they? Still, she was having a hard time reconciling the Aidan she'd met as someone who would be involved with another man's wife. Or cheating on someone he was in a relationship with, she thought, recalling the women in the photographs.

Then again – how much did she really know about him? Yes, he seemed like a nice guy and had been lovely about the fact that she had almost killed him the other morning, but oftentimes the most disarming men turned out to be the real lady-killers. Hadn't Darcy come across that in real life and indeed fiction, all the time?

And thinking about it, wasn't there a very real chance that the woman who had called Aidan sounding so frantic about him being a no-show somewhere yesterday (and who for good reason couldn't reach him on his cell phone) had tried calling the house again later from home?

Which meant that at the moment, this woman was Darcy's best option in finding out who Aidan was, and reuniting him not only with his memory, but his loved ones.

She wondered then if this Mrs Kensington was the blonde woman in the photograph by Aidan's bedside. If so, and she happened to be married it explained why the picture had been hidden away like that. Aidan was no doubt trying to keep their relationship secret. Darcy was dying to know. Lovers or not, this Mrs Kensington clearly had *some* connection to Aidan. She just needed to find out what it was. But how could she realistically turn up at the spa and ask to speak to the woman when she didn't even know her first name? Darcy once again cursed her lack of technological savvy.

Finishing her coffee, she went back downstairs and using the work computer, summoned up Google, typing in the name 'Kensington' and adding 'Manhattan' for good measure.

Scores of references to city residents evidently sharing the same name came up.

Damn ... how to narrow it down? Darcy thought about what she knew or what she was assuming about Mrs Kensington – the housekeeper, pricy salon, possible society friend of Aidan's? Amending the search terms to 'Kensington, New York society' and pressing enter, she took a deep breath while Google quickly considered her query then spat out a response.

Darcy smiled – she had guessed right. Aidan's Mrs Kensington was a society swan. Though to suggest that this particular Mrs Kensington (first name Tabitha) was simply a member of New York society was the understatement of the century. The woman was of a breed that clearly *ran* the island of Manhattan.

Her name was listed on countless charity events, and like Aidan, she clearly had money to burn. Bloggers and columnists alike heralded her impeccable taste and sense of style.

Lists of donations, with figures that literally made Darcy's head spin, cluttered the screen. The woman's patronage of everything from the Chanel flagship store on Fifth Avenue, to auctions at Christie's, to her chairwomanship of various causes at the New York Public Library, were all highlighted. Truly, Tabitha Kensington was, as Katherine might say, a *big deal*.

Darcy clicked on a link to the *New York Post*'s Page Six section, and was met with a picture of a stunningly beautiful blonde. Bingo.

Unfortunately, she couldn't recall from memory if Tabitha Kensington was the same blonde in the picture that she had found by Aidan's bedside, but she too was model gorgeous. Looking not a day over thirty, the woman was either very young or very well-preserved. Darcy pondered this for a moment, thinking that it could well be a combination of the two, and then automatically wondered how old Mr Kensington was.

The inevitable gold-digger moniker quickly popped into her brain, but then she just as quickly pushed the notion away when on another website, she came across a picture of the couple together. Miller Kensington looked to be older than his wife by about six or seven years. Tabitha, it was revealed, was no slouch. She had graduated from Columbia with a degree in History and a Master's from Harvard in Historical Preservation, had served as an assistant curator at the National Archives and taken time to oversee some preservation work at the National Gallery in London, before coming back to the US to serve as the lead curator at the Met. Which is where she met her husband, whom she'd married only five years ago. Tabitha certainly didn't need Miller's money – Darcy learned that she was wealthy in her own right as the only child of multi-millionaires Stanley and Martina Washbourne, who owned a series of five-star European hotels. To say the least, Tabitha Kensington was certified blue blood.

Whether or not she was currently having an affair with Aidan Harris had yet to be determined. Darcy hoped in her heart of hearts that Aidan wasn't that kind of guy.

Chapter 14

My only conclusion as to why I'm putting myself through something like this is that I really must be a glutton for punishment.

God knows I can be an eejit sometimes.

And I'll be an even bigger one if I go and mess this up.

My newly organised iPhone buzzed and whatever Jenna had done to it that time at the store, now it automatically told me just what was happening at that particular moment. In this case, Siri's cool voice announced, 'An incoming text, from Mel.'

The robotic voice nevertheless warmed my heart.

Accessing the message, I read the words and smiled. *Hi, I miss you. Are you coming over later?*

I typed a quick response and said that I would be there as soon as I could, but that I had to finish up some errands first – hopefully make some progress on one big errand – and then I would swing by and pick her up.

This earned me a smiley face along with an *xoxo*. My heart swelled. Even though I had been with her less than forty-eight hours before, my arms still ached to hold her. I thought of everything that had happened over the past few years and acknowledged that I would do anything for her, anything to make her happy.

At that second, I was broken from my reverie as Bailey tugged on his leash and put on the brakes. I almost tripped over my feet as I realised too late that we had reached our destination. Regaining my composure, I decided again that Bailey really was too smart for his own good.

How many dogs know the exact location of Christie's Sales Rooms? Probably not many, and probably even fewer outside of Manhattan.

What a pampered pooch.

I smiled down at him. 'You know you are a real snob, don't you? I didn't learn where Christie's was until recently. I guess you might be a bourgeois dog, huh?'

Bailey gave a low 'woof' as if agreeing that yes, he was in fact part of that socio-economic crowd of canines and then looked at the building, wondering if I was going to go inside.

'Yes, I'm going. I'm going,' I said, leading Bailey over to yet another hydrant and fastening his leash around it. 'Unfortunately, you are stuck out here, pal. No offence. I just don't think the guys at Christie's need you drooling on any of their Renoirs or Fabergé eggs, or any of that racket. Wait out here.'

Bailey met my gaze knowingly and again, I felt like he wanted to roll his eyes and sigh at me, as if the last thing he would do is engage in anything so crass as drooling. I had no doubt that this was true, and that if given the opportunity to walk the hallowed halls of Christie's, a dog like Bailey would, in fact, display impeccable manners. However, I was pretty sure that Christie's formidable staff would not have the same perspective on it.

'Just take a load off, bud. I promise I'll be quick.'

The temperature was dropping quickly out here, and although I knew that Huskies were built for the cold and he had a nice winter coat, I still worried about him sitting on the chilly pavement. That couldn't be fun, warm coat or not. I had a warm coat on and *I* didn't want to do it. I felt bad for the people and animals who had no other choice.

So I was a softie. Just because I was in the position I was in didn't mean I didn't have a heart. I always felt bad for individuals, be it people or animals who didn't have what they needed to get by. And yes, I knew that what I was able to do was all well and good, but I also believed in the need to give back. And I wanted to ensure that I associated with people who had the same belief structure. After all, while it was one thing to be fortunate, it was another to be fortunate and not consider the welfare of the least of us. My mindset might go against traditional thinking in some places, but at the end of the day, I was just a guy from Dublin who happened to hit a stroke of luck in New York. That's all. Being exposed to money and nice things might change some people, but not this guy.

I petted Bailey's head and once again promised I wouldn't be long. He sighed and resigned himself to the pavement. I stood up at the same moment when he looked at me as if to say, 'OK, go on, get a move on.' He gave a little wag of his bushy tail.

I turned on my heel towards the entrance of the auction house in Rockefeller Plaza, a famed and prestigious destination. I knew there was a good chance I could get what I needed here. And if not, well, maybe they would be able to point me in the right direction.

I pulled open the doors of Christie's and walked into the lobby that was designed specifically to receive guests. Guests with money.

I put the phone into the pocket of my trousers as the receptionist looked at me and smiled. Over the past couple of years, she and I had become reasonably well acquainted and I knew that she would immediately take me to the right people.

I just hoped that the saying, 'Money talks,' would, in fact, prove true today.

Just for luck, I crossed my fingers.

Chapter 15

It may be normal, darling: but I'd rather be natural.
Holly Golightly

Saying goodbye to Joshua at five that evening, Darcy left Chaucer's, got on her bike and made a beeline for Fifth Avenue.

Although the fresh air allowed her to clear her head, and she enjoyed feeling the positive endorphins that came with riding the bike, by the time she reached the corner of Fifty-Third Street, she was still no closer to figuring out just how she was going to get to speak with Tabitha Kensington.

Parking her bike half a block away from the salon entrance, she joined the crowds on Fifth Avenue, marvelling at how her life had done a complete one-eighty since she had got out of bed forty-eight hours before.

Until then she had been living her life according to her own

169

rules and going by her usual unexciting daily routine, and now here she was shackled with a dog, an attractive millionaire who couldn't remember his own name, and presently hunting down a New York socialite on a street whose stores she couldn't even afford to walk by.

Running a hand through her hair and brushing off her dusty jeans, she looked at the understated façade of Elizabeth Arden's Red Door salon and took a deep breath.

'All right, Archer,' she whispered. 'Here goes nothing.'

She was about to push open the glass door when at that moment, her phone buzzed in her pocket. Pulling it out and checking the display, she discovered it was Katherine. Darcy bit her lip and wondered if she should ignore it, but knowing that her aunt would continue to call until she reached her, decided she should just get the conversation over with right now.

'Katherine, hi.'

'Hello, dear. I just wanted to tell you that Oliver Martin was very taken with you the other night.' Her aunt launched into a spiel without preamble and typically without bothering with hellos or a how are you? 'It was such a shame you had to rush off like that. Still, I have his number, so all is not lost.' Darcy shook her head. Clearly everything she'd said to her aunt that night had gone in one ear and out the other. 'Where are you? I guessed you'd be finished work by now. Not riding that awful bike through town again, I hope; it's going to snow later and—'

'I'm on Fifth Avenue, just about to go into one of your

favourite haunts actually,' Darcy said mischievously, explaining where she was and knowing full well that her aunt would be mystified; it was generally known that Darcy often failed to bother getting a simple haircut, let alone take the time to attend a high-end beauty salon.

Katherine was suitably bewildered. 'Did one of your beloved books finally fall off the shelf and hit you over the head?'

Darcy smiled and leaning against the wall next to the doorway, went on to explain all that had happened, how she'd run down Aidan Harris on the street and ended up taking care of his dog and trying to track down anyone who knew him. Barely pausing for breath – mostly because she didn't want to give her aunt the opportunity to say *I told you so* about the dangers of the bike – she recounted the story quickly.

'Which is why,' she concluded, 'I'm hoping for the opportunity to waylay Tabitha Kensington here, since it seems she is not only a scholar and beautiful, but apparently richer than Mitt Romney. And seems like she could be Aidan's friend.'

Silence came from the other end of the line.

'Katherine?' she asked, wondering if she was still there. It wouldn't be the first time she had wished her aunt would have hung up mid-conversation.

'I'm here,' Katherine replied with a flat voice. 'I just can't believe you ran somebody over – though actually I can. How many times have I—'

'I know, I know.' Darcy groaned inwardly. 'And I've learned

my lesson.' Not enough to quit riding the bike though. 'But luckily it wasn't serious, and I'm trying my best to make amends. Have you heard of Tabitha Kensington, by any chance?' Given her aunt's connections, and Mrs Kensington's apparent high profile within New York society she figured her aunt might be familiar with the name.

'Indeed I'm aware of the woman, to say nothing of her reputation,' Katherine replied in an ominous tone that made her niece gulp. 'And you intend to do what now?'

Darcy looked at her scruffy boots and gave a small, swift kick at the sidewalk. She looked over towards the door of the salon. 'Honestly, I'm really not sure. I know what Tabitha looks like, as there are lots of pictures of her on the internet, so I figured I would just go in and ask for her, and if that didn't work, well, maybe I would wait for her outside or something.'

There was an additional beat of silence and then Katherine tut-tutted. 'Sometimes I wonder if you and I truly are related. That is the worst idea I have ever heard. Do you have any idea how long a spa day at Elizabeth Arden might last? No, no, of course you don't,' she said, answering her own question. 'That woman could *literally* be in there till midnight. Don't you realise that?'

Darcy shrugged and remained silent. How the hell would she know how these things worked?

Katherine sighed. 'So Tabitha Kensington is the only lead you have when it comes to helping this man – who sounds like a very interesting prospect, by the way.'

Darcy shook her head. Of course – she'd mentioned that Aidan was young and wealthy, so naturally her aunt was already viewing him as a potential match for her.

'And your plan is just to behave like a stalker?' Katherine enquired.

Darcy ignored her aunt's last question and focused on her first. 'I don't know what else to do. Aidan's phone is broken, the hospital won't give his details out to just anyone, and the Kensington number was on his caller ID at his house. Tabitha, or someone at her house, called him. And then there's the gift he was carrying, and the message on the answering machine … Look, it's *my* fault all of this happened in the first place,' she said then, trying to convince herself more than anyone else. 'Because of me Aidan missed an important date or a special occasion, and I need to help him find out who he was trying to deliver that gift to, never mind help him remember who he is—'

Katherine cut her off. 'Darcy, it's really not your job to play nursemaid.'

'I know that,' Darcy said patiently, 'but like I said, it's my fault he is where he is right now. I just want to help him. And besides taking care of his dog, this seems the only way I can.' For a moment, her voice wavered and she thought she might get blubbery. The drama-filled forty-eight hours were catching up with her.

'All right,' her aunt said on the other end of the phone as she took a deep resolving breath. When she spoke again, her voice had softened, but there was a touch of something else in it too. Darcy knew that tone well: Katherine was going into problem-solving mode. 'I think the broken phone might be a better option frankly, but we can deal with that later. So long as you are at Elizabeth Arden right now, and we know that Tabitha Kensington is inside, I might be able to help, but I want to let you know that I am calling in a *big* favour, OK?'

Darcy's eyes widened. Was her aunt going to use her influence to get past the gatekeepers in the salon?

But it seemed Katherine was considering a more direct route. 'I am of course familiar with Mrs Kensington, but more importantly one of my very good friends in the industry happens to be a close acquaintance,' she said, then added: 'I'm rather impressed that you've got this far actually, given that Tabitha Kensington is not easy to track down. Her maid committed a major boo-boo by letting this slip; you would normally need a GPS to locate that woman. So don't think you can just stroll up to her at the pedicure station.'

Darcy's ears perked up. Her aunt was usually willing to help her with little requests now and then, but it was something different when Katherine had to call in a *big favour*. With some difficulty, she remained silent as she waited for her to continue.

'Let me make it clear first off, darling, that I do not know this woman personally, and I have no strings to pull with her directly. So therefore, I have to appeal to my friend and hope that she is in a good mood and willing to help me. I can't make any promises but I just may be able to find a way to get you an audience with Tabitha without getting yourself arrested. Understand?'

'Yes.' Darcy felt as though she should stand to attention and salute.

Katherine breathed deeply again. 'OK. I want you to stay put exactly where you are. I do not want you to move a muscle. I do not want you to go one step closer to Elizabeth Arden than you are right now. The last thing we need is for you to blow it. If you walk inside and start asking for her and spouting this crazy story, you will be turned away and probably escorted from the grounds by their security team. Are you understanding me, Darcy?'

There was no denying that her aunt would have made a great drill sergeant. 'Understood, Captain,' she chided.

'Darcy, I'm serious. No joking right now,' Katherine replied, her voice devoid of humour.

'OK, I'm sorry. Yes, I promise I will not get any closer to the doors of Elizabeth Arden than I am right now. I will not darken their doorway lest they believe that I am stalking Tabitha Kensington.'

'Good. Now, just wait there and I will call you back shortly. I may have good news and I may not. It depends.' Darcy didn't have time to respond because at that moment, the line went dead.

Looking around nervously at the crowds of people populating the shopping mecca that was Fifth Avenue, Darcy fiddled with her ski jacket, tapped her foot and then stepped backwards, leaning flush against the building.

She couldn't deny that she felt conspicuous just then, and indeed very much like a stalker as she accepted that she'd actually believed she could just walk into a place like this and expect to bump into a woman like Tabitha Kensington. Her aunt's words had given her a little perspective and Darcy realised that sometimes she didn't think things through. Heck, she couldn't help it if she had such an optimistic attitude, and in any case, she didn't think that anyone – wealthy or not – should be that *unapproachable*. But then again, Katherine's words spoke volumes too.

Aidan obviously ran in circles that were completely beyond Darcy's ordinary existence, and clearly Katherine understood that when it came to society swans like Tabitha Kensington, you needed connections in order to connect. She guessed she was lucky that her aunt had had the chance to intervene before she'd made a complete fool of herself and blown her only chance to help Aidan.

Darcy took another glance at her watch as she waited. She guessed that Katherine wouldn't be able to get her answer within minutes, but how long would it actually take? What type of convincing did this 'good friend' need? She hoped it would be soon because her ears were numb and her fingers almost ready to fall off with the cold. Combine this with the fact that she was tired and hungry after a long day's work and Darcy was just about ready to give up or take her chances in the salon.

Right then, her phone buzzed in her hand and she jumped.

However, before she could answer it, the glass door of Elizabeth Arden swung open and a severe-looking woman, in her early fifties, stepped outside and looked around. She had a red power suit on, her hair was pulled back in a tight bun at the nape of her neck, and her face looked recently Botoxed. Either that or she was really not amused. Darcy thought that if anything, she was probably upset by the fact that she had been forced to step outside of the salon into the chill permeating Fifth Avenue on this icy December day.

The woman looked around, searching the crowds that meandered down the street. Then her eagle gaze zeroed in on Darcy as if she'd identified exactly who she was looking for. Darcy looked down at the phone again, which stopped ringing just as the woman from Elizabeth Arden pointed a well-manicured finger at her.

'Darcy Archer?'

Nervously and taken somewhat off-guard, Darcy nodded her head. 'Um, yes, that's me.'

The woman snapped her fingers and motioned for her to approach. 'Come with me.'

Darcy's eyebrows flew into her hairline out of shock as her phone beeped, signalling an incoming text. Feeling like a fire was starting under her, she wordlessly followed the woman into the inner sanctum of the Elizabeth Arden salon.

Stealing a glance at her phone as she entered the calming interior, she saw that the text was from Katherine. Quickly clicking on the message, she swallowed hard, out of both nervousness and anticipation.

The message read simply, *You're in*.

Chapter 16

Money can't buy happiness but it can buy books, which is kind of the same thing. **Unknown**

Darcy was quickly ushered through the reception area and led past rows of women getting blow-dried, straightened, keratined, coloured and curled. She momentarily pawed at her limp ponytail and secretly wished that she had taken just a little more time to make herself presentable while she waited. Her eyes roved around just enough to take in a style or two that she liked, filing it away in her mind in case she ever got a crazy notion and fancied a change.

Then, guessing that she would have been wind-blown one way or the other regardless, she brushed her insecurities aside and decided that she shouldn't allow herself to be intimidated by these people. Having more money and being well-groomed didn't mean anything, after all; at the end of the day everyone put their pants on the same way.

She smiled politely as a few technicians moved to let her and her escort, who had since introduced herself as Olivia, through a doorway which led to the inner sanctum of the spa. She was pretty sure by the fearful expressions on the technicians' faces that Olivia wasn't someone to be trifled with.

Olivia took her through a series of hallways and as they approached a door at the end of one, she turned sharply to meet Darcy's gaze.

'Mrs Kensington is in this treatment room. As a valuable customer of Elizabeth Arden, her happiness and comfort is important to us. Moreover, I would not want anything to trouble her or otherwise impact on her relaxation experience here today. Is that understood?'

Darcy shook her head lamely, the only appropriate response to this woman.

'Good,' she said. Her gaze flickered across Darcy once more, as though resigning herself to the fact that she couldn't do anything to make her more presentable before they entered the room. Turning around to face the door, she raised her hand and knocked softly. A low murmur came from inside and she twisted the door knob, which didn't make a single sound.

Darcy wondered if the staff here treated each bit of metal on-site with the spa equivalent of WD40, just to make sure that there wasn't ever an unwarranted or unwanted squeak. Stifling a giggle, she pictured a Code Red lock-down if, God forbid, a door knob whined when it was turned.

Olivia opened the door solemnly and Darcy had to give the

179

woman credit, she truly was the epitome of calm. In fact, there was a good chance that she might have been a closeted nun in a previous life.

Once inside the private treatment room, Darcy breathed in deeply the comforting scent of lemongrass that permeated the air. The place was so dim, lit only by candlelight, that she needed a moment to adjust her eyes – and then she noticed a woman reclining in a spa chair, swaddled in a robe with another person at her feet, carrying out a foot massage. A third woman, a tiny Asian lady who at first glance could pass for an eleven year old, massaged the robe-clad woman's right hand, and a fourth was painting her face with a clay-like mixture. Two cucumber slices were placed over the client's eyes.

At this point, Darcy had to guess that the woman being pampered in the chair was Tabitha Kensington for she couldn't see her face or her long, shining blonde hair as it was secured up in a towelled turban.

'Mrs Kensington?' Olivia said, her voice barely more than a whisper. 'The woman you asked for is here. Miss Archer.'

Tabitha Kensington raised one graceful hand and gently shooed away the woman who was applying the clay mask to her face. She removed the cucumber from her eyes and sat up in the chair, encouraging the woman who was doing the pedicure to move.

When Tabitha spoke, Darcy realised that she was not following the apparent whispering policy.

'Ah, I see. Thank you, Olivia. I appreciate you fetching her.' Not waiting for a response from Olivia, she turned her attention to Darcy, and immediately launched into a line of questioning. 'Now, what is this about? Alexa Falcone called me directly, asking me to speak with you.'

Crikey, Alexa Falcone, the famed New York portrait photographer? Almost on a par with Annie Leibovitz in terms of reputation. Darcy had no idea that the woman was one of Katherine's 'friends', but then again the connections her aunt had established in the city over the years were more intricate than any spider web.

And while Darcy was grateful for the introduction she was also now keenly aware of the calibre of the woman she was dealing with.

'She didn't say what this was about or how she was involved, but Alexa is a dear enough friend that if she asks me to do something for her, I do it.' Tabitha had such an air about her that it was easy to guess that she was used to getting her own way.

Darcy nervously cleared her throat. 'Actually, it was my Aunt Katherine who arranged for me to meet with you.' She felt silly alluding to the idea that getting an audience with the woman was akin to getting one with the Queen of England, but it was how people like this made her feel. 'Founder of Ignite Event Management?' When Tabitha looked blank, Darcy added, 'Her company did the Level 42 grand opening earlier this year,' mentioning a hip new lifestyle emporium in Soho that, partly down to the fanfare created by Katherine in the lead up to the launch, was currently one of the city's trendiest shopping hotspots.

Tabitha raised a perfectly arched eyebrow and motioned for the woman next to her to continue her application of the clay on her face. 'Oh yes. Wonderful place, some fantastic up and coming designers there,' she nodded enthusiastically, and Darcy made a mental note to pass on this reaction to Katherine, who would be pleased.

'Now, the thing that I don't understand is what I can do for you,' Tabitha continued. 'I don't usually speak to PR people without an appointment, and certainly not—'

'No, no – I'm not here for anything like that,' Darcy reassured her quickly. 'Actually it's a bit of a long story.' She wasn't sure if she should just set off on a blow by blow account of Aidan and his amnesia.

'Well, sit down for a start; you're disrupting my aura,' Tabitha commanded, signalling to one of the ladies assisting her. 'And if your story is that long, then you should have a treatment while you're here.'

'Oh no, I really don't think—' Darcy protested, but before she knew it she was being helped into a robe by one therapist and the other was determinedly leading her onto a treatment chair.

'Perhaps a manicure, madam?' the therapist suggested, pointedly eyeing her bitten-down nails. Darcy, who had never even used a nail file in her life and was terrified of the prospect of any kind of 'treatment', instinctively shrank away.

'I'm fine, honestly.'

'Don't you realise how difficult it is to get an appointment here?' Tabitha interjected sharply. 'I wouldn't look a gift horse in the mouth if I were you,' she added, her tone ominous enough that Darcy felt she had to relent.

Unsure what to expect – to say nothing of how much this ordeal was going to cost – she had to fight not to hold her breath when the therapist asked her to sit forward and then proceeded to dip her hands in some kind of solution.

Relax, Darcy, she urged herself – *it's not like you're having a pap smear*. Though right at the moment she figured that, given the choice, she might well opt for one instead; she truly had no idea what she was facing here. Though, seeing as women all over the world chose to have such a procedure on a regular basis, it couldn't be *that* scary, could it? She'd just never been into all that kind of stuff.

The truth was that Darcy hated feeling out of control and was always much happier keeping within the confines of her own little world, where nothing terribly out of the ordinary could happen. Much better to keep such surprises restricted to within the pages of a book.

'Wonderful.' Tabitha Kensington seemed satisfied that she was willing to join in the fun. 'So then, tell me what's so important that you needed to gate-crash my facial today?'

Trying not to wince at both Tabitha's tone and the therapist coming at her with nail clippers, Darcy began telling the socialite all about the accident and how her path and Aidan's had crossed. In keeping with the low-key mood of the room, everyone remained scarily silent as she talked, and Darcy instinctively spoke in hushed tones as if confessing something, while throughout it all, Tabitha appeared unmoved.

Eventually wrapping up the story, Darcy turned to look at her, hoping for a reaction. Tabitha's eyebrows were indeed raised under her mud mask.

'OK,' she said. 'Nice story, but I'm still in the dark as to exactly how I tie into this tale.'

Darcy smiled pleasantly – at least as much as she could while the therapist squeezed her fingers agonisingly hard while pushing back her cuticles. She wondered if the woman had worked as a torture specialist in another life. 'Yes, I was just getting to that part. So the poor guy asked me to go to his house and check it out – see if I could find anything that might help him there. And well ...' Saying it out loud, Darcy realised this part sounded a bit iffy. 'I went to the house, found a few things that I thought might help and then checked his caller ID – just in case anyone was missing his absence. Your number, or rather the telephone number of your house, was on it.'

Darcy stopped talking and took a tentative sip of the camomile tea that had appeared in front of her as if by magic. She returned her gaze to Tabitha, who was now staring at her blankly. Darcy felt even more unnerved; she couldn't read anything in her stare.

'You said that my number was on this guy's caller ID?'

'Yes,' Darcy nodded, hoping that she wasn't guilty of something. Though she supposed she was past that point a long time ago. She decided to provide additional clarification. 'So I called the number earlier today, and spoke to somebody there who mentioned that you ... might be here this afternoon.' She purposely didn't mention Maria's name for fear of getting her in trouble. 'She also informed me that your husband is in Europe just now so I'm assuming it wasn't he who called the house.'

'What did you say your friend's name was again?'

Darcy frowned, because she was pretty sure that she had already mentioned it many times already.

'Aidan Harris. He lives off Central Park West, in the Upper Seventies?'

Tabitha's brow furrowed under her clay mask. 'Well, I'm sorry, but I'm afraid I really can't help you. I have absolutely no idea who Aidan Harris is.'

Chapter 17

After saying hello to the receptionist at Christie's, I was led to an office at the rear of the building by another woman who told me, very nicely, that I could wait until one of the managers was able to meet with me. I was sure I wouldn't be waiting too long; Christie's didn't make anyone with a chequebook like mine wait around.

I deposited myself in a chair and the woman offered me a drink. I told her that black coffee would be wonderful and as she left, I felt momentarily guilty that I had not asked what her name was. I hated only to think of someone as a member of the 'support staff'. It was important to call the people you worked with and who helped you by the name their parents gave them. Or at least the name they wanted to be known by.

After all, some parents had crap taste in naming children. I once knew a couple who had called their kid 'Leia' after the princess in *Star Wars*. Mel told me she knew a girl at school whose name was 'Aquanette' like the hairspray. Not surprising that these days, the girl insisted on being called 'Etta'. Smart move.

As I waited for my coffee, I looked around the office. It was a nice room, tastefully decorated with a few focal pieces scattered about. There was a Matisse on the wall and a vase on a stand in the corner. I looked closer at the vase and identified it as dating from the Ming Dynasty. I smiled, wondering what my father would think if he could see me now, and laughing a little at the notion that life had changed so much that I could now pinpoint things like that on sight. It was a long, long way from O'Connell Street, that's for sure.

I settled back in my chair and thought about taking out my phone again, if only to touch base once more with Mel. But I knew she had a busy day today, and she would more than likely be tied up if I did text her, so I decided to do the next best thing, and look at her beautiful face instead.

Selecting the gallery, I smiled as I scrolled to the photos – happy memories taken over the last few weeks once she'd laughingly shown me how to work the camera function on the new iPhone.

I had to admit, it had been a good year all round – better than the one before, certainly. But we seemed to have got over the worst of that now and these days she was feeling secure and happy and back to her old self again.

A huge relief, as the last thing I'd ever want to do was make her unhappy.

Still, I think we both appreciated that sometimes life just didn't work out how you planned it and as much as I enjoyed my own company, I also lived to spend time with her as often as was possible.

I looked at the pictures – snaps I'd taken in a variety of places at different times and moods. In all of them though, her blonde hair floated about her smiling face.

There was one of her, grinning and dancing around the edge of the Bethesda fountain in the Park. Another of her on top of a wooden horse at the carousel – again in the Park. She was wearing the kind of 'bursting' expression she had when she was working to suppress laughter, but failing miserably.

Before I could reminisce any more, the door of the office opened behind me and a man I recognised walked in. The younger woman following behind carried a silver tray. Even though I had told her that I take my coffee black, I'm sure there was something in the Christie's operational handbook that said you couldn't give a guest a simple cup of coffee and instead you must break out the fine china.

I accepted the cup that she poured for me and appreciated her efforts, but at the same time, I'm a paper cup kind of fellow and happy as long as the coffee is hot and fresh.

Before I could say anything other than thank you, or even ask the woman her name, the man in charge here, a guy by the name of George Stafford, cleared his throat, took a sip of his own coffee – cream, sugar – and sat back in his chair.

'Mr Harris, it's so nice to see you again. I trust that you are doing well?'

I nodded and said I was, but thinking of Bailey waiting on the cold street outside I decided to dispense with the niceties and stay on task. When I extended my query to George, he nodded and said that he had already been briefed on what I was looking for.

'Of course, it's not that something of this nature cannot be procured ...' I nodded but raised my eyebrows, waiting for the inevitable 'but'. 'However, I must ask. Are you sure this particular edition is exactly what you are looking for?'

'Quite sure,' I responded. 'Is there a reason you ask?'

George pursed his lips. 'Well, the fact is, we had an auction just a month ago, during which we sold that very one.'

Dammit.

I ran a hand through my hair. If I had known I wanted it a month ago, I would have done something about it then. Except that I didn't and it was more of a last-minute idea. Impulsive, but that didn't matter. What mattered was whether or not I could get it – and most importantly, get it in time for the big day.

'Do you think that the person who bought it at the auction would be willing to sell again?'

George grimaced. 'Unlikely. This individual is a serious collector, and had been in the market for this for quite some time.'

I exhaled, disappointed. 'OK, well, what are my other options, do you think? There has to be a solution. I know it's

a long shot, but there must be a willing seller out there somewhere. Isn't there always?'

George nodded thoughtfully. 'I would normally agree that
yes, a seller can usually be found. However, I am also keenly
aware of your deadline. Mr Harris, you know I appreciate
your business and I certainly appreciate the fact that your
company is such a loyal patron. But I'm sure you also realise
that it is nearing the end of December. People are getting
ready to go to St Barts or St Tropez, if they are not there
already. Anyone with the ability to help you is probably not
going to be available for such a transaction, at least not until
after the New Year.'

I knew what he was telling me. That anyone who had the
ability to sell me something like this was already on their
yacht. But at the same time, I also knew that there were plenty
of jet-setters who still stuck around for the holidays.

I wasn't going to give up that easily. Too much was riding
on it.

'Well George, I struggle to believe that there are no options
at all,' I said in my most unnerving tone. The tone that usually bade people into doing what I asked. 'Especially when I
am ready to spend this kind of money. So what else can be
done?'

George took a deep breath and locked eyes with me, understanding that I was truly serious about this. 'Well,' he began
hesitantly, 'I suppose there is the possibility of ... a list.'

I nodded. A list was good. 'What kind of list?' I encouraged.
'Tell me more.'

George seemed to be carefully considering his next words. 'Christie's aren't directly involved in such transactions, but we do know that there are items being bought and sold privately. We are often kept abreast of many of those sales, simply because it is good business practice to keep an eye on such things – especially for our most valued customers.' He paused, laying it on thick, and I waited. 'As such I have a private list of collectors situated in the New York area who may have the item you seek.'

'Excellent,' I said, heartened. 'So can you reach out to these people on my behalf?'

'Well, firstly, Mr Harris, as I said, we very much appreciate you as a client. And secondly, we don't normally reach out to collectors, not unless we understand that they are seriously considering selling. I'm sure I don't have to tell a man such as yourself that these are people who don't like to be solicited unannounced. They aren't exactly running eBay auctions, if you catch my drift.'

I smiled. If only it were possible to find something like this on eBay, I would have done it already.

'I see,' I said, indeed catching his drift. 'So are you suggesting I should approach them myself?'

'Yes. If you promise to keep this exchange quiet, I would be happy to turn over such information to you. I can't guarantee anything will come from it, as I'm naturally not au fait with the particulars of each collection, but at least it may point you in the right direction for the future. Like I said, your deadline is a little ... unrealistic.'

I nodded. I got it. I had waited too long to do this and now I might be screwed.

'Very well,' I said. 'Let's go ahead and we'll see what happens, won't we?'

Seemingly satisfied, George stood up and promised that he would return very soon. I sat back in my chair and thought that at least I would not be leaving Christie's empty-handed. Granted I hadn't expected it would be easy, but at least I now had something else to go on.

When George finally returned about ten minutes later, he was carrying a folder. He rounded his desk and once again sat down. Opening the folder, he looked at me, seemed to be considering something in his own mind, and then said, 'I trust you understand that this information is strictly confidential.' He pushed the folder across the desk.

'Of course I understand,' I told him. I picked up the folder but refrained from opening it. I didn't want to spook George by appearing over-eager. Instead, I needed to say something to allow him to rest easy.

'You can trust me,' I said. 'And this is for a good cause, I promise. No one will know how I came by this information and I will not even breathe Christie's name when I speak to these people.' I stood, thanked him and shook his hand.

Leaving his office, I pulled my phone from my pocket and asked Siri to remind me to get George a gift for his trouble. Going back out front I looked around for the receptionist, wanting to thank her, but she was nowhere to be seen, so I went out into the street.

Bailey was sitting up on his haunches, as if he knew I was going to appear right at that moment. I untied his leash as he looked up at me, silently questioning me over what had happened and what might be happening next. I checked my watch. It was late afternoon, but there was still time to get started on this right away. After all, time was of the essence.

'All right, Bailey,' I told him. 'Let's head home. I need to make some phone calls and I'm guessing you could do with some chow.'

He wagged his tail happily as we set off back towards home. As we walked, I opened the folder that George had given me and looked at the single sheet of paper that it contained. I recognised some of the names on the list.

There were six of them and they all possessed – or at least *had* possessed at one point – exactly what I was looking for.

The question was: would any of them be willing to part with it?

Chapter 18

The world is full of obvious things which nobody by any chance ever observes. **Arthur Conan Doyle**

Even though Darcy spent the next few minutes with Tabitha Kensington, trying to piece together the reason why her home phone number might been on Aidan Harris's caller ID, they were unable to figure it out.

Despite Darcy's original fears about the socialite being some kind of monstrous lioness, Tabitha had actually turned out to be more of a pussy-cat. Not only did she insist on paying for Darcy's (hellish) manicure, but she was also kind enough to check through her cell-phone contact list trying to find anyone of that name, or a female friend or acquaintance who on the off-chance shared Aidan's surname.

In much the same way that Aidan too had turned her perception of wealthy New Yorkers on its head, Tabitha's generosity was proving to Darcy yet again that appearances and reputation could so often be deceptive.

'I'm sorry that I couldn't be of more help, really I am,' Tabitha said in conclusion. 'I guess it's always possible that someone at my home might know him. I have a large staff, so I could ask around, check with my assistant?' she offered.

Darcy gave a half-hearted smile. She certainly appreciated the other woman's kindness, but she doubted that it would have been one of the 'staff' – especially as Aidan seemed to be on the same level society-wise as the Kensingtons. She couldn't understand how they didn't seem to know each other; she'd thought that all the New York glitterati flocked together and moved throughout the same circles. But maybe that was another assumption that simply wasn't true.

At the same time, she doubted that Aidan would be hanging out with Tabitha's housekeeper or butler, or whatever profession wealthy people like her employed to run their households.

Even so, she remained polite. 'That would be great, Mrs Kensington. I'd really appreciate it, Aidan too.'

'Please call me Tabitha.' The socialite gave a warm smile and her clay mask cracked just a little around her mouth. 'Of course, it's also possible that someone simply misdialled. Have you thought of that?'

Darcy admitted that the thought had crossed her mind. But the Kensington number had been the only phone call logged on Aidan's machine, outside of the private number that his stood-up date must have been calling from. It just didn't make sense. She was sure there had to be a connection.

195

Unless she was once again guilty of judging a book by its cover? Maybe Aidan *was* involved with someone on the Kensington staff. There was certainly no rule to say that people needed to date within the same social class or circle, and knowing Aidan and how down to earth he seemed to be, it was as much of a possibility as anything else.

One thing Darcy did know for sure was that if he did happen to be involved with one of Tabitha's staff, it certainly wasn't Maria, given how unmoved she'd been throughout Darcy's earlier phone call and explanation of Aidan's condition.

Having exchanged phone numbers with her, Darcy bade Tabitha goodbye and once again apologised for interrupting her spa day. Tabitha had promised to have her assistant get in touch if she discovered anything, and in closing, made Darcy swear that she would not tell anyone, like a reporter from Page Six, that she had seen her in the state she was. Namely, clay mask on, face off. Darcy assured her that she wouldn't utter a single word.

She half-worried that the woman might ask to see her phone, flip though it and make sure she hadn't taken any sneaky pictures while she was here. Darcy supposed that was the kind of life these women led and she briefly felt sorry for Tabitha – but only briefly. What she wouldn't give to be able to sit around all day being pampered and doing nothing. Granted she could keep the being pampered part though. Darcy's cuticles were still smarting from the effects of her first manicure, though admittedly her hands did look nice and feel soft, and the length of each nail was now perfectly aligned. A short spell opening boxes of books at Chaucer's would soon put an end to that, she thought wryly.

Still, she had her day off tomorrow to look forward to and was hoping to get in some long-overdue reading time. She'd been so busy the last couple of evenings running around trying to help Aidan that she hadn't been able to keep her eyes open at night, let alone get in a couple of chapters before sleep. Which was seriously unlike her.

But it was also very difficult to concentrate on reading when you were trying to share your bed with a fifty-pound lump of fur. Bailey had been making himself at home on Darcy's couch, floor and her bed too.

As she left the salon, she sent a quick text to Katherine to thank her for arranging the introduction and telling her that she owed her one, even though her meeting hadn't yielded any helpful results.

Going back to pick up her bike, she checked her watch and decided that, seeing as she was already in this part of town, she might as well head a few blocks down to the Apple store and see if there was any hope of saving Aidan's smashed iPhone.

Pulling up by the Pulitzer Fountain, Darcy jumped from her bike and fastened it to the parking rack on the concrete plaza just across the street from the huge glass box building that housed some of the most up-and-coming technology on the market.

Darcy's technology aversion was well known by her friends.

She felt that sadly, technology stores and their wares were beginning to take the place of bookstores or libraries as a place for kids to spend time. How could any piece of kit ever replicate the feel and smell of a real book or the joy of turning the pages and creasing the spine? A book was so much more than simply words on a page. Darcy still had every single book she'd bought and read for the last twenty years or so, and had reread many of them multiple times over. She'd even bought second copies of books she already owned because the cover on the other one was even prettier. And in the case of some of her absolute favourites, she had two copies – one to keep, unspoiled, and the other to read. For her, books were physical memories, portable magic.

As far as Darcy was concerned, a simple piece of plastic could never even begin to compete with any of that, and while some of the new reading devices might be convenient for some people, she herself would never be a convert.

Checking once again that she did in fact have Aidan's phone with her, she entered the glass box and proceeded downstairs to the basement area in which the Apple retail store was situated. Immediately she was struck by sensory overload. It was so bright and white and clinical – and all these people were wandering around looking slightly spaced out as they perused the devices with a visible sense of wonder and awe.

Darcy dodged the crowds and waited her turn to speak to a sales assistant. She'd heard somewhere that the store didn't have cash registers *per se* and that the clerks simply rang you up from wherever they were helping you via little hand-held computers.

'How can I help you today?' a friendly male assistant asked, when after a few minutes' wait, he finally became free.

Darcy took Aidan's iPhone out of her bag. 'Well, this phone is broken, and I wanted to—'

'Do you have an appointment?' he asked kindly, and Darcy wasn't sure if she'd heard him right. Whoever heard of making an appointment to ask a simple question?

'I'm sorry? No, I don't actually but I just wanted to ask—'

'I can put you on the waiting list then,' he interjected, his tone so pleasant, yet so decidedly *un*helpful that Darcy felt like screaming.

'The waiting list?'

'Yes. It should only be a fifteen to twenty-minute wait at the most.'

Her eyes widened. How did such stores stay in business? If they operated a similar policy at Chaucer's – making customers wait around for fifteen minutes to ask a mere question, they'd be out of business in no time.

But perhaps this was simply another part of the appeal of Apple. Almost like a guy who played hard to get, and you merely wanted him more because of it?

Right then Darcy didn't have the patience for some technological pseudo-mating ritual. 'Can you just answer a quick question for me?' she pleaded. 'Is it possible to get a person's data from a broken phone?'

'I'd really love to help you but I'm afraid you'll need to talk to somebody from our Technical Support team,' he replied in the same infuriatingly kind tone.

Granted the guy seemed lovely but Darcy was in two minds about whether to storm out of the store or wait around for somebody who could help her. Then, reminding herself that she was here not for her own benefit but to try and help Aidan, she decided she might as well bite the bullet and hang around.

She checked her watch. It was now well after 6 p.m. and she felt guilty enough as it was about leaving Bailey with Grace for a second night running, let alone another late one. But at least she wouldn't have to burden her neighbour again tomorrow, and with luck if she got this sorted, Bailey would be going back to his owner sooner rather than later.

She leaned against a nearby wall while she waited, remaining determinedly unmoved by the various paraphernalia that everyone else seemed to view as manna from the heavens.

Fifteen minutes later she had successfully moved along on the waiting list and a young female employee who looked about fourteen approached her. 'Are you Darcy?' she asked.

Caught offguard, Darcy said, 'Oh yes, that's me. Is it my turn now?'

The girl smiled. 'Yep. You were pretty lucky to get seen to so quickly without an appointment,' she said, and Darcy smiled wryly. Lucky indeed. But again, this Apple employee seemed like a sweet girl. 'My name is Jenna, and I'm going to be helping you today. I understand you have a smashed device? That's tough.'

Darcy nodded and showed her Aidan's phone. 'Yes. I was wondering if it can be fixed?'

Jenna took the handset from her and engaged in a quick examination. 'Hmm, it is pretty banged up.' She went on to point out the damage to various ports and points using language that sailed straight over Darcy's head. 'Well, unfortunately such things can rarely be repaired, and it's usually more cost-effective to get a new phone,' she told her in conclusion.

Darcy grimaced. 'That's what I figured. But what about the information – the contact numbers and everything: would all of this have been damaged too?'

'No, no, there's nothing actually wrong with the phone memory. And the only reason the screen is blank is because the battery's dead,' Jenna informed her knowledgeably. 'So we can easily transfer all of your data to the new one.' She turned her attention to a little hand-held device that pulled up account information. 'So, what's your full name and billing address, Darcy? And I can get a replacement iPhone sent down for you right away.'

'Oh no – you see the thing is, the phone isn't mine,' Darcy told her hastily. 'I'm just checking for a friend who really needs to access his information – contacts, photographs, diary entries, that kind of thing.'

'Oh, OK.' Jenna's face gave nothing away but Darcy guessed that no doubt employees like her heard countless versions of sob stories from people coming in with phones that weren't theirs, but wanting to access the information just the same. It sounded like a situation normally faced by the spouses of cheaters and scorned significant others.

But before Jenna could shut up shop and tell her that she wouldn't be able to access anything without the account-holder's permission, Darcy launched into the story of the accident and how she was trying to help Aidan overcome his amnesia. She really needed Jenna's help, even if she knew that the story she was telling made her sound a little bit crazy. And she wasn't even sure how effective she was being, considering the younger girl was staring at her in open-mouthed silence.

When Darcy finally stopped to take a breath, she decided that she needed to reinforce her desperation. 'Please, Jenna. I know that this is unusual, and probably goes against company policy, but I really do need your help. All of this is my fault and I am just trying to make it right.'

Jenna finally closed her mouth and regarded Darcy sceptically. 'You're right, this really is against company policy.'

'Please. It's only five days till Christmas and I am sure someone is missing him but nobody's been able to get in touch with his family to tell them where he is. They're probably going out of their minds,' she added, thinking about the woman on the answer machine who must be distraught by now.

Darcy guessed that if she could just access the iPhone information there would be countless and increasingly desperate calls from the same woman, and possibly more of Aidan's loved ones too. 'You and I both know that most people's lives are contained in their phones. Please. Would a stalker pay to have a phone fixed or buy a new one for a guy she barely even knows?'

Jenna's face was neutral even if she was thinking that a stalker might indeed do any and all of those things. Finally, she spoke. 'So, what's this guy's name? I'm assuming you know that much at least.'

Darcy nodded, happy that she did have this information. 'Yes. It's Aidan Harris.'

Jenna went to work tapping the information into the device. Then she frowned. 'There are actually quite a few Aidan Harrises in the system. Do you by any chance have an address?'

Darcy duly relayed the address of Aidan's place off Central Park West. After Jenna input the new information, she nodded.

'Ah, I see it here now, but it's listed under a company name.' Then suddenly the younger girl's eyes lit up in recognition. 'Actually I *remember* this guy. He was just here – I don't know, about a week ago, maybe? I remember thinking the company sounded pretty cool from the name.' She looked up at Darcy. 'Tall with dark hair and eyes? And kinda hot, if a little old.'

Aidan couldn't be more than late thirties, not much older than Darcy but she supposed he seemed positively *ancient* for young Jenna.

'Yes, that certainly sounds like him.'

The girl's green eyes sparkled. 'Yes, I *totally* remember him. He was having issues with his contact list. I set up Siri for him.' She looked back down at her little computer screen. 'So he's in the hospital now? You ran him over – seriously?'

203

Darcy bit her lip. 'Well, kind of. But it was an accident. And it was with my bike. It's not as though I crashed into him with a car or anything. But in light of this, do you think we can get him a new phone? And how much will it cost?' Her stomach clenched, not having a clue if she had enough credit on her Visa card to pay for it.

Jenna smiled. 'No need to worry; there is insurance with the phone and instructions that any repairs, issues, bills, et cetera are to be charged to the company account. I can arrange for a replacement, and then we can set up the data transfer.'

'So he won't lose any of the existing information and will be able to access contact numbers, photographs – all that?' Darcy felt heartened; the stars were finally aligning in her favour.

'Yes, but first we will need written authorisation from the company to order the replacement.'

Darcy frowned, wondering how she was going to get round this. She guessed that if he worked for the company or even owned it, Aidan could sign some kind of authorisation?

Then a thought struck her. 'Of course,' she told Jenna distractedly. 'I'm sure that would be no problem. Thanks so much for your help. Can you tell me the name of the company so that I can arrange it?'

'Sure.' Jenna looked back down at the device in her hand and gave Darcy another piece of the puzzle that was Aidan Harris. 'Like I said, I thought it sounded kind of interesting. The name on the company account is Thrill Seeker Holdings.'

Chapter 19

Life's under no obligation to give us what we expect.
Margaret Mitchell

Later that evening, back home with Bailey curled up alongside her on the couch, Darcy powered up her ancient Vaio laptop and did an internet search for Thrill Seeker Holdings.

She'd been curious from the outset about what Aidan did for a living; finding out more about the company would provide her with the answer.

Like Jenna, she thought the name sounded intriguing, and wondered if he was one of those guys who was involved in adrenaline-type extreme sports, like snow-boarding and sky-diving – a view bolstered by the photographs she'd seen in his house. When the search came back she was expecting to be faced with pages of listings detailing the company's various high-octane offerings.

She couldn't imagine that such a business would generate the kind of serious money that Aidan seemed to have though, and she considered for the first time the possibility that his wealth might indeed have been inherited, after all. Perhaps he was actually American by birth but had picked up the Irish lilt while attending college there or something? She knew Trinity College was an old and prestigious Dublin university, and sometimes the place of choice for second- or third-generation Irish-American families seeking to reconnect with their heritage.

She resolved to ask Aidan if the name of the college meant anything to him, and then turned her attention back to the internet search.

But unfortunately Google yielded scant results on Thrill Seeker Holdings; just a link to a general information page and a brief paragraph confirming that its office was incorporated at the Upper West Side address. Nothing at all about what activities the company engaged in, or information on its directors, shareholders or employees. Odd.

Darcy recalled from her brief introduction to the mechanics of business during her time at *Celebrate* magazine that holding companies were often set up for legal or taxation rather than operational reasons, and she guessed this was one such situation. The question remained: was Aidan an employee of the company or its founder?

Well, she could ask him about it tomorrow and see if the name kicked anything loose in his memory. Despite her best intentions to fill her day off tomorrow with reading and relaxation, now Darcy was anxious to arrange the necessary authorisation to replace his iPhone, which meant that she would have to pay Roosevelt Hospital another visit. And of course she'd also promised to fix him up with a temporary phone, which would be helpful to both of them for keeping in touch.

And possibly most important of all, she needed to drop off the package to him too, she thought, reminding herself of it. Setting the computer aside, she rose to her feet and went to the drawer in which she'd stashed it the other night.

Taking it out and sitting back down on the sofa, she withdrew the gift box from the paper bag and studied it again.

It was probably five inches by eight inches or so, and the luxurious box and grosgrain ribbon signified that it had come from somewhere very upmarket indeed. She couldn't put her finger on why exactly, but it gave off an air of expectation, almost as if the air around it was charged with electricity.

And was it her imagination, or did it have the weight and dimensions approximate to a hardback book?

Could *this* be the key to unlocking Aidan's memory? She hugged the package to her, taken by the romantic notion that a simple book could well be the answer to all of this, and it took every ounce of her willpower not to open it there and then.

At that same moment, Bailey sat up and nudged her elbow, as if interested in sharing in her musings. Darcy stared at him, wishing for the umpteenth time that the Husky could talk. He could tell all there was to know about his owner.

Looking back down at the gift box, she gently positioned the nail of her index finger under the lid, wondering if there was any way she could identify what was inside by getting a tiny peek.

As she did so, Bailey whined faintly and cocked his head. She bit her lip, wondering if he was trying to tell her to 'go ahead' or 'hold on, you might not want to do that.'

She looked at him, trying to figure out what the Husky was thinking. Then she looked again at the box, sorely tempted. 'What do you think, boy?'

Bailey put his head on her knee and fixed those disconcertingly intelligent blue eyes on her face.

Darcy sighed and patted his crown. 'I know, I know, you're right. When all is said and done, I don't think your owner would be too happy with me for interfering.' Especially if the gift was something very personal.

No, she would leave the decision up to Aidan about whether the contents would be helpful when she returned it to him tomorrow. Darcy hoped against hope that he would put her out of her misery by tearing the gift open there and then, as she knew her curiosity about whether or not it was indeed a book (and if so, what book?) would drive her crazy. Much as her curiosity about Aidan Harris was driving her crazy.

Who had he bought it for? His mother? A sister? Girlfriend? Her heart deflated a little at the thought and she fought off disappointment that the first guy she'd felt close to in an age should be involved with someone else. It had to be some lucky loved one of his who was worthy of such a beautifully presented token.

Thinking of loved ones, Darcy decided to call Katherine and thank her aunt properly for her help in arranging the meeting with Tabitha at Elizabeth Arden.

'So how did it go?' her aunt asked once Darcy had assured her that she hadn't let the family name down.

'Not terribly well. She didn't seem to know Aidan Harris at all.'

'You know, that woman is only a few years older than you,' her aunt replied in an apparent non-sequitur.

'Nine,' she corrected, remembering the details from her internet biography earlier. 'I think she's nine years older than me, why?'

'She had already met her husband by the time she was your age. Just so you know," added Katherine.

Darcy rolled her eyes – some things would never change. 'Katherine ...'

'Yes, yes, I know, you are happy being single and independent and responsible for your own destiny blah, blah, blah ... I've heard it all before. I only say things like this because I worry about you, darling. I'm not going to be around forever, you know, and before you say it, yes, of course I know all women don't need husbands. But still ...'

Darcy frowned at her aunt's uncommonly emotional tone, wondering where all of this was coming from.

'Is everything OK?' she asked quietly, her heart rising in her throat. If something was wrong with her aunt, her only remaining living relative, she didn't know what she would do.

'Of course I am – never better!' her aunt replied, sounding much more like her usual robust self and immediately relieving Darcy's unease. 'So tell me more about the redoubtable Mrs Kensington. She has quite a reputation ...'

Sticking firmly to her promise to Tabitha, and knowing how quickly word travelled in her aunt's profession, Darcy was reluctant to disarrange the socialite's carefully-cultured public image by confessing to her aunt that in reality Tabitha was actually quite sweet.

'Yes, the meeting was somewhat of an ... ordeal,' she replied evasively, looking down at her hands, 'but seeing as you're familiar with Tabitha, I wonder would you have heard of Aidan somehow too? Given the Rothko and the antique rugs and everything, you would think someone like him must be in the thick of things in New York society.' It was something that she'd thrown out there merely to change the subject, but she wondered now if the idea had some merit.

Katherine was silent for a moment. 'Perhaps. I will ask around for you. And I agree – someone who has the sort of aesthetic appreciation you describe may well be known amongst the establishment. And if he's wealthy then he almost certainly is a donor to some cause or another. You mentioned he owns a Rothko?'

'Yes.'

'Goodness. And it's just sitting in the hallway? That, my dear, is what I call "stupid money".' Katherine paused again while the wheels seemed to be turning in her head. 'And you are *absolutely* sure he's not single?'

Darcy let out an exasperated sigh. 'Look, I've just told you about the fresh flowers and the pictures of various women in his apartment. And one of these women left a breathy message on his answering machine concerned about his missing some significant date.'

But her aunt wasn't giving up without a fight. 'Which proves what, exactly? And you didn't answer my question.'

Darcy flushed, despite herself. 'Yes, he seems like a very nice guy but at the moment I am simply helping him piece together the details of his life, that's all. And once he does this and goes back to that life – which I may add is a world apart from my own – and the people close to him, then I'm sure we'll have nothing more to do with one another.'

'Hmm,' Katherine replied, a smile still in her voice, and no doubt some form of plot being hatched inside her head. 'Well, let me ask around about collectors or donors in the name of Aidan Harris. Eligible or not, I'm sure somebody must have heard.'

'Oh, I forgot to mention – I know the name of his company too. It's called Thrill Seeker Holdings.'

Her aunt was silent for a moment. 'Thrill Seeker?'

'Yes, why? Have you heard of it? I was Googling it earlier but I came up blank.'

'It does ring a bell somehow. Let me think about it, and if I can find anything on this mystery man of yours I'll be sure to let you know.'

'Thank you. I appreciate that, Katherine.' Darcy knew that if anyone could track down more information on Aidan it would be Katherine Armstrong. Never one to turn her back on a challenge – nor indeed give up on any cause without a fight –it could only be a matter of time before she unearthed something useful.

'In the meantime, darling, I'm sure it'll do no harm to continue playing nursemaid to the man. Maybe by the time all of this is sorted out, he'll have forgotten all about his other woman and have fallen completely in love with you,' Katherine added jokingly, but Darcy knew her well enough to recognise a note of seriousness in there too.

She couldn't help but laugh. Trust her aunt to think that trying to hit on a hospitalised amnesiac millionaire was a good idea.

Chapter 20

So far, I think it's safe to say that I am striking out with my mission. To suggest that I was unmercifully screened on the first two calls I made to the names on George's private list would be an understatement.

First the Monroes – a family who had just recently come into money via some minor connection to the British Royal Family, and who very much liked to make everyone Stateside, where something like that was sure to impress, aware of it – flat out refused to entertain me.

Then the Benningtons, a family name that I did not recognise until I was reading Page Six of the *Post* this morning and realised the connection between Arthur and Miriam Bennington, the individuals I had been trying to get in touch with, and the LA socialite Tiffany Bennington, who was recently photographed falling out of a Bentley wearing no underwear.

Obviously, the screener didn't understand how modern media worked and Arthur and Miriam were currently not in Cannes as I had been told but according to the *New York Post* were out in LA reportedly bailing out their daughter.

It seems that falling out of a Bentley with no underwear on wouldn't have been that big of a deal in the scheme of things, but the fact that Miss Bennington happened to do so on Sunset Boulevard at 3 a.m. with a gram of cocaine on her ... well, that was a different story altogether.

Ah, rich people's problems.

At least I didn't have to deal with too much of that. Probably because I had solid Irish roots, and growing up in such a family certainly had its advantages when it came to navigating one's way through Manhattan's business circles.

Such an upbringing is probably why I am able to keep in perspective much of what I now experience on a daily basis. Though I can appreciate how, if a person has been born and raised with money, they might find it easy to forget about the things that really count.

Like family, relationships, and being happy with yourself. I find comfort in the fact that even with everything that has happened to me and no matter what good fortunes I have been granted, I can still close my eyes at the end of every day and sleep soundly.

Just then, Bailey decided to grace me with his presence. The big dog entered the room, took note of the fact that I was sitting at my desk, then settled into his usual place under the desk and on top of my feet.

I took a sip of coffee and pulled my laptop closer, along with the list that George from Christie's had so kindly provided.

Who was next?

'The Cleaver-Parks,' I muttered to myself. It always made me laugh, the way the ultra-rich never had everyday names like Smith, Jones, or O'Brien.

I pulled up Google on my browser and typed in *Nathaniel Cleaver-Parks, Sr*. A moment later, I was given the full low-down on the gentleman's background and very quickly decided to make it easy on myself by forgoing the litany of newspaper write-ups and other supporting information, choosing instead to consult Mr Cleaver-Parks's Wikipedia page.

Call me lazy, but at the end of the day I'm not writing this guy's biography; I simply need enough basic information with which to arm myself before I call.

I skimmed Wikipedia and learned that Mr Cleaver-Parks was in his late fifties. He inherited the majority of his fortune from his mother's side of the family and had generated the rest of his wealth through a successful career on Wall Street. He regularly gave to charity, and had been a big supporter of the Republican Party until his twenty-year-old son came out of the closet three years ago. Following that incident, Nathan, being the good father that he was, decided to side with the political party that was most likely not to judge his son based on sexual orientation or deny him rights.

I smiled. I had to give respect to a guy who put the love of his family above politics and his wallet. His son should be accepted for the person he is and I knew I would do the same thing if ever faced with such a situation.

Feeling confident about contacting the man, and praying that he was in reality the kind of stand-up guy he sounded like online, I picked up the phone on the desk and started to dial. The list detailed a home number and a cell number and out of courtesy, I decided to try the home phone first.

Moments later, a man with a distinctive clipped New York accent picked up. 'Cleaver-Parks residence,' he said.

'Hello,' I began warmly, 'I'm looking for Nathaniel Cleaver-Parks.'

'Speaking,' the man replied and I frowned. He sounded too young. Then all too quickly, I realised my mistake.

'Er, actually I think I might be looking for Nathaniel Senior.'

'Oh right, sure,' said the man I guessed to be the son for whom Nate Sr had switched political parties. He must be home on Christmas break. According to the Wikipedia page, Nate Jr was in his senior year at Harvard. 'I'm sorry, but Dad is actually travelling right now.'

My heart sank, but then I asked, 'Do you think he would be taking calls on his cell?'

The son paused for a moment. 'Do you mind telling me who this is and what it is about?'

'Sure. My name is Aidan Harris,' I introduced myself before getting to the purpose of my query. 'I believe that he has an item in his collection that I am interested in and was wondering if he might be inclined to sell.'

'Which one are you looking for?'

I felt my heart soar just a little. Maybe there was hope here. When I outlined the details of my request, as well as my ideal timeline, he sucked in his breath a little.

'As in one week from today?'

'Yes,' I said, all at once feeling completely hopeless. 'Let's just say the eighteenth is significant and if I don't get it by then, well ... it just wouldn't be the same.'

Nate was quiet on the other end of the line. 'OK, so I'm guessing this isn't an early Christmas gift to yourself then.'

'Correct.'

'Look, Aidan. You seem like a decent guy. And judging by the sounds of it, you are trying to do something really nice for someone whom you care about. So here is what I am going to do.' At this my ears perked up and my spirit lifted. 'If it were up to my dad, who is also a good guy by the way, and if he had answered the phone just now there's probably no way that you would be able to get your hands on one of his precious babies in just a couple of days. I also know that my dad isn't going to sell the one you want because it's one of his favourites. I might as well tell you that straight, OK?' At this my heart sank again. 'But I might be able to help you out. Frankly, I'm kind of bored at the moment; I had an invite to St Barts, but decided not to take it because I don't want to be around a bunch of fake, annoying people I don't like to begin with. So I'm going to make your little project my project too, if you don't mind.'

217

I admitted that I didn't mind at all. While I knew that I might have some ties to this particular world, at the same time, those ties were few and far between. Whereas this kid had been born into the environment I was navigating and might be able to throw some more names my way.

I told him that any help he could give me would be great.

'OK, so tell me, who else is on your hit list?'

I read off the names and Nate made little comments after almost every single one. Clearly, he was familiar with these other collectors and the reactions I might expect to face.

'So what I think you should do is first off tell the others that I referred you to them,' he told me. 'Someone is going to dig deeper about where you are getting your info and will not be as forgiving as I am. Trust me when I say that one of these days our boy George is going to get his ass handed to him.'

I breathed a sigh of relief. 'You're sure you don't mind if I say that you are the one referring me?' I enquired.

'Absolutely. All of those people know me. But still, there are some others not on the list who I think you should call as well. I need a day or two to think about it though.'

'Thank you, you don't know how grateful I am,' I said, relieved that another potential avenue had opened itself to me.

'Final question, Aidan, and this is just for my own reference. If I do come by anyone who has what you're looking for, I'm going to need to know who you are.'

I felt momentarily confused.

'Um, what exactly do you need to know?'

'Well, in order to arrange the trade. My father won't do business with just anyone out of the blue so I need some background.'

I felt a light go on. 'Oh, yes, of course. The transaction is on behalf of my company, Thrill Seeker Holdings.'

'OK.' He paused and I waited for some form of recognition but there was nothing. 'OK, so you're not just some hotshot enthusiast shouting his mouth off about something he probably can't afford?'

'Absolutely not,' I confirmed briskly. 'Affordability is not a problem here. And I'm also more than happy to compensate you for any help you—'

'OK, OK, I get it. New money, huh? I love you guys.' Nate laughed but it wasn't scornful or dismissive, the way some of his elders tended to be about people like me. Nate began to wrap up the conversation. 'All right, Aidan. Good talking to you. You get working on that list, and I will be in touch if I find out anything, I have your number from my caller ID.'

'Great.' I gave him my cell-phone number too, seeing as I would be doing so much running around over the next few days.

'Actually I've just thought of someone else you should definitely talk to because she's in the know about pretty much anything and everything when it comes to stuff like this.'

'She?' I repeated, surprised.

'Oh yeah, you have no idea. She may not be an enthusiast herself, but boy does she have connections – a bigger network than AT&T. But I also have to make sure she's in town. She's kind of like the mayor, if you know what I mean.'

'Whatever you think is best, Nate. I'm at your mercy, just so you know.'

'I know you are, Aidan. And it's cool. This is just the distraction I needed. We'll track down your perfect gift before the eighteenth if I have anything to do with it.'

After I got off the phone with Nate Jr I took his advice and started going through the rest of the list, calling one person after the next, assuring them that I was contacting them with Nate Cleaver-Park's blessing.

Although I made notes along the way, keeping a record of whether I'd left a voicemail, talked to a real person, was forwarded to another phone number, or whatever else, when I eventually got to the bottom of the names, I still hadn't made any definite progress.

Feeling perplexed about what to do next, and antsy over the idea of just sitting around waiting for Nate to call me back, I took to the internet, my best friend in so many other less challenging situations but perhaps not so much with this one.

After about half an hour I felt stiff from sitting in the same position for so long, essentially repeating the same information over and over. I had no idea how telemarketers did it and knew for sanity's sake, I needed to take a break. So, I pulled up Facebook and logged into the account that Mel had convinced me to register about a year ago. It still freaked me out a little, the sheer amount of information that people put out into the ether about themselves, what they were doing, where they were, what they were thinking about, what they desired.

I momentarily considered posting a status update outlining my own query, but quickly reconsidered, knowing that there were certain things that firstly, didn't need to be broadcast to all and sundry and secondly, were unlikely to garner any type of response except useless 'likes'. After all, the small group of people I was 'friends' with on the social network weren't exactly specialists in this area.

I scrolled aimlessly through the recent posts of friends and some family, and immediately spotted the recent check-in at Hong Kong International. Then I smiled when I saw a check-in at Macy's from Mel with the comment *Shopping till I drop*. Feeling like an idiot, I gave both statuses a thumbs-up and signed off.

Maybe some time away from this desk and the house would do me good.

Maybe I could meet up with Mel for a coffee, or a late lunch? I pulled my phone out of my pocket and sent her a text. She quickly replied, reporting that she was with a friend but that lunch would be great.

Excellent. I sighed and reached under the desk.

'Come on, boy,' I said to Bailey. 'Time for a walk. I need to stretch my legs and I am sure you do, too. How does a ramble to midtown sound?'

Bailey certainly didn't need to be asked twice. He jumped up from under the desk and left the room ahead of me in a hurry. Like any semi-literate dog, he knew the word 'walk' – probably even knew how to spell it.

I shut my laptop and opened the desk drawer, putting George's list in its folder and placed it inside. Then reaching under the desk blotter I extracted the key and locked the drawer.

Slightly over-cautious perhaps, but at the same time, I was respecting Nate Jr's request to be careful with such information.

I replaced the key under the blotter, thinking that if I truly felt there was anything to worry about I should just take the key with me. But a person would have to be really searching to look under the blotter and I had a feeling if this place was going to be burgled, the culprit was undoubtedly much more likely to go for the Rothko by the front door instead of dilly-dallying around a boring office, looking for a key to a desk drawer.

So off Bailey and I headed to Thirty-Fourth Street. Fitting perhaps, as I was definitely in need of a miracle.

Chapter 21

The only true wisdom is in knowing you know nothing. **Socrates**

Darcy closed her eyes as the wind swirled around her skirts and birds sang overhead. It was as if all of nature understood that *this* was a magic moment and was required to set the scene appropriately. The smell of lavender filled her nose.

Yes, she realised. This time it really was going to happen.

She took a deep breath and hoped secretly that her face was elegantly flushed in a ladylike way, rather than looking like she was suffering from an extended bout of heat rash. Despite her somewhat olive complexion, at times she could seem downright ruddy. Especially during moments like this.

Don't think about that now, her subconscious chided her. *Think about the man in front of you.*

Darcy opened her eyes briefly to see him leaning forward.

There was something different about the way he looked today, but for some reason she couldn't place exactly what it was. Before she could ponder the difference any further, he leaned in closer to her. They were so close now, the kiss was inevitable. She just knew it. Her lips moved to meet his and as they did so she heard a sound come from his mouth. Some kind of amorous murmur or passionate sigh or ... wait a minute, was that a *growl*?

Waking suddenly, Darcy sat up in bed and strained her ears, listening for the sound again. After a beat, she heard it a second time and decided that yes, it was very definitely a growl, but not a hostile or threatening one. She got out of bed and went to look for Bailey, wondering why he wasn't sprawled in his usual spot at the bottom of her bed. What was he up to?

Going into the living room, she saw the big dog lying flat on the ground in front of the TV, his attention fixed on something between his paws. Something, Darcy realised with a sinking heart, that he seemed to be munching on.

While Aidan's dog was for the most part dignified and well-behaved, in the few days Bailey had been her house-guest she'd come to learn that when bored, his breed liked to entertain themselves by chewing on whatever random item came their way. He'd tried on numerous occasions to snatch Darcy's little homemade books down from the Christmas tree, to say nothing of their real-life counterparts on the shelves, and she'd had to move her book piles to loftier locations like the top of her closet or stuff them inside so as to keep them out of reach of prying paws. And as it was no longer safe to leave a book on her nightstand, she'd taken to placing them under her pillow for 'safe-keeping'.

But what had he managed to purloin this time?

Creeping up slowly behind him in her bare feet, Darcy got a glimpse of something long and metallic between his paws, and relaxed a little, since whatever he was gnawing on, at least it wasn't one of her treasured books. But what *was* it? Bailey gave another growl of satisfaction and she bent down, trying to get a better look at what was keeping him so happily engrossed.

And then, when Darcy caught sight of the object's gold-coloured twin, tossed carelessly beside him on the rug, she understood. 'Bailey!' she gasped, her heart going to her mouth as she wrenched a shoe from his grasp. But not just any old shoe, oh no – it had to be from the most expensive pair in her closet or indeed, the priciest items in her entire apartment – the Jimmy Choos!

He must have swiped them from the closet earlier. Darcy realised she'd stupidly left it open last night. The Neiman Marcus sticker was still attached to the sole, or what was left of it, she thought, horrified by the piercing toothmarks all over the metallic gold leather. The four inch heel was almost completely gnawed through and the ankle strap was in pieces. And as for the dust bag ...

Darcy stared at the ruined designer shoe, but when she looked back at Bailey, tail wagging, blue eyes shining innocently and tongue lolling happily, she couldn't help but laugh.

'I suppose I should be glad somebody's getting pleasure out of them,' she giggled, knowing that she was unlikely to have ever had occasion to wear the shoes in any case. 'But it's probably best to keep this between ourselves for now, OK?' she whispered conspiratorially. 'I have an inkling Katherine wouldn't appreciate her generous gift being used as a doggie toy.'

The Husky gave another joyous wag of his tail, and as Darcy cleaned up the mess she couldn't help but muse that you could take the dog out of the Upper West Side, but evidently couldn't take the Upper West Side out of the dog. The mutt had taste.

Afterwards, having made sure there was nothing else in range for Bailey to turn his attentions to, she stepped into the shower, readying herself for the day ahead and thinking about how she was going to spend her time. First up she needed to pay Aidan a visit at the hospital, she mused. Putting her head under the spray, she ran her fingers through her hair and allowed her thoughts to revert to that morning's dream.

She recalled the moment she had run her fingers through Mr Rochester's hair as he bent low to kiss her and how something had been confusing.

Over the years, Darcy had had countless dreams that featured Edward Fairfax Rochester, and during that time, he had always looked the way her mind's eye had pictured him and had always spoken with a clipped English accent. Tall, dark, handsome and absolutely polished . . . he looked the way that a Regency gentleman should – clad in a distinguished cravat, waistcoat and breeches. However, this dream had been different. *He* had been different.

'Oh,' she said, reddening a little, as understanding dawned. She bit her lip and stood limply in the shower as she worked to come to terms with what her subconscious had done to her dream.

It seemed her subconscious thought it would be interesting to give Mr Rochester a faint Irish accent. And have him bear a rather close resemblance to the man she was about to visit in hospital.

'Thrill Seeker Holdings means nothing to you at all? Are you sure?'

Darcy was back at the hospital by Aidan's bedside. She couldn't help but remember Katherine's reference to her last night as a 'nursemaid' and felt slightly embarrassed by the notion. To say nothing of that morning's dream.

She was still a little confused by that and certainly hoped Aidan Harris didn't think she had any designs on him, or was helping him out of anything other than the goodness of her heart. That and guilt, of course – and no small measure of curiosity.

Especially about the gift.

He was sitting up when she walked in, flipping through the usual Christmas movies, *A Wonderful Life, Holiday Inn and A Christmas Story* on nearly every channel at this time of year. When he saw her, he turned the set off.

'Hey there.' His voice was still hoarse, but not as much as last time.

'Me again,' Darcy greeted him shyly. 'I hope you still remember me?'

He chuckled, laying his hands on top of the blanket. 'Of course I do.'

Tiny butterflies danced in her stomach. 'So how are you feeling today?' she asked. 'Any improvement at all?'

He thought for a moment. 'No, it's all still a blank. But the doctor says it should improve as time goes on.'

'That's good, isn't it?'

'Not really,' he replied, throwing the remote control across the bed in frustration. 'It's been three days already. How long do I have to wait? It could be weeks – months even, until things get straightened out. In the meantime, I'm still stuck in this dump.'

Darcy looked at the ground. 'I'm sorry – I really wish there was more I could do.' She sensed that he was used to being on the go all the time. The thought reminded her of the company, and its thus-far elusive information.

'I'm sorry. Ah shit, I didn't mean to sound ungrateful,' Aidan added then, looking chagrined. 'God knows, you've done more than enough, and gone miles out of your way already to help me.' He gave her a broad smile, and his eyes twinkled. 'I've been trying to think of a way to thank you, actually. I'm not sure if you're a ballet fan, but ...' He took his wallet out of the bedside locker and opened it. 'Remember I told you I had these?' Aidan held up two tickets and she recalled him mentioning something about tickets for the theatre before. 'Well, I had a proper look and they're actually for the New York City Ballet.' He shrugged. 'Again, it beats me why I'd have them, but seeing as I do and the performance is tomorrow night …' He looked at her, and for one brief moment Darcy's heart almost stopped as she thought he was about to ask her out. Then she remembered where they were. Or more to the point, where Aidan needed to stay. 'Like I said,' he continued, 'I'm not sure if the ballet is your thing, but maybe you'd like to give these to a friend?'

All of sudden, Darcy pictured Mrs Henley's pink and white Christmas tree. She didn't know the first thing about ballet, so probably wasn't the best person to appreciate the gesture, but was sure that Grace would. And wouldn't it be the perfect way to thank her for all her help in taking care of Bailey over the last few days?

'Thank you, that's really very kind of you.' Taking the tickets from Aidan, she glanced down at the details. 'The Koch Theater. I'm never been there; I've heard it's beautiful though.'

'I guess so, I couldn't tell you.' Aidan shrugged again, as if such cluelessness was becoming the norm for him. Which of course it was. 'You'll take them then?' he urged and she nodded. 'Good. Like I said, I really appreciate all you've been doing. You're a lifesaver, Darcy.'

Well, at least he seemed calmer and a little less frustrated than he had been, Darcy thought. Granted, she might not have been able to find something or someone to help him just yet, but she was sure it was only a matter of time before she did.

In the meantime, she had to admit that she was enjoying the journey. It was a long time since she'd been on an adventure – a quest of her own instead of vicariously experiencing such escapades through the pages of a story – and she wanted to make the most of this opportunity to take a brief glimpse into another person's considerably more exciting life.

'I also found this in my wallet – I forgot to show you the other day.' He held out a small photograph, creased from being folded, and Darcy wondered if the person in it might be the same as one of the others at his house. But it was soon obvious that this was different altogether.

Shot in black and white, it was a picture of a young woman obviously taken a long time ago – possibly during the 1960s, to judge by the fashion. Darcy smiled at the classic beauty of the woman and the way she posed so elegantly, sitting with a full skirt laid out around her that would likely have been a light pastel colour, her bow-shaped lips sharing a secret smile with the camera.

'It's my mother,' Aidan said, and Darcy looked at him, heartened.

'Well, that's wonderful!' she exclaimed happily. 'If you remember her, it means that things are starting to come back, doesn't it?'

'Not necessarily. I know it's my mother and I also know she's dead, but that's about it.' His tone was glum once again. How awful that this sad memory was the only thing that stood out for him. And she wondered then if he had perhaps lost his father too, and if so, then clearly they had that much in common, if nothing else. Both were all alone in the world.

The fact that Aidan carried such a beautiful picture of his mother around with him merely made her like him all the more. She watched him closely as he put it back into the wallet, a strange expression on his face.

Hoping to move on to happier things, she picked up her messenger bag and carefully withdrew the gift box, as well as a shopping bag from Verizon. 'I just picked you up a prepaid phone on the way, and this is the package I was talking about before, the one you were carrying before I hit you.'

Aidan studied it for a moment, but the package, much like the company name, clearly meant absolutely nothing to him, and he seemed much more interested in the phone.

'Maybe you should open it?' she suggested, trying not to betray her anticipation. But perhaps he wanted to do that in private. Darcy hoped not, as she really wanted to know what was inside. What had he intended to give to the person he was supposed to meet that day?

He looked doubtful. 'I don't know. I'm not sure how it would help if it's supposed to be for someone else. Is it OK to put your contact details on this?' Much to Darcy's disappointment, he immediately lost interest in the package and was instead fiddling with his new phone. She couldn't really blame him – this would be his first lifeline to the outside world in days, but still . . .

'Sure.' She quickly inputted her own and Chaucer's details

into the prepaid phone. 'Be sure to call me at either of those numbers if anything happens.'

'I was just thinking about that actually,' Aidan said, looking thoughtful. 'You working in a bookshop, I mean. It's weird, but it's the only other thing that is sort of ringing a bell for me. Faintly,' he added, as Darcy looked up.

'Really? How so? Would you have visited our store in the past maybe, or ...?'

'No, I don't mean the actual bookstore, just ... well, it's strange but I was watching this quiz show yesterday; in here there's nothing else to do but watch TV, something I normally hate.'

'Oh!' Darcy said excitedly and Aidan looked at her, his brown eyes widening as he realised it too. 'You remembered that you don't like TV.'

'I did, didn't I?' He beamed, looking so pleased with himself that Darcy almost wanted to hug him. Instead, and feeling even more like an idiot, she just high-fived him, his big hand warm and firm against her own.

'That really is something.' He scratched his chin, beneath which signs of dark stubble had begun to appear. It made him look even more attractive and just so ... masculine, Darcy thought, trying hard to concentrate on what he was saying. 'Maybe I'll be out of this place sooner than I thought.'

'I'm so pleased for you,' she said, meaning it. 'If you can remember that then I'm sure other things will gradually start coming back to you too.'

'Yes, but as I was saying – about the quiz show – it's weird but I was able to answer all the literature-related questions, stuff that I didn't have a clue I even knew.'

'Like what?' Darcy asked, intrigued. Besides that reference from *The Princess Bride*, she hadn't pegged Aidan as the literary type. Far from it, given that his home was apparently devoid of books, and he clearly led much more of an outdoorsy kind of life.

'Well, one of them was about Joyce, something about a certain day?' He scrunched up his eyes, remembering. 'Yes, the question was: If you were to celebrate Bloomsday, on what day would you celebrate it?'

Darcy immediately knew the answer to that one, but he answered ahead of her. 'June the sixteenth. And not only that but I knew the year too – 1904.'

'Could be it relates to your heritage?' she suggested. 'James Joyce was Irish, as is your name, and you do have a touch of an Irish accent.'

'Yes, but that's not all I knew,' he continued, sounding mightily pleased with himself. 'I also guessed correctly that Agatha Christie is the world's biggest-selling author, that *Freeman's Oath* by Stephen Daye was the very first book published in the American colonies, and …' He sat up, as if readying himself for a challenge.

Or, as it turned out, to offer one. 'OK, you're the books expert, let's see if you know the answer to this one,' he said, playfully raising his eyebrows as he threw out the question.

She grinned and sat forward in her chair. 'Fire ahead.' Darcy was only too happy to play along.

'It's a quote. But what book is it from? *For Where Your Treasure Is, There Will Your Heart Be Also.*'

Darcy smirked. Easy-peasy. '*Harry Potter and the Deathly Hallows*,' she replied confidently, but Aidan was shaking his head. 'What? Yes, it's the inscription on the tombstones of Dumbledore's mother and sister,' she insisted defensively, knowing full well that she was right.

'Nope. It may well appear in the book, but from where does it *originate*?'

'The author's mind?' she said somewhat belligerently, not liking to be contradicted.

Aidan was grinning. 'Actually it's in the Bible. Matthew Chapter Six, verses nineteen to twenty-four, and it's also in Luke.' Then he added: 'The show contestants didn't get it right either.'

'Are you sure?' She was genuinely stumped by this – had had no idea that the phrase had come from the Bible.

'Very sure. Like I said, nobody else got it either. But when the question was called out, I knew right away that it was in Harry Potter but also that it didn't originate in that story. I don't know how, but clearly the information must be stored somewhere in the recesses of my brain.'

'Interesting,' Darcy said thoughtfully. 'So you think that maybe books and literary knowledge are a part of who you are?' she asked, now feeling even more of a kinship towards him.

'Hard to say for sure, and unfortunately it doesn't get me any closer to finding out what the rest of me is about,' he said, looking dejected once again. Then: 'Sorry, here I am feeling sorry for myself again, when I know all of this must be a complete pain in the ass for you.' He smiled, and his eyes did that cute crinkly thing again.

'It's fine,' she said. 'Honestly, I'm happy to do it.' Once again Darcy tried to get him to concentrate on the positive. 'So how should we deal with Apple's request for authorisation to get you a new cell phone? I've tried tracking down more information on your company, an office address even, where I might be able to get official business literature for you to sign.'

Aidan scratched his chin. 'There's nothing but the house address listed, you say?'

'Yes.'

'Well then, I guess that's where we find the answer.' He reached towards his keys again and gave her a sheepish grin. Was he flirting with her? Darcy felt that same blush from this morning creeping once again up her neck. *Settle down*, she chided herself.

'That is, if you're up for another visit to home sweet home?' Aidan asked.

She shook her head indulgently, already powerless to resist that smile.

So much for her day off . . .

Chapter 22

I have always imagined that Paradise will be a kind of library. **Jorge Luis Borges**

Darcy took her time on her way back to Aidan's house. The city was alive with lights and music and the threat of fresh snow as the morning stretched on, but in truth, she didn't mind doing what was necessary to help him out. He was a lovely guy and she guessed they'd formed a friendship of sorts by now. It was nice, as such relationships had never come easy to her, and even as a small child she had tended to seek out books for solace and companionship.

She was also touched by his insistence that she should make use of the ballet tickets. It was a long time since Darcy had felt appreciated by anyone – not that she expected or wanted praise for any extra shifts her boss automatically assumed she was available for, or any favours she gave to the staff re. time off, etc.

A Gift to Remember

The fact of the matter was, the more time she spent with Aidan Harris, the more curious she became.

As she made her way back uptown, she had the fleeting thought that she had not yet done any of her holiday shopping – most pressingly, found a special gift for Katherine. Four days to Christmas and she was knee-deep in someone else's affairs. The city landscape blurred as she rode by on her bike, a steady stream of coloured Christmas lights and steamy windows and the scent of freshly baked bread making her stomach rumble as she pedalled past the snooty cafés and ritzy bistros on the Upper West Side – all of them brimming with people, in perfectly cut winter coats and hats, displaying manicured nails, whitened smiles and spa-day hair, showcasing New York's unmistakable winter glamour.

As she passed, Darcy started to wonder if Aidan had dined in each one, whether he was the kind of regular everyone greeted with a hearty 'hello' and a 'welcome back'. Was he a good tipper? And had he brought the women in the photographs to any of them?

Soon, five blocks turned into four, four to three, three to two then one, and at last she turned the corner to Aidan's street. The snow was coming down as she climbed off her bike, her limbs still a little tender from the collision of the other day.

Reaching Aidan's house, Darcy rapped twice before unlocking the door, just in case somebody was home this time, but once again there was no reply.

'Hello?' she called out, still almost expecting someone, a

237

housekeeper even, to be there this time. But the silence remained.

Stepping into the hallway, she glanced quickly at the Rothko hanging on the wall, checking that no one had since broken into the place and swiped it. She'd hardly slept that night after her first visit, worried that she'd failed to properly lock up the house, and had left all of its treasures exposed.

Satisfied that no larceny had been committed on her watch, she continued inside, taking a moment to reacquaint herself with the space.

Closing her eyes, she took a deep breath, hoping that when she opened them, she would be able to look upon the contents of the house with fresh eyes.

She was intent not only on finding something related to Thrill Seeker Holdings, but based on what she'd learned about Aidan in the meantime, discovering something of relevance that might help him, something that had been out of reach the first time she was here, when she was still feeling flustered by what she was supposed to be doing.

Darcy looked down at the puddle rapidly forming at her feet and on the polished oak flooring. Hurriedly slipping out of her slush-covered boots, she left them beneath a side table in the hallway. Moving stealthily in her socks, she proceeded straight to the kitchen, planning to pick up some more food for Bailey, who had an appetite like Tolkien's trolls, and had gone through the initial lot in no time.

She opened the pantry door and extracted the bag of kibble

and some more cans and treats, placing them on the counter to take with her when she was ready to leave.

Then she started opening the other kitchen cabinets, checking to see if anything looked out of order, or if there were any signs that a third party – a friend, housekeeper, Aidan's lady friend? – had been here in the meantime.

As expected, the contents of Aidan's cabinets were pretty standard: plates, mugs, bowls, although far from ordinary, all bearing the Williams Sonoma branding. But there was nothing to indicate that the kitchen had recently been used or indeed held any secrets.

She opened his refrigerator again and wondered if maybe she should toss some of the items in there that might spoil. She didn't want to overstep her boundaries – well, any more than she already had, that is – but nor did she want Aidan to come home from the hospital to a nasty-smelling mess either.

Darcy removed a couple of containers, opened them, sniffed, and decided they would be OK for another day or two. She was about to close the fridge and keep going when she realised how thirsty she was from all the cycling this morning; Aidan would likely not mind if she helped herself to a bottle of water.

Grabbing a bottle of Fiji and cracking it open, she shut the fridge and walked through to the ornate dining room she'd checked out on her first visit, taking in once again the fixtures; the gleaming walnut dining table, the exquisite chandelier, hanging from the ceiling, the sideboard that displayed elegant crystal glasses and decanters filled with a golden liquid that Darcy assumed was some eye-wateringly expensive scotch.

She wondered if Aidan had dinner parties often. And she somewhat enviously wondered who helped him plan said dinner parties. Darcy allowed herself to imagine what it would be like playing hostess in this very room. Or having romantic dinners by the beautiful bay window, drinking wine of some fantastic vintage and raising glasses in a toast to each other and their blissful happiness.

Feeling ridiculous, Darcy banished the thought from her head, even though she could almost hear the sounds of glasses chinking as the imaginary couple celebrated some special occasion.

At that thought, she stopped walking and stared at the table, a question forming in her mind.

Moving out of the dining room, she carried on, up the steps to the next floor, towards the entrance to another room into which she hadn't ventured the last time she was here.

Stepping inside, she had to pause and catch her breath.

The sunlight coming through the window filled the entire space with a kind of austere glow as Darcy stared awestruck, unable to believe what she was seeing, and wondering how on earth she could have missed this before.

Rows and rows of books were housed in a gigantic wooden bookcase that ran the entire length of the room: it reached so high it needed a ladder like the one they had at Chaucer's – a series of rollers running across the top and bottom to allow the ladder to move along the length of the entire case.

On the shelves looked to be classic editions of Austen and

Beckett, Hemingway and Molière, Wilde and Woolf, and a complete set of *Sherlock Holmes*, all richly bound in varnished leather.

In fact, the entire room smelled like leather, from the buttersoft taupe couches sitting opposite one another, to the oxblood Louis XV wing chairs set in front of a fireplace.

What an amazing place to curl up in – your own private library. Despite the opulent furnishings, Darcy only had eyes for the books, her gaze moving hungrily over the shelves.

If Aidan Harris couldn't remember owning this, there was something seriously wrong with him, she mused.

A copy of *Wuthering Heights* that looked like it could well be a first edition caught her eye. Pulling it carefully from its space on the shelf, she confirmed her hunch within seconds, and lovingly ran her hands over the red leather cover.

Returning the book to the space, she brushed her fingers along the spines of the others, finding titles by so many of her own favourite writers. There was a very old-looking copy of *The Prince* by Machiavelli, which she actually felt too nervous to touch, as well as *Dido, Queen of Carthage* by Christopher Marlowe. *Dido* was attributed as Marlowe's first work.

Darcy extracted the tome from its place on the shelf, and delicately opened the cover. Too late, she wondered if she should be wearing gloves, or at least something to keep the natural oil from her hands rubbing off on the treasure. Painstakingly raising the cover, her breath caught in her throat. A scribble of ink dotted the flyleaf – handwritten words. The sentence ended with the name *Kit*. Gasping in shock, Darcy ran her index finger over the words as if the action allowed her to travel across the centuries and connect with the man who had written them.

There was little doubt in Darcy's mind that the book she was holding at the moment had also been held four hundred years ago by the Elizabethan tragedian himself.

She felt tears prick at the corner of her eyes from the wonder and amazement of it all. Then, though it killed her to do so, she placed it back on the shelf, vowing that she would take a proper look again sometime, ideally with Aidan's full permission.

She recalled what Aidan had said earlier about his curious knowledge of books and literature. Well, the explanation for that was right here in front of her eyes, and she couldn't wait to tell him what she'd found, although she was kicking herself for not checking this room first time out. But she'd been in a hurry, and had been actively looking for personal objects and photographs that might help his memory, rather than taking a full account of every room.

Darcy guessed that if she owned a collection of books like that, she'd remember them in an instant; if her position and Aidan's were reversed, it would have been those that stood out in her memory.

But who knew how these things worked? And the fact that he was obviously such a dog lover said something good about him too.

Darcy continued to skim through the titles, and back in

the A-section soon came across her beloved *Pride and Prejudice*. The novel had originally been published in 1813 in three separate volumes, and Darcy gasped aloud as she saw the three spines facing her. Scarcely daring to breathe, she lifted out the first volume and set it down on a nearby side table. Leaning over it, she inspected its weathered brown leather cover.

As she examined the black morocco double spine she couldn't help but wonder how Aidan had procured this. 'He must really be a man of means,' she muttered out loud as she remembered reading what such editions typically went for at auction. Eighty-five grand or so?

Wow. Never mind Elizabeth Arden. This was something that truly was a million miles outside of her pay grade.

This particular set of volumes seemed extraordinarily well-preserved. Again, she wondered where Aidan had come across them.

She traced her fingers over the title page and its simple statement: *By a Lady*, wondering what Jane Austen would have made of her own current adventure.

'She probably would have considered it too far-fetched for a plot,' she said with a grin.

Then, turning to the first page, Darcy began to read out loud the iconic opening sentence. '*It is a truth universally acknowledged, that a single man in possession of a good fortune, must be in want of a wife.* Certainly sounds like a best-seller to me,' she added. As her gaze travelled over the text, Darcy remembered a maxim that she'd adhered to all her life: you could tell a lot about a person from simply looking at their bookshelves.

And if Aidan Harris was anything like his book collection, she sighed, then he was a very special person indeed.

Chapter 23

What in the hell has happened to all this time I thought I had?

Yesterday and today have been a blur. I don't even know how the time has got so far away from me. Sure, I've checked off some of the things on my To Do list. But not the most important things. The big day is looming large now and time is seriously running out.

When did life become so complicated?

Now, as I sit at the kitchen counter, laptop in front of me, Bailey at my feet begging, and practically willing me to drop this forkful of noodle on the floor so he can gobble it up, I'm doing my best to not be completely consumed by the fact that 17 December is now less than three days away.

So I really only have two days, if I want to get everything organised and ready for delivery beforehand.

Christ.

And even worse, my new buddy Nate has not called, despite his promises.

Today I ended up getting nothing done except fielding enquiries from LA and making follow-up calls to the names on George's list. I had to cancel a planned outing with Mel, something I know she was terribly disappointed about but I just have to hope she understands. She gets how things can be and how busy I am sometimes, yet I know that she doesn't completely understand why she has to suffer because of it. It makes me feel so guilty to have to let her down like that but there's really nothing I can do.

I'll make it up to her though, and I already have an idea how, but for the moment, I need to concentrate all my energies on getting this thing done.

At least this morning I managed to get Bailey out for a good amble in the Park, and he enjoyed sniffing around and meeting up with his buddies, some of the other regulars around the Great Lawn.

But realising I hadn't actually eaten anything since our hot dogs mid-morning (I'm not really a fan but Bailey has a thing for Gray's) I took the easy option and microwaved some noodles for lunch.

I have to admit, this readymade stuff from Whole Foods was pretty good. That Californian Petite Syrah from the rack was good too. So good, in fact, that I might just drink the whole bottle – I am starting to feel that desperate.

'How about that idea, Bailey? Maybe getting drunk will give some answers. It worked for Hemingway.'

Bailey stared up at me with those incisive blue eyes of his, perhaps mulling over the idea that if I got drunk, I would be much more likely to drop food on the floor.

I rubbed my forehead, refilling my glass while I offered Bailey a small piece of chicken from the plate.

He gobbled it up as if it was the finest Kobe steak.

'Good, isn't it?' I asked him. He licked his chops and stared at me intently, looking for more and giving me my answer.

Feeding him again, I finished off the last few bites myself and pushed the plate away. Then I pulled the laptop close and started half-heartedly typing in some search terms, just on the offchance that Google would feel sorry for me today and answer, 'Here you go, Aidan. Right here, at this location, is exactly what you want, ready and waiting to be sold to you.' The search engine would show me a big map with an 'X' on it and I would put on my coat and rush off, chequebook in hand.

But Google didn't work that way, did it? And so I lost yet another hour's worth of time, still hoping I might get lucky.

Remind me not to head to Atlantic City anytime soon; I would probably lose my shorts.

I got up from the stainless-steel kitchen counter, picked up my wine glass and meandered into the library. Flicking a switch, I turned on the Christmas tree and stared at the glittering lights and twinkling orbs, making me all too aware that the holidays were approaching and time was almost up.

Turning my gaze from the tree, I walked slowly along the bookshelves, lightly caressing the spines. They comforted me as books always do.

Many people would kill for a collection like this, I knew, and no doubt for a house like this. In a place as perfect as this you'd expect to have a perfect life, and that everything would be easy.

But I knew better. I knew that you could spend a fortune filling shelves with rare books, travel all over the world and take pictures of exotic locations that most people could only ever dream about visiting, but at the end of the day, if the books remained unread and the journeys were mostly taken alone, then there was something missing.

And really, I guess that's the saddest thing in the world. I know for sure that I would rather have memories with another person in some cheap, out-of-the-way place on the map, than travel to Paris alone, stay in the finest hotel and take a picture of the Eiffel Tower that I could get from any stock photo website.

I sat down in one of the big wing chairs next to the fireplace and took another sip of wine. A moment later, Bailey came in and joined me, sitting down next to the chair and balancing his big warm head on my knee. I put a hand on his head and petted him.

'Good boy. You're a good boy.' I scratched his ears and he

leaned into my hand as if wanting to comfort me. 'Don't worry, buddy, we'll get this sorted,' perhaps reassuring myself more than him. 'Something will come up; I'm sure of it.'

Chapter 24

Let me tell you about the very rich. They are different from you and me. **F. Scott Fitzgerald**

Very reluctantly replacing volume one of *Pride and Prejudice* back on the shelf next to its sister volumes, Darcy managed to tear herself away from Aidan's library and began to move further along into the house, trying other rooms that she hadn't ventured into previously.

Next she encountered another bedroom – smaller than the one she'd seen on her last visit – and while it was well-appointed just like the rest of the house, it also looked relatively lived in, or at least recently used, unlike other areas that seemed pristine in their appearance.

A remote control for the plasma TV on the wall was haphazardly thrown on the bed, which was made, but it also appeared somewhat rumpled, as if someone had been watching TV while lying on top of the covers.

Curious, Darcy moved to the antique rosewood closet and opened it. Inside were men's clothes: shirts, trousers, and a couple of folded-up sweaters.

Granted, Aidan probably had a lot of clothes, but she wondered why he kept them in here instead of his own bedroom. Then she reminded herself of F. Scott Fitzgerald's words about the rich being 'different', and guessed that this closet was used as an overflow, or to store away his wardrobe depending on season.

She would have given anything for a closet that was big enough to store what few clothes she had, let alone have the luxury of a separate room altogether. As it was, she sometimes had to use the kitchen cupboards to put away seasonal stuff. If she wasn't careful she could soon end up storing T-shirts in the freezer and socks in her cutlery drawer.

Turning, she left the room and headed again in the direction of the larger bedroom, the one in which she'd tried to find useful mementos for Aidan on her last visit.

She flung open the doors to the walk-in closet and turned on the light to check if her suspicions about the smaller bedroom being an overflow were correct. In front of her was yet another wide assortment of men's clothes. She pulled a shirt off the rack and examined the label. Valentino. Nice.

Placing the shirt back where she'd found it, she looked around briefly again and turned the light off, closing the closet door behind her.

Darcy turned to her left and found herself in the master ensuite bathroom. Here, too, she immediately noticed that everything looked perfect, as if it hadn't been touched in days.

Granted she was not the most experienced of girlfriends, but every guy she'd ever been involved with had at least offered her a drawer if ever she stayed over, someplace to store spare underwear and socks, or a toothbrush.

But Darcy realised now, despite her initial impression that Aidan lived here with a female companion, there were no women's clothes anywhere, no stray shoes, or any make-up or face creams in the master bathroom. Actually, now that she thought about it, other than the flowers in the hallway, there were few feminine touches *anywhere* in the house. Despite herself, Darcy was heartened by the notion.

Perhaps he preferred to live alone then? While he was a guy who clearly had no shortage of female attention, she guessed he enjoyed his own space, preferred things the way he liked them – particularly his books and his organic food and fancy cookware ...

Well, Darcy couldn't blame him. If she was lucky enough to own a house like this, to say nothing of what was inside it, she'd be quite possessive of them too.

She opened the bathroom cabinets and idly ran her gaze across the contents, which consisted of a typical selection of toothpaste, and luxurious male toiletries such as Tom Ford pore gel and Bulgari aftershave, though one of the bottles gave her pause.

Rogaine? Darcy frowned as she studied the hair-loss treatment bottle. Picturing Aidan's healthy head of hair, she wondered why on earth he would need this. Or was his glossy mane in fact a good advertisement for the product? If so, the company should definitely use him in their marketing campaigns, she thought, smiling at the notion. But it was a curious find all the same.

Her attention moved to a small container of pills immediately recognisable as some form of prescription medicine.

'Diamox ...' Darcy read the words on the label out loud and was wondering what the pills were for and if by chance their absence might be affecting Aidan's memory recovery, when she noticed that they were in fact labelled as effective for altitude sickness.

Altitude sickness ... No doubt for all that high-adrenaline travel, in mountainous places like the Swiss Alps or indeed, scaling the heights of Mont Blanc.

She found herself craving to hear Aidan – in that lovely lilting voice – tell her about what it was like to have reached the top of K2 or Everest even, and bring those adventures alive for her. She frowned. What was she really doing here? Poking around in someone else's life? She should be out there, concentrating on her own. Was all of this helping of Aidan actually an excuse to put her own run-of-the-mill existence on hold?

Feeling slightly maudlin, she closed the bathroom cabinet and headed back into the bedroom, finding herself in front of the large bay window which overlooked some of the balconies in the luxurious apartment building across the road. She soon discovered that if she leaned to the far right side of the window, shoved her shoulder into the corner and slightly tilted her head to the left, she could just about make out the inside of some of those residences.

Peering into the windows of the homes across the way, she saw that some had Christmas trees displayed, others had lights strung round their windows and piles of wrapped packages piled on the window seats. There were vast, open loft spaces and tight, tidy family kitchens, all well-lit and festive, fairy lights blinking on the trees. In one, kids played games on the floor, and in another, an elderly couple sat reading companionably side by side on the sofa, the way Darcy's mum and dad used to do; in others, people were wrapping presents, baking cookies or simply sipping coffee by the window while gazing across at snow-covered oak trees in the Park.

She could have stayed there all day, watching families go about their daily business. Darcy loved watching families period, and wondered if she'd ever have one of her own, to help recreate some of those special times she'd enjoyed before her parents' death.

She turned away from the window then, suddenly uneasy about making herself too comfortable here, to say nothing about prying beyond what was necessary.

But on her way out of the bedroom, Darcy's eyes were drawn to a small cabinet in the corner; it was set into an alcove which made it difficult to see when you first walked into the room. As she approached, she could see that it was a brass and glass display case sitting on top of an antique rosewood table.

The back of the case was lined with etched mirror and Darcy thought that it had probably sat proudly in one of Fifth Avenue's finest furniture stores once upon a time. Inside the case was a selection of medals and medallions, set apart from each other in an obvious display.

She was about to check what the accolades might be for when her eyes landed on a framed photograph just alongside the medals. It was a group shot of people mostly dressed in sports gear, and the location was obviously somewhere with a hot climate, judging by the camera subjects' tanned skin, sunglasses and hats protecting them from the glare of the sun.

Darcy scanned the faces, trying to seek out Aidan; it was a huge group, probably about 150 people. Some of them were adorned in colourful tribal dress, with dark complexions and bare feet. What exotic location was it this time? she wondered, taking in the oxide red dust beneath their feet. Several white-skinned members of the group could possibly be him, given the clothing, but it was difficult to pick anyone out at the distance the photograph had been taken to get the entire group in frame.

But curiously, right beside the photograph and on its own stand was a book entitled *Born to Run*. Darcy scratched her head as she thought of all the expensive first edition classics and collectors' items downstairs – yet here in the only lockable display case was a very ordinary-looking paperback.

Curious ...

But taking all of the contents in the case into account she realised that there was a definite theme forming.

The large medallions and belt buckles with various logos and dates all detailed running competitions and races of some kind. *Western States Endurance Run: 100 miles – 1 day* read one of the large silver belt buckles. 100 miles in one day? Who in their right mind would undertake such a thing? Darcy thought incredulously, reminding herself that merely walking ten or so blocks put her out of breath. Yes, she managed to stay reasonably fit from cycling, but compared to Aidan, she was an absolute slouch.

Yet it fit with the photographs she'd seen in the living room, the prescription pills and what she suspected Thrill Seeker Holdings was all about. Aidan was indeed one of those adventure-loving, adrenaline-seeking activity types.

She reached for the clasp on the side of the display case and giving it a gentle tug, found the door was unlocked. Opening it, she thought about poor Aidan in the hospital bed, and so many hard-earned, precious memories out of his reach. The only thing Darcy could think of worse than having to run 100 miles was running 100 miles and not being able to remember it.

Deciding immediately to bring one of these medals back to him, she looked through them, trying to select the best one.

There were certainly lots to choose from: the first, detailing the ING New York City Marathon, was a race Darcy recognised well, recalling the inconvenience of closed streets and inaccessible parks one weekend every November. Several other medals on thick ribbons recorded similar achievements from various years – all attached to a wooden holder that looked like it could have been custom-made.

Where on earth did he get the time to maintain a hugely successful career, sit and enjoy the wonderful contents of his own private library, and at the same time train to run hundreds of miles? Trying to figure out who Aidan Harris really was, was turning out to be a true conundrum.

Darcy knew for sure which hobby she'd prefer, she thought, picking up the book – the one thing in the case she had some chance of understanding.

The book jacket was not pristine or particularly attractive: it was cream with a black imprint of a bare foot, and the title printed within the footprint beneath the outline of a man running partly silhouetted against the sun.

She held it in her hands, guessing that it was easily the least valuable book in the house by a mile. Then she opened the first page and saw two signatures, one by Christopher McDougall the author, and beneath this the name 'Cabello Blanco'.

Well, it might seem insignificant to her, but it must mean a lot to Aidan if it was the only book on display. Carefully placing the book in her bag to take back to the hospital, Darcy was about to close the cabinet when an inscription on one of the medals caught her attention.

NYRR. Which Darcy knew stood for New York Road Runners.

Joshua often spoke of the running club – his health-conscious medical family were all avid runners and all members of the club. His dad even sat on the board apparently, and

Joshua often joked that no matter what time you went to Central Park there was always a Bishop running around it.

She looked again at the contents of the cabinet – so many proud mementos of races Aidan had run. And she thought again about how he seemed so full of contradictions.

Every time Darcy thought she was getting closer to figuring out who Aidan Harris was, something else came along to blow her assumptions out of the water.

Chapter 25

All those who wander are not lost. **J.R.R. Tolkien**

Trying to think like Miss Marple, but actually feeling more like Goldilocks, Darcy left the master bedroom and ventured back down the hall to the room she had to assume was a guestroom. She took in every detail and decided that yes, someone had been sleeping in this room, recently. Strange ... with the other room available to them as a first choice, no one would realistically pick the smaller room.

She entered the guest bathroom and was again confronted with signs of use. Taking in the aftershave, the deodorant and the nose-hair trimmers, she deduced that it had to be a man.

'Have you recently had a house-guest, Aidan?' Darcy murmured into thin air.

Maybe someone had been staying at the house and had been locked out since Aidan hadn't returned after the other day.

Feeling anxious now, she wondered where this person could be. Her thoughts flashed to Aidan's phone, out of action for the last few days. How horrible it would be if his house guest had been trying to get in touch with him, thinking he'd disappeared or that something bad had happened to him. Darcy thought of hanging around for a while longer, just in case the person might come back.

But then again, how would she know if they were who they said they were?

Too many confusing thoughts were bumping around Darcy's head, and she was starting to feel overwhelmed.

Casting a final glance at the room, she headed in the direction of the office she'd glanced through the other day. It hadn't held her interest at the time as it contained little other than filing cabinets, the heavy wooden desk and Aidan's laptop. But this time, on her way in she noticed another photograph, tucked away on a shelf nearby.

A striking woman – again incredibly radiant and beautiful – was pictured in a gold string bikini, evidently in some tropical location. Sunshine glistened off her blonde hair and she was deeply tanned. Darcy made a face as she took in the woman's model physique. Difficult to be 100 per cent certain, as this image was in colour, but it seemed likely to be the same blonde that she'd seen in the other photograph shut away upstairs in Aidan's bedside drawer.

'OK, it's official,' Darcy sighed. 'The girlfriend is beautiful.'

She glanced balefully down at her own frame and tried to imagine what she would look like in that same bikini. There was a litheness about this woman that she knew she would never have.

She tried to remind herself of the statistics – that Supermodels were merely genetic abnormalities. Whereas she was normal and should be proud of it.

Still, Darcy couldn't help but feel a pang. Despite the odds, why did it always have to be women like this who attracted men like Aidan?

She put the picture back on the shelf, deciding not to go there. Besides, *everyone* had cellulite, and Miss Universe probably did too, it's just that the lens wasn't picking it up. And everyone knew that PhotoShop could work wonders.

Determinedly putting Aidan's love interest out of her mind, she wandered back to the desk, upon which sat a Vaio laptop, a considerably more expensive version than her ancient clunker. If by some miracle she could access Aidan's computer, then a whole world of additional information would become open to her *and* him. She wondered if there was any point in packing up the laptop and taking it back to the hospital with her just in case his brain might remember how to access it. She knew the mind worked like that, that a person's fingers sometimes automatically moved to the relevant keys, without having to think about what they were typing.

Darcy placed the bottle of water she'd been carrying on the desktop blotter and sat back in the chair, wondering where she might start looking for company information or stationery that would act as sufficient authorisation for Apple.

Seeing a drawer to her right, she reached out and grasped the handle. Tugged it gently, and then a bit harder.

Nothing happened.

Foiled yet again, she sat up straight in the chair and turned her attention to the phone on the desk. She wondered if a separate phone number was fed into the office, or whether it was just another extension of the downstairs phone. As she looked, she noticed that the message light on the phone was blinking again. Darcy started to scroll through the caller ID. Immediately recognising the Kensington number, she realised that this was indeed the same line as downstairs, but quite a lot of activity had taken place since the last time she'd checked it.

She was dismayed to see that there were now *seven* private number entries after the Kensington one, as well as a couple of others. Clearly somebody was frantically trying to get in touch with Aidan.

A small pad of paper sat next to the phone, along with a Mont Blanc pen, and Darcy quickly wrote down the numbers that came up, marvelling at how smooth the nib was.

Interspersed with the private number calls was a listing displayed as 'Bennington' with a 212 number, as well as 'Cleaver-Parks', also in Manhattan. Wondering if either of them might be the woman who was calling from the withheld numbers, Darcy scribbled the details down.

Then, feeling no sense of guilt this time around, she pressed Play on the answering machine.

Aidan, hey, it's Nate. Just wanted to follow up. I heard you since made contact with my friend, and I hope all went well. I'll try you on your cell but if I don't get you, really happy that you got what you needed before the big day. Ciao.

Her eyes widened. *Happy that you got what you needed before the big day?*

Now Darcy was more certain than ever that Aidan had been on his way to meet someone and deliver that gift on the day of the accident.

She bit her lip. It was all her fault he never made it.

Hearing a beep and then some background noise she listened closely, feeling a sense of dread as she guessed it would be the woman again.

'*Pick up, goddamn you!*' said a female voice, clearly upset, and this time very angry. '*I just can't believe you're ignoring me like this! If you wanted to end things, OK fine, but the least you could do is tell it to my face instead of this pathetic, idiotic ... juvenile behaviour. Well forget it, I get the message. I'd like to say it was fun but I'd be lying. Have a nice life, asshole. Oh, and this is Melanie by the way, just in case you're having trouble keeping track.*'

Darcy sat there, stunned. Clearly the meeting that Aidan had missed was very significant indeed. But, more importantly, she realised, playing the message back again, the mysterious caller now had a name: Melanie.

Melanie. Aidan and Melanie. Darcy turned the combination over in her mind. So Melanie had to be the gorgeous blonde in the bikini – the voice matched somehow. And she was a somewhat forbidding type, judging by her parting shot.

She guessed that beautiful women like that didn't tolerate being messed around too easily, especially when there were bound to be lots of other men lined up to treat them as they expected to be.

But what event had Aidan missed the other day? Clearly it was something significant, to Melanie at least. She wished the woman hadn't withheld her number though, since Darcy could have just called her up and told her that no, Aidan hadn't done anything wrong, that it was actually all *her* fault, and if it hadn't been for Darcy he would have made it to wherever he was supposed to be and delivered the gift to her.

But now she wondered again what the gift could be. She guessed that a woman like Melanie would have expensive tastes and habits. Which meant that the gift Aidan had chosen for her must have been something very special. Her mind racing, she thought of the other message, the one in which the man had mentioned about Aidan getting 'what he needed in time'. Could this guy, this Cleaver-Parks person, be somehow involved in that?

Quickly scribbling down the caller's number, she dropped the pen and tore off a piece of paper from the pad. But as she did so, Darcy's elbow knocked against the open Fiji bottle, spilling water all over the blotter and on top of the desk.

She jumped up from her chair. 'Oh crap! I'm sorry, Aidan, I'm sorry!' she called out to the air. 'I just keep ruining your stuff.'

Looking around desperately for anything to sop up the mess, she ran from the room and returned a moment later with a hand towel that she'd grabbed from a small washroom just off the hallway. Rushing to wipe up the blotter, she realised that she should be more concerned about the desk's expensive-looking walnut surface.

Darcy pulled the wet blotter from the desk and tossed it to the side. As she did so, she heard something clink on the floor. Something distinctly metal.

Pausing briefly, she glanced at the ground, wondering what else she had broken.

And spotted a key. Her hands shook ever so slightly as she bent down to pick it up. A tiny silver thing, it looked to be the kind of key that would fit a padlock, or a suitcase.

'Or a desk drawer,' she whispered out loud.

Darcy picked up the key and placed it on the desk. She made another cursory swipe of the surface with the hand towel, making sure it was completely dry, and then turned her attention to the water-stained blotter.

Horrified, she took note of the brushed silver handle and expensive fine leather base, and knew she was looking at a couple of hundred dollars'-worth of damage or more. For a simple ink blotter. She shrugged. Next time she'd be sure to run down a poor guy.

Darcy sat back down in the chair and picked up the key. She started on the left side of the desk, and tried each individual keyhole for each drawer.

Her efforts were foiled every time; the key didn't seem to fit in any of them.

Feeling her frustration grow, she turned her attention to the other set of drawers on the right side of the desk. And felt her spirits soar as the key fit effortlessly into the lock of the top one.

Darcy took a deep breath, turned the key, and the lock clicked.

Opening the drawer, she was struck by how neat and orderly the contents inside seemed to be. Once again, in keeping with the rest of his house, Aidan was not one for clutter or mess.

Darcy thought of her own place and grimaced, wondering what he would think if he saw the dishes clogging the sink, the discarded clothing on the back of the chair, the pile of ironing in the corner calling out to be tended and, of course, the contents of her book collection gathered on every available surface.

For the most part, everything in the drawer looked rather normal and uninteresting. Rubber bands, paper clips, a few Mont Blanc pens, a small notepad and ... aha! Beneath a manila folder lay a small stack of A4 stationery with the Thrill Seeker Holdings company letterhead printed on each page.

Eureka!

Delighted to have come across something she was actually looking for, Darcy set aside the folder and picked up a few sheets then put them in her messenger bag, carefully folding them over. She would get Aidan to scribble a quick note authorising the Apple Store to order the replacement iPhone and drop by Fifth Avenue with it later today. One thing off her list.

With any luck, Aidan would have a working phone and his

contacts back in no time. Arranging the drawer back exactly
as she'd found it, Darcy put back the folder which she
noticed was so thin, it couldn't possibly contain anything.
But flicking it open briefly to check, she found that it did in
fact contain a single sheet of paper listing various names and
addresses, handwritten in precise cursive script. Alongside
this were some other, less elegant scribbles, and Darcy wondered which of the two writing styles was Aidan's. There
were some other names and numbers listed below, again in
the messier handwriting, and a couple of numbers which
looked to be dates.

Darcy peered closer at the names and addresses and one
immediately caught her eye. Nate Cleaver-Parks.

Cleaver-Parks? The guy who she'd just heard on the
answering machine was on this list.

Turning the paper over, she read through some more
names, written again alongside a 212 phone number, as well
as a couple of 917 numbers, also a New York area code.

Darcy scratched her head, wondering what it was all about.
At the very least she could call back Mr Cleaver-Parks. Unlike
the Kensingtons, this guy seemed to know who Aidan was,
and from what she could recall from the phone message, had
even called him by name. So she figured he was as good a bet
as any.

Replaying the message to confirm that Cleaver-Parks had
indeed referred to Aidan by name, she compared the number
on the list with the one on the caller display: they were indeed
one and same.

Suddenly indecisive, she picked up the handset, realising that she felt nervous, possibly because this phone call might well mean the end of her involvement with Aidan Harris and his mysterious life. And the thought made her feel despondent.

Was the fact that she'd discovered he was a book-lover like herself clouding her judgement? Loving books didn't automatically make you a decent human being (although in Darcy's eyes it went a hell of a long way towards it), nor did an affinity with animals, or a love of hot dogs and still taking the subway even when you were loaded ... And really, that was about the sum of what she knew about him. All the ideas she'd built up around Aidan and his world: his loves, likes and dislikes, hopes and dreams, were mostly products of her admittedly sometimes vivid imagination, and she guessed that anyone who really knew Aidan might well end up ruining the fiction, quickly disabusing her of any presumptions she had made. She wondered too what would happen when Aidan got his life back and didn't need her to help or run errands for him any more. Would he want to keep in touch once she'd served her purpose?

She guessed she was going to have to deal with all of that sometime anyway, and her priority at the moment was to help him get back on his feet and set things right.

Darcy consulted the sheet of paper again and punched in the numbers. She waited a moment and knew that somewhere else, here in Manhattan, a phone was ringing. A moment later, a voice came on the line. A disturbingly gruff voice.

'Cleaver-Parks residence.'

Darcy's stomach clenched. 'Uh, hello yes, I'm calling for Nate Cleaver-Parks, please?'

'Speaking,' the voice barked, without hesitation.

Darcy's brow furrowed. That was odd; the voice on the answering machine didn't sound anything like the belligerent man on the phone now.

'Oh, I see. I was actually calling with regard to a message that was left on my friend's answering machine—'

'Who is this?' Cleaver-Parks snapped, cutting Darcy off.

'I'm sorry, excuse me, I should have introduced myself. My name is Darcy Archer, and I'm calling on behalf of someone I believe you know – Aidan Harris—'

The man interrupted her again before she could finish speaking. 'I have no idea what you're talking about.'

'Well actually, I believe it was you who called him, sir. There was a message on his answering machine, and well—'

But Nate Cleaver-Parks was apparently intent on not letting Darcy speak. 'I'm sorry, I haven't a clue what or who the hell you are talking about. I just got back into town this morning and have called absolutely no one. And with that being said, I am also incredibly jet-lagged with a long To Do list to get through before the holidays. I suspect you have the wrong number. Goodbye.'

The line went dead in Darcy's ear, indicating that he had hung up. She pulled the phone away from her head and stared at it. She had just been hung up on! Double-barrelled surname or not, this guy clearly was no gentleman. What type of person wouldn't let another finish a sentence? And hang up without listening to what she had to say?

Nate Cleaver-Parks, that's who.

Darcy shook her head. It didn't make sense. She knew this guy had called Aidan. She had the voicemail on the answering machine to prove it. Yet, much like Tabitha Kensington, the man she had just spoken to insisted that he had no knowledge of Aidan Harris or anything to do with him.

Another dead end. Darcy felt like banging her head on the table. Whatever elaborate fantasy her mind might concoct about Aidan Harris and his mysterious life and elusive friends, it couldn't possibly be any stranger than the reality.

Chapter 26

All that we see or seem is but a dream within a dream. **Edgar Allan Poe**

'So which ravishing hero delayed you this time?' Joshua teased Darcy the following morning when she arrived a couple of minutes late to open up at Chaucer's. 'Heathcliff or Rochester? Don't these Regency cads realise you have a job?'

'It was Mr Darcy actually.' Going inside, she switched on the lights and went about readying the store for a busy day ahead, given there were now only a few days left till Christmas. 'And I don't believe he approves of my employment actually,' she joked, grabbing a stack of books from the countertop and moving them to the side.

'And for him, being late is worth it, is it?' her colleague asked.

'Maybe, I don't know. Actually, I'm mildly frustrated,' she

271

told him. 'My subconscious keeps putting a lake in my dream and it's annoying as everyone knows that entire lake scene with Colin Firth in the TV series isn't in the book at all. Granted, in my dreams Mr Darcy never appears with a wet shirt, but for some reason the lake is there.' And it wasn't the only trick her subconscious was playing on her, Darcy thought uncomfortably, not about to admit to Joshua that once again the object of her affection had borne a striking resemblance to Aidan Harris.

Joshua laughed. 'I think you might be the only girl in the world who has a problem with a dream that involves a guy in a wet shirt. Your subconscious should be *rewarded* for its creative embellishment, I think. But then again, maybe you wouldn't have so many of those dreams if you found yourself a *real* man. There's a gallery-opening in Soho tonight I'm invited to. You should come along – it'll be a hot crowd, and we'll have a blast.' He rolled his eyes at Darcy's immediate hesitation. 'Let me guess, only three more chapters to go in the current tome,' he teased, repeating one of her oft-used excuses to turn down the prospect of a night out.

And while normally he'd be right, tonight Darcy had a genuine excuse for not accepting his invitation because for once, she actually had a prior engagement – a night at the ballet.

'Ooh very swanky,' Joshua replied when she told him about the tickets to the Koch Theater which Aidan had so kindly given her.

But thinking about Aidan made Darcy remember something else.

'Hey, you run the city marathon every year, don't you?' she asked him, outlining what she'd found at the house the day before, including the running medals.

'Sure do – me and forty-five thousand others. It's not like we all know each other, sweetie,' her colleague replied playfully.

'I know that, but I just wondered if Aidan might have something to do with your running group.' She went on to tell him about the New York Road Runner connection. 'There are medals from some smaller races in the Park too. You running types are pretty cliquey, aren't you?'

'Well, if he's as rich and attractive as you say, I'm sure some of the girls in the club might well be running after him, so to speak.' Joshua winked. 'You could try searching the results section of the club's website. That would tell you if he ever ran with us, when and where, that kind of thing.'

Darcy bit her lip. 'Doesn't really help me though. I was hoping I might be able to get in touch with his family through the club. Maybe there's an emergency contact number on record or something?'

Joshua thought for a second. 'We have a group session tomorrow night, I can ask around, if you like. Though I don't know … he sounds pretty bad-ass if he's doing ultras and stuff.'

Darcy looked up. 'Ultras?'

'Ultra races,' he clarified. 'As opposed to simple marathon running.'

She smiled wryly. Only a running nut like Joshua would ever refer to a marathon as 'simple'.

'Western States 100 is some serious shit, Darcy: a hundred

miles through the Sierra Nevada over mountains and canyons,' he told her, and she shook her head, unable to imagine Aidan (or indeed anyone) putting themselves through this kind of endurance. 'And that book, signed by the White Horse himself? I'll bet that's worth a few hundred, especially now.'

Darcy looked doubly confused. 'White Horse?'

'Signed by Cabello Blanco, you said. The White Horse – that's what the local Mexicans called him. He's dead now, but the guy is a *legend* in running circles.' Joshua went on to tell her in reverent tones the story of an American who'd dropped out of regular society and travelled to live and run in the copper canyons of Mexico with the Tarahumara Indians, whom he believed were a hidden tribe of super-athletes. 'Seriously, you've never read *Born to Run*? It's the runner's bible.'

'Well, you know that outdoorsy stuff has never really been my thing,' Darcy said, shrugging. Needless to say she had always preferred to be curled up cosy and warm indoors with some choice reading material, rather than outside pounding the pavements.

'Take it from me, if your guy is in that picture he must have some serious kudos or clout; the first few years of the Copper Canyon Ultra-marathon were invitation only. Tell you what, one of the older guys in the club has definitely competed in the Western 100 and I think he might even have done the Copper Canyon one time too. I'll ask him if the name means anything.'

'Thanks, Joshua, that would be a huge help,' Darcy said, looking thoughtful. 'You could be right about him having some kind of clout though.' She told him about Thrill Seeker and what she suspected it might be about. 'Judging by the photographs, it looks like "ultra" sports and races are right up his street.'

'Whoa, so I wasn't far wrong – this dude really is a real-life Jason Bourne,' Joshua said, replenishing candy canes in the countertop favours jar. 'I can see why you're smitten,' he teased, and despite herself Darcy flushed.

Was she smitten? she asked herself, trying to get her thoughts in order as she went about restocking shelves. *Was she attracted to Aidan?*

Sure, she had immediately thought him handsome on first seeing him at the hospital. And of course she couldn't help but feel a huge affinity with someone who was evidently a book geek like herself; never mind his nice eyes, lovely smile, lilting accent as well as his obvious affection for Bailey. To say nothing of his generosity in trying to pay her back for her help by insisting she take those ballet tickets.

And then there was the matter of his appearances in her dreams of late ...

Still, what she thought – or indeed felt – didn't matter, did it? For one thing, Aidan was attached to a beautiful woman called Melanie – or at least he had been until Darcy had thrown a spanner in the works.

And for another, as far as he was concerned, Darcy was just the girl who'd run him over in the street, and who was trying to make amends by dog-sitting, and helping him over a few administrative hurdles.

That was all.

Chapter 27

'So would you believe that I get all the way over here, only to spend less than forty-eight hours with those assholes, who then tell me they are not going to need me for as long as they thought? I've barely got started with my jet-lag when I'll be getting another plane home!'

I'd answered the phone and barely got out a hello before she launched into her latest diatribe. My lovely sister could always be depended upon for a rant. Smiling, I looked at my watch and calculated the time. 'It's past one a.m. there,' I said, as if Ciara was not aware of what time it was in Hong Kong.

'Right. And your point is, caller?' she replied dryly.

'So when do you think you will be home?' I knew that she wouldn't be going anywhere right at that moment, but in

276

Ciara's eyes, putting herself on a plane tomorrow or three days from now was all relative.

'Er, I'm not sure. I just know it won't be next week like I originally thought. I know this probably throws a monkey wrench in your life, but do you mind if I come to you a bit earlier? I know what your schedule is like.'

'Of course not. That would be great. I mean, you already know it's a crazy week for me workwise, and we have a lot of stuff going on just now, but as soon as I put a couple of other things to bed, so to speak, I'm all yours.' I welcomed her suggestion, really. It would be nice to have her around; I didn't see her nearly enough. 'Mel will be thrilled too; she's dying to see you.'

'Same here, and I'm glad everything seems back to normal for you guys now.' There was a brief pause. 'Don't take that for granted though.'

I frowned. 'What do you mean?'

'I mean you and your workaholic ways. I hope you've learned from past mistakes by now. Part of the whole problem was you taking so much on – often a lot more than you should. You aren't Superman you know, much as you refuse to believe it.'

I smiled patiently. My beloved sister didn't really understand how things in my world worked. No one I knew did really; they just assumed it was all fun and games, parties and launches and rubbing shoulders with celebrities … Sure, it could be like that sometimes, and most of the time it was great.

Except when the pressure was on, like now.

'Don't worry, sis, today is an easy day; my blue tights and cape are at the dry cleaners.'

'Aidan, are you listening to me? I'm serious. If you keep working at this pace, I can assure you that it's going to catch up with you – and when it does, you're going to be knocked to the ground. Not literally, of course, but this type of constant stress can't be good. For you or for Mel.'

'Well then, what would you have me do?' I retorted, my hackles rising at the insinuation that I was neglecting Mel. 'Throw in the towel and just walk away? That wouldn't be any good to anyone, would it? Anyway, it's not like that. I do love my job, but like everything there are good days and bad days. You more than anyone should know that.'

'I sure as hell do.' Then Ciara's voice softened on the other end of the line. 'I just wish you'd take some time off now and again. Look, maybe when I get there I can help somehow? If you'd let me, that is. I know what a control freak you are.'

I smiled at the idea. My sister was one hell of a tornado when she wanted to be, but I'm not sure even she could whip up what I needed in time.

'It'll be fine. I'll get there eventually. I always do.'

'Well, like I said, try not to work too hard. You deserve to have a life of your own sometimes, even though I'm not sure you actually realise that.'

She told me again that she would keep me posted on when she would be arriving and I wished her goodbye. When I hung up, I had to admit I was glad she had called – though still a little annoyed at the suggestion that I was jeopardising my relationship with Mel, when she had to know that it would be the very *last* thing I'd do.

I placed the phone on the side table and thought again about Ciara's words. Maybe my sister was right, maybe I had been taking too much on lately, and that's the reason I was feeling a little dejected at the moment.

I resolved to make sure she and I spent some quality time together while she was back in the city, maybe try and arrange a night out or something, just the two of us. Unlike the previous visit, where something last-minute had come up and I'd barely had enough time to see her for a cup of coffee.

Trying to shake the gloom, I picked up an advance reading copy of a book by an author named Oliver Martin that an editor friend gave me a few days ago.

I wasn't sure if the storyline sounded like my thing but by all accounts the author was very popular and I needed something to distract me in any case.

I was about to start reading when the phone piped up again. It must be Ciara, I thought, calling back to say something she had forgotten the first time around (or to tell me off again).

But this time it was a male voice on the other end. 'Aidan? Is that you?'

It was Nate Cleaver-Parks.

I sat up straight in the chair, feeling a surge of energy rush through me. Please let him be calling with good news.

'What's up, Nate? I was wondering if you had forgotten about me.'

'Sorry. Got tied up with that whole LA Tiffany Bennington mess. Her parents bailed her out, you know, but they also toted her back to New York. And because she's bored, she called me.' I was about to ask if he had spoken to the Benningtons about my query, but before I formed the question, Nate answered it for me. 'And no, just in case you're wondering, it's not them that I'm calling you about. I actually have someone else for you to talk to. And well, OK, you will be talking to his assistant, but she'll be able to speak on her boss's behalf, OK?'

'Fantastic. OK, who do I have to call?'

There was a pause. 'Do you have a pen?'

'Not with me. Hold on.' I raced up to the office where I had left the list, grabbed the key, unlocked the drawer and extracted the folder and a pen. Then I picked up the extension handset, ready for business. 'OK, shoot.'

'All right. I want you to talk to Stephanie Everly.'

I wrote down the name and as Nate gave me some background on the woman and her employer, I hoped that this new avenue would actually lead somewhere and wouldn't be as fruitless and exhausting as everything that I had already tried.

'Thanks, Nate. I owe you one,' I said, breathing an inward sigh of relief. Here's hoping that this Stephanie Everly, whoever she is, may be able to help me.

'Not a problem. Let me know how it goes, OK?' he said, wrapping up the call. 'Interested to know if you hit the jackpot and I hope it all pans out.'

Chapter 28

Let us read, and let us dance; these two amusements will never do any harm to the world. **Voltaire**

'Whoever will watch Bailey?' Grace fretted later that evening, pacing in front of her blinking pink and white Christmas tree, as Darcy waited for her neighbour to get ready for their impromptu night out.

'Ricardo's going to come check on him during his break,' she replied, not exactly proud of how she'd lured Luigi's waiter in and taken advantage of his interest in her with the promise of a home-cooked meal sometime. She was grateful that Luigi hadn't yet made a stink about her house-guest overstaying his welcome – in fact, both her landlord and Ricardo had taken a bit of a shine to the Husky. She'd had little option but to curry favour with Ricardo if she and Bailey's fall-back dog-sitter were to take advantage of Aidan's tickets. 'Anyway,

Grace, why all the worrying? I thought you'd be happy. It's the ballet!'

The older woman softened. 'I know, dear, and it's awfully sweet of your friend but I have to confess, it's been years since I've gone out on the town. I'm not ... I'm not sure I'm ready.'

'Nonsense,' Darcy answered, urging Grace into her bedroom so they could choose an outfit for the 7.30 performance of *The Nutcracker* at the Koch Theater. 'You eat out at Luigi's almost every night, don't you?'

'That's different, dear. The place is a dive. But the Koch is legendary in ballet circles. This is a big deal.'

'It is?' Darcy asked, glancing down at herself and her boring black trousers and purple merino sweater combo. Now she was starting to wonder if *she* was up to it.

'Why yes, dear. I told you, I danced there myself, many, many moons ago.'

Darcy strengthened her resolve. 'Then all the more reason to go back tonight and enjoy it. Listen, I think I might do a quick change myself, but I'll come back over to get you in ten minutes, OK? We both need to be ready to leave soon if we're going to make the performance on time.'

Darcy dashed across the hall, digging out her vintage wrap dress, about the only vaguely glamorous item of clothing she had in her closet. Though what she wouldn't give to have those Jimmy Choos now! she groaned, giving Bailey a murderous look. The Husky remained sprawled lazily on her bed as though he didn't have a care in the world.

Well, she did have a cute pair of courtesan-style heels that just might work, Darcy thought, rummaging deeper into the closet.

Once dressed, she stood in front of the full-length mirror on the wardrobe door and looked appraisingly at her reflection, frowning at the sight of her habitual ponytail and face devoid of make-up.

She was lucky in that her skin was in good condition and mostly blemish-free, but Joshua was right; she really did need to try harder. Perhaps then a guy of Aidan Harris' calibre might be interested enough to ask her out.

The feminist in her immediately berated herself for thinking that way, deciding that any man concerned primarily with appearances was hardly worth her time, but Darcy had to admit that she wasn't exactly making the most of her femininity. She should tame her wayward hair for a start. It was actually quite soft and shiny, though she rarely wore it down. And everyone always commented on her eyes, which were a curious shade of green that looked especially vivid when accentuated with mascara or eye-liner.

Rummaging around in a drawer, she located her old cosmetics bag and proceeded to apply foundation, eye make-up and some faint blusher. Then, untying her hair, she shook it out and let it fall casually around her face, surprised at how long it had grown. The ends now reached well past her shoulders. The longer style definitely gave her a somewhat more glamorous – and yes, definitely sexier – look, she decided approvingly.

Smearing on some bright red lipstick to finish the job, she

re-examined her appearance, feeling a little taken aback by the transformation and moreover how good it felt. Maybe she really should take the time to glam up a little more now and again.

She was just slipping on a faintly vintage-style grey cape she remembered Katherine buying her in Macy's last year as she knocked on Grace's door. Her neighbour appeared in the doorway, a stunner in a silver gown that hit her mid-calf and showed off her high, elegant neck and still-strong arms. A black shawl was draped across her shoulders and fell to the middle of her back, accenting the diamond pendant earrings that glittered on either side of her nervous smile. Now *this* was a lady who really knew how to glam up.

'Wow, Grace, you look beautiful!' Darcy gasped, amazed at how, since she'd got to know the older woman better, it was as if the years had simply fallen away. She'd always viewed Mrs Henley as a grumpy old lady, but since Bailey had come into their lives a few days before, she'd begun to understand that Grace was simply a lonely middle-aged woman.

Not too unlike herself perhaps, Darcy admitted; though scratch the middle-aged bit.

Since her conversation with Joshua earlier she had been thinking about that, wondering if this was the real reason she'd been so eager to throw herself into helping Aidan Harris.

Was she lonely?

Yes, she was surrounded by lovely people who cared about her, like Katherine, Joshua and Ashley from the bookstore, and indeed she had stayed in touch with many of Chaucer's staff over the years. But ultimately, and while it might sound a little pathetic to some, her beloved books had always been her closest friends and confidantes.

It had been that way since childhood. Sure, she'd always talked about doing things; travelling more and experiencing adventures in faraway places, but as she routinely did so vicariously through the pages of a book, the ambition never seemed to go any further than that – talk.

Like most New Yorkers, Darcy adored the city. It had so much to offer that one truly didn't need to leave it at all, but now she wondered if she clung to the place, almost like a life-raft, safe in the knowledge that it was her constant – and that no more bad things could happen as long as she remained cocooned in the city's embrace.

But since she'd met Aidan and had had a chance to examine the exciting life he seemed to lead it had somehow turned the spotlight on what was lacking in her own. She didn't mean the money or the incredible house – though there was no question it was the stuff of dreams – but it was almost as if her quest to help Aidan reconstruct the story of his life was also helping Darcy discover the missing pieces of her own.

And she wondered if she was a little too guilty of using escapism as a means to avoid confronting the reality of her own life, and what it might be lacking.

'Look at us,' Grace whispered as they clomped down the steps in their heels, putting an end to Darcy's musings. 'We look like a couple of real gals.'

The taxi she had called for them was waiting, and through the steamy windows of Luigi's Ricardo waved at them both, a dishtowel slung over his shoulder.

'Don't look now, dear,' joked Grace, lowering herself into the cab. 'But I think you have an admirer.'

Darcy chuckled, sliding in next to her and giving the driver their destination. 'Who says he's admiring *me*?'

As the taxi headed uptown, she couldn't deny feeling more than a little excited. A night at the ballet in one of New York's premier theatres was yet another thing that had thus far been out of her realm of experience, and it would be a chance to experience a tiny part of Aidan Harris's glamorous lifestyle.

She wondered again if these tickets had been bought by him and if so, who had he planned on accompanying him tonight?

The woman called Melanie who had sounded so indignant on the answering machine yesterday had certainly given the impression that Aidan might have been stepping out with more than one woman recently, yet on the other hand, hadn't he taken the time to arrange that beautiful gift for someone special? Notwithstanding that in the short time she'd known him, he'd come across as a down to earth kind of guy, and wasn't in the least bit flirtatious with her. Although perhaps, Darcy thought somewhat glumly, it was that she simply wasn't worthy of his interest.

The driver dropped them off right in front of the steps up to the Lincoln Center, where the Koch Theater was located, and the two women made their way up the steps and onto the main plaza. As they neared the top and the backlit fountain came into view – the water sparkling like a diamond in the darkness – Darcy was immediately struck by something.

The black and white picture of the blonde woman in Aidan's apartment . . . it had been taken here at the plaza right in front of the Revson Fountain. She couldn't understand why she hadn't realised it before now, since the fountain's backlit jets and circular arrangement were so distinctive. However, she guessed that she'd been so focused on the woman herself she'd hadn't paid close enough attention to the background.

And now that she thought about the photo again – the woman's confident, arching pose, her arms over her head . . . Darcy took the tickets out of her purse and looked at them, the cogs turning in her brain. Could it be that the woman in the photograph was a ballerina? It might explain why Aidan had the tickets. Then she wondered, her heart racing as she tried to put the pieces together while she and Grace made their way to the entrance of the theatre, could it be that the same woman was performing here tonight?

Once inside, Darcy hurriedly opened the programme she and Grace had been given, and scanned through the names of the performers, trying to find a dancer by the name of the only person she could so far confirm was missing Aidan and was worried by his absence.

Granted it was a long shot, but she figured it was worth a try.

If she could find her, then she could at least explain why

Aidan had let her down, and if Melanie turned out to be Aidan's girlfriend – the love of his life and the one who was supposed to receive the gift from him – then Darcy could put things right.

But there was no Melanie listed on that night's programme.

'What's the matter, dear?' Grace asked as an usher directed them to their seats, and they both sat back. 'You seem distracted.'

Darcy was in two minds whether to share her thoughts with Grace, but she figured it would do no harm to have someone else's perspective on the matter. There were so many mysteries surrounding Aidan that she could barely get her head straight.

'My, my, such a muddle,' Grace said, when Darcy finished the tale some minutes later. 'But I think you may be right about this lady being a ballerina, at least. It's almost obligatory for any dancer talented enough to perform at the New York City Ballet to be photographed at the fountain – a rite of passage, if you will. I have one of myself tucked away somewhere – though the fountain was quite different back then.'

Darcy heart raced; she was on to something now, she was sure of it. The question was, could the reason he had those tickets be because his blonde friend was actually performing *The Nutcracker* here tonight? And if so, would Darcy be able to recognise her?

The auditorium was beautiful – a hybrid of traditional and continental-style seating on the orchestra level, and five balconies adorned with jewel-like faceted lights. Hanging from the gold-panelled ceiling was a large spherical chandelier.

A Gift to Remember

'Is it how you remember?' Darcy asked Grace.

'Would you believe, it's *exactly* as I remember,' the older woman replied fondly, a tear in her eye. 'It's as if I've stepped back in time. And these are Fourth Ring, the best seats in the house.'

Darcy didn't understand; she was actually a little underwhelmed that the two of them were seated on a balcony three rows from the back, and thus such a distance from the stage, but Grace explained that the further away from the dancers, the better to view the detail of the dance.

There was a jovial feel to the evening, as everyone – the men decked out in smart suits and the women in festive sparkling clothes and fine jewellery – took their seats. Temporarily putting aside all other thoughts as the lights dimmed and the performance began, Darcy sat back, the hairs standing on the back of her neck as the first performer dashed onstage; wearing a soft red helmet, gorgeous satiny blue jacket with bright gold buttons and shimmering red tights. And right then it hit home just how lucky she was to be experiencing a night at the magical New York Ballet.

She had never been to a performance before, and to watch was almost to forget oneself; to fall in love with the dance. It was a stunning spectacle, and Darcy was breathless throughout as she saw the graceful performers leap lithely around the stage, muscles defined and motions fluid, as if they'd been born to dance.

Afterwards, she gripped Grace's hand. 'Just incredible!' she whispered as the curtain fell. The crowd roared its approval but none more loudly than Grace and Darcy, high up in the balcony where Aidan Harris and an unknown companion should have been.

And though she'd tried her utmost to see if she could pick out the woman in the photograph, it was impossible to get a proper look at the dancers from this distance. Even if she had been able to get any closer, Darcy doubted she'd be able to identify her beneath the greasepaint and costumes.

As other patrons moved past them in the aisle she stood to go but Grace held her back. 'Let's just enjoy it a moment longer,' she suggested. Darcy noticed the older woman's eyes glittering and she was grateful once again to Aidan for his generosity.

'Grace Clarke?' a voice called out from nearby, and the two women looked to find an older man, humbly dressed in an old driving cap atop a head full of stringy white hair moving up the aisle steps towards them.

'Chalmers?' Grace gasped, a hand to her throat. 'I can't believe you recognised me.'

'Or you me,' he chuckled.

The two embraced, and Grace introduced the man as one of her former dancing partners; she explained that Clarke was her maiden name.

'I haven't seen you since you got married and crossed to the dark side,' Chalmers said, smiling at her fondly, and Darcy knew that tonight had meant a lot to her neighbour and was bringing back special memories in more ways than one.

Chapter 29

Reality can be beaten with enough imagination.
Mark Twain

The following morning, Darcy walked along the footpath on Central Park's West Drive, Bailey at her side. The place was truly spectacular at this time of year, low winter sunshine illuminating the surrounding buildings, a light dusting of snow on the ground and on bare branches set against a brilliant blue sky.

She had no choice but to take Aidan's dog to work with her today, as following Grace's happy reunion with Chalmers last night at the ballet, it seemed her neighbour now had a lunch date with her old friend.

Darcy didn't mind, she'd imposed too much on her as it was, and furthermore she knew that the gentle Husky would be perfectly behaved. Anyway, the customers might appreciate it, though she knew the same couldn't be said for the staff – one of them at least, she thought with smile.

There were hundreds of joggers, walkers, cyclists and fellow dog-walkers taking full advantage of the bright winter's morning. Bailey tugged hard on his leash, sensing the freedom of the wide open space that lay behind a row of trees just off the path.

'Sorry, boy. Much as I'd love to let you go crazy, I'm not going to be the one telling Aidan that I lost you after you went chasing squirrels.' She felt terrible though. There he was, a Husky, by an open expanse of recently fallen snow; born to race across it. Still, dogs weren't allowed off the leash in the Park, something she guessed Bailey knew if Aidan exercised him here on a regular basis.

When she walked into the bookstore with Bailey in tow, Joshua was standing behind the counter with Ashley, logging new inventory into the computer. He looked up, stricken at the sight of her four-legged companion.

'What. Is. *That*?' he shrieked, eyeing Bailey. 'If that ... *wolf* does his business in here, there is going to be hell to pay. Liam Neeson will have nothing on me.'

Bailey regally returned Joshua's gaze, and if Darcy was correct, his eyes faintly narrowed at the uncivilised notion of actually doing his business inside.

'Oh Joshua, cut it out. This is Bailey and I can assure you he'll be fine. He's probably better behaved than you or me. Maybe even better read too.' Darcy dropped her bag behind the cashier's desk and took Bailey off his leash. Immediately, the dog took to sniffing about, making himself at home in his new surroundings.

Joshua eyed him warily. 'What if he pees on the merchandise? You know there is a reason for the sign on the door saying: *No Dogs Allowed*.'

'Except assistance dogs,' Darcy retorted. 'And he's assisting us today.'

Her workmate shook his head, his Santa hat bobbing furiously as he did so. 'You are insane.'

Ashley wandered around the counter and dropped to her knees, coaxing Bailey to her. Darcy watched as he introduced himself to the younger girl, first sniffing tentatively and then laying a sloppy kiss on her cheek. He nudged himself so close to her that she almost fell backwards and Bailey wagged his tail happily as Ashley tried to get the upper hand on their spontaneous bout of wrestling, giggling the whole time.

'He's fabulous.' She looked up at Darcy. 'I'm so sorry again about the other day. If I hadn't asked to change shifts that morning then you wouldn't have had to rush and none of this would have happened.'

'No need to apologise; it was completely my fault for not setting my alarm.'

'Joshua told me all about Jason Bourne,' she added smiling, and Darcy glared at Joshua, who shrugged. 'I think it's really great that you're trying to help him.'

Darcy reached for her Chaucer's apron. 'For the record, his name is Aidan Harris, and I'm not sure I'm actually helping at all, to be honest.'

'Well, speaking of Mr Bourne,' Joshua said, unpacking one of the newly delivered boxes, 'I guess with that new movie coming out, we should put a bunch of these Will Anderson thrillers at the front.'

Darcy had to smile as she noticed a pile of books by the author Katherine had tried to set her up with before. Her aunt had been right about the thriller author being a 'big deal'. She began to wonder if Katherine had had any luck in finding someone via her famous connections who might know Aidan. Though if she had, Darcy knew she would have heard about it by now, despite the fact that her aunt was tied up with the countless holiday events Ignite hosted at this time of year.

Making sure Bailey was comfortably situated on the rug behind the counter near the store's heater, she tried to focus her attentions on the day ahead, but her thoughts kept drifting back to Aidan.

While her last visit to the brownstone had thrown up a lot of interesting stuff, it didn't really get her any further down the line in helping him. When she'd shown the medals and *Born to Run* paperback to him on a quick visit to the hospital after work yesterday, he'd looked just as clueless about the idea of being some kind of ultra-fitness aficionado as he had about everything else she'd presented him with so far.

And much to her disappointment, he seemed even more perplexed about the existence of the library. Darcy had been truly expecting that the books would be just the thing to trigger his memory. Especially as he'd already shown he possessed some kind of literary knowledge.

In the meantime, she'd even gone so far as to enquire about Aidan at Gray's Papaya, but the guy behind the counter at the hot-dog joint had looked at her as if she was mad. 'Do you know how many people we get here every day?' he'd asked incredulously.

Which meant that it looked like the ballerina angle was the only option left to her at this point, and if she was wrong about that – if Aidan's lady friend Melanie was no longer a dancer, or never had been – then she was well and truly sunk.

Plain and simple: Darcy just didn't know what else to do.

More than anything, she didn't want Aidan to have to spend another night alone in that sterile, flower-free hospital room.

But with only three days left till Christmas she couldn't help but wonder why nobody had yet sought him out in the hospital. It had been four days since the accident now and still he remained to all intents and purposes 'unclaimed'. She knew it was starting to get to him too; she guessed he was feeling hurt and even more despondent as the days went by and with the holidays just over the horizon.

No one should be alone at this time of year, especially not when they had a beautiful, talented and accomplished girlfriend out there who loved them and who, thanks to Darcy's efforts, might well now believe that Aidan didn't care about her.

Darcy knew she couldn't let that happen, and having gone

this far, would try her utmost to make things right. She'd deliver the gift herself to Melanie if she had to.

Yes, it was proving difficult to get to the bottom of it all, but at the moment she was Aidan's only hope – and didn't she owe it to him to try?

Chapter 30

For Christ's sake, doesn't anyone ever answer their phone in this city? I have tried to reach Stephanie Everly twice now – once immediately after Nate passed me her number and once again this morning, hoping out of dumb luck that I would get her to pick up.

Though it seems luck is not on the cards for me lately. She didn't pick up, not last night, and not this morning either.

Don't these people understand my urgency at this point? I'm fifty shades of desperate and I think that my next step may have to be running across Manhattan with a sign attached to my chest advertising my needs.

Not sure who would pay attention to me though. Maybe if

I did it naked it would work, perhaps generate some attention in the papers?

Ah no, Aidan. Don't even go there. You would more likely get arrested.

But back to the matter at hand.

It has now been four hours since I last called Stephanie's cell phone and I reckon it's time for me to try again. I don't want to come across as a stalker but I just really, really, really need to talk to her.

I dialled her number and heard it ring – one, two, three, four times – and then it went to voicemail.

'Once again,' I muttered as I listened to Stephanie's cool voice tell me to leave a message and that she would call me back. At this point in the game, I didn't believe her.

But of course, I didn't tell her that.

Injecting a warmth into my voice that I didn't feel, I began to speak.

'Hi, Stephanie. It's Aidan Harris – again. Don't mean to be a pest, I really don't, but Nate Cleaver-Parks – Junior, that is – said that I should talk to you about something I'm seeking urgently. He tells me that your boss is a keen collector in this area and may be willing to sell. And just in case Nate might-n't have mentioned it, I'm anxious to expedite a deal and as such am willing to pay top dollar.' My stomach hurt when I said that – old habits die hard – but it was the truth.

'Anyway, I'll leave you my number again, 212-555-4343. So give me a call and we can chat. Again it's—'

Beep.

An automatic voice told me that my message had exceeded the maximum time allotted. Irritated, I pulled the phone away from my ear. It would be an understatement to say that I was frustrated by the silence. Then, no sooner had I thought this than karma answered by making my phone buzz with several incoming text messages.

Due to the frequency, I could guess who they were from, and the knot of anxiety that had been forming in my stomach tightened as I read through them.

I typed a quick response and flung myself down on the bed, aimlessly turning on the TV.

Bailey, sensing an invitation, jumped up next to me on the down-filled duvet and rested his head on the pillow next to mine. He sniffed briefly, possibly picking up the remnants of Mel's strawberry shampoo from the other night, and then rolled onto his back, as if he'd identified the source of the smell and was satisfied.

I flipped channels for a moment and as usual found nothing worth watching. It was all Christmas specials featuring the Kardashians or the *Jersey Shore* cast or some other reality show family, news about whatever was happening in Washington and who was picking fights with whom.

I tossed the remote control to the side, leaving the news channel on as background, and closed my eyes. I knew I should be doing something, anything other than lying here, but God, I was getting so tired and worn out.

'Thirty-six hours, Bailey. Thirty-six hours to D-day. Either I succeed by way of some miracle, or I fail miserably.'

Bailey sighed as if he felt my pain. I opened an eye and looked at him.

Nope, not feeling my pain actually, just falling asleep. Typical ...

Chapter 31

There was nowhere to go but everywhere, so just keep on rolling under the stars. **Jack Kerouac**

It was early afternoon the following day, and there were few things prettier than a winter sky over Manhattan in December. It was so blue it almost hurt to look at it, and the crispness in the air made the pedestrians smile, red scarves bright and matching berets crisp, as they passed Darcy's little lunch table for one on the East Side.

That morning at work she'd printed out a copy of some of the most prestigious ballet academies in Manhattan, as suggested by Grace's old dancer friend Abe Chalmers, who was still in the business.

The name Melanie didn't immediately ring any bells with him amongst the New York City Ballet professionals he was aware of, he'd told Darcy the other night at the theatre when she had enquired, but that didn't necessarily mean she didn't exist.

'It merely suggests that she may be part of a company elsewhere. Bring your photograph along to the academies,' he told her. 'If she happened to attend any of the schools in the past, then somebody is sure to recognise her.'

She'd planned to visit the others after work later, but there was one on the Upper East Side, not far from Chaucer's, that she was heading to now during her lunch break.

The spot was cubist and modern, all glass and chrome, and Darcy could see a ballet class going on as she walked off the street straight into a blindingly white reception area. Initially she got a shock, thinking she had hit pay dirt on her first stop; the receptionist was an almost spitting image of the woman in the photo.

Stiff and pale and dressed all in black, with strawberry-blonde hair pulled back severely from a thin but moon-shaped face, she took one look at Darcy's blue jeans and worn coat, and a veil of frost seemed to crystallise across her already stiff face.

'Class has already started,' she said, looking back down at some kind of sleek, paper-thin tablet on her desk.

'Oh, that's OK, I don't attend a class here.'

The woman glanced up, gave her the once-over and made a 'that's obvious' sneer. 'So, why are you here then?'

The frosty exterior and haughty tone put Darcy a little off-kilter. 'I'm enquiring about someone who might have been a student here,' she babbled, visibly wincing as she did so.

She started reaching into her messenger bag for the photo, realising she should already have it out, when the frosty woman – who probably wasn't all that much older than Darcy – inched back in her chair. 'Hold up,' she said. 'You understand I can't give out any information about students who go here. It's against policy, and in any case you could be some kind of ... stalker.'

That word again. 'Really?'

'Yes, really. Keeping in mind that you outweigh most of these girls by a good twenty-five pounds and—'

Darcy threw her hands up and turned around. 'All right, all right, forget I asked.'

She left, rounding the side of the building, and leaned against a wall just out of sight of the sheer glass wall facing the street. She sighed, looking at the picture.

What would it take, she wondered, to penetrate this woman's glittering world?

Where had she and Aidan met? At a party after one of her performances? Or some fancy benefit do at which the good, great and most attractive Manhattanites gathered to admire each other?

She looked so flawless, pale and chic, her smile beaming and confident as the Revson Fountain sparkled behind her. '*Who are you?*' Darcy muttered to herself as the glass door to the ballet studio opened, and a dozen or more spindly legs stampeded down the steps.

As the dancers split off into the wind, she called out to whoever might listen. 'Excuse me, can you help me?' She held out the photo to three girls who had stopped, impatient but standing still, at least. 'I'm looking for this dancer.'

Before even glancing at the picture one of the girls, taller than the rest and looking sharper somehow, asked, 'Why?'

Having taken time between being rebuffed by the secretary and the end of the dance class to concoct a vaguely realistic story, Darcy said confidently. 'I saw her a few weeks back at a benefit performance and she was just stunning. But I had to leave before it was over and couldn't approach her myself. I was hoping she might stage an encore show for a private audience.'

The girl blinked and thought for a second. 'Who is this private audience for?'

Darcy blinked back. 'Well, it wouldn't be very private if I told you that, now would it? But it means a great deal to my client. You see, he's researching a part for his new movie and I know she'd be just perfect.'

She surprised herself at how easily the fiction tripped off her tongue, but at the mention of the word 'movie' the girls all straightened, as if auditioning themselves. Darcy felt vaguely guilty about the fib, but if it got her one step closer to her quarry, and she wasn't promising these girls anything, who was it hurting?

'Let me see,' said the tall girl, taking the photo from Darcy. 'She looks familiar, but she doesn't dance here. I might have seen her in *Swan Lake* last year, or maybe *Serenade* but I can't be sure.'

Another girl nodded. 'Try Madame Song's two blocks over. She looks like she could be one of her girls.'

And so later that day after work, Darcy bounced like a pin-ball from one ballet studio to the other. From Madame Song's she went to the Studio Academy, and from the Academy Group she want to Slippers Studio, and on it went … Some of the classes were held in little more than basements in the bottom of massive brownstones, others took up entire floors above Chinese restaurants or dry cleaners.

It was a journey she'd never expected to take, through parts of Manhattan she'd never ever seen before; some exclusive, some gritty, some flashy, some classical.

She'd quickly learned never to actually go inside but instead to lurk around the corner, down the stairs, at the intersection or more effectively the juice bar a few doors down from the class. As the girls filed out, she would usu-ally find a cluster or a gaggle who were friendlier than the rest.

She got a lot of recommendations, but by the end of that day she was no closer to the dancer's identity than when she'd started.

Later that evening, she sat across from Grace, sipping another cup of strong, hot, instant coffee that revived her as much as the sight of Bailey did on her arrival. 'I'm really having a hard time tracking this girl down.'

Grace nodded. 'Well, of course you are, dear. This is a very busy time of year in ballet.'

'It is?'

She nodded, smoothing out the lap of her pink housedress. 'Oh yes. From private benefits to holiday performances and end-of-season extravaganzas, professional dancers hardly rest until after the New Year.'

The butter cookies from Darcy's plate disappeared but after a trip to the kitchen by Grace, more soon reappeared. She looked up, almost powerless to move after cycling to and from so many dance studios on the island. 'I don't know what I ever did without you, Grace.'

Bailey sat next to the older woman on the sofa, his head on her lap. She petted him gently, cooing to him. 'Believe me; you've already done so much. I'm really going to miss this pooch when your fellow takes him back.'

'He's not my fellow,' she corrected Grace. 'He's just somebody I'm helping.'

'Are you sure?' her neighbour asked, eyeing her shrewdly.

Darcy coloured. 'What do you mean?' she asked.

'Well, forgive me if I'm speaking out of turn, but it seems to me that you've been going to an awful lot of trouble over the last few days to help out a man who is to all intents and purposes a complete stranger.'

'But it's entirely my fault he's in this situation, Grace,' Darcy insisted yet again. 'It's three days till Christmas and he's all alone in some hospital bed, while the people he loves and who love him must be driven crazy with worry.'

'Some would say that you've paid your dues by offering to take care of his dog. Nobody could expect any more. Unless ...' she glanced meaningfully at Darcy, 'unless your reasons have gone beyond mere obligation.'

Darcy sank back on the sofa and sighed. 'Oh, I don't know.

It's silly really, maybe I have developed a bit of a crush. I mean, Aidan is successful, obviously smart, handsome, kind, well-read – pretty much everything a girl wants in a guy, I suppose. But it doesn't matter what I think because from what little I have learned about Aidan's life, he's definitely not available, and *of course* a man like him would be snatched up by someone. And *of course* that someone would just happen to be a drop dead beautiful model-type with a perfect body, glamorous clothes and is likely super-successful to boot. Whereas I –' she smiled crookedly. 'Let's just say I'm no catch.'

Grace shook her head. 'Oh Darcy, come on, you know better than that. So you aren't dripping in silly designers from head to toe, how many of us are? And who cares? I already know that there is plenty about you that makes you special – your kindness, for one. Don't ever sell yourself short like that,' she finished earnestly.

Darcy was touched by her neighbour's kindness. 'Thank you, Grace, I appreciate you saying that and I appreciate your friendship too. I can't believe we spent almost three years living side by side, barely saying hello when we passed each other by.'

'That was my fault,' Grace said gently. 'I was still grieving for my Ralph and didn't want to know anyone, didn't want anyone in my life. I remember you smiling at me that first day you moved in, but I knew I wasn't ready for friendship – in truth, I wasn't able for it. But that was my mistake.'

'And that was then,' Darcy finished, reaching out and

squeezing the older woman's hand. She cocked her head at Bailey and smiled. 'And they say this guy is *man's* best friend?'

Grace laughed and patted Darcy's hand in turn. 'What I said just now, I'm not just being polite. I mean it. Sure, every man might dream about being with a Supermodel, and some guys might even get to date them once in a while, but it's gals like *us* that are real. And there are more of us in the world, too. Last time I checked, plenty of them get their happy ever after.'

Darcy nodded, wondering just who would get their happy ever after in *this* story.

Chapter 32

Once she knows how to read there's only one thing you can teach her to believe in and that is herself.
Virginia Woolf

'Hey, you don't happen to know anything about ballet, do you?' Darcy asked Joshua the following day at work, explaining about her latest potential lead in tracking down one of Aidan's elusive loved ones.

''Fraid not. Not really my thing. Musicals, however ...'

'Yes, we know.' She smiled fondly. A devoted Broadway fan, her colleague was known to periodically break out in bursts of 'Defying Gravity' or 'The Wizard and I' at any opportune moment. It was a most effective tactic for clearing the store at closing time.

Darcy took the photo of the ballerina out of her messenger bag and showed it to him.

309

Joshua's eyes went wide. 'Who's this?'

'I think it might be Aidan's girlfriend, and I'm trying to track her down.'

'Classy,' he said, handing the picture back. 'If a little cold for my taste.'

Darcy looked at the photograph for the umpteenth time. 'She really does look like a ballerina though, doesn't she?' She went on to tell him about the significance of the pose and picture outside the Revson Fountain, and about her and Grace's night out at the Koch Theater, ending with her trundle through the various ballet schools the day before in the hope that somebody might recognise the woman.

'I've only got one more place to visit and if that doesn't work out, I'm stumped. I just don't know how else I can get in touch with somebody Aidan knows.'

'You're really dedicated to this, aren't you?' he said, echoing Grace's gentle probing from the night before.

'Yes. He'll be coming home from the hospital tomorrow, but I can't really relax until I know he's OK, and that somebody else will be there to look out for him.' She'd spoken to Aidan on the phone a little earlier and he'd informed her that despite his doctor's protests he was checking out of the hospital and going home. 'There's no point in sitting here in an empty room scratching my head when I could be doing the same at home, surrounded by things that I will surely recognise,' he told her, and by the sound of his voice she knew he'd reached the end of his tether. 'I can't have you keep to-ing and fro-ing here with various bits and pieces either, Darcy. It's not fair; you have your own life and I've taken up more than enough of it. '

But Darcy didn't want to admit to him that she was enjoying the adventure, the brief distraction from her humdrum routine. His life had become her life.

'When will Apple have the phone back? I'm sure that will straighten things out once and for all. Better than you cycling around Manhattan on a wild-goose chase. Or should it be swan, seeing as you think she's a ballerina?'

'Ha. And the phone is due back any day now. Just waiting on Apple's Head Office to authorise the replacement and then the store can do a data transfer.'

'Well, if I were you, I'd concentrate on that,' Joshua said with a carefree shrug as he got ready to finish his shift. 'Let the wizards of Apple sort out the confusion once and for all.'

But for Darcy, things were no longer that simple. She was by now way too deep into this story, and the romantic in her almost didn't want to rely on the phone data to fill in the gaps, tie up the loose strands and wrap everything up in a big red bow. Less satisfying somehow.

She wanted to find Aidan's girlfriend, and let her know that Aidan's gift was still there waiting for her. That her lover hadn't let her down and was likely still as much in love with her as ever.

'Well, I just think you're crazy,' Joshua said, when she tried to explain this to him. 'But then again, since when did anyone around here care what I think? See you tomorrow!' With that, the door chimed and he was off like a blast, all ninety-eight pounds of him, reindeer antlers bobbing as he went.

When he left, Darcy was almost grateful for the silence and the opportunity to be alone with her thoughts as she moved through the shelves, rearranging the children's section to face out the more seasonal titles, and finding a home for new stock. She adored Joshua, but sometimes he was like a black hole, sucking dry everything around him with his manic energy. She also felt as if she'd never spent so much time around people as lately. She was used to her solitude and it felt strange to be in the middle of so much activity.

Later that evening, once she'd closed up the store, she made her way to the last ballet school on her list. The bike was trusty and sleek beneath her as she dodged traffic all the way to Lamont's, on the Upper East Side, the only place she hadn't visited.

This academy, located just off Madison Avenue, was according to her research well-respected and exclusive, and the beautiful Renaissance building in which it resided was definitely the most upscale of all of the schools she'd visited.

She'd also learned from her mistakes, and wasn't going to risk ruining what was possibly her last and only chance at finding the dancer she was looking for by actually going inside and flashing the picture around like some amateur.

Instead she found a juice bar at the end of the same block and, as she had with so many of the other schools and studios in the last twenty-four hours, decided to hide in plain sight. Locking her bike up nearby, she went inside and ordered a banana and low-fat yogurt smoothie with an immunity boost and sat at a window table waiting for classes to finish.

After about thirty minutes, the door opened and in walked half a dozen girls, leg warmers pink and high, throats flush with perspiration, their hair in six identical ponytails. The girls ordered in synchronised high-pitched voices and paid with six separate cheque cards, and it took forever for them to collect their drinks, gossip about their classmates and eventually drift towards the tables on either side of Darcy.

She'd finished her own drink almost twenty minutes ago and sat there, turning the photograph over and over in her hands, the plastic wrap worn from constant handling. As the girls launched into their smoothies Darcy turned to the table behind her, clearing her throat. They looked up at her, so young and thin, instantly suspicious.

'Hi, there. Sorry, I don't mean to bother you,' she began, smiling as they inched back in their seats. 'I won't waste your time but I'm just wondering ... this woman is a dancer and I heard she used to attend your school.'

She'd learned by now never to sound uncertain or hesitant, as people naturally responded to confident authority. Still, Darcy didn't think she'd ever quite make it in the NYPD.

She showed the girls the picture and despite their snootiness, they all craned their necks. One of them spoke up. 'Yes, she looks kind of familiar.'

'I think her picture is on the wall somewhere?'

Another shook her head. 'Nope, never seen her.'

Then without another word, they turned around and left

Darcy still holding out the picture. She turned to the second table, who ignored her completely and stood instead, and took their smoothies out the door. The first table quickly followed and Darcy sat there, deflated, her palms moist and head throbbing. Well, that was it then. No more academies to visit, no more ballerinas to ask.

Sorry, Aidan, I really tried.

She went to slide the picture back in her messenger bag when a shadow crossed her table. She looked up to see a girl about her own age, but razor thin and with reading glasses sliding down her nose.

'Excuse me,' the girl said. 'But could I see that picture for a moment?'

Darcy slid the photograph over and, immediately, the girl smiled. 'It's Melanie Rothschild,' she said, nodding in recognition, and Darcy's heart almost stopped.

Melanie – she'd found her.

'When I heard Emily, one of the dancers, say just now that she'd seen the woman's picture on the wall, I suspected it might be one of ours.'

Darcy's heart was pounding. 'Are you an instructor?'

'Me? Heavens, no. I was actually a dancer until a few years ago when I tore a hamstring. Madame Scarsdale, who owns Lamont's, was kind enough to give me a receptionist job, and I've been there ever since. I see Melanie's picture in the hallway every day, along with the rest of Lamont's success stories.'

Darcy breathed a giant sigh of relief. 'So she *is* a professional ballerina then?'

'Yes, she performs with the Boston Ballet, last I heard. Lamont's is really very proud of our graduates; many of them do go on to truly great things.'

The Boston Ballet. 'So she's not based here in New York then?' It made a certain sense, as the majority of the missed calls on Aidan's phone had come from a private number with no area identification. And it matched up with him living alone for the most part.

Darcy felt heartened.

'What was her surname again?' she asked the girl, taking a pen and paper out of her bag. 'Rothschild, did you say?'

'Yes. Respected old New York family.'

A blue blood. Of course. What else? But it was good news in a way as it might just make it easier to track Melanie down.

'I don't suppose I could take a look at that photograph in your building?' she asked then. 'Just to be sure.'

'In the foyer? Sorry, no,' the girl laughed. 'I'm afraid today was our last day of term before Christmas. But can I ask you why you're looking for her?'

Darcy bit her lip. 'How long do you have?'

Chapter 33

I had so much restless energy that I had been walking all over Manhattan with Bailey since that morning.

Stephanie Everly still had not called me back and here I was, the day before The Day, wondering how the hell I was going to pull this feat off in time. This was seriously bad.

Currently, I was walking down Sixth Avenue, somewhat aimlessly, passing Radio City Music Hall on my left, taking note of the throngs of tourists waiting in line for the annual *Rockette's Christmas Spectacular*.

I thought of last year, when Mel insisted that we go to see it, even though the attraction was a mecca for tourists. She said that she didn't care, she just loved the Rockettes, and despite my cynicism I had to admit that it was good fun. Still, most things she suggested turned out to be fun; that was one of the joys of spending time with her. That and her boundless enthusiasm for life.

I had an idea for something different this Christmas though, something I knew she'd enjoy, and had picked up the tickets from the Koch Theater box office earlier. The New York City Ballet's performance of the *The Nutcracker* was as much a city tradition as the Rockettes at this time of year. One that I figured Mel was especially likely to appreciate.

Trudging on, I stopped at Magnolia Bakery on the next block. While it had always been popular, it had now gone interstellar thanks to being featured on that TV show. Perhaps not surprisingly, I'd never watched it.

Still, regardless of the fact that the place was now almost always overrun with glamorous city-girl wannabes who don't look as if they eat a lettuce leaf let alone a cupcake, I stopped off to pick up a red velvet for Bailey and a chocolate vanilla for myself.

Un-macho perhaps, but it was still an old favourite for both of us.

The sugar gave me a temporary boost but I couldn't escape the feeling that I was like an inmate on Death Row. Here I was, less than twenty-four hours from when I should be making the delivery, and I was currently standing around empty-handed. Well, apart from the cupcake.

'What now, Bailey?'

He peered up at me with those big blue eyes that said, '*No idea; let's just keep walking.*'

And so we did. And the cold barely even affected me. In fact, we walked so long that I felt I was taking in most sight-seeing tours around Manhattan.

I wished that I had more time like this to take in the sights and the sounds that made the city just so special at this time of year. I remembered something Tom Wolfe had said about how 'one belongs to New York instantly, one belongs to it as much in five minutes as in five years'. That resonated with me and indeed spoke of how I felt about this city.

I knew that some people didn't get it – Ciara a case in point. As worldly as she was, she was happiest in California. I tried to get her to move across one time but she wouldn't. 'Only for fun and shopping,' she said. 'I couldn't do perma-nent.' And I think she had an eye on returning home to Dublin sometime too, though that would never be a consid-eration for me. That was where we grew up, where our family home had been, and some people found it much harder than others to abandon their roots. It pained me a little to realise that I hadn't been back to the place in over seven years. But life – and admittedly work – always somehow got in the way.

Suddenly Bailey came to a stop and I emerged from the fog I had been in and finally paid attention long enough to realise that we were all the way down in Greenwich Village. I looked in the direction that we were heading and saw that Washington Square Park loomed ahead of us.

'You want to take a breather, big guy? Get some water?' I asked. He panted, his tongue almost dropping to the ground and I took that as a yes.

We headed into the Park where I found a drinking fountain and filled up his portable mesh and plastic dish that I always carried with me. I sat down on a bench and placed the water dish at my feet.

Bailey drank happily and I took a moment to slip my wallet out of my pocket. Thinking about family and Ireland and all of it had made me feel slightly melancholy. Maybe because it was so close to the holidays.

I opened my wallet and flipped through the pictures, finding the black and white one I wanted. Mam.

I don't think she was more than seventeen or eighteen in this picture. All dressed up to go to Mass or something. Ciara and I had only found it after she'd died and I wished that there had been an opportunity for her to tell me where she had been going, or what she had been doing, or if she had met Dad yet when the picture had been taken.

Hell, I wish I even knew what colour her dress was. I know it sounds silly, but with this picture I felt that there was a whole other side to my mother that I didn't know about. Something that she didn't tell Ciara and me as kids. I always said that if and when I ever had kids I would make sure they knew whatever they wanted to know about me. History was important at the end of the day.

Bailey finished drinking and then looked up at me, sending the signal that he was ready to start walking again.

Crossing Sixth Avenue again we headed back uptown. Several times I felt myself pulling Bailey back towards me, aiming to avoid being hit by a bicycle messenger – a crazy breed who effortlessly rule Manhattan's streets while also endangering each and every one of us in their path.

I'm all about physical fitness and being kind to the environment by using alternative transport methods and all that, but seriously, watch where you are going.

Or, to quote many a New Yorker: 'Hey, I'm walking here!'

Chapter 34

You are braver than you believe, stronger than you seem, and smarter than you think. **A.A. Milne**

The following morning, people seemed to look at Darcy differently this time as, leash in hand and dog at her heels, she strolled along the Upper West Side passing by the same fancy bistros, the same five-star restaurants, modelling studios and funky furniture stores. Although she was wearing the usual comfortable work clothes, and her usual messily-tied ponytail bounced on her shoulders, now she noticed an accepting nod from the other city-dwellers as she passed them by.

The old women in their silken scarves and two thousand-dollar bags gave her space on the path. The hipster dudes in their Converse hi-tops, three hundred-dollar skinny jeans and designer stubble grinned at her and Bailey.

The couples with their shopping bags from places like

Henri Bendel, Bloomingdales and Comptoir des Cotonniers beamed at the dignified Husky, their eyes warm and suddenly neighbourly.

If a pure-bred dog was all it took to feel like you belonged in this part of town, Darcy thought to herself, Bailey gliding jauntily along at her heels, she should have got herself one years ago. And she couldn't deny that these days she was feeling emboldened with the people she'd spoken to and the places she'd been to in her quest to try and help Aidan. It was almost as if she'd found a new sense of connection with the city and was more certain of her place in it.

But while she would be happy to see Bailey reunited with his owner, she was really sorry to see him go, though not nearly as sorry as Grace, who'd showered the big dog with beef jerky sticks and kisses almost all the way down the stairs on their way out this morning.

'Do you think he could come back and visit sometime?' her neighbour had pleaded as Darcy affixed him to the lead, the big dog licking her hand as she caressed his head, reluctant to let him go.

'I'm sure Aidan will want to thank you for taking care of him,' Darcy reassured her, although she herself had no idea what was going to happen next; if any of them would see either Bailey or indeed his owner again after today.

Aidan had wanted to arrange a car to collect them both from her apartment but Darcy had refused, preferring to take her time and enjoy one last walk with Bailey on this bright clear Manhattan morning. As such, the journey to work would take a good hour longer than usual but she decided it was well worth it.

The weather was brisk, and having chosen to take the more scenic path, she stopped en route at Bryant Park for breakfast – a bagel and orange juice for her, and a hot dog and bottled water for Bailey.

Darcy sat on one of the chairs beside the Park's ice rink – still empty at this early hour – and watched the artisan vendors of the holiday shops ready their prettily decorated huts with souvenirs, crafts and artwork for the day. Bailey lapped water from the bottle as she held it out for him and scarfed the hot dog – even the bun – down in seconds flat.

He licked his lips, full of energy now and circling her feet as they continued onwards, the city coming alive with the early rush, and the threat of fresh snow as the morning stretched on.

Bailey had gradually been getting more and more skittish and excited as they skirted Columbus Circle and wandered along familiar territory, and by the way he was pulling against the leash Darcy knew he was looking forward to being reunited with his owner after the last few days' separation.

Either that, or being reunited with his Dean & DeLuca dog food!

Though the hospital had reluctantly agreed to let Aidan discharge himself, Dr Mandeville was insisting on a final check-up that morning before he left her care, which meant that Bailey would be home before his master, given that Darcy needed to drop him off early to make it in time for work.

But Aidan shouldn't be too much later, and if anything it would be a nice opportunity for man and dog to get reacquainted on familiar territory. She just hoped that something would click for Aidan once he was back in his own environment, surrounded by his own things, and a space in which he felt comfortable.

Aidan had promised to call her to confirm that he'd safely retrieved the key (she hoped he'd remember that they'd agreed to hide it in the soil of the potted maple) and was settled – and after that, well – Darcy wasn't entirely sure what would happen.

Based on what she'd learned at the ballet school last night, she was going to try and track down Melanie Rothschild and explain what had happened. Given that there was a genuine reason behind whatever mix-up had occurred on the day of the accident, Darcy hoped that this, combined with the revelation that Aidan had been on his way to deliver a special gift to her, should mollify the woman.

But even if Aidan's memory remained problematic in the meantime, it wouldn't be long before all the people who'd been trying to get in touch and were worried about his safety would eventually make contact, and no doubt everything else would fall into place after that.

She felt saddened by this, and it wasn't all down to her admission to Grace the other night. It was more the fact that her quest to figure out Aidan's story would be over.

And Darcy could never abandon any tale until she knew the ending.

Chapter 35

There is no friend as loyal as a book. **Ernest Hemingway**

Later at Chaucer's, Darcy updated Joshua and Ashley on her recent adventures.

'You'll be glad to know that you won't need to worry about sharing your workspace with any wolves from now on,' she teased Joshua.

He listened, eyebrows raised, while Ashley unpacked boxes nearby. 'What was that you said about talking to somebody called Cleaver-Parks?' he asked, looking thoughtful. 'I recognise that name from somewhere.'

Darcy looked at him. Where on earth would her flamboyant man-about-town, book-geek colleague have come across a decidedly older, crotchety gent like the one Darcy had recently spoken to?

At this Ashley perked up too. 'Senior or Junior?' she asked.

Both Joshua and Darcy turned in unison towards the younger girl. 'What do you mean?'

'Nate Cleaver-Parks – which one were you trying to get in touch with?' she asked simply. 'There's a Senior and a Junior.'

Then it clicked. *Father and son.* 'So that explains it!' Darcy exclaimed. 'I'm guessing that the guy I talked to was Senior and maybe the one who actually phoned Aidan was Junior?'

Ashley nodded. 'Yes, Nate Junior is my age or so.'

Darcy blinked, surprised. 'Sounds like you might actually know this guy then? Nate Junior, that is.'

The younger girl shrugged. 'Of course I do. I've known him since I was a kid. Our families are good friends.'

'Wow.' Darcy couldn't believe what she was hearing. 'Well, he obviously knows Aidan too, so if I could speak to him then maybe I can let him know what's happened and maybe he might even know Melanie,' she said, her anticipation running away with her.

Ashley waved a hand and smiled. 'Sure, I can give him a quick call now. Like I said, I've known him forever, it's no big deal.' She stood up straight, brushed book dust off her jeans and headed towards the cash desk, taking out an up-to-the-minute designer handbag from underneath.

'I honestly don't know why you're even paid to work here, considering you carry around a bag like that,' Joshua commented balefully. 'If anything, this place should be asking *you* for financing.'

Ashley grinned. 'Oh come on. It was a gift. You know I'm just a starving college grad.'

326

He rolled his eyes. 'Daddy's girl.'

Ignoring their banter, Darcy waited for Ashley to place the call, berating herself for giving up so easily the other day. But how could she possibly have guessed there would be two Nate Cleaver-Parks?

Ashley hit some buttons on her phone and a moment later she cooed, 'Nate, sweetie, I haven't spoken to you in forever ...'

Darcy watched her intently, hoping they'd get through the preliminary chitchat soon so Ashley could get to the point of the call. The girl made eye-contact with Darcy and winked.

'Anyway Nate, yes, I am totally up for some fun on New Year's Eve. I heard something about a bash that Kanye is promoting downtown? I'm sure we could get in.' She laughed and Joshua tutted, mouthing the words 'unbelievable' with an incredulous glance at Ashley. She ignored him. 'So anyway, there is a purpose to my call ...'

The young woman paused, listening to whatever Nate had to say. Darcy made circular motions with both of her hands, urging her to speed things up as the suspense was killing her. Luckily for Darcy's heart-rate, Ashley duly moved the conversation on. 'I'm here with a friend of mine, my boss at the bookstore. She's trying to find this guy, it's actually a really crazy story, but we're pretty sure you know him—' Ashley stopped talking abruptly, obviously cut off. She let out a giggle. 'No, I'm pretty sure you aren't dating this guy. In fact, I think that he is straight, at least my friend thinks so.'

Darcy gulped, a bit taken aback, but it was certainly an angle she'd never even thought to consider.

327

'Anyway. So like I said, you must know him or have talked to him or something. You left a message on his answering machine earlier this week. His name is Aidan Harris?'

Ashley went quiet as she listened intently to whatever Nate was saying.

Darcy paced the floor, dying to know what they were talking about or what was developing.

Soon Ashley continued her end of the conversation. 'Well, that's interesting,' she said, 'and it does fit in with a lot of what my friend has been thinking. She's been running all over the city trying to track down someone who knows him.' She paused. 'No, no, I get that. But maybe what you know can help Darcy?' Another pause. 'Yes, that's my friend. The one who knows Aidan. Well, sort of. It's kind of a weird story.' Ashley listened again. 'Well, he couldn't have got your message because he is actually in the hospital right now.' She nodded. 'Sorry, yes, of course you didn't know that.' More listening, and Darcy felt like wrenching the phone away from her. 'OK. Yes, she's right here.'

Ashley held the phone out to Darcy.

'Here you go,' she said. 'Nate wants to talk to you.'

Chapter 36

'Aidan Harris? Stephanie Everly here. I understand that you have been trying to get in touch with me,' a woman said in clipped tones on the other end of the line. Before I could continue, she went on: 'I heard from Nate Cleaver-Parks that you are interested in Miller's collection.'

'Yes,' I said, wanting to punch the air. Instead I crossed my fingers. 'I am. And I would seriously be thrilled if he might consider brokering a deal with me, say today?'

I bit my lip, trying not to sound so desperate. I really would be slaughtered in Atlantic City.

'I see. Well, I can't arrange anything that quickly without consulting him first, and he's travelling in Europe at the moment, but we will be back in contact later today. However,

I can confirm that like most collectors, Miller is always willing to entertain any interest in his portfolio, particularly at the right price.'

She left the obvious implication hanging and I closed my eyes, not sure whether to be relieved or frightened.

So it could happen – but only if the price was right.

'In the meantime, would you like to come out to the house and inspect the collection – see if the edition in question meets your requirements? I'm aware of your tight timeline.'

'What – now? Today?' I asked, in some disbelief.

'Yes, now,' Stephanie said simply. She recited an address in Westchester County, a good forty-minute taxi ride from Manhattan. 'I'll meet you there.'

I hung up the phone, unable to believe my luck. Two days to D-day and finally I had a lead. A good one.

I took off at a pace, practically dragging Bailey along beside me. He was looking at me as if I had lost my mind. I briefly considered going back to the house and dropping him off, but I was all the way downtown and there was precious little time to waste.

Finally I found a cab that would take us to Westchester County and allow a dog like Bailey in the car. When I say 'a dog like Bailey' I'm referring to his size and the fact that he is obviously not of the tea-cup variety that Paris Hilton made famous.

Of course, the reason the driver accepted us was obvious as soon as we sat inside. The cab smelled like a mixture of falafel, sweaty gym socks, curry and quite possibly ferret, and appeared as if it had not received a good cleaning in about a year and a half.

Nonetheless, beggars, choosers and all that ...

We reached the address that Stephanie Everly had given me in just under thirty-five minutes; it was a sprawling country estate upon which sat a steep-roofed three-storey stone Beaux Arts mansion with a view of the city skyline twenty-five miles to the south.

It immediately brought to mind the Pemberley Estate in *Pride and Prejudice*. I paid the driver and helped Bailey out of the car. Damn, I thought, looking from the Husky to the house and back again. Definitely not a good combination. But maybe they were dog-lovers here? Estates like this usually had a couple of resident dogs ambling around somewhere.

Holding tight to Bailey's lead, I walked up the stone steps towards the front entrance, whereupon one of a pair of heavy wooden doors opened and there, waiting for us was a woman I assumed to be Stephanie Everly.

She wore a black pant suit that looked specifically tailored for her petite size two frame, and her shocking red hair was pulled expertly back into an elegant knot at the nape of her neck.

'Aidan Harris?' she asked.

'That's me.'

Stephanie's gaze flickered to Bailey and she looked as if she was calculating the approximate amount of dog hair that would be left behind in the house after his departure.

Uh-oh.

'And this is Bailey,' I offered lamely. 'Sorry, I came here immediately after your call and didn't have time to—'

'Great name.' Much to my surprise, she gave a broad smile. 'I grew up with Huskies. They are dreadful shedders though.'

'Should I ask him not to do that while he's here?' I joked.

Stephanie gave a small laugh. 'Between you and me, I'm a total dog person,' she said, 'but the lady of the house is not. Do you think he could possibly wait here in the foyer?' Before I could say anything, she offered further explanation. 'It's not that she doesn't like dogs. She is just allergic. Terribly so. I apologise.'

I held up a hand. 'No worries, I'm not offended, I completely understand and I don't plan on taking up too much of your time in any case. Bailey can certainly hang back, can't you, boy?' I asked my four-legged friend, who looked up at me and seeming to acquiesce, promptly took a seat on his haunches.

'Smart,' said Stephanie with raised eyebrows. 'Well-trained too.'

'Smarter than me most days,' I said, giving him a last pat on the head.

I followed Stephanie deeper into the bowels of the luxurious home, taking in the décor. While I was used to nice surroundings, this place put the townhouse to shame.

Though many of the people I mixed with in New York these days had come into money, I could tell that the people who lived in this place had been born with it and had certifiable blue blood coursing through their veins.

As I walked, my heels clicked on the marble floors, echoing off the walls around me. My eyes met with antique after antique. Sterling-silver frames littered tables and could be seen within the built-in bookcases. I was able to catch a quick look at some of the pictures, and it appeared that Stephanie's employers were definitely well-travelled, and also knew some very important people. The proof was displayed everywhere.

However, as she guided me through a sitting room, past a formal dining room containing a table which could easily fit thirty people, and onwards into a formal library that had floor-to-ceiling mahogany shelves and countless displays with what had to be rare manuscripts held under glass, I discovered something else.

This entire place was like a museum. It was a house, but not a home.

I thought back to the brownstone and recognised a couple of startling similarities between the two – and then I thought back to my family home in Dublin, my old house, and even some of the apartments that I had lived in over the years. Those were homes. Those were all places where you could hang your hat, put your feet up and let your dog roam around without worrying about making a mess.

Stephanie looked at me evenly. 'Just to say that when it comes to such dealings it's usually the prospective buyer who throws out a number initially. Especially when they reach out to us first, and we haven't advertised our intent to sell through the auction houses or some other resource.'

Ah, so that's how this was going to go. They wanted to see just how serious I was by what I was willing to offer right off the bat.

No matter.

I nodded. 'Understood.'

'Nate didn't tell me why your timeline was so tight but I can only assume delivery needs to be imminent.' She looked sideways at me. 'I'm aware of your company. Thrill Seeker Holdings has an interesting reputation.'

Ah, so she was going to take this route. Call me out on the fact that she knew my needs were urgent and that the company had the tendency to splash the cash.

'I must also admit that I'm a fan,' she added with a quiet smile, and I glanced at her, surprised and proud of how far and wide the franchise had reached.

'Delighted to hear it, thank you.' I nodded. 'But, you are right. I do need this wrapped up soon for various reasons – today, if possible.'

Stephanie considered what I had said.

'I see. Well, I will convey any offer you might have to Miller when I speak to him later. May I assume that there will be a first bid today and you are open to negotiation?'

I wasn't going to say more and overplay my hand.

'I think it might be good to take a look before we get into specifics, don't you?'

'Absolutely,' she said, leading me down some steps into a completely different part of the building. 'But rest assured, Miller has extremely high standards and everything in his collection is in impeccable condition. I don't think you'll be disappointed.'

'That's good to hear.' I took a small breath and thought about the leeway I had with the numbers. I knew what something like this should be worth on the open market, but this was a completely different market altogether.

Doing the elementary math, I kept my face impassive, realising that these days I seemed to no longer have any real appreciation for money, which if I wasn't careful could prove dangerous.

Opening another door, Stephanie led me into a huge open space, almost hangar-like in its appearance. 'Here we are. I moved it up to the front for you to take a better look.' She smiled. 'I assume this is what you are looking for?'

Following her gaze, I took in the rows upon rows neatly lined up together, and then let out a low whistle as I finally laid eyes on my prize.

And it was perfect.

Chapter 37

Beware of false knowledge; it is more dangerous than ignorance. **George Bernard Shaw**

Walking brusquely with the cold wind in her face, Darcy went to meet Nate Cleaver-Parks. She'd wanted to arrange something after work or at least during her lunch-hour, but Joshua had been insistent. 'Are you kidding me? Go – Ash and I will hold the fort. And I want to see how this thing works out as much as anyone.' He'd even gone so far as to rustle up one of his famous 'Joshua bucks', agreeing to stay on and cover her for the later shift as he bustled her out of the door.

Darcy was just as eager to hear what the only person she'd come across so far who definitely knew Aidan had to say, so she made her way to the arranged meeting spot – Bomboloni, a popular Upper West Side eaterie and an apparent favourite of Nate's. Darcy had heard of the little Italian

bakery but had never sampled one of its famed bomboloni –
miniature light pastry doughnuts filled with various fruit and
crème flavourings.

Turning on Sixty-Ninth Street on to Columbus Avenue, she
looked up and saw a sign for the place up ahead. There was
plenty of outdoor seating, and despite the cold almost all of
the tables were full, the overhead heat lamps helping the
bakery's customers brave the elements.

Nearing the entrance, Darcy began scanning faces beneath
the red-striped awning. While she didn't know what Nate
looked like, he'd told her on the phone that he would be wearing a red velvet Prada jacket (though Darcy couldn't tell Prada
from JC Penney), was about six foot tall and had sandy-blond
hair. She'd thought that was a pretty run-of-the-mill description, but when she clapped eyes on Nate Cleaver-Parks, she
realised that he was anything but run-of-the-mill.

In fact, he was drop-dead gorgeous. Of the male model
variety.

Sitting at a table closest to the building and (thankfully)
right beneath a heat lamp, he was in his mid-twenties, had a
finely chiselled jaw and bright blue eyes that caught your
attention, broad muscular shoulders and the build of an ath-
lete. She wondered if he played lacrosse for Harvard.

Nate seemed to know Darcy right off the bat; probably
because she'd said she would be carrying a book. And as Nate
stood up to greet her, every female in the vicinity turned to
look, as if envious that he had his sights set on her.

If only they knew.

She smiled and walked forward to say hello.

'Darcy? Darcy Archer?' he enquired, indicating her copy of *Pride and Prejudice*. 'Hardly surprising you'd be carrying that book, given your name,' he added jokingly, and for this Darcy liked him immediately.

'Lovely to meet you, Nate,' she said, holding out a hand to shake his. 'And thanks so much for taking the time to talk to me.'

'Not a problem,' Nate said pleasantly. 'I was heading down this way anyhow, and seeing as you weren't far ...' He held out a chair for her and Darcy sat down right beside the window that looked into the little bakery.

Tiny inside, it was decorated with pretty Sicilian tiling and handcrafted wooden honeycomb on the ceiling, but most important was the big glass display case filled with a selection of mouth-watering pastries.

'Anything in particular you like?' Nate said, following her gaze. 'My favourite's the Nutella and passion fruit – a strange combination but it somehow works.'

'I'm not sure, I've never actually been here,' she admitted.

'Ah well then, we'll have to find you a favourite. I'll order a mixed half-dozen,' he said. 'Coffee too?'

'Tea thanks,' she replied. A half-dozen? While the doughnuts were small they still looked like they could pack a punch, but Darcy had to admit she was interested in trying out some of the delicious flavours Nate talked about: pistachio, tiramisu and blood orange to name but a few.

Ever the gentleman he went in to place the order, while

Darcy waited outside, grateful for the warmth of the heat lamp.

'OK, so tell me all about your friend Aidan Harris,' he said, once they were both settled with the hot drinks and a box of fresh pastries in front of them. 'Given that I barely know this guy, I'm intrigued as to why you or Ashley think I can help.'

'You barely know him?' Darcy was disappointed. She'd hoped that Nate was a good friend or at least a business acquaintance of Aidan's.

'Yes. Just helped him out with a favour recently, but that's it.'

But it was this 'favour' that might just hold the key to everything, Darcy thought.

She bit into a delicious honey-flavoured bomboloni and began her story, filling Nate in on everything that had happened since she'd quite literally run into Aidan a few days before, and how the phone message Nate had left on his answering machine had led her to him today.

When she'd finished, he looked briefly past her and down the street as if considering something, and then returned his gaze to peer inquisitively at her.

'OK, a couple of things aren't adding up for me here.'

'How so?'

'I realise that you've since found this dancer Melanie, and that she was leaving messages on his phone too, but how do you know she's his girlfriend?'

'Well, I don't know for sure,' Darcy replied, 'but it certainly points in that direction, doesn't it? The first message on the answering machine, especially. She was clearly expecting Aidan on that day – a significant day for her or the two of them even, maybe an anniversary – and then when he failed to turn up ...'

'But why would she be so furious with him for not turning up? Surely if she is a love interest, then shouldn't she be *concerned* rather than angry?'

Darcy sat back in her chair. 'I suppose that depends on how significant the occasion was.' But he was right; all those missed calls and the venom in Melanie's words during the most recent call didn't exactly suggest love's young dream.

Especially coupled with her parting shot.

'She did say something along the lines of how she didn't know how Aidan could keep track or something. I'm not sure – I'd have to listen to the message again.' Darcy knew she wasn't likely to get an opportunity to do that though, not with Aidan now safely ensconced in his home and once again in control of his phone messages, if not his life.

Reminded of this, she noted the time and surreptitiously checked her phone to see if there were any missed calls from him. It was almost midday and she figured he'd be home by now. She hoped Bailey was OK. She was missing him already.

But there was nothing.

'Well, if she thinks he can't keep track then maybe he can't,' Nate said. 'Granted I only spoke to him once or twice, but I must admit I didn't think he seemed the type.'

'Type?'

'To have a string of women running after him.'

Darcy felt a bit nauseous at the thought. 'Well, I guess it takes all kinds. So you think I might be wrong then about him being on his way to deliver the gift to Melanie?'

'I really can't say. I'm just pointing out that you can't assume that she was the person he was on his way to meet. Heck, what's to say he was going to meet anyone? Maybe the guy was just taking his dog out for a walk, have you considered that?'

'But the package ... it's so beautifully wrapped, very considered, and with all the mention of D-day, it has to be a gift for ...' Then Darcy remembered why she was here with Nate in the first place. 'In your message to Aidan you said something like you hoped he got what he needed before the Big Day. Were you involved in that somehow? Arranging the gift, I mean?'

Nate looked dubiously at her. 'Me? How so?'

'Well then, why did you say it? And why were you phoning him in the first place?'

'To follow up. He was looking to do some business, and I put him in touch with a contact who could help him but,' he chuckled, 'believe me, this was no little wrapped package. Unless ...' He took out his phone.

'Unless what?'

'I just want to check something with Stephanie; the contact I mentioned. See if Aidan did in fact get what he needed from her. Hold on.'

Thoroughly confused, Darcy stayed silent while Nate waited for the call to go through.

As he did so, she thought about what he'd said. Maybe he was right; maybe there was no big meeting, no special romantic occasion that Aidan was missing because he wasn't the romantic type. A part of her desperately hoped Nate was right. A big part, she secretly admitted.

Perhaps he'd let Melanie down somehow but it might have nothing to do with the gift or a meeting, and there was no denying that she did seem uncommonly angry for someone who Darcy assumed was very important to Aidan.

Then there was the suggestion that Aidan was a womaniser, in which case the gift could have been meant for anyone.

And what did Nate mean when he'd said that his involvement in the whole thing was something very different?

'I just got voicemail.' Nate's eyes narrowed. 'Honestly, Sherlock Archer, I think there's something off about your theory. We're missing something – apart from the fact that you have a crush, of course,' he added with a mischievous grin.

'I don't have a crush,' she said defensively. 'I barely know Aidan.'

'Oh sweetheart, please,' Nate replied. 'Tell it to someone else. You would have to be blind not to notice.'

Darcy was silent, not trusting herself to speak, while Nate tapped his fingers rapidly on the table. 'No, something is definitely not adding up here.'

'You think?' she chuckled, as she tried to cover her embarrassment. 'There is so much not right about this situation, I don't even know where to begin.'

Nate thought for a second. 'You said you have a picture of the woman you think is Melanie?' She confirmed that she did as Nate continued, 'Well, the other thing that I find weird is that if Aidan travels in the circles that you say he does, I feel like I would have heard of him long before all of this. And frankly, I haven't. On the phone, I certainly got the impression that he was new money – but not big-shot arrogant like the way these guys can be sometimes. Can I see the picture of this alleged love interest?'

Darcy reached inside her bag. 'So it *is* a rule that all rich people in New York have to know each other then,' she said, extracting the picture and sliding it across the table. 'I mean, it is a big city.'

Nate took the picture and peered at it. 'No, it's not a rule *per se*, it's just how things are. I'm not trying to sound like a snob, but it's just a fact. You see the same people at parties and events. Dullsville. It is what it is. People with money know other people with money.'

Darcy pointed at the picture. 'So? Do you know *her*?'

Nate concentrated. 'She looks familiar, but she also has to be older than me by at least eight or ten years, and that's depending on what kind of work she's had done. Unfortunately, I'm not the right person to ask about this. I might know some of the players, but I'm not into the cocktail-party scene just yet. Did you show this to Tabitha Kensington when you met her?'

'No, I didn't know if it was important at the time, and anyway Aidan had it at the hospital. Why, do you think she might be a friend of Tabitha's?' Now that *would* make some sense. But if Tabitha and Melanie knew each other, then why wouldn't she have recognised Aidan's name that time at Elizabeth Arden? It was all very confusing, but interesting that Nate had mentioned Tabitha Kensington all the same. Clearly she tied into this thing somehow.

'All right. That settles it.' He grabbed his velvet jacket and extracted his wallet from a pocket. Throwing a couple of twenties on the table, he put his coat on and motioned her to follow him. 'I've left her a message. Come on. We're done here. We can kill two birds with one stone. Stephanie is sure to be able to fill in the missing pieces.'

Chapter 38

When all the details fit in perfectly, something is probably wrong with the story. **Charles Baxter**

Nate led Darcy through the gilded doors of a stunning Park Avenue apartment building. Feeling intimidated by the opulence of the lobby, she hung back momentarily, but her companion continued on with the air of someone who felt completely at home in such an environment.

Still confused as to where they were going, she followed Nate to where he stood at the concierge desk. The man on the other side of the podium seemed to recognise Nate and allowed his eyes to flicker over Darcy.

'We're here to see Stephanie Everly in the penthouse,' said Nate.

The concierge picked up the phone, confirmed something and then nodded in their direction. 'Ms Everly has said you should go straight up. Take this elevator for the pent-house.'

Darcy gulped nervously, wondering what to expect. Moments later they were whisked up from the lobby to the top floor, where the elevator doors opened immediately into a large reception area. A woman stood, waiting to greet them.

Nate quickly made the introductions. 'Darcy meet Steph. Steph, Darcy.'

'Nice to meet you,' said the beautifully dressed and perfectly made-up woman. She then turned to Nate. 'I must admit, I was rather bewildered by your message.'

Nate put a casual arm around Stephanie's shoulder. 'Steph, like I said, Darcy here has had a mixed-up couple of days, to say the least. Can we go inside? Then we can tell you the whole story.'

Stephanie agreed and led the way into a nearby living room. When all were seated comfortably, she looked in expectation at Darcy and Nate.

Darcy sighed forlornly at the realisation that she would have to tell the entire story of how she had come to know Aidan once again, but hopeful that she was close to finding some answers, she went ahead. When she finished speaking, Stephanie was nodding thoughtfully.

'Oh dear, I'm very sorry to hear about Aidan's amnesia. He seemed like a nice man,' she said.

Darcy sat forward, pleased that Stephanie had revealed that she'd actually met Aidan and also that her opinion of him concurred with her own. 'Yes, he is.'

'I'm not entirely sure how I can help you, though,' Steph went on. 'I only met him once last week when he came out to Westchester – where the main residence is,' she added for Darcy's benefit, 'to see Miller's collection. I originally called him to set up a viewing and then afterwards to confirm the deal and arrange delivery. Then once more a couple of days ago to confirm receipt of the wire, but I couldn't get him on either his cell or the office.'

So it seemed this Stephanie was some kind of personal assistant to the guy Aidan had been dealing with, and was involved in the sale of something in her boss's collection. Which explained at least one of the missed phone calls to the house, Darcy thought, her mind racing now. The boss's name 'Miller' seemed familiar for some reason, but she couldn't recall why.

'Ah, so he did get all that figured out in time,' Nate was saying.

'Yes. Thanks for the recommendation, by the way,' Stephanie smiled at him. 'Miller was very pleased with the sale price.'

Now Darcy was even more intrigued about the gift. Given that Aidan had bought it from a millionaire's 'collection', it seemed like her suspicions were correct, and it was indeed some kind of rare or collectable book. But which book? she wondered, desperate to find out.

'Arrange delivery?' Darcy repeated, tuning back into their conversation. 'So Aidan wasn't going to deliver it himself?' Delivery was an awfully impersonal word to describe presenting an important gift to a girlfriend or someone you loved, she thought.

Stephanie smiled as if she'd said something funny. 'Not if he needed it in LA by the following day, no.'

'LA?' Now she was baffled. Darcy studied Stephanie and asked the question that had been bothering her all the way over here, but which Nate wouldn't reveal until he'd spoken to his friend. 'Stephanie, do you mind telling me what exactly Aidan was buying from you?'

'I'm sorry – I thought you already knew that,' she said. 'And he was buying it not from me but from Miller, of course. It was a car. A special edition vintage Shelby Mustang, to be exact.'

'Oh.' Now Darcy felt a bit silly. The rich truly were different. And so much for Aidan being eco-friendly.

She was about to ask Stephanie more about it, when somebody else walked into the room.

'Stephanie?' a woman asked in a harried voice – one which Darcy recognised immediately. 'You haven't seen that invitation to the Library benefit on New Year's Eve, have you? I remember the invite coming in and realise that it's on both Miller's and my calendar, but I've just received a call from the steering committee and they said—'

Then Darcy understood exactly why the name 'Miller' rang a bell and exactly whose house this was.

Things were finally starting to fall into place.

It was Tabitha Kensington, this time without the Elizabeth Arden robe and mud mask, who was married to Miller Kensington, the man from whom Aidan had bought a car last week.

Tabitha was obviously in a rush, and was caught offguard by the fact that her husband's assistant had guests. 'Oh, I do apologise Stephanie, I didn't realise you were in a meeting, but— oh, don't I know you?' she said, gazing at Darcy for a moment as if trying to recall where exactly she had come across her before. 'That's right, at Elizabeth Arden a couple of days ago. Daisy, isn't it?'

Darcy stood up and shook Tabitha's extended hand. 'Darcy actually, and it's nice to see you again.'

The woman's gaze flicked to Nate. 'Home for the holidays, I take it? How's your father?' The two duly exchanged niceties and once that was over, Tabitha turned again to Stephanie. 'So you'll check on that invite?' she asked again, before turning to leave.

Stephanie nodded. 'Right away.'

Then Tabitha stopped and looked at Darcy again, as if only then remembering what they'd talked about. 'So I hope everything worked out with your friend – what was his name again?'

'Aidan. Aidan Harris.' And Darcy now understood that it was Stephanie who'd made the call to Aidan's house on the day of the accident from the Kensington residence to, as she'd said, 'confirm the wire transfer'.

For a car. Her head was well and truly spinning. 'Yes, I think I'm just about getting some answers,' she added politely.

'Aidan Harris is the man who bought Miller's '66 Shelby last week,' said Stephanie, and Tabitha's face lit up with recognition.

'Ah. And this is the same guy you ran down with your bike, is that correct?'

She nodded mutely.

'Well, Darcy, I'm awfully sorry for not being able to clear this up when you met me at Elizabeth Arden, but as you can see, I wasn't involved in the deal. To be honest, I can't keep up with my husband and his dealings in any case. Boys and their toys, eh?' she tittered pleasantly. 'But I do know Miller was very pleased to see it splashed across the papers in LA last week though. That Will Anderson seems quite a showman. Well, I'd better go and leave you to it – busy busy!' she trilled. 'But it was so nice to see you again – you too, Nate.' With that Tabitha Kensington left the room but Darcy barely noticed her go.

'Will Anderson, the thriller author?' she repeated. The one her aunt had tried to set her up with before. Now Darcy was seriously confused. Chaucer's sold dozens of Will's books per week. Right now, their front window display featured the movie tie-in edition of his first novel *Thrill Seeker* ...

Suddenly, something else clicked into place.

'Yes,' Stephanie said. 'I couldn't understand why Aidan was so desperate to secure the car, but then he explained all about how Will wanted it in time for the movie premiere in LA.' When Darcy remained silent she continued, 'If you read the *Thrill Seeker* books, I'm sure you know that Max Bailey drives a '66 Mustang Shelby. Aidan said Anderson was desperate to roll up to the première of his own movie in it.'

'Like James Bond and his Aston Martin?' Nate raised an

immaculate eyebrow. 'I must admit I've never read the books, but it sounds like the guy has style.'

'Oh, you really should,' Stephanie said. 'Max Bailey is amazing.'

Darcy was dumbfounded. And yet, little by little, things began slotting into place: the name of the company – Thrill Seeker, after Will Anderson's series of super-successful books. And then . . . Bailey. Named after Max Bailey, the action hero star of those same books?

But then how did Aidan come into it all? Was he an author too, a friend of Will's who worked under a pseudonym maybe?

The discovery was very exciting, and completely fit with Aidan's apparent fixation on literature, and of course his wonderful book collection, Darcy thought happily.

He truly was a kindred spirit.

'I know Aidan was really delighted to have secured the car in time, though relieved too, I'd imagine,' Stephanie said before Darcy had a chance to say anything further. 'Will Anderson has a reputation for being . . . difficult, and I'm guessing an egotistical multi-millionaire author isn't the easiest person to work for. I don't envy your friend's life. Not for one minute.'

Chapter 39

The truth is rarely pure and never simple. **Oscar Wilde**

Afterwards, Nate offered to travel back in the taxi to Chaucer's with Darcy, lending her his ear and letting her talk through her confusion about all that she'd just learned.

'So Aidan works for Will Anderson? I can't believe it.'

Stephanie Everly seemed 100 per cent certain that Aidan was Anderson's assistant, business manager, fixer and general dogsbody. 'All of the usual things people like us are employed to do,' she'd explained with a patient smile.

Darcy's brain was reeling with the implications of the discovery.

'No wonder there was never any improvement in his memory,' she said, feeling truly idiotic now, 'when I constantly fed him the wrong information. Bringing him things that didn't even belong to him, and insisting that he was filthy rich and lived in this amazing— oh no!' she gasped as the thought struck her. 'The brownstone must be Will Anderson's house and Aidan had the keys simply because he is Will's assistant. And not only is the house not Aidan's, but Bailey must not be his dog either.'

'Unless he decided to name his dog after Anderson's fictional character?' Nate suggested. 'Anderson might be his boss but Aidan could well be a big fan too.'

'No, definitely not,' Darcy insisted. 'I'm pretty sure Bailey must be Will's, which is why he led me to the house in the first place, and—' Remembering something else, she leaned forward to talk to the taxi driver. 'Slight change of plan – can you take me to Seventy-Seventh and Park, please?'

She turned to Nate, panicked. 'I dropped Bailey off at the brownstone this morning, leaving him to wait for Aidan to come home from hospital.'

Oh Christ, this was such a mess. As far as Aidan knew, he lived in the Park Avenue house, and was probably there now trying to figure things out. Darcy could only imagine the poor guy's reaction when she had to explain that all of the information she'd been giving him over the last few days was completely wrong, that the house and the dog really belonged to someone else, and that ultimately she didn't have the first clue about Aidan's life - his *real* life.

She thought about Nate's description of him being a general dogsbody. Would this have extended to his literally walking Will's dog too?

Why else would they have been together on that fateful

morning, and why was Bailey the only thing that Aidan could remember when he came to after the accident? And then there was the gift . . .

There were so many things that Darcy still couldn't get her head around, and she struggled to figure out what to do next.

'Well, just drop me off at the end of Fifth then,' Nate said, patting her arm. 'And try not to worry; I'm sure Aidan is fine. With the way things happened you couldn't have known that the house wasn't his, and you were only trying to help the guy, after all.'

'Yes, and look what an almighty mess I made of that,' Darcy said, biting her lip. In trying to reconstruct Aidan's life for him, her imagination had completely run away with her and had created something a million miles from reality.

'Like I said, I'm sure Aidan will understand,' Nate soothed. 'It was an easy mistake to make. It'll all work out for the best and everyone will live happily ever after.'

Easy mistake? Darcy just hoped Aidan felt that way when she had to break the news to him that he wasn't after all a super-wealthy millionaire.

She then thought about how she herself felt upon discovering the truth about the man she had become quite close to over the last few days, and realised that for her at least, the new information didn't change anything.

True, she knew for sure that Aidan was smart, handsome and well-read, but she'd also assumed that he must be sophisticated, go-getting and worldly, based on his house, hobbies and possessions. Darcy definitely didn't care about the money aspect; that was something that wasn't even on her list of attributes the way it might be to some women, and she'd grown to be much more interested in Aidan as a person, what made him tick, his likes and dislikes.

But she couldn't escape the fact that in the midst of creating her own fairy tale, she'd overlooked many aspects to the story that were still unaccounted for, some now glaringly obvious pieces in the jigsaw of Aidan's life that she couldn't decipher.

Why for example had nobody come looking for him over the last few days? Granted Will Anderson was away in LA and busy with his film première all week, which might explain why Aidan's boss hadn't missed him, but what about others, especially the intended recipient of the gift? And if he didn't live in the Upper West Side house, then where did he actually live? As the taxi snaked its way through the traffic along Fifth Avenue, she heard her phone ring.

Her heart pounding as she caught sight of the display, she answered it quickly and immediately launched straight into conversation. 'Aidan, are you OK? Have you reached the house yet?'

'I'm really sorry to bother you again, Darcy, but this is weird,' he said, sounding confused. 'I'm actually in Long Island. The hospital ordered a cab to drop me home and then I notice the guy brings me straight out of town – so I check my ID and funnily enough ...'

Darcy's mind raced. She remembered the doctor talking about how they'd got Aidan's address from his ID, which would of course, she realised now, have shown his real address.

Long Island, the Mets keyring – it all made sense.

But because Bailey had been so insistent about taking her to the brownstone, and the fact that Aidan had keys to it, she had never once queried his address or thought to double-check it on his ID. Notwithstanding that people's addresses weren't always up to date in any case; not everyone made it a priority to inform the authorities every time they moved.

'OK,' she said to Aidan, trying not to betray her anxiety. 'Tell you what, can you ask the driver to come back to Manhattan? I'll meet you somewhere, say ...' Darcy racked her brains trying to figure out a place nearby where she could sit down and try to explain everything, somewhere quiet but not too quiet, just in case Aidan didn't take the news so well. Nate nudged her and she looked out the window to where he was pointing further down the road. The Plaza Hotel. 'The Park,' Darcy said, shaking her head. Nate was rolling his eyes but there was no way she was going to break the news in a place like that, which would merely serve to remind Aidan of all that he had lost. Or rather never had. 'I'll meet you at the corner entrance across from the Plaza Hotel, right in front of the carriages?'

Aidan chuckled a little. 'I don't know – I'm not sure I have enough cash on me to make it back.' And Darcy winced afresh as she remembered how she'd practically cleaned out his wallet in order to get him that prepaid phone. 'Well then, the subway,' she blurted out, thinking on her feet. 'Travel back in the cab as far as you can and then take the subway from there, OK? Just be sure you have the phone with you too and I'll meet you outside the Park subway entrance.'

'OK, thanks – are you sure it's convenient for you? I know you're probably at work. Look, Darcy, I'm really sorry to be such a pest again; I still don't really know what happened. Is Bailey all right?'

She wanted to cry. How on earth was she going to explain to this lovely trusting man that she'd completely fabricated a life for him, one that seemed a world away from the actual truth?

He thought he lived in an amazing house with an incredible library, had travelled all over the world and seen exotic places, had his pick of gorgeous women and Bailey ... how on earth Darcy was going to break the news to Aidan that his beloved Husky wasn't actually his dog was beyond her. And she felt fleetingly annoyed at Bailey for allowing the confusion to happen at all, let alone allow it to continue. If he was smart enough to lead her to his house then surely he should have been smart enough to lead her to the truth. So much for the Lassie comparison.

'He's fine,' she said evasively. 'See you soon.'

Having said goodbye to Aidan, she sent a brief text to Joshua, apologising for her absence and saying that she'd be back at the store as soon as she could. He replied almost immediately telling her to take her time and that everything was under control. At least something was.

She took a deep breath and sat back for a moment, relieved at least that her colleagues were so generous and easy-going.

She wondered what Will Anderson was like to work for. Darcy only remembered him briefly from that time a year or so ago when Katherine introduced them at that party, but there was no denying that he was arrogant and completely in love with himself. She hoped he wasn't too hard on Aidan.

The day had become blustery and the wind had picked up, swirling the snow flurries around the car. Traffic was becoming slower and heavier as they inched alongside the Park on Fifth Avenue.

Darcy jumped as once again the phone buzzed in her pocket. She worried that Aidan had since got into some kind of fix or another, but it was a private number.

'Darcy? How are you? It's Jenna from the Apple Store.'

'Oh hi Jenna,' she replied tiredly, not really able to cope with the young girl's perky approach right then.

'Just to tell you that Head Office have since authorised a replacement iPhone for Mr Harris so we're ready to do the data transfer if you'd like to bring in the old handset.'

'OK – great, thanks.' Darcy had forgotten to leave the broken phone at the brownstone that morning, which had turned out to be a stroke of good luck. If she went to Apple now and did the data transfer, it should be much easier to break the news to Aidan, having to hand his information, photographs, et cetera – all the details of his life that had proven so far elusive. 'How about I call in now, in the next five minutes or so? I'm in the area and I have the phone with me. Or do I need to make an appointment?' She groaned inwardly at the thought.

'No, it's fine; I'll slot you in. The transfer should take just a few minutes anyway. See you then!'

'Great,' Darcy said dully, disconnecting the call. At this point, she felt like her brain was going to explode and wasn't entirely sure if she could actually handle one more piece of information about Aidan or his life – his *real* life – today.

She already had too many loose ends that she didn't understand. Still, it looked like today was truly the day for finding answers, and she thought about what Nate had said earlier about happy endings.

But life didn't always result in happy endings, this Darcy knew well. And when it came down to it, reality usually trumped fiction.

Chapter 40

Saved by the bell. Stephanie Everly had come through at the last minute, thank goodness.

Granted I had to offer a little more than I'd hoped to secure the car and to arrange immediate delivery to LA, but thanks to Nate Cleaver-Parks and his reliable contacts network, Thrill Seeker Holdings was now in possession of a beautiful Special Edition '66 Mustang Shelby.

It was an amazing vehicle and no doubt would soon be resold once it had outlived its initial usefulness, but for the moment it was Will's new toy, and a fitting way to mark the occasion and all the excitement surrounding the movie release in LA.

Sipping coffee, I glanced at the heavy snow falling outside the window this morning and wished I'd accepted the invitation to go out west for last night's première, but then remembered how much was still going on here. I checked my watch, knowing I'd better get a move on if I wanted to make it on time, but (at least for the moment) my work was done and today was my own.

Not to mention that I would have felt terrible going to LA and leaving Bailey in doggy care. Admittedly another famed 'prop' related to my employer's fiction (a grey Husky featured in the second *Thrill Seeker* novel, spurring a short-lived obsession and subsequent purchase), but I knew he was loved. It was just that Will's day-to-day lifestyle simply didn't afford dedication to such an energetic creature, and being a longtime dog-lover I was more than happy to take Bailey's care upon myself. It was the reason I'd been here all week at the townhouse and would be for most of next until Will returned home on Christmas Eve in a blaze of glory.

And although I loved taking the Husky round the city with me on various errands, there were some places I couldn't take him – which was why today I'd have to drop him off at daycare. Just for a few hours, and I knew he loved the interaction with the other dogs, to say nothing of all the attention he got from the girls there. First, I'd bring him for our regular walk through the Park before heading on down to the usual place just off Eighth Avenue.

Feeding Bailey and pouring another cup of coffee for myself, I sat in the kitchen and switched on the laptop, immediately bringing up TMZ and its red-carpet coverage of last night's event.

Will and the car were everywhere. The elaborate stunt had worked, and based on the coverage the event had got across many of the entertainment websites, my boss was now the hottest ticket in Hollywood.

People could say what they liked about Will Anderson but he knew how the entertainment business worked. He knew that if you wanted to make it in either books or movies, then you needed to create a persona for yourself that was even bigger than the ones you wrote about.

People liked to pass him off as a mere peddler of pulp fiction, but every day I witnessed first-hand the blood, sweat and tears that went into not only the writing but the marketing of his stories, and knew that he took his work, like most things in his life, very seriously indeed.

As was evidenced by the rapid rise in popularity of the Max Bailey books over the last four years and now, no doubt, the movie franchise too. A tough taskmaster, Will brought the same energy and dedication to his work as he did to his leisure pursuits, like the various high-endurance marathon races he'd put himself through over the last few years.

I sometimes wondered if he had a death wish, such were the high-octane activities he signed up for, like death-defying skydives, cave jumping, deep sea diving – all for the sake of personal improvement. I guess in that way he embodied his character Max Bailey's thrill-seeking spirit.

Flicking through the online entertainment reports, I gave a crooked smile. If I had thought the last couple of years had been busy, I wouldn't know what hit me once the movie side really took off and I had to start jumping through hoops for producers in Hollywood as well as publishers on Park Avenue.

Still, it had to be said that I was more than recompensed for my efforts and the perks of the job were second to none. Yes, Will drove me crazy sometimes with his more bizarre requests (especially the last-minute ones like the Mustang – a case in point) but I loved being involved in the business as well as the creative side of Thrill Seeker, and wouldn't change it for the world.

Any profession that allowed me to be surrounded by books made me a very happy man. The job had given me a chance to dig deep, and had helped me to overcome the big changes and disappointments in my personal life over the last few years. And while some might argue – like Ciara – that my dedication to the cause may have been partly to blame, my belief is that some things just aren't meant to be. In any case, life is pretty good these days, and Mel and I have never been closer.

And while my boss might be a tough taskmaster, I also know that my efforts are appreciated and my input respected.

For example, I can take personal credit for some of Max Bailey's quirkier personality traits, like his preference for vintage Mustangs (yes, my own fault) and his secret love of great literature – the latter surprisingly at odds with his kickass renegade persona and, I like to think, one of the reasons that makes him so popular with female readers.

Hence Will's beloved library. I had helped him with much of the selection and indeed procured – thanks to George at

Christie's – many of the rarer first editions, most notably the Marlowe, who happened to be Max Bailey's favourite writer. Will routinely joked that his popular character was as much my creation as his and to be fair, routinely credits me in the book Acknowledgements, thanking me for my input.

And he was very understanding all throughout my domestic issues a while back, offering to let me stay here at the brownstone for a while until I managed to get things sorted.

I guess that's a side to the guy that people like my sister don't understand, and one of the reasons I will go to the ends of the earth to find what Will wants when he wants it – because we aren't just boss and employee; over the years we have in a way become good mates, albeit from completely different sides of the tracks.

Will has always been wealthy, after all, hailing from a family of well-to-do Scandinavians who made good in the US, whereas I'm just a Dublin immigrant still making my way in New York.

To say that benefits at the Met, Rothko paintings and skiing holidays in Val d'Isère are beyond my usual sphere of existence is an understatement, although by the nature of the job, I get the opportunity to sample the more glamorous side of Manhattan – repeated dealings with Christie's and my open-ended chequebook a case in point. I like it. But 'not permanent' as Ciara would say.

Pouring another coffee, I checked my emails and immediately spotted one from Will which, judging by the time, he'd sent yesterday a few hours before the première.

A Gift to Remember

Man, I can't believe you came through for me! You're a miracle worker, Aidan, and I don't know what I'd do without you. This baby is beautiful! I can't WAIT to drive down Hollywood Boulevard, pull up outside Grauman's and step out onto the red carpet from this. James Bond who?

Seriously, man, I owe you one and wish you could be here, but I know you're taking good care of my buddy back home. Hope he's OK. In the meantime, I wanted to get you a little something to show my appreciation – not for Christmas, because needless to say that's gonna be a kickass bonus – but something that I hope you'll like. Hell knows, you deserve it. I left it all wrapped up in the office; in the top desk drawer on the right-hand side. Key's in the usual place.

So thanks again, man, and wish me luck for later. We're really going to blow 'em all away in these wheels. See you on the 24th!

Will

Chapter 41

Longest way round is the shortest way home.
James Joyce

In the Apple Store, Darcy pulled Aidan's broken iPhone out of her bag and sat it on the countertop as Jenna powered up the new one.

'Hmm,' the younger girl said after a beat.

Darcy looked up and sighed, wondering what the problem was now.

'Just to make you aware that not everything will transfer. Anything that wasn't backed up to iCloud likely wasn't saved. Images, apps, things like that.'

iCloud? It was all gobbledegook to Darcy. 'Well, I never back up my phone. Does that mean I would lose everything if something happened to it?'

Jenna remained polite but Darcy could sense that *oh you're one of those people* was running through her mind. 'Do you want to know how many people come into the store who lose everything because they don't religiously back up their device?' the younger girl chided gently.

Darcy felt somewhat heartened that she, along with Aidan apparently, weren't religious backer-uppers. 'Well, forgive me for not being a techie,' she said as Jenna continued to mess about with the iPhone.

'It has nothing to do with being a techie,' the assistant said simply. 'It has to do with something like this.' She gave Darcy a knowing look. 'Imagine if you were knocked unconscious and had a broken phone causing a data loss, making things so much harder for the person trying to help you?'

Darcy had to smile. 'Honestly Jenna, perhaps you should use Aidan's situation as a new case study for Apple.'

'OK, here we go. The new device is now up and running.' Jenna pushed the handset across the table to Darcy, who suddenly felt her hands begin to tremble a little, as if it was a bomb waiting to be detonated. Today's phones were surely comparable to personal diaries of old; given the opportunity, you were likely to learn both bad and good about the person who owned them.

She couldn't deny feeling somewhat melancholy, knowing that the contact details of everybody whom Aidan knew and loved were assuredly in this phone, which meant that her role in his story would undoubtedly soon be over. Aidan was sure to be furious and would never want to see her again once he figured out the incorrect information Darcy had been feeding him.

'Well, I guess I'd better get going,' she said, pulling herself together. 'Thanks again, Jenna. I really appreciate your help with this; I know Aidan will too. And I promise to back my phone up in future.'

'Good, and not a problem – any time.'

Saying goodbye to the assistant, Darcy checked her watch and went back upstairs and outside, but knew it would likely be some time before Aidan made his way back from Long Island. So she'd been right about the Mets keyring then at least. *But* she'd been wrong about so many other things.

As per Aidan's instruction on the written authorisation to Apple, the password protection on the new phone had not yet been activated, because it was unlikely that Aidan would remember the old one. Which meant that his personal information was available for all to see. Darcy took the handset out of her pocket again and stared at it, wrestling with her conscience. She would be seeing Aidan in a few minutes, and with this, hopefully empowering him with all the information he needed to get his life back.

Very different information to what Darcy had provided.

But just how different? she wondered. OK, so instead of being a millionaire, Aidan worked for one, which if she thought about it actually sounded reasonable, given that he'd never shown signs of having any airs or graces whatsoever. And while he might not own that amazing library, he was still extremely well read and, Darcy guessed, likely appreciated the book collection perhaps even more than its owner did.

She thought then about the travel souvenirs, running

medals and pictures of someone she'd assumed was Aidan, skiing and skydiving, but were likely of Will – a genuine mistake, given that his features had been partly obscured in almost all of them, and Darcy wouldn't have known to think otherwise in any case.

Aidan may not have travelled to all of these places or done any of those activities – which went some way towards explaining why he had absolutely no memory of them – but did that matter in the grand scheme of things?

He might not be Bailey's owner either, but clearly he loved and cared for the dog just as much if not more, given that his only memory when waking up had been of the gorgeous Husky.

And it was also unlikely that Aidan was in a relationship with a ballet dancer called Melanie. It was much more probable that she was in fact Will's girlfriend, or at least one of them, given her diatribe on the answering machine and the author's known reputation as a ladies man. And now that she thought about it, Darcy did recall noticing that the author's hair was thinning a little bit at the top ... hence the Rogaine.

Thinking about it all she felt a faint glimmer of hope about the prospect of Aidan being unattached, and she gradually felt calmer as the wheels began to turn and some of the pieces started to fall into place. Though she cursed herself for all the time she'd wasted over the last five days chasing down blind alleys trying to help Aidan, when in reality she'd likely been delaying his recovery. So much for trying to make amends.

Then she thought of something else. The gift box – where *did* that come into it? If the item Aidan had been so eagerly chasing for the last few weeks had actually been a vintage car, then where had the gift he'd been carrying that day come from, and who was it intended for?

Darcy thought back and tried to figure out why she'd immediately assumed that the gift was important. She recalled that it was because of the first message she'd heard on what she now knew was Will's answering machine. But the woman phoning about being 'let down' had definitely been looking for Aidan – had even mentioned him by name, she was sure of it.

So maybe Darcy had been right in guessing that Aidan was on his way to meet someone on the morning of the accident. But who? And was this person the gift's intended recipient?

Suddenly, out of nowhere, Aidan's iPhone started to ring in her hand, and Darcy almost jumped out of her skin. She looked down at the display and her eyes widened.

Mel calling.

Darcy's mind raced. Mel? As in Melanie Rothschild?

OK, so maybe she hadn't got everything completely wrong, after all.

She glanced quickly across the road to the subway entrance to see if there was any sign of Aidan yet, but even if there was, Darcy knew she wouldn't be able to reach him in time for him to answer this call. And Mel, whoever she was, must be going out of her mind with worry by now.

'Hello?' Darcy answered, not sure if she was doing the right thing. 'This is Aidan Harris's phone.'

'What ... where is he? What's going on? Who are you?'

gasped the person on the other end of the line, and Darcy could hear the desperation in her voice and realised that it had to be one of Aidan's loved ones, or someone who'd be at least concerned about his absence. Finally!

'It's OK,' she soothed. 'Aidan's OK, I promise. Please don't worry. He was in a slight accident a few days ago, and his phone was damaged, which is why he's been out of contact for a while, but he's just got it back and—'

There was a loud cry and then a muffled voice saying something like, 'I don't know,' and Darcy winced, wondering if she should have tried to phrase it all better. But she had assured the caller that Aidan was OK and tried her best to explain why he'd been inaccessible, which was the most important information, wasn't it?

Then a different voice appeared on the other end of the line.

'Who is this?' a decidedly less emotional and more assured older woman asked sharply. 'Where is Aidan? And what have you said to upset my daughter?'

'I'm sorry ... Mrs Rothschild, is it?' Darcy ventured hesitantly, trying to figure things out.

'Who is this? Where is Aidan?' the woman demanded.

'I didn't mean to upset anyone, Mrs Rothschild,' Darcy babbled.

'Well then, for goodness' sake explain! And I'm not Mrs Rothschild, whoever that is,' the woman added irritably. 'I'm Mrs Harris, Aidan's wife.'

Chapter 42

I sat down with my coffee, delighted that Will was so happy with the car – it truly made all the stress and strain of trying to secure it worthwhile. Just as I was about to close out of the email, however, I noticed a P.S. underneath his sign off.

> *P.S. Oh and by the way, if that crazy Melanie calls the house while you're there, just ignore it – she's still not getting it, and has left about a hundred screaming messages on my cell since I got here. My own fault for dating a psycho ... hey you know what I mean, you saw* Black Swan ...

I smiled. Checking the time, I realised that I really needed to get a move on if I wanted to take Bailey for a run, then drop him down to the daycare place before meeting Ciara.

I stood up and took my coffee into the office, curious about Will's so-called 'thank you' gift. But at the same time, I knew better than to get too excited.

For a man so incredibly imaginative in many ways, he very often came up short in others, especially when it came to choosing gifts.

If it weren't for my intervention, at Christmas his mother would be getting a blender from Pottery Barn instead of cashmere from Bergdorf, and his girlfriend gloves from Macy's instead of earrings from Tiffany's.

Or girlfriends even. It was proving increasingly difficult to keep up with those, especially lately when he'd been meeting lots of new people out in LA, and thus neglecting some on the East Coast.

My gaze rested on the bikini shot of Melanie Rothschild on the shelf nearby – a case in point. She'd evidently put it there during a stay-over one time, evidently not realising that this wasn't Will's office but mine.

Preferring to keep work and home life separate, he rented a space in the Trump Office Tower on Fifth where he wrote when he wasn't travelling, surrounded by all the various editions of the Max Bailey books to inspire him.

And since we'd decided that part of my role should encompass taking care of Bailey (actually I'd insisted), it made sense for me to have a base at the townhouse, especially for the accounts part, though in reality most of my work involved being out and about, gathering specifics for research, meeting with publishers, or like last week, chasing down some of Will's more obscure requests.

I'd recognised right off the bat that the ballet dancer was dangerously smitten with Will – not a good idea when the same man hadn't committed to one girl since preschool – and I had once even tried to gently warn her, obviously to no avail.

Finding the key under the blotter, I opened the desk drawer, curious to see what Will had chosen for me. But seeing as his last gift to me was rather disappointing – being a replica of some dagger that had featured in one of the Max Bailey books – I didn't have high hopes.

And taking out the beautifully wrapped but suspiciously book-shaped package, I realised that my instincts had been right on the money.

Will had a habit of gifting me signed first editions of his own work – a kind gesture certainly – and seeing as the new Max Bailey book was due out in the New Year, I guessed that this was exactly what was contained in the package.

Never mind, I thought, absentmindedly tidying the desk and shoving the file from Christie's back into the drawer; like they said, it's the thought that counts.

Back in the kitchen I tidied everything away; put the laptop back in its rightful place in the office and my cup in the dishwasher before attaching a skittish Bailey to his lead.

'Come on, boy, time to get moving. We have a busy day ahead of ourselves today.' I clapped my hands and Bailey yawned. Clearly, he didn't share my urgency.

I hurriedly shoved the gift box into a bag I found in Will's pantry, deciding I'd open it later. If anything, Ciara would get a kick out of it.

Smoothing down my Cole Haan coat in the hallway, I brushed some lint off the sleeve. It really was a nice coat. Way too nice truthfully, but in my line of work, I thought, glancing at that insanely expensive Rothko – another impulsive purchase of Will's upon selling the movie rights – you had to keep up with appearances.

Bailey and I walked quickly through the snow-filled streets, and I couldn't help but notice that today, everything looked fresh and new to me. It was often like that after I'd finished a difficult assignment; as if a great weight had been lifted and I could concentrate on something other than the task in hand.

Looking around, and for the first time in days truly taking in the beauty that the city had to offer, especially at this time of year, I felt my heart and my spirit soar.

Going up to the Park entrance on Eighty-Sixth Street, I took our usual meandering route around the reservoir and then down past the lake and out at Central Park South, before heading back in the direction of Eighth Avenue where Bailey's occasional daycare place 'Puppy Love' was located.

I tapped my foot on the ground and out of nowhere started humming 'It's Beginning to Look a Lot Like Christmas' to myself. Bailey looked up at me as I hummed and I glanced down, throwing him a wink.

I smiled benevolently at the Apple Store, the target of so much of my bewilderment not two weeks before, and took in the holiday window displays over at Bergdorf, as Bailey and I effortlessly weaved our way through the holiday shoppers and late-morning commuters. And for once, I didn't feel the slightest bit annoyed by the sea of people that seemed to hit our path at the junction of Fifth, where a plethora of carriages waited to take tourists around a snowy romantic Central Park.

Then I checked my watch and realised that my thus far relaxed attitude was turning out to be seriously misplaced. It was after ten and Ciara's flight from San Diego was due in at Newark at eleven. I would have to get a move on if I wanted to make it there on time. Distractedly sending a text to the company's regular town car service, asking them to pick me up at the daycare address, I quickened my step.

Bailey hurried along in tandem, immediately noticing my sudden change of pace, and I looked up ahead noticing that the crosswalk light on Sixth was on a flashing red.

I glanced sideways at the driver of the FedEx van stopped at the lights; he was on the phone and didn't look like he was going anywhere too fast.

'Come on, boy, we'll just make it—'

But I didn't get to finish my sentence, as out of nowhere I thought I heard a female voice scream, 'Hey, look out!'

And then out of the blue, something crashed into me – the van? – I wasn't sure. It felt as if I was witnessing the entire scene from afar, as if I was having an out-of-body experience. My legs were suddenly flying towards the clear, blue winter sky as my head and upper body were headed towards the ground. As I guessed what was coming next, I had a sudden moment of clarity: I was going down hard.

And that was it. After that, the world around me went black.

Chapter 43

Logic will get you from A to Z, but imagination will get you everywhere. **Albert Einstein**

'Darcy? It's Aidan. I'm sorry, but I'm still here on Long Island, at my house actually, and you won't believe this, but now that I've seen it, things are coming back! Turns out you were wrong about my place being on the Upper West Side, but I think I have an explanation for that ... So listen, just to say that there's no need to meet me now. I'm fine here and I think everything's going to be OK. Sorry again for bothering you, and I hope I haven't put you out. Talk soon.'

Darcy had played back Aidan's phone message about a hundred times, trying to figure out how she'd got it all so wrong.

It had come in while she'd been talking to his wife – his *wife* – trying to explain to the woman what had happened

378

over the last few days and why she and her daughter Amelia – Aidan's daughter – had been unable to contact him.

Assuring Mrs Harris that she'd have him call them as soon as she met Aidan outside the subway entrance a few minutes later, she'd ended the call and proceeded to the agreed meeting place. Only to find the missed call from him on her own phone, telling her that he wasn't going to show.

His tone had sounded so jovial that Darcy guessed that upon reaching home, he would have immediately reconnected with his family and everything would go from there.

And they all lived happily ever after.

She could only assume as much, as that was almost forty-eight hours ago and she hadn't heard anything from the family – or indeed Aidan – since.

She would need to return his phone and, of course, the keys to the townhouse which she'd in the meantime removed from beneath the maple tree when checking on Bailey, and that would be the end of her involvement in Aidan Harris's life. She'd sent him a follow-up text telling him he could pick up the phone (and Will's keys) from her at Chaucer's whenever it was convenient for him to do so. She also assured him that she'd keep an eye on Bailey too.

But she guessed he and his family had quite a bit of catching up to do.

The Husky seemed happy to be back home, and because she knew Aidan had enough to think about just then, Darcy had topped up his feeding bowl and taken him across to the Park for walks the last couple of mornings on her way to work. She guessed his real owner would return soon, but she wasn't going to abandon his needs in any case.

Darcy still cringed when she thought how badly wrong she'd been about Aidan, and how she'd fallen for an idea of the man – a sophisticated, charming book-geek like herself, but with an enviable, glamorous New York lifestyle – a far reality from who he actually was.

Married and with a daughter Amelia (Mel), maybe even more children for all she knew.

Yet, it wasn't just the fantasy she'd created for him either; Darcy had genuinely fallen for his kindness, his gentle laugh, those twinkling eyes and wonderful Irish lilt in his voice as he teased her about her doggedness in helping him, and challenged her book knowledge.

And all along he was married.

Darcy wanted to kick herself for not even considering it and felt guilty afresh for allowing herself to think so fondly of another man's wife. Yet she distinctly remembered checking for a wedding ring that first night she met him and he absolutely wasn't wearing one, she was sure of it.

Still, she thought shrugging, as Katherine made her way to the table Darcy was sitting at now in the restaurant, there was bound to be a simple explanation for that one too; maybe the hospital had removed it for some kind of medical reason, or he'd forgotten to put it back on after a shower that morning.

She could speculate endlessly, but at the end of the day, it was no longer her business to speculate, nor was there any point.

'Hey there, why the long face, darling?' Katherine asked, sitting down and promptly summoning a waiter. They were at the Gramercy Tavern for their annual pre-Christmas lunch date before Katherine left for St Barts; Christmas now only two days away.

Darcy raised a smile at her aunt's all too familiar behaviour and knew that she could always rely on Katherine to behave according to character. 'Nothing – just daydreaming, that's all.'

The waiter duly obliged and without consulting Darcy, her aunt ordered a bottle of some unpronounceable wine that was sure to be both expensive and delicious.

'Well, I have something to cheer you up,' Katherine went on. 'Turns out I managed to get some interesting information about your gentleman friend. That library you told me about was the key.'

'Katherine . . .'

'Now, I did make some phone calls, and spoke with a gentleman at Christie's – I think his name was George? And while some of this information is confidential, George revealed that a copy of Christopher Marlowe's *Dido* was sold about eighteen months ago. It was the only one sold in New York in recent history; in fact, it seems to be one of the only copies in the United States. Although, and here is the important bit,' she paused, smiling in satisfaction, 'it was not sold to your friend himself but to a company called Thrill Seeker Holdings, which you did mention and which I thought at the time sounded familiar.'

'Katherine ...'

'So I enquired further about Thrill Seeker Holdings, which wasn't an easy task, believe me – holding companies are notoriously lacking in public information. I persisted, and you might even say I threw a small bribe at the records clerk – nothing serious, of course, but it did work, the man apparently is a fan of Le Cirque. And you'll never guess what I discovered and the reason it sounded so familiar.' She paused dramatically, waiting to make her announcement, Darcy having decided by now to just give up and let her have her say.

But at that moment the sommelier arrived with the wine, and Katherine went through her usual routine of tasting and swirling before declaring it agreeable and continuing with her story.

'The holding company is owned by none other than Will Anderson!' she exclaimed incredulously. 'Will Anderson, don't you remember him? That thriller author I introduced you to before,' she pressed when Darcy didn't immediately react with surprise, or indeed gratitude.

'Yes, I know.'

'So I was thinking that perhaps your gentleman friend is simply an employee of the company – in which case he's not that much of a catch after all, darling. So best not to completely disregard Oliver Martin. You might think he is a little ... different, but I saw him the other day again at a restaurant in midtown, and he asked about you. So, just know you have options. Anyway, cheers,' she said, finally pausing for breath, but only to raise her glass.

'Cheers,' Darcy replied dully, her thoughts drifting to Hemingway and his belief that alcohol was the rose-coloured glass of life.

Then out of the blue she felt her eyes well up.

'What's the matter, dear?' Katherine asked, looking vaguely horrified. 'I had no idea you disliked him *that* much.'

'No, that's not it.' Darcy gave a shaky smile. 'It's just – oh, I've been such an idiot!'

It all poured out – everything that had happened over the past few days: the crash, Bailey, her trek all over the city to try and help Aidan, then the realisation that she'd got it stupidly, horribly wrong.

Especially the notion that there might have been some kind of connection between them.

Katherine listened silently as she recounted the story.

'It's my own fault for spending so much of my life in make-believe worlds, so much so that I can't seem to tell the difference between fiction and reality any more,' Darcy said, her voice shaking. 'I created a storybook life for Aidan, actually hampered the poor guy's recovery because of it. And I was so taken with my version of the man I believed him to be, and the narrative I'd formed – imagining mystery and romance where there was none – that I completely failed to see that he was just an ordinary guy with a family and a whole other life. Instead I imagined him as some enigmatic romantic hero – the star of this mysterious love story.'

Katherine spoke softly. 'But I'm guessing you might have fallen for more than just the fiction where your hero is concerned?'

She sniffed. 'Yes. And that's the stupidest thing of all. Oh Katherine, why am I such an idiot? You're right, you know – I do spend too much time between the pages of books instead of confronting my own reality, and look how far that's got me.'

'Ssh.' Her aunt laid a comforting hand on her own – something Darcy couldn't remember her doing in a very long time. It felt good. 'Oh sweetheart, I know I give you grief sometimes, but you know I love you and I am so proud of you. And it's hardly a surprise that you spend so much time in imaginary worlds when the real one let you down so badly early on in life.'

Darcy looked up, surprised. She guessed she'd never thought about it that way before, that after her parents' death, her beloved books had been a form of solace, escapism in its truest form.

'You know, I miss your mother every day,' Katherine continued, in a rare maudlin tone. 'Lauren was not only my sister but also my best friend, and I miss your dad too; Steven was such a wonderful person, the kind of man I wish I could have met back then, and they loved each other so much. They loved you too.'

Darcy watched her carefully. Her aunt had never been one to dwell on emotion or regret, and it was strange for her to hear this now.

'I remember when they asked me if I would agree to act as your guardian in case anything was to ever happen to them, and I honestly questioned their sanity. After all, Steven had sisters and brothers, married with children of their own, people who were already properly equipped for parenthood. Unlike me,' she said sardonically, 'a childless, husbandless New York spinster completely dedicated to her work. We both know I'm not exactly the warm and cuddly type.' She briefly met Darcy's gaze and the two exchanged knowing smiles. 'But you know, your parents were wise too. They knew that if anything were to happen to them, that you and I would need each other. Your aunts and uncles and cousins could have raised you, and I know you would have been fine with any of them. But my sister, she knew *I* would need someone. And I feel terrible for admitting it, but it really was the best thing that ever happened to me. *You* were.'

Darcy couldn't believe what she was hearing, and her eyes welled up afresh. She'd always felt that she was an inconvenience in Katherine's life. Yes, she loved her aunt who had always done her best for her, but still Darcy always got the sense that becoming a surrogate mother overnight was the *worst* thing that could have happened to Katherine Armstrong, who until then, had had the world at her feet.

'I suppose you could say that you saved me from myself,' her aunt was saying. 'I was becoming – had become – completely immersed in the city girl lifestyle. I was drinking too much, and yes, sometimes using drugs too,' she admitted to a completely flabbergasted Darcy, 'not to mention getting involved with inappropriate men for inappropriate reasons. And then you came along, twelve years old and completely lost, sending my life crashing down to earth. Yet while I know

I've let you down in so many ways, ultimately you gave me the opportunity to get a handle on my life and concentrate on something of real worth.'

Darcy was shaking her head. 'I truly had no idea and I always worried that I'd held you back.'

'Only in the best possible way. Who knows where I'd have ended up by now? But clearly it was too one-sided, as I suspect I deprived you of the emotional support you needed – something I know you found in your beloved books. But Darcy, that was no bad thing, and please try not to view it that way. You have always been wonderfully imaginative, optimistic and open to the greatest possibilities life has to offer, which is a true gift. And it will certainly prevent you from going down the same path as a jaded old cynic like me.'

'That's so not true. *You're* the most optimistic person I know. You haven't given up on me yet,' Darcy joked. 'Whereas I already know I'm a lost cause.'

'Don't say that,' Katherine begged. Then she paused and took a deep breath. 'But seeing as we're bringing things out into the open …' she paused a little, '… I think now might be as good a time as any to come clean with you about something.'

Her aunt sounded so serious all of a sudden that Darcy looked up, terrified that she was going to tell her that she was ill or something just as terrible.

'I've been seeing someone recently – a man,' Katherine confessed softly, and Darcy looked up, amazed. Her aunt never, ever talked about her romantic life. 'A very nice one and I think – hope – you'll like him. Because it seems he's going to be a big part of our life from now on.' With that, she tentatively extended her left hand upon which sat a beautiful sparkling diamond.

Darcy's mouth dropped open. 'Oh my goodness!'

'Do you mind?' Katherine asked, her tone hesitant. 'I've wanted to tell you about him for a while, but I wasn't sure how you'd react.'

'Are you crazy? How could I react with anything other than absolute delight!' Darcy jumped up from the table and went to give her a huge hug. 'Oh Katherine, I'm so pleased for you. Congratulations, this is wonderful news!' But she couldn't believe that her aunt had felt she needed to keep her relationship secret.

'I suppose I was worried that you might feel I was abandoning you,' Katherine said gently, answering Darcy's unspoken question. 'After all, it's been just the two of us for such a long time.'

'Is this the reason you've been trying so hard to get me coupled off?' Darcy laughed, as comprehension dawned as to the true purpose behind Katherine's repeated matchmaking attempts.

Her aunt looked guilty.

'But I'm thirty-three years old, and I thought – well, at least I *hoped* – that you didn't feel responsible for me any more. I can't even imagine what it was like for you, all those years ago, being landed out of the blue with me. Which is why I wanted to give you your life back as soon as I was able to.'

'Oh sweetheart, any sense of responsibility that might have

existed was replaced a very long time ago with affection, pure and simple. I love you, Darcy, and all I ever wanted was to make sure that you were happy. I suppose I wanted you to have someone to share your life with, someone a hell of a lot better than me.'

'Please don't say that – you did a wonderful job.' Darcy's eyes shone with fresh tears, unable to believe that her aunt was pouring out her heart to her like this.

And as Katherine told her more about Francis Cartwright, a widowed businessman she'd been friends with for many years before the relationship had recently blossomed into something more, she was amazed to discover the depths of her aunt's actual feelings for her.

'I'm fifty-three and way past any big white-wedding nonsense, but he was insistent on the ring,' Katherine said airily. 'Whether we actually bother going all the way to the altar or not doesn't matter. I know he's the one for me.'

'I'm so thrilled for you, really I am, and I can't wait to meet him,' Darcy said. She made a face. 'Though I'd imagine he thinks I'm a right ogre, seeing as you were afraid to introduce us before now.'

'Absolutely not. With two daughters of his own Francis completely understands the situation, and it was my own issue, rather than anything to do with you. Though to be truthful, I am pleased to have it all out in the open now,' she chuckled. 'You know how terrible I am at keeping anything under wraps.'

'So you two are going to St Barts together then?' Darcy asked.

'Yes, and I was wondering if you wanted to join us?'

'Sounds wonderful, but if you don't mind I think I'd rather stay home this year,' Darcy said. 'I have a few things to catch up on and I'm not sure I could take the time off work in any case.'

In truth, all she wanted to do after the drama of the last few days was curl up at home surrounded by the comfort of the things she loved. As much as she wanted to meet her aunt's fiancé, she just didn't have the energy.

'Well, if you're sure? We can always arrange something for when we get back. Perhaps New Year's dinner at my place? Nothing fancy, just a nice easy-going evening.'

'Sounds perfect.' Darcy smiled dully and her aunt reached across the table and clasped her hand.

'Try not to fret,' Katherine said, as if understanding yet again exactly what was on Darcy's mind. 'Yes, you might have come to a few unrealistic conclusions where this man of yours is concerned. But don't let that dampen that wonderful spark of imagination you own – that belief that in this world, anything is possible. It's one of the greatest traits a person can have, and I sorely wish I possessed even a smidgen of it.'

'Thank you,' Darcy said, feeling a whole lot better all of a sudden. Katherine was almost making it sound as though her imagination running away with her was a good thing, and she guessed that in certain cases it had worked to her advantage.

But not in the case of Aidan Harris. In this scenario, she thought sadly, lifting her wine glass, her imagination had been well and truly out of focus.

389

Chapter 44

Everything has to come to an end, sometime.
L. Frank Baum

Darcy stood at the counter with Joshua in a packed Chaucer's on Christmas Eve. She'd been on her feet all day, restocking shelves, helping customers with recommendations, but mostly ringing up holiday purchases, and she couldn't wait for her coffee break, when she planned to indulge in one of the café's cinnamon mochas upstairs. Heaven.

'I wonder if you can help me,' the next customer in line said. 'I'm looking for a book ...'

Darcy looked up, surprised at the familiar-sounding voice. And to see the even more familiar person standing in front of her at the countertop.

'Aidan!'

Despite herself she felt somewhat irritated. Helluva time

he'd chosen to come and pick up his phone and keys. But it seemed he'd also fancied doing some shopping while he was at it.

'The story is about two people whose lives collide one snowy morning once upon a time in New York,' he continued, his brown eyes twinkling and his voice full of humour. 'It has kind of a slow beginning as the girl and the guy take a little while to get to know each other, but the one thing that's obvious from the get-go is that they have a lot in common. Still, there are many misunderstandings along the way, like when the guy gets knocked on the head and can't remember who he is, and the girl gets the impression that he's rich and successful when really he's just a regular Joe . . .'

He eyed her closely, and Darcy was unable to move her gaze away. 'And an even bigger misunderstanding when his worried but *estranged* wife might lead her to believe they're still together.'

Darcy's heart did a little somersault.

'Possibly causing her to go right off the guy, and preventing her from getting to know him better – the *real* him. Oh, and there's a cute dog in there too.'

'I quite like the sound of that one myself,' piped up the young female customer next in line. She looked at Darcy. 'So what's it called?'

Joshua sniggered. 'I think maybe you and Jason Bourne should take this outside now – you're confusing the customers.'

'But it's so busy. I can't leave you in the lurch again,' Darcy protested weakly, though she was dying to speak to Aidan properly and find out what else he had to say.

'It's Christmas Eve, honey; people will be worried if they *don't* have to wait in line. Anyway, Ashley will be back from coffee break soon. So go, go!'

Her heart pounding, Darcy duly grabbed her jacket from beneath the counter and followed Aidan outside.

She was *dying* to ask more, but didn't want to interrupt the story – Aidan's version of it.

He moved closer to her as they walked, close enough to touch. 'So do you think you might know the one I'm talking about?' he asked, those twinkling eyes causing her heart to break all over again.

'I'm – I'm not sure,' she replied, playing along. 'I think it might ring a bell, but there are a few gaps. Estranged wife, you said?'

'Yes. Separated almost two years now. We're – *they're*, the guy and his ex, I mean – still good friends, and love their twelve-year-old daughter. Who is a huge fan of books, by the way, and incidentally her current favourite is *The Princess Bride*. Which the guy happened to be reading with her just a couple of days before he got run over.' He shook his head. 'Inconceivable.'

At this, Darcy couldn't resist a smile and she listened as he continued.

'So the daughter was starting to get concerned when she hadn't heard from him for a little while, and couldn't contact him. As was the guy's sister, whom he was supposed to collect from the airport the morning he got hit, so she had to make her own way to his house on Long Island – after leaving several messages on every contact number she had for him.'

'Sounds like a real mess,' Darcy said, as they strolled on down the street, heading almost instinctively towards the Park. It was cold but she barely felt it, she was so wrapped up in Aidan's 'story', which was providing her with so many answers about the last few days. 'I'm so sorry for getting things all wrong, Aidan,' she said then, feeling that an apology was way overdue. 'But when Bailey led me to the brownstone and you had the keys, I didn't think to question anything.'

'Of course you didn't, and it's perfectly reasonable. And now that everything's come back to me, I can completely see why the fog took so long to lift, as can Doctor Mandeville,' he added, looking sideways at her.

Darcy coloured. 'The woman must be cursing me. So much for trying to help.'

'Darcy, you went above and beyond the call of duty – way beyond – and I can't thank you enough for all you've done.'

'All I've done? You mean delay your recovery by goodness knows how long and no doubt sending your poor family into convulsions wondering where you were these last few days.'

Aidan approached a nearby bench and sat on it, a melancholy expression on his face. He looked at Darcy, who sat a respectful distance beside him. Then he sighed deeply. 'Would you believe they didn't really notice anything until the day I came home?'

She looked at him, and though his voice was light, she could tell by his face that he was wounded.

'What? But surely they were going nuts trying to find you, checking with the hospitals and phoning everywhere they could think of? I'm sure they were getting close to sending out a missing persons report.'

But Aidan was shaking his head. 'You must understand. Like I said, Tessa and I are separated so I don't live at the family home in Long Island any more. I got a place nearby and I see Mel, my daughter, a lot of course – as much as I can outside of when she has school, but most of the time she and her mother live their own lives, separate to mine. And I work in Manhattan so I spend a lot of time here.'

OK, so if he didn't live with them, Darcy could maybe understand that they might not have missed Aidan for a couple of days at least, if they didn't realise anything was wrong.

'But what about your sister, the one you were supposed to meet at the airport that morning ... surely she was worried when you didn't show?'

And Darcy suddenly realised then that it was she – Aidan's sister – who had left that first message on Will Anderson's phone, the one about him forgetting and letting her down.

He looked embarrassed. 'I'm sorry to say that it wasn't that out of the ordinary. Ciara knows how I am with work, and while I hate to admit it, the truth is I've let her down before. She lives in San Diego and was stopping over for a quick visit on her way home to Dublin for Christmas. And because she knows I can often get caught up with work stuff, and also knows that this was a – if not *the* – major flashpoint for the marriage breakup … well, she kind of covered for me.'

'Covered for you?'

'Yes. She made her own way to my place, the townhouse I moved to after the separation, and assuming I'd again got waylaid by something at work, went to visit Tessa and Mel, but didn't mention anything to them about me standing her up. Then the following day she went back to the airport and took her onward flight to Dublin as planned. She was pissed off that I didn't show and hadn't returned her calls, but like I said, this kind of thing has happened before and so there was nothing to make her think anything out of the ordinary might have happened.' He looked at Darcy. 'She actually joked about it not long before she arrived, telling me I thought I was Superman.'

Darcy couldn't get her head around the fact that someone wouldn't have noticed his absence. 'So your daughter and your … wife, they didn't think it strange not to have heard from you either?'

'Like I said, they know how my work is, and that last week was a particularly busy one. Mel stayed over with me at the brownstone one time and I'd been telling her that I had a pressurised few days ahead. So I guess they just figured I was caught up in all of that.'

Darcy frowned. All the time she'd spent trying to find a friend or family member of Aidan's, assuming they'd be going out of their minds with worry, when they had barely even noticed his absence.

Judging by the hurt in his eyes, she guessed the realisation had hit him hard too.

'So Will Anderson is tough to work for then?' she asked.

'Ah, so you figured out that part of the story since,' he replied with a lopsided smile. 'Yes, I'm sorry to say that I'm not the wealthy man about town you imagined. That would be my boss.'

'No need to apologise. It was my mistake for being so stupid for assuming things.' Then Darcy thought of something else. 'You said on the day of the accident that you were on your way to the airport to pick up your sister. Then how come you had Bailey with you? And what about the package? Was that for her, Ciara? And what about the ballet tickets?'

Aidan sat forward and put his hands on his knees. 'Mel is crazy into the ballerina stuff at the moment and I was planning on taking her to *The Nutcracker* as a treat, though I hadn't told her anything about it yet, thank goodness. And as for the package ...' He smiled. 'Just so happens that it was a gift from Will to me, which I hadn't yet had the chance to open. I was running late and was just about to drop Bailey off to doggie daycare. Which is why I took that chance at the crosswalk.' He looked guiltily at her.

Darcy's eyes widened. 'So the gift was yours all along – meant for you, I mean, not some special person.'

'You don't think I'm special?' he teased, and she blushed a little.

'So what was it – the gift, I mean?' Darcy asked, though she figured it hardly mattered now. Still, the contents of the package had been driving her crazy all along and she needed to satisfy that final curiosity.

He reached inside his jacket. 'I kind of figured that, which is why I thought it best not to open it until you were here too.'

She laughed. 'Seriously?'

'Yes. Don't get too excited though,' he warned, his tone oddly flat. 'I already have a pretty good idea what it is.'

The wrapped gift box lay between them on the bench, and Darcy wondered what he meant by that. He picked it up and handed to her. 'First things first: are you a Will Anderson fan, by any chance?'

'Not especially.' Darcy wasn't going to admit that she'd come across Aidan's illustrious boss in person once before, and hadn't thought all that much of him. 'Why do you ask?'

'Because I think we've both figured out by now that this is a book, and I sort of have an inkling which book it might be too,' he said, sliding open the ribbon. Then he handed the package to Darcy. 'Might as well let you do the honours.'

Surprised at his downbeat tone, she gently lifted off the lid of the box, and pushed back the tissue paper, only to discover that inside was a copy of one of Will Anderson's forthcoming Thrill Seeker books, *Hard Knocks*. Darcy couldn't resist a smile at the altogether fitting title.

But now she also understood Aidan's lack of enthusiasm about the contents. Talk about a let-down.

'Oh.'

'He does that all the time,' Aidan sighed as Darcy handed the hardback book to him. 'I have signed first editions of all four Max Bailey books now. Nice, if not exactly inventive, if you know what I mean.' He opened the book to the title page, intent on showing Darcy the signature, and as he did so, a white envelope slid out.

'What's that?' she asked.

Aidan was frowning. 'I'm not sure. He doesn't usually put anything else in there.' Opening up the envelope, he took out a small sheet of paper attached to what Darcy thought looked like airline tickets.

Reading the note, Aidan said slowly, 'I don't believe it. Just when you think you know someone . . .' He handed Darcy the note for her to read.

Saw these and I thought of you. Take a break, wingman – you've earned it! Thought your little girl might like to go along for the ride too. Go nuts on Guinness and thanks again for everything. W

Darcy looked closer and saw that the destination listed on the airline ticket was Dublin and the date was the 27 December, three days from now.

'I haven't been back there in almost eight years,' Aidan was saying, his eyes glistening a little. 'It's just my dad left at home now and the last few years, with the separation and everything, have been tough. And before that Tess and I weren't making enough money to go over.'

He went on to explain that the relationship had struggled since their move from Dublin to New York ten years before, especially when in the early days Aidan unexpectedly lost his job and was out of work for a time.

'Then when I got the job with Will, I was determined to do the best I could, but the long hours and being constantly on call ... it took a real toll on us as a family.'

Darcy didn't need too much imagination to fill in the blanks this time. Ultimately his commitment to the job had cost Aidan his marriage.

'It wasn't just that,' he admitted when she gently suggested this. 'Tessa never really took to the States. She's a home bird, always has been, whereas Mel and I really love it here, but for as long as Mel is happy, she'll stay.'

Reading between the lines Darcy guessed that there were still a lot of issues surrounding his wife and his commitment to Will Anderson at the expense of their daughter. It was a difficult position to be in. But it also highlighted how sad it was that his family were so used to him being at work's beck and call that they had barely noticed him missing.

Will Anderson was right about one thing: Aidan deserved that break.

'Mel will be over the moon when she hears about this; she hasn't seen her grandfather since she was a kid.' And then, as if suddenly remembering something, he said to Darcy, 'I'll only be gone for a week, you know – to Ireland, I mean.'

She looked at him, not sure what he was getting at. He put the tickets back into his pocket and turned towards her on the bench.

'So about that story I was telling you,' he said, his eyes crinkling in amusement again. 'Seems that many of the loose ends have been tied up by now, but there's still a major plot strand that needs resolving.'

Darcy's heart lifted a little. 'Well, I believe you've read enough books to realise by now that not all stories end in happily ever after,' she said, smiling.

'I know that.' His hazel eyes were soft and warm as he looked at her. 'And I really don't expect everything to be tied up with a big red bow, but for me there's nothing worse than an unsatisfying ending.'

Now she was smiling broadly. 'With some stories, you really can't rush things,' she told him, 'and it's often best just to sit back and enjoy the journey for what it is.'

'I know what you mean. But you do recognise it though – the story I'm talking about?' He reached for her hand and she turned to meet his gaze, those dark eyes now completely earnest. 'Because if you don't, I think I'll go out of my mind not knowing the ending.'

'Ah, but the thing about books is that there *are* no real endings,' Darcy said, gently moving towards Aidan, 'only the place where you decide to stop the story.'

Epilogue

I opened my eyes from where I lay in the bed.

I heard a small snore come from next to me and rolled on to my side. She lay there, an arm across her forehead, mumbling something in her sleep. I listened intently to what she was saying but couldn't make out the words

Dreaming again, I thought indulgently.

I moved closer and nuzzled her neck, laying some slow kisses along her collarbone. She jumped in her sleep and relaxed when she realised it was me, then blinked sleepily as she opened her eyes and adjusted to the bright sunlight streaming in the windows. Another beautiful summer morning in New York City.

'Mmmm, good morning,' she smiled.

I put my arms around her waist and we lay face to face on our sides.

'I'm assuming that one was a Heathcliff dream?' I teased her.

She laughed. 'Those guys are so persistent. But thanks for waking me up. My reality is so much better than anything my subconscious can come up with.'

Six months ago, I thought. Six short months since my whole life changed for the better. Of course, my living space is a little bit more cramped than it was before, but things are working out. And I couldn't be happier.

I kissed her gently and ran my hand down her face. I couldn't believe just how much things had changed for me. For her. For us. I loved the fact that she lived here now. With me.

Even though there was barely any room for the two of us, and the extent of Will's library now pales compared to the size of our combined book collections.

I loved the fact that Amelia loved her. And Tessa too.

Even Will seemed to have taken a shine to her. Although I'm not entirely sure if *that's* a good thing.

And her terrifying Aunt Katherine seemed to approve of me too. I wasn't even scared when the woman asked openly about how well Will paid me, and when Darcy could expect a ring.

All in good time.

First, we wanted to master living together, figure out the mechanics of the delicate matter of sharing our book collection, and helping get our new Manhattan Literary Walking Tours business up and running. It's early days but with Darcy's city knowledge and my business know-how, I think we make a good team.

And then of course there was the whole distraction of the baby.

Almost as if they could tell I was thinking about them, I heard rustling noises on the other side of the door. 'Dad! Darcy! Are you guys up?' Mel called out, knocking on the door. 'Lizzy's awake.'

'Hold on, I'm coming.' Darcy sat up. She kissed my nose and grabbing a robe draped over a nearby chair, put it on.

I swung my legs over the side of the bed and picked up a T-shirt, just as our bedroom door burst forth, and in came a jumble of legs and fur.

My beloved daughter and three-month-old Lizzy – one of Bailey's progeny following Will's recent decision to sire him. Can you guess who named her?

Surprisingly, it was Mel's choice, suggesting it after Darcy had educated her on the finer points of Austen's strong and witty female characters and immersed her in a Regency romance reading marathon.

'Can we go into the city and take Lizzy to the Park?' asked my beaming daughter, who as always made my heart want to burst with love for her. 'And when we're there, can we ride the carousel?' she wanted to know, rubbing her face in the young Husky's soft fluffy coat.

'Ask Darcy, it's her weekend to pick what we do this time.'

All heads turned in Darcy's direction and she smiled mischievously.

'Can we, Darcy, can we?' Amelia cried.

Darcy tapped her finger on her lips, as if she was trying to determine if that's what she wanted to do while drawing out her response for as long as possible. 'Hmm ... I suppose that's OK. As long as we can make a pit stop for something yummy while we're there.'

'Hooray!' The cheers that came from my daughter's mouth almost raised the roof.

I playfully rolled my eyes and she laughed, dragging Lizzy out of the room.

Darcy snuck up behind me, wrapping her arms around my waist. 'It'll be fun. Maybe we can stop off at Will's and pick up Bailey too.'

'Something yummy, you said – maybe Serendipity?' I suggested, thinking that one of their famed frozen hot chocolates sounded good. 'Though I suppose we should probably phone and make a reservation,' I added, going automatically into work-mode.

'Nah, don't bother. I know a better place – less touristy. And I was thinking doughnuts.' Darcy ran a brush through her long, silken black hair and began the process of getting ready.

'Doughnuts? Sounds intriguing,' I said, reaching for her and pulling her close.

'Mini-doughnuts. Trust me, you'll love this place.'

I leaned down to kiss her, realising I must be the luckiest guy in the world, to have literally been knocked off my feet by Darcy Archer.

I smiled. 'As you wish.'

Acknowledgements

Lots of love and thanks to Kevin and Carrie and my family and friends for their continued support.

Big thank you to my wonderful agent, Sheila Crowley and all at Curtis Brown – I don't know what I would do without you.

To my amazing editor, Maxine Hitchcock, who makes every story infinitely better for having worked her magic on it – especially this one – thank you.

Many thanks to the brilliant S&S team in the UK, and the Hesses in Ireland for looking after me so well.

Huge gratitude to the fantastic booksellers all over the world who continuously give my books such amazing support, and to my international publishers for offering me the opportunity to combine my favourite things: books and travel.

As always, special thanks to readers everywhere who buy and read the books. I'm so very grateful and I love hearing from you. Please do get in touch via my website www.melissahill.info or Facebook and Twitter.

I very much hope you enjoy this one.